JENNIFER BOSWORTH

STRUCK

SQUARE
FISH

Farrar Straus Giroux New York

SQUARE
FISH

An Imprint of Macmillan
175 Fifth Avenue
New York, NY 10010
macteenbooks.com

Square Fish and the Square Fish logo are trademarks of Macmillan and
are used by Farrar Straus Giroux under license from Macmillan.

Square Fish books may be purchased for business or promotional use.
For information on bulk purchases, please contact the Macmillan Corporate
and Premium Sales Department at (800) 221-7945 x 5442 or by e-mail at
specialmarkets@macmillan.com.

Library of Congress Cataloging-in-Publication Data
  Bosworth, Jennifer.
      Struck / Jennifer Bosworth.
         p.   cm.
      Summary: After a major earthquake devastates Los Angeles, seventeen-year-
   old Mia wants only to take care of her younger brother and traumatized
   mother, but two fanatical doomsday cults vie for her powers, drawn from the
   multiple lightning strikes she has experienced.
      ISBN 978-1-250-02740-5 (paperback)
      ISBN 978-1-4299-5470-9 (e-book)
      [1. Supernatural—Fiction.   2. Cults—Fiction.   3. Lightning—Fiction.
   4. Thunderstorms—Fiction.   5. Brothers and sisters—Fiction.   6. Mothers
   and daughters—Fiction.   7. Los Angeles (Calif.)—Fiction.]   I. Title.
   PZ7.B6532Str 2012   [Fic]—dc23   2011018298

Originally published in the United States by Farrar Straus Giroux
First Square Fish Edition: 2013
Book designed by Andrew Arnold
Square Fish logo designed by Filomena Tuosto

10 9 8 7 6 5 4 3 2 1

AR: 4.9 / LEXILE: 720L

To Ryan, for believing

It never rains in California
But girl, don't they warn ya
It pours, man, it pours
—Albert Hammond

PROLOGUE

When you've been struck by lightning as many times as I have, you start to expect the worst pretty much all the time. You never know when that jagged scrawl of white fire, charged with a hundred million volts of electricity, might blaze down from the sky and find its mark on you; sear a hole like a bullet right through you, or turn your hair to ash; maybe leave your skin blackened to a crisp, or stop your heart; make you blind, or deaf, or both.

Sometimes lightning plays with you a little, lifts you into the air and drops you twenty yards away, blows your shoes off, or flash-fries the clothes from your body, leaving you naked and steaming in the rain. Lightning could wipe the last few hours or days from your memory, or overload your brain, short-circuiting your personality and rendering you a completely different person. I heard about a woman who was struck by lightning and cured of terminal cancer. A paraplegic who was given the ability to walk again.

Sometimes lightning strikes *you*, but it's the person standing next to you who ends up in the hospital. Or the morgue.

Any of that could happen, or none of it, or something else no one's ever heard of. The thing about lightning is you never know what it's going to do to you. Lightning could turn you into some kind of freakish human battery, storing up energy, leaving you with the persistent feeling that any day now you're going to spontaneously combust. Like a bomb is going to go off inside you and do, well . . . what bombs do best.

Or maybe that's just me.

My name is Mia Price, and I am a human lightning rod. Do they make a support group for that? They should, and let me tell you why.

My name is Mia Price, and I am a lightning *addict*.

There. Now you know the truth. I want the lightning to find me. I crave it like lungs crave oxygen. There's nothing that makes you feel more alive than being struck. Unless, of course, it kills you. It does that to me from time to time, which is why I moved to Los Angeles. As the song says, it never rains in Southern California. But the song also says when it pours, it *pours*.

The song is right.

My name is Mia Price, and it's been one year since my last strike, but that doesn't mean I've stopped expecting the worst. Lightning only strikes in L.A. a handful of times every year. The problem is, I traded thunderstorms for earthquakes, one earthquake in particular. The one that changed the city, and my life, forever.

That day, the day of the worst natural disaster to hit the United States, oh, pretty much ever . . . it rained.

Actually, it poured.

PART 1

Lightning never strikes twice in the same place.
— Proverb

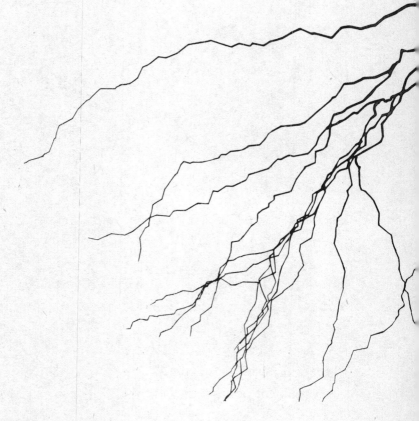

APRIL 14

Three days until the storm . . .

I don't sleep much. An hour here. Two hours there. Chronic insomnia, it's one of my more tolerable lightning strike aftereffects. Not as bad as the veiny red scars that cover me from neck to toes, or the burning in my chest that flares hotter when I get a little emotional. Insomnia? Eh. It could be worse (and usually is). Most people wish they had more hours in the day. I keep almost the full twenty-four.

When I go to bed at night, it's not with the intention to sleep. If sleep happens, great. If it doesn't, well, that's something I've gotten used to.

So when I opened my eyes and saw a guy standing over my bed, I had to assume I'd finally fallen asleep. And when I noticed the shiny silver knife gripped in his hand—the kind of pretty, decorative blade that has no practical application but murder—I decided this was not a dream I wanted to see through to the end. It would have been nice to stay asleep a bit longer, but now I was going to have to wake myself before Nightmare Boy used his knife to gut me.

"Wake up, Mia," I told myself in a voice that came out hoarse and scratchy, like it would have if I'd actually awakened.

The guy startled back from my bed. He dropped the

knife and it fell straight down and stuck in the wood floor with a *thunk*. Must be sharp. He scrambled to yank it free, but looked unsure what to do with it after that. His face was in shadow, but his wide, white eyes and jerky movements told me he was as scared as I was supposed to be. As far as nightmares went, he wasn't too bad. I decided to stay asleep.

I closed my eyes, hoping I'd open them to a new dream.

But there were no more dreams that night, only Nightmare Boy's soft, retreating footsteps.

When I opened my eyes again, feeling as though I hadn't slept at all, it was the morning I'd been dreading. The morning when my brother, Parker, and I would return to school for the first time since the quake.

We had a dream dictionary kicking around the house somewhere. If I consulted it, I was pretty sure it would confirm my suspicion that a knife in your dream was a bad omen. Not that I needed an omen to give me the heads-up that this day was going to suck.

As I dragged myself out of bed, I noticed a small split in the floor, right about where Nightmare Boy's knife had lodged itself in the floorboards. Strange. Then again, there were plenty of other little cracks and splits on the old floor of my restored attic bedroom.

I put thoughts of the dream away. I had bigger problems—real problems—to worry about. I didn't know what to expect back at school, but if the changes that had taken root throughout the rest of the city were any indication, I should probably give in and expect the worst, as usual.

Thanks for the warning, Nightmare Boy. Not that it'll do me any good.

2

I stood outside Mom's bedroom door and listened to Prophet's muffled voice. I couldn't make out what he said, but after a month of Mom obsessively watching his televised sermons, I could guess the subject matter.

The end of the world is at hand.

Those who surrender their souls to Prophet will be saved.

Those who don't will suffer and die and suffer some more.

Yeah, yeah, yeah. We heard you the first time.

"Mom?" I tapped on the door before turning the knob. It was seven in the morning, and outside the sun was doing its job, but Mom's bedroom was a cave. She sat at her window in the grungy bathrobe she hadn't shed in days, peeking through the slats in the blinds. Her eyes traveled back and forth between the window and the TV, which was playing *The Hour of Light*, Rance Ridley Prophet's morning broadcast. He did three shows a day: morning, midday, and evening. Ever since we brought her home from the hospital, Mom had been obsessed with Prophet. The only way she missed his broadcast was if the electricity or cable went out. I almost looked forward to those outages now.

"Brothers and sisters," Prophet intoned, "God will soon

make His final judgment. You must decide now on which side you will stand, on the side of heaven, or on the side of earth and its wicked, worldly pleasures. Will you be lifted up, raptured to paradise, or laid low by God's terrible vengeance?"

Prophet's voice drowned out my entrance into the bedroom. Sometimes I wondered if Mom's hearing was somehow damaged during the quake. She seemed so oblivious to what went on around her. The doctor who attended to her for all of five minutes before he gave her bed away to someone more needy said she was fine. Malnourished and dehydrated, but she'd live. After three days trapped under a collapsed building, she had some bad bruises, a few cracked ribs, and a dozen lacerations on her face and arms—caused by the wall of glass that had exploded near her when the building started to buckle—most of which had nearly healed by now. Physically, she was as sound as could be expected. Mental health was another matter.

The Internet—along with our utilities and cable—had been in and out since the quake, but when our connection was working I'd researched Mom's symptoms until I determined what was wrong with her: Acute Stress Disorder—Post-Traumatic Stress Disorder's evil twin on steroids—caused by a traumatic event, which is re-experienced in flashbacks, anxiety, delusions, emotional detachment, even amnesia.

Mom had all the symptoms and then some. She should have been in a hospital, under the care of a psychiatrist and a team of nurses tending to her around the clock. But the hospitals were still full of patients with actual life-threatening injuries, people with broken backs and crushed limbs and infected burns. People suffering from earthquake fever, an immunity disorder caused by mold released from the ground during the quake. People so malnourished and dehydrated from the lack of food and water in the city that the only way their bodies would accept nutrients was through a tube. There were no beds for those with functioning bodies but malfunctioning minds.

The upside was Acute Stress Disorder usually lasted a maximum of four weeks, and it had been four weeks to the day since the earthquake. Three weeks and four days since rescue workers pulled Mom's unconscious, dehydrated body from beneath several tons of rubble. It was a miracle she'd still been breathing. The people who'd been found with her were not so lucky. Some were crushed instantly. Others suffocated, and it was their deaths that saved my mom's life. There wasn't enough oxygen in the small cavern beneath the wreckage to go around.

Four weeks since the quake . . . it seemed like four thousand.

"Mom?" I said again. I kept my voice low, gentle, as though my words might hurt her if they came out too hard. She stiffened and her shoulders hunched as she craned her head around. It had been so long since she'd washed her hair that it appeared wet with grease. The scars on her face stood out in waxy, salmon-colored lines against skin that hadn't seen the sun in weeks. It was an effort not to flinch every time I looked at her. At least my face had been spared from the lightning scars that etched the rest of my body. Mom's face, on the other hand . . . she would need plastic surgery to remove the scars if she didn't want to be reminded of the quake every time she looked in a mirror.

"We have already begun to witness God's wrath," Prophet continued. "He whispered to me that He would strike Los Angeles only minutes before His fist came down. The end of all things is at hand, brothers and sisters, and it will commence right here, in Los Angeles. For this is not the city of angels, but a city where devils rule from their hillside mansions and immense studios, spreading their corruption like a plague through your television screens and movie theaters and the Internet. Is it any surprise, in a city so amoral, that our young people—the ones who call themselves 'rovers'—dance and drink and cavort on the graves of the dead in the Waste?"

I turned the volume down, averting my gaze from the milky orbs of Prophet's eyes. His snowy hair avalanched over his shoulders, thick and frosty as a polar bear's pelt, though he couldn't be older than thirty-five, with that peanut-butter-smooth, tanned face. That bleach-white crescent of a smile. But mostly when I looked at him I saw the eyes, empty and opaque, filmed with cataracts.

"Mom, Parker and I have to go," I said.

"What?" she finally responded. "Where . . . where are you going?" Her voice dragged, weighted with the antipsychotics and anti-anxiety medications I'd procured for her through less than legitimate means. Even if I could get Mom an appointment with one of the overburdened doctors in the city, they'd just give me prescriptions I couldn't fill. Pharmacies had been looted within the first days after the quake. Supplies of food, water, and medications were trickling back into the city by air, but with most of the freeways shut down, and the trucks that did make it in being looted, there wasn't enough to go around.

When the quake hit, there were nineteen million people living in the greater metropolitan area. The population had thinned since then. Those who could manage it had abandoned the city like the proverbial sinking ship. But there were still too many people to feed and medicate. Even counting the private jets celebrities loaned to aid organizations, there were only so many planes and helicopters available to import goods. Supplies were divided up for the area hospitals and clinics and consumed as soon as they left the trucks. *If* the trucks made it from the airports to their drop-off destinations.

The only option I was left with for getting Mom's meds was the black market. I knew I was buying the same pills that were being stolen, but I couldn't afford to care. My moral compass didn't point the same direction it used to.

"Mom," I said again. I could tell she was having a hard time focusing on me. Half her attention was on the window and half on Prophet. "Parker and I have to go back to school today. But we'll come straight home after. You'll only be alone for a few hours."

A look started to surface on Mom's face. Terror at the prospect of being left alone in the house, with rioting and looting still going on throughout the city, water and power and cell service still unreliable.

Mom twisted her hands together in her lap, like she was trying to mold them into some new shape. "What if someone tries to get in while you're gone?"

"I checked the doors and windows. Everything's locked up tight. No one's getting in." It was a good thing I'd checked the windows again this morning. I'd found the one in the garage unlocked. It was a small window, but someone could squeeze through if he or she really wanted to.

Mom unraveled her fingers and parted the blinds again. "There was a boy watching the house earlier. A boy your age with glasses. I've seen him before. I can't . . . can't remember where. He saw me looking and he went away. I know him from somewhere, Mia. I *know* him, but I can't *remember*." She pounded both fists against her temples so hard I jumped. "Why do you both have to go? Can't one of you stay here with me? I don't want to be alone in this house with him out there watching."

I didn't want to tell her why it was so important that both Parker and I return to school, why it couldn't wait another week. We were down to our last cans of food, and the few schools that had reopened not only offered free lunch, but the kids who started attending classes again got priority aid. Parker and I would each receive a ration of food to take home with us for every day we showed up.

This was not about education. It was about survival.

Mom's fists were curled against her temples, her body hunched like she was bracing for impact. Was there really someone watching the house, or was she seeing things again?

"Mom . . . *Mom*, I need you to take your pills before we leave." Xanax for anxiety. Thorazine for the hallucinations and flashbacks.

She pulled her chin against her chest. "I already took them."

"Are you sure?" I sounded patronizing, but Mom hardly

ever remembered to take her pills. Most of the time she hardly seemed to remember her own name.

She gave me a sharp look. "I'm sure," she said.

A soft knock at the open door. Parker poked his head in, his thick, straw-colored hair, still wet from the shower, hung in his eyes. The water was on today. That had been a relief. I hadn't taken more than a handful of showers since the quake, and I didn't want to return to school smelling like one of the Displaced.

Parker went to Mom, put his arms around her. "Love you," he said. "We'll be back before you know it, okay?"

Mom tensed at his touch. Parker released her, trying not to look hurt by her rejection, but I knew he was. Out of the two of us, Parker had always been the sensitive one. "Empathetic" was the word Mom used to describe him, but it was more than that. Parker didn't just empathize. He was a "fixer." When someone was hurting, he tried to find a way to make them better.

But Parker couldn't crack the wall Mom had put up around herself, and it was killing him. Mom's rejection wasn't personal, though. At least, that was what I told myself. But she didn't like people to get too close anymore. Every day she seemed to fold more tightly into herself, growing smaller and smaller, as though she were still being crushed under that fallen building.

"I'll wait in the car." Parker avoided my eyes as he walked past me, but I saw they were wet, and I felt emotion close my throat.

When he was gone, I went to Mom. I wanted to hug her, too, even though I knew she would be as rigid and unresponsive as a twist of wood. But more than that, I wanted to grab her by the shoulders and shake her and demand she come back to us. We needed her.

My eyes strayed to the TV. On-screen, the camera panned back, revealing the stage. Several identically dressed teenagers—the boys wearing crisp white shirts and white slacks, the girls in long white dresses—flanked Prophet on each side. Two of them were twins, a boy and a girl, with white-blond hair a shade more ivory than Prophet's; both so tall and thin, they looked like they'd been stretched. Prophet's entourage of adopted children. His Twelve Apostles, he called them, though I only counted eleven on stage with him.

Considering how Prophet had managed to brainwash millions of people into believing he was not just a man named Prophet, not just *a* prophet, but *the* prophet God had chosen to let us know the world was about over, I didn't want to imagine the conditioning that went on in the privacy of the man's home.

"He's out there again . . . watching the house," Mom said urgently. "The boy. Look."

I bent to squint through the blinds into the bright sunlight. People passed by on the sidewalk, wandering aimlessly. The Displaced. Those whose homes had been destroyed by the earthquake. But I didn't see any boy watching the house.

"What does he want?" Mom asked. Her hand fluttered to her face; fingers traced the knotted line of a jagged pink scar along her jaw.

"I don't know," I told her, hearing the despair in my voice, thick as an accent.

Her voice shook. "Everything is coming apart, and Prophet says things are only going to get worse. He knows what's coming, Mia. God speaks to him."

God. Oh, God, God, God. I was sick of hearing about God, maybe because I hadn't heard much about him (or her, or it) since Mom's mom—our fanatically God-fearing, Bible-thumping grandma—passed away a couple years ago. After that, Mom was free to stop pretending she bought into Grandma's fire-and-brimstone theology. Grandma went to the grave thinking her daughter would someday join her in fluffy white-cloud heaven, instead of plummeting straight to hell, where my father was roasting on a spit with the rest of the unbelievers.

Mom always claimed she was firmly agnostic despite her extreme evangelical upbringing. She didn't believe in anything in particular, and she was perfectly content to wait until she died to find out the real deal. I figured her obsession with Prophet was a phase born out of desperation, like people on an airplane who start praying when they go through a nasty bit of turbulence.

I touched Mom's shoulder. It was a hard, protruding angle. She was nothing but bones under her bathrobe.

"Everything's going to be okay," I told her, even though the words had lost their meaning from too frequent use. I was always saying them to someone now, to Mom, to Parker, or to myself.

"Be careful out there," Mom said, touching me briefly on my gloved hand before pulling away. "Take care of your brother."

"I will." I turned to go, and Prophet whispered over my

shoulder, like he was standing right behind me. *"And I beheld when he had opened the sixth seal, and, lo, there was a great earthquake; and the sun became black as a sackcloth of hair, and the moon became as blood.*

"The time is coming," Prophet said. "The end is coming."

3

Parker sat in the front passenger seat of my silver hatch-back, watching the Displaced wander past on the side-walk, looking as tattered and lifeless as a herd of zombies. I wished, not for the first time, that we had a bigger garage so I didn't have to leave my car on the street. So far the Displaced hadn't messed with it, but I expected every morning to come outside and find a window busted out, and maybe a family sleeping inside.

Our Craftsman bungalow was located only a few blocks east of Venice Beach, where so many of the Displaced had migrated after the quake and set up tents as temporary homes. A lot of them made their way up to our neighbor-hood to knock on doors and ask for food or clothing or clean water.

But sometimes they didn't ask.

I looked around again for the boy Mom mentioned. I didn't want to think someone might be casing our house, but I also didn't want to believe Mom was hallucinating again. The Dealer—that was the only name I knew him by—told me the Thorazine was supposed to control that.

For some reason I thought of the dream I'd had about Nightmare Boy and that knife he'd been ready to plunge into me. And I thought of the unlocked window in our garage. Then I forgot those things as a middle-aged man with grime etched deep into the lines on his forehead spotted Parker in my car and stooped to knock on the window.

I hurried down the walk, bracing for trouble. The Displaced weren't like people who'd been homeless before the quake. They weren't used to going without, and it made them more aggressive, a fact Parker often chose to ignore. He probably would have turned our house into a temporary shelter if it weren't for Mom.

By the time I reached the car, Parker had already rolled down the window. He held out several rumpled bills to the man.

"It's all I've got," Parker said. I caught his eye over the man's shoulder and shook my head. A few dollars was more than we could spare these days. Black market meds weren't cheap.

Parker ignored me.

"Thank you," the man said, nodding over the money. "This helps. Everything helps. I have a family, you know. It's for my family."

A militiaman I'd seen patrolling the area jogged up the sidewalk toward us, one hand resting on the Taser fastened to his belt. He was dressed head-to-toe in black, like he thought he was a Navy SEAL or something.

When riots and looting broke out after the quake, it quickly became apparent that the LAPD didn't have anywhere near enough officers to control the chaos, and the National Guard and FEMA were tied up elsewhere. Droughts and wildfires in the Midwest had destroyed over a million acres of farmland, resulting in food shortages all over the country. A series of unseasonal hurricanes had ripped through the Gulf of Mexico, killing thousands and wiping out the fishing industry. Fierce tornadoes were showing up in states where they had no business existing, tearing up whole communities. Add to that the United States was involved in more wars at the moment than I could keep track of, and military forces were deployed overseas. Humanitarian organizations were occupied with famine in Africa and mass outbreaks of some new pandemic in India.

Our federal government was too busy saving the world to focus on Los Angeles, and our city government wasn't doing much better. A number of high-ranking officials, including the mayor, had perished during the quake, and those who were left couldn't figure out who was in charge, much less make any decisions about a riot solution. It was up to the people to protect themselves, so that's what they did, forming neighborhood militias composed of ordinary citizens.

"Move along, sir," the militiaman called out to Parker's charity case, who shoved the money into his pocket and shuffled away. The militiaman gave him a little push to hurry him along. The guy stumbled, probably weak from hunger.

"Hey!" Parker said, getting out of the car and facing the militiaman. The man had several inches on my brother. Still, Parker didn't back down. "You didn't need to do that. He was already leaving."

The militiaman narrowed one eye at Parker, probably the way he'd seen someone do it in a cop drama. "You shouldn't give them money. They know where to get handouts, it encourages them to come up into the neighborhoods instead of staying in Tentville where they belong."

Parker glowered at the man, but wisely chose to stay quiet when he saw how the militiaman's hand rested so lovingly on that Taser.

I cleared my throat to get the militiaman's attention.

"Hi," I said, holding out my hand. "My name's Mia. I live here." I nodded toward our house.

The man eyed my fingerless leather gloves, took note of my black turtleneck, my black jeans, and my boots. It was warm out, even this early in the morning. Not turtleneck and gloves weather, for sure, but I needed the coverage at all times, or someone might catch sight of my lightning scars. It occurred to me that the militiaman and I were dressed in nearly identical outfits. He nodded approval.

"Brent," the militiaman said.

"We appreciate what you're doing," I said, casting Parker a keep-your-mouth-shut look.

"Someone has to make sure we're not overrun by these drifters," Brent said. "I feel sorry for them, losing their homes and everything, but it's time things got back to normal around here."

I didn't have to fake a nod of agreement. What I wanted more than anything was for things to get back to normal.

"Could you do me a favor?" I asked. "My mom saw a guy watching our house. She said she's seen him before."

"You think he's planning a break-in?"

"I don't know, but I wondered if you could keep an eye out for him."

"What's he look like?" Brent asked, eyes suddenly bright with interest.

"Um . . . he was around my age . . . oh, and he had glasses."

"Dark glasses?"

"Um . . . yeah," I decided. Mom hadn't been specific.

"I'll find him," Brent said, caressing his Taser again. "And you might want to tell your brother to wise up. You leave crumbs on the floor, eventually you get roaches."

Parker muttered something I didn't catch, and I hoped Militiaman Brent didn't either. It wouldn't hurt to have this guy watching our backs.

"Thank you so much," I told Brent, gushing a bit to make up for my brother.

Brent was standing in front of my house with his thumbs hooked in his belt loops when we pulled away. I wondered if Mom was still peering out the window. I hoped Brent made her feel safer.

Parker barely spoke during the drive to school. I wasn't sure if he was annoyed with me for enlisting Militiaman Brent to keep an eye on the house, or if he was upset about Mom, or nervous about returning to school. Probably all of the above, with an added emphasis on the latter. Parker hadn't heard much from his friends since the quake. Once the Internet was up he'd exchanged a few brief e-mails with them, so he knew they were alive, but not much else. With riots and looting still rampant, and so many people sick or injured or starving, not knowing if his friends were okay was almost more than he could handle. He didn't say much, but he didn't have to. I knew my brother. At least, I used to.

Nothing was the same as it used to be.

Parker and I were only two years apart in age, and we'd always been close. But he'd changed since the quake, grown quieter, more introverted. I thought tragedy was supposed to bring people closer, but Parker was pulling away, same as Mom. I should have been the glue holding us together, but apparently I wasn't sticky enough.

Ocean Avenue, which ran parallel to the Pacific, was the quickest way to Skyline High School, and as far as I knew the road was intact and clear of debris. We passed several groups of road crew volunteers in orange vests still working to haul mounds of rubble from collapsed buildings out of the road, but at least we could get through.

But as I drove, I began to wish I'd chosen a different route. The drive along Ocean Avenue offered a view of the vast shantytown known as Tentville that had been assembled on the sands of Venice and Santa Monica. Ten square miles of the city had been destroyed, including downtown Los Angeles. People called it the Waste now, because that's what it was. A wasteland of fallen high-rises, shattered cement and glass, and empty, ruined buildings. Only one tower remained standing in the Waste, dominating the cityscape like an enormous monument to the dead.

But even miles from the epicenter of the quake, buildings had sustained major damage, especially those that were not up to code. Roofs caved in. Walls collapsed. Fires broke out and raged unchecked, while firemen and rescue workers were distracted by the catastrophic devastation downtown. On the west side, the damage was random. You'd see a dozen normal houses, and then one that looked like it had been stepped on by a giant. Even our house, which had been built around the time when people were still building houses "right," had cracks running up the walls and across the ceiling. I didn't want to think about what Parker and I would have done if our house had collapsed or burned to the ground. We'd be living in Tentville with the rest of the Displaced, caring for Mom in the midst of the chaos.

We drove past a woman sitting on the sidewalk, surrounded by plastic bags full of her belongings and holding a large umbrella, though the sun had barely climbed over the horizon. I wondered if she didn't have a tent, if the umbrella was the closest thing she had to shelter.

"Was the Internet up this morning?" Parker asked, squinting at the woman with the umbrella. "Did you check the weather?"

"Don't I always?" It was a ritual of mine to check at least three weather sites every morning, even though it wasn't necessary. When a storm was coming, I *felt* it. My skin would tingle and my bones would ache, and the fire in my heart and my blood, the feeling that had been growing inside me since the first time I was struck, would burn hotter.

Except on the day of the Puente Hills Earthquake. That day the storm had materialized out of a clear blue sky. I'd seen storms do that where we used to live in Lake Havasu City, but only during the sweltering monsoon season, and those storms were usually over as soon as they began. But storms in L.A. didn't just *happen*; you could always see them coming.

"So, what's the forecast?" Parker asked.

"Clear skies all week."

He nodded. "Good. The last thing we need right now is . . ." He trailed off, casting a glance my way. "You know," he mumbled.

I did know. The last thing we needed was another electrical storm, and not only because people were saying lightning might have caused the Puente Hills Quake . . . because that day I felt lightning cracking the sky even from fifteen miles away, and I had wanted nothing more than to put myself in its path. It took every ounce of my self-control not to get in my car and race downtown toward the storm so I could get a piece of it. Even when the shaking started, when it seemed like the whole world would crumble if it didn't stop, the only thing I could think about was pulling the lightning down into me. The aliveness I would feel. The perfect pain that might do anything to me. Even kill me.

Yeah, the last thing we needed right now was another storm.

Up ahead, what remained of the Santa Monica Pier tilted like a ramp into the ocean. The longest of the wooden pilings that supported the pier had bent and broken during the quake, pouring hundreds of tourists and a dozen or so chintzy restaurants into the Pacific. A section of the famous Santa Monica Ferris wheel still protruded from the water, like the spine of some Lovecraftian sea beast emerging from the depths.

Laid out on the sand on either side of the downed pier were thousands of tents and makeshift lean-tos. Scores of people milled about on the sand. Aimless. Waiting to get their lives back. And in the midst of the disorder, Prophet's great White Tent, where he held his midnight revivals, stood out like a mirage, glowing incandescent in the morning sun, its white canvas walls flapping in a light breeze. Followers, dressed in pristine white, wandered through the crowds of beach dwellers, offering to trade bottles of water or oatmeal cookies for a moment of the beach dwellers' time. Even from the road, it was easy to distinguish the Followers from everyone else, like white doves among dirty park pigeons.

Even from a distance, I could see how willing people were to follow the Followers into the White Tent.

Faintly, I heard the sound of shattering glass and the scream of an alarm.

"Mia, look out!" Parker grabbed the wheel and cranked it right. Just in time, too. We barely avoided mowing down a guy as he sprinted across the street, his arms loaded so high with stolen electronics he couldn't see over them. He made it across Ocean Avenue without getting creamed and disappeared into an alley, headed toward Tentville.

I screeched to a halt at the curb and waited for the inferno in my chest to cool. My heart was in my throat, my whole body trembling with the rush of adrenaline.

A group of Followers approached the car, holding poster board signs raised above their heads.

The End Is Coming, one sign read.

The Sixth Seal Is Cracked, another read.

We Have Been Warned.

The Real Storm Is Still to Come. I stared at the Follower who held this sign. She smiled and waved, like we were old friends, and gestured for me to roll down the window.

I hit the gas and probably left streaks of rubber behind as I burned away from the curb.

Parking at school was madness. There were buses and cars jamming up the whole lot. No one seemed to know who was coming and who was going. Normally there was someone on-site to direct traffic, but apparently that person hadn't shown up for work today.

As soon as we got out of the car, we were immersed in shouting and honking, whistles blowing as kids shuffled off the buses. To reduce traffic on the roads—which were still barricaded or blocked off by debris in many areas—returning students were advised to take the buses, even if they had cars or their parents could drop them off. But with Mom at home alone, I wasn't comfortable being stuck at school until the buses came at the end of the day. I wanted to be able to rush home and check on her if I needed to.

Two militiamen tried to herd the flow of people into a line, but they were ignored. Kids pushed and shoved and fought their way toward the school, even though we wouldn't receive our rations until the end of the day. Someone rammed past me and crunched my toes. Someone else nailed me in the ribs with an elbow. It wasn't that there were more people than usual heading to school; there were far fewer. But they were frantic. Desperate. Starving. Crying. Sick.

Scared.

But not the Followers. The Followers were perfectly calm and removed from the rest of us, their eyes bright as little lightbulbs, knowing smiles playing at the corners of their mouths. Somehow they managed to disturb me more than the rest of the crowd, even the kids who were suffering from earthquake fever, their skin rash-red, lips and eyelids and the rims of their noses and ears crusted with yellow sores. Earthquake fever caused the immune system to go into overdrive, so white blood cells started attacking healthy cells. Their bodies were essentially waging war on themselves.

Looking at the sufferers turned my stomach, but seeing the Followers up close like this, in real life, not on *The Hour of Light*, made me feel like turning and running away. Running as fast as I could, and taking Parker with me.

But we couldn't run away, not either of us. Not unless we wanted to starve.

The first bell warbled like a sick bird as Parker and I made our way through the crush of people and toward the main building. The bell system must have been damaged during the quake. One more thing that was off-kilter, knocked askew by our city being shaken like it was contained in a snowless snow globe.

I thought of what Militiaman Brent had said. *It's time things got back to normal around here.* Looking around at how many of the students wore Followers' white, and how many others looked like they'd come from a refugee camp, so skinny their eyes were sucked into the sockets, lips cracked and skin chalky from dehydration, I had a sinking feeling I wouldn't find anything close to normal at Skyline.

Approaching the school, I heard raised voices and then a squawk of pain and surprise. Parker and I froze in place, earning growls and shoves from the students behind us. A group of boys with mean, feral eyes and dirty skin and clothes surrounded a much smaller, weaker-looking kid.

One of the feral boys bent the smaller kid's arm behind his back, and another jabbed a fist into his kidney. The kid cried out again. His backpack hit the ground.

I searched the flow of students moving toward the school, hoping someone would step forward. Do something. I saw people watching out of the corners of their eyes, and people pretending not to see at all. I saw people walking faster, probably worried they might be the next victims.

Heat pulsed in my chest, thumping like a second heartbeat. The sound boomed in my ears. I breathed deep.

Keep it together, Mia. You made it through the last four weeks without imploding; you can make it through the next few minutes.

The feral boys released the kid and shoved him away. He staggered and grabbed onto the flagpole to stabilize himself. Tears leaked from his eyes and he wiped at them angrily with his sleeve.

Parker's paralysis broke, and he started toward the attackers. I grabbed him back.

"No," I told him firmly.

Parker's eyes were livid. "They can't get away with it."

"They already did."

The pack of boys tore open the kid's backpack, scattered his books and papers, and took off with whatever was left inside, probably a bottle of water or an energy bar. The backpack looked close to empty.

Parker wrenched away from me, and for a second I thought he would go after the pack. But he had acted too late. They were already gone.

My brother rounded on me. "I could have done something."

"You could have gotten your ass kicked."

"Better than standing here watching!" His voice was rising, so I forced mine to sound calm even though I felt like I was boiling on the inside.

The crowd parted around us, now pretending not to see my brother and me having it out.

"What do you think would happen if you came home from school battered and bruised? Mom would go into free fall. Think about it, Parker. Think about *her*."

Parker glared at me. "Mom's not the only one in the world who needs help."

Those were the words he left me with as he plunged back into the tangled procession of students.

I turned once again to the kid still holding the flagpole. He had one hand pressed to his side where he'd been sucker punched, his mouth set in a grimace of pain and his eyes turned toward the sky, maybe so no one would see his tears; maybe to look at the flag that was at half-mast to honor the dead, where it would probably stay for a long, long time.

A girl dressed in white approached the kid, holding out a tissue. She was smiling as though nothing could possibly be wrong in the world. She spoke softly to him, but I was close enough to catch her words.

"Have you accepted the Word of Rance Ridley Prophet as the Word of God?" she asked.

The kid shook his head but accepted the tissue.

I moved on before I could hear more, but I glanced back once and saw they were still talking, and I felt a chill dance up my spine. I fell in with the rest of the disheveled, hollow-cheeked kids trudging into the school, keeping my distance from the Followers. When I reached the cement stairs, I saw that someone had tagged them in white spray paint. One word on each step.

WHICH
SIDE
WILL
YOU
CHOOSE?

My head pounded as I climbed past the question.

I was heading through the door when a girl with long black hair veered in front of me, knocking me aside and sloshing half of her to-go cup of coffee onto my turtleneck.

"Hey! Watch it!" I stood there with my arms spread, dripping.

The girl stopped and turned slowly to face me. A line from some kid's show I used to watch played through my head. *One of these things is not like the others . . .*

The girl didn't fit. Where nearly everyone else here looked like they'd been through a war, this girl seemed to think she was in line at a nightclub. She wore a tight black dress and tall black boots. Her lips were painted a shade of red that made me think of stop signs. I didn't remember ever seeing her at school before the quake, and she was the kind of person you remembered. If she wasn't registered at Skyline, she wouldn't be eligible for aid. Maybe she thought she could seduce some food off the aid workers. The way she looked, it would probably work.

I glanced around and saw the crowd had thinned. Now it was just me and the girl in black.

"You could say you're sorry," I told her when she only stood there, saying nothing. The smell of her coffee soaking into my turtleneck made me salivate. I hadn't tasted coffee in weeks.

"Sorry," the girl said perfunctorily, staring straight into my eyes in a way that was too direct; smiling the way people smiled when they had a secret they couldn't wait to tell. "I didn't see you," she added. "What a klutz, huh?"

She didn't seem like a klutz. She seemed like the kind of person who could walk on ice in her spike-heeled boots and never slip.

"Which side will you choose?" she asked.

"Huh?"

"The question on the steps. Which side will you choose?"

"What are my options?"

"Us," she said, putting a hand to her chest. "Or them." She nodded at the Follower still talking to the boy near the flagpole.

"How about neither."

She laughed. "But you haven't even heard my sales pitch. It's a good one. I think you'll like it."

The second bell warbled then. Perfect. I was officially late for my first day back at school. The girl in black better hope that didn't disqualify me from getting what I came for.

"Not interested," I told the girl. Her mysterious smile dropped, and she opened her mouth to say something else, but I didn't give her the chance. I weaved around her and into the school.

And stopped.

My mouth fell open. I heard a sound in my throat like air leaking from a punctured tire.

The whole length of the entryway, about thirty feet, was completely wallpapered in photographs and flyers from floor to ceiling, and the tile along one side of the floor was littered with bouquets and stray flowers. The air was heavy with their mingled perfumes. I resisted the urge to cover my nose and mouth like I'd caught a whiff of garbage. The whole place reeked of funeral.

I stepped to one wall and examined a collage of photographs. Faces. So many faces. Adults. Children. Elderly men and women. Babies. Dogs. Cats. And captions, most of them handwritten on scraps of paper, pinned beneath the photos.

We miss you so much.

I will love you always.

We'll never forget you.

I know you're in a better place.

There were poems, and longer notes, and obituaries, and I felt my eyes burning.

"This wall is for the dead."

I jerked in surprise. I hadn't noticed the girl in black come up beside me.

I blinked the tears out of my eyes before looking at her. "Yeah, I figured that out."

She turned around and faced the opposite wall. Her sharp heel speared a white rose petal. "That wall is for the missing, people who disappeared after the quake. People who have not been found."

I thought of my mom, buried in the Waste with the rest of the dead, waiting for her air to run out. What if she'd never been found? Would I have posted her picture on this wall, hoping that someone had seen her? Hoping she was still alive, lost in the shuffle at some hospital or clinic?

I felt panic rising inside me. I tried to breathe, but I couldn't seem to get any oxygen to my lungs. The heat that lived in my chest flared, like a hot coal that never quite went out.

The girl in black tilted her head and watched me curiously, a dreamy sort of expression on her face. "Are you okay?" she asked.

I bolted. I needed out of that hallway, with all those dead and missing people gazing at me from their photographs. With its stench of flowers that belonged in a funeral home, not a school.

And more than anything, for reasons I didn't understand, I had to get away from the girl in black.

4

I couldn't go to class. Not yet. I needed a moment alone to get myself under control. I was already late, so what was another few minutes?

I found myself in the ladies' lounge on the first floor. I wasn't sure who had started calling the girls' restroom "the *lounge*," like you'd step inside and be greeted with velvet sofas, blood orange martinis, and downtempo remixes, but the name stuck. Still, it was just a school restroom, like any other. Gray walls. Gray tile floor. Gray-painted stalls. Even the light humming from the flickering fluorescent tubes overhead had a grayish hue. If a person wanted to know what she'd look like after being embalmed, all she had to do was check herself out in the lounge mirror.

It was silent inside except for the *drip-drip-drip* of a leaky faucet, but I peered beneath the stalls to make sure I was alone before removing my gloves. People probably wondered if I had scales under my clothes. Nope, just Lichtenberg figures. That's the technical name for the lightning scars, which are supposedly caused by electron showers through the skin. For most people struck by lightning, the marks fade within a few days. Mine never did. They kept growing every time I was struck. Only my face had been spared, and I had to be thankful for that. It wasn't a bad face. Big gray eyes. A kiss-shaped mouth. Round cheekbones. But if I were to be struck again . . . the lightning scars would almost certainly grow, and they had nowhere to go but up.

I ran the water until it was ice cold and then splashed it on my face. That's what movie characters always do when they're feeling overwhelmed. Splash a little water on the face, right? But somehow the women manage to do it without messing up their makeup. There must be some trick to it, because I ended up with heroin-addict eyes. I tried to rub off the mascara stains drizzling down my cheeks and only smeared them around, staining my hands.

This day just kept on getting better.

I squirted soap into my cupped palms and rubbed them until they were frothy, used a foamy fingertip to scrub the mascara from my eyes, leaving them red and irritated and a little gray around the sockets. Then I felt the sting of soap in my eyes and squeezed them shut.

"Excuse me. May I ask you a question?" The voice was polite, inquisitive, and it immediately put me on high alert. I peered up with my face dripping water to discover who had crept up behind me and was now trespassing on my personal space.

Her long-sleeved white shirt was buttoned so tight at the neck it was a wonder she could breathe, and her hair was pulled back severely enough to make her eyes bulge from their sockets. But even without the masochistic ponytail and strangulating collar, I imagined her eyes would bug out. She had that kind of intensity about her. That fervor the Followers of the Light, the Followers of Rance Ridley Prophet, seemed to possess.

But she hadn't always looked this way. Squinting at her reflection in the mirror, I recognized her. It was like looking at one of those optical illusions where a 3D image pops out of a pattern. The image that popped out at me now was of a girl named Rachel Jackson who sat a few seats in front of me in biology, only the Rachel Jackson I remembered had blue streaks in her goth-black hair, and a tattoo of a Celtic cross on the back of her neck. And now she was a white-is-the-new-black Follower? Maybe the world *was* coming to an end.

I wondered how long she'd been standing behind me. Had she seen the lightning scars on my hands? No, they were still covered in lather. I didn't rinse, just shut off the water and slid my soapy hands into my gloves, grimacing at the squish.

"Excuse me. May I ask you a question?" Rachel said this like it was the first time.

"You know, there are about ten other sinks you could use." Gloves securely in place, I turned from the sink. Our noses were two inches from an Eskimo kiss.

"My name is Sister Rachel," she began.

One of my eyebrows went way up. "Yeah, I know who you are," I said. "Biology, remember? We have it together." Apparently I was invisible. But that was fine with me. After the way I'd left things in Lake Havasu City, I was perfectly happy to live out the rest of my high school career in anonymity.

Rachel blinked once, slowly. "Is it Maya?"

"Mia."

She smiled. The Rachel Jackson I'd known never smiled. "Well, Mia . . ." I guessed the next words out of her mouth before she spoke them. "I was wondering, have you embraced the Word of Rance Ridley Prophet as the Word of God?"

"No," I said, "and I'm not—" She went on as if I hadn't spoken.

"Then I'd like to invite you to attend a midnight revival at the Church of Light this evening held by Rance Ridley Prophet himself." She conveyed the scripted words in a single breath.

Before the quake, there had been maybe three students who wore the white of the Followers. Back then, most sane people still considered the Church of Light to be one more group of extremist evangelical whackos. Then Rance Ridley Prophet accurately predicted a few natural disasters and world crises on *The Hour of Light,* and people across the globe started taking him and his church seriously. When he predicted the Puente Hills Quake, right down to the minute, people in Los Angeles started taking him seriously. Too seriously.

I didn't get it. So Prophet had predicted the earthquake before it hit. California was earthquake country! Everyone knew we were overdue for "The Big One." Prophet probably had a pet scientist locked up in the basement, calculating earthquake probability and feeding him information. The idea that God told Prophet the exact dates and times cataclysmic events were to happen was not on my list of logical explanations.

Aside from that, I had a special dislike for any organization, religious or otherwise, that pointed their finger at this person or that person and condemned them as evil, maybe because I'd had that finger of condemnation pointed at me in the past. A lot of people back in Lake Havasu City knew about my human lightning rod weirdness and avoided me, but some went out of their way to let me know being struck by lightning was a punishment from God, and that I must have done something terrible to deserve His wrath. My own grandmother had been one of those people.

My skin itched from the soap drying inside my gloves.

Rachel was still waiting for my response.

"You know . . . thanks for the offer," I told her, "but revivals . . . . they're not my thing."

"Are you sure?"

"Pretty sure. Very sure. One hundred percent, actually."

"Sister Mia—"

"Just Mia is great."

"We're all brothers and sisters in the eyes of the Lord," Rachel said.

"Uh-huh." I preferred a less incestuous worldview, but I kept that thought to myself.

Rachel cocked her head and studied me. "Mia, can I tell you what I see when I look at you?" She didn't wait for my answer. "A girl with the troubled countenance of someone in search of something."

Way to keep it nice and vague, I thought. But I couldn't help myself. I took the bait. "Something?" I said, daring her to convince me of "something." Anything.

"Truth. Purpose. Comfort." She smiled. "Light."

"All four, or is this multiple choice?"

"In these dark times, we are each in need of something," she said. "Whatever it is you seek, Prophet can provide it. You only have to ask."

I'd had enough. "You know what I want? I want you

Followers—and I mean this in the nicest way—to leave me alone. I didn't come to you looking for answers to my problems, and I never wear white, so you're wasting your time with me."

"I think you should reconsider," Rachel said, but now her voice was cold, nearly threatening. She still had not moved out of my way. The feel of the soap drying inside my gloves was getting to be unbearable, and the heat inside me, flickering in my chest like one of those birthday candles that won't blow out, was waking up, starting to pulse again, to cook my blood. I needed to get out of there. Was no place in this school safe?

I tried to ease past her, but suddenly Rachel's hand was on my arm. Her smile was gone, but her teeth still showed, as did the white around her muddy irises. Her lips peeled back from her teeth like strips of dried fruit. The lighting in here really was terrible.

"You have something Prophet wants. You *will* come to him, or you will die when the storm arrives and the sixth seal is opened completely. You will suffer and die with the rest of the unbelievers, and then you will burn in hell forever. When you deny the Word of Rance Ridley Prophet, you deny the Word of God!"

I jerked my arm, trying to shake her loose, but she was on me like a barnacle.

"Let. Go," I said, the words barely making it past my clenched teeth.

She ignored me. "*Cynic.*" She spat the word, and I do mean spat. Spots of wetness actually flecked my cheek. I used my free hand to wipe them away, shaking with rage.

The heat collected inside me, concentrated in the center

of my chest. It smoldered in my heart, an ember that would burst into flame and consume me from the inside out. At least, that's what it felt like. I tasted metal. There was a scent coming off me, like burning wires and ozone. Like the moment before a storm cracks the sky wide open.

Get a hold of yourself, Mia. Deep breaths. Happy thoughts. Zen state—

"The Day of Reckoning is at hand, and when it arrives you will burn with the rest of the cynics who refused to heed Prophet's warning," Rachel said. "The time is coming and soon. You will suffer and you will *burn* and your ashes will be cast into darkness! You will—"

The lounge door swung open.

In walked the girl in black, like she'd been waiting for the right moment.

A slow smile curled at the corners of her red lips. Her finger twisted a lock of her dark hair. If anyone was the antithesis of a Follower, it was this girl, clad in black that clung to her curves like paint; boot heels sharp enough to commit murder.

Her eyes lit on Rachel's hand. The hand that was still gripping my arm. The girl's smile stayed in place, but there was nothing friendly about it. There was glassy darkness in her eyes, like mirrors pointed at a starless night. Whatever Rachel saw in those eyes, she must not have liked it. She released me and finally stepped back.

"You're one of *them*," Rachel said. I thought she was talking to the girl in black, but when I glanced at her I saw her eyes looking at me with clear accusation. I didn't even know who "them" were.

Rachel and the girl faced off. I was reminded of a nature

documentary I'd seen, stags ready to lock antlers over a doe. I felt like the doe.

"Is this Follower bothering you?" the girl in black asked me.

"Oh, um . . ." The answer was a resounding yes, but for some reason I couldn't admit the truth. Rachel's eyes cut toward me, waiting for me to give her up. A change had come over her the moment the girl in black entered the lounge. She looked afraid. Defensive and defiant, but also afraid. "She was just leaving," I said.

The girl in black wasn't convinced. Her dark eyes narrowed on Rachel. "What did I tell you?"

The Follower slid toward the door. "I don't remember."

The girl in black sidestepped into her path. "Are you sure? Because it really was *such* a simple message. How about I give you a hint?"

"Stay away from me," Rachel muttered.

"On second thought, I'll repeat myself." The girl punctuated her statement by poking a finger into the Follower's chest. Hard. Like she was trying to break through the breastbone. "This school is Seeker territory. We claimed it first. That means you and the rest of your sheep do your recruiting elsewhere. If I catch you proselytizing here one more time, there are going to be consequences, and I promise you aren't going to like them." She pinched Rachel's cheek, leaving behind a splotch of red. "Try to remember this time."

The girl in black stepped aside, and Rachel scurried toward the door. Then she stopped and looked back at me.

"Don't join them," she said. "Come to Prophet. He will forgive you. Whatever you've done, no matter how great the sin, he will accept you. Think of it, Mia. Redemption. That's what you seek, isn't it? Redemption and forgiveness for the wrong you've done."

I started to tell her to shut her mouth, but my throat wouldn't release the words.

The girl in black took a step toward Rachel. "Get gone," she said.

Rachel puffed up her chest, and for the briefest moment I caught a glimpse of the goth-chick she used to be before she was swallowed by her new persona. "I'm not afraid of you," she said. "There is no light in you. In her, yes." She nodded at me. "I felt it. But there is no light in you, Seeker. The only thing you'll ever be is a recruiter, hiding behind those in your cult who possess real power."

It seemed impossible for the girl's eyes to get any darker, but they did. She didn't have a chance to respond, though. Rachel pushed through the swinging door. Before she exited, I caught a glimpse of the back of her neck. The Celtic cross tattoo was gone, replaced by a ragged patch of scar tissue, as though it had been burned off.

Then I was alone with the girl in black.

The heat in my chest eased as soon as Rachel was gone. I drew in a deep breath and released it, shaking my head. What was wrong with me? I hadn't come that close to losing control since Arizona, since the day my family had fled the city we'd lived in our entire lives. But I was on edge. It was that kind of day. It had been that kind of month.

Think of it, Mia. Redemption. That's what you seek.

Another round of chills climbed my spine like a ladder.

"Goddamn Followers," the girl in black said, turning to me.

"God *saved*, you mean." My voice came out shaky.

She laughed once, a short burst. "So your name's Mia? Sorry about the coffee this morning," she said. "I'm glad you were wearing black. I can't even see the stain."

I could very clearly still see the stain.

"I'm Katrina, by the way." She held out her hand. Her nails were painted the same red as her lips. The color of stop. And displayed on the center of her palm was a reddish scar in the shape of a perfect ring. It looked like a burn scar. A brand.

I hesitated before clasping hands with her. I wasn't sure why. Maybe because I didn't want to draw attention to my gloves, didn't want her to hear the wet squish if she squeezed my hand. Or because it seemed like an oddly formal thing to do in the lounge.

Maybe because that circular scar warned me to be careful.

When our hands came into contact, Katrina closed her eyes. Then she gasped and released my hand quickly, and shook hers a little. She grimaced, like I'd hurt her.

"You've definitely got it," Katrina said. "Good thing I bumped into you this morning. I felt it then, but it happened so fast I couldn't be sure."

My stomach filled with dread. "I have no idea what you're talking about."

"The Spark." She reached into the tiny black leather purse that hung on a long strap across her shoulder and removed something small and flat and rectangular. A deck of cards bound with a strip of black satin. She did a quick midair shuffle, like a magician, and then fanned the deck out for me, the cards facing the floor.

"Pick one," she said.

"Is this a trick?"

"It's an invitation."

I eased toward the door. "I should get to class."

"It will only take a second."

The cards were larger than normal playing cards, and looked soft, almost antique with age. I chose one and slid it from the deck. It felt even softer than it looked, like cloth. I turned it over, holding it so only I could see it.

I'd never had a tarot reading, but I'd seen plenty of fortune-tellers on the Venice Boardwalk doing them. The card I held between two fingers bore a picture of a stone tower perched on a cliff. Of lightning striking that tower, and people falling from the top, screaming on their way to the ground. The eyes of the fallen seemed to stare out of the card at me, accusing.

I didn't need to read the caption at the bottom of the card to know its name.

The Tower.

During the earthquake, the Tower was the only downtown skyscraper to survive. It was the newest and tallest structure, built in response to the kind of massive, glittering high-rises going up in Dubai. Construction on the monstrosity had finished only a few months before the earthquake, and it was dubbed, simply, the Tower, as though height alone excused the need for further description.

"Show it to me," Katrina said.

My throat was dry. I turned the card around so she could see it, and her eyes grew.

She snatched the card out of my hand, reinserted it into

the deck, and shuffled again, muttering to herself as she did so.

She fanned the cards again. "Pick another."

"Why?"

She shoved the cards at me. "Do it."

I caught another glimpse of the knotted red scar tissue on her right palm, but it was mostly obscured by the cards.

"All right, all right." I slid another card from the deck, shaking my head, bewildered. I'd had some strange days in my life. Some *very* strange days. But this day definitely made it into my top ten.

I turned the card over so we both could see.

"The Tower." Katrina exhaled the word.

I tried to hand the card back to her. "Nice trick," I said. "What's the secret?"

"I told you, it's not a trick." She stared at me with those glassy eyes. Her voice lowered. "It's an invitation." She wouldn't take the card. "Keep it for now," she said. "You can return it to me after school. Meet me in room 317."

"What? Why?"

"We'll talk about it then."

I shook my head. "I can't be there." I was becoming more convinced with each word Katrina spoke that I wanted nothing to do with her.

She gazed at me a moment longer, and then nodded to herself. "You'll come," she muttered, and before I could assure her she was wrong, she walked out of the lounge, leaving me with the Tower card in my hand.

5

Lunch. It was half the reason Parker and I had returned to school, but scanning the crowded cafeteria, I didn't see my brother anywhere.

Considering how many people were lined up at the lunch counter and jammed in shoulder to shoulder at the tables, it was strangely quiet inside the cafeteria, especially compared to the chaos in the parking lot that morning. There was no horsing around, no chatter. Students ate with concentration, and those in line for food had expressions of extreme focus on their haggard faces.

I couldn't help but notice that the usual cliques were a thing of the past. There seemed to be only two divisions now: Followers sat with Followers; everyone else sat with everyone else. Roughly half the tables were white. Seeing the Followers massed together like that, I was shocked at their numbers.

I didn't spot Parker, but I did notice Rachel Jackson sitting at a table near the windows, surrounded by Followers. The light pouring through the glass made their white clothing seem to glow so bright I had to turn my eyes away.

I couldn't remember the last time I'd eaten school lunch,

but the smell of hot food, even though I knew it came out of an industrial-sized slop bucket, made my stomach cramp with hunger. Still, I felt like I should go look for Parker. After what we'd witnessed that morning—and what had happened in the lounge—I was worried about him being on his own. We needed to stick together.

But I was almost to the front of the line, and I didn't want to lose my spot. Most likely, Parker had tracked down his friends and they were on their way to the cafeteria. He'd be here.

I was turned around, looking for Parker, when I felt a nudge at my back. I faced forward and suddenly there were two girls in front of me who hadn't been there before, a tall one and a stocky one, both with tangled, greasy hair and a sour smell coming off them like they hadn't showered in a while. I said a silent thank you to the plumbing gods that our water had been on that morning.

The girls kept their backs to me.

"Hey," I said, and was ignored. *"Hey."* I tapped the tall one on the shoulder.

"What?" She glanced back, annoyed. I recognized her and her friend. They were pitcher and catcher on the soft-ball team, emphasis on *were*. Maybe they hadn't figured out yet that their season was over.

"You cut in front of me," I said, thinking that if I called them out, they'd leave.

"We didn't cut," Pitcher said.

"Yeah, you did."

"Prove it." She snarled the word with such unnecessary viciousness, it made me take a step back, bumping the person behind me. Pitcher had a look I recognized, feral, like the pack of boys from that morning. A look that said she would stomp anyone who got in her way.

She faced forward again as we reached the front of the line and she and Catcher grabbed their food trays from the stacks.

I bit my tongue and told myself to let it go. There were only two of them. I'd get my food, only a few seconds later than I would have. Still, it wasn't fair. I glanced at the people lined up behind me. They looked angry, but too tired to do anything about it.

"Hey, you guys, over here!" Pitcher waved, and several more of her friends joined her, enough of them to fill a dugout.

I bit my tongue harder as what was left of the softball team grabbed their trays. Apparently I had been wrong about the usual cliques dissolving. The softball girls were tough, a force to be reckoned with, and they knew it. If they stuck together, very few people would dare to mess with them. Or stand up to them.

It's not fair . . .

The heat began to gather in my chest again, and the sound of forks scraping on plastic faded until the only thing I could hear was the rush of hot blood parading through my veins, pounding in my ears.

Let it go, I told myself. *It doesn't matter. Let it go.*

But it wasn't fair . . . Parker was right. People shouldn't be allowed to do whatever they wanted. To take whatever they wanted simply because they were bigger and stronger and ran in a pack.

Fire crackled like static in my heart, and I felt myself

reaching for Pitcher, even though the more rational side of my mind had questions.

What do you think you're going to do to her? The same thing you did to that man back in Lake Havasu City? He didn't deserve it and neither does this girl. Let. It. Go.

I sighed, knowing the voice was right. The crackling fire in my heart stilled. I let my arm drop as I was distracted by motion in my peripheral vision.

About half a dozen kids approached the line-cutters. The group was random, made up of guys and girls ranging in age from freshmen to seniors, popular kids to geeks like Andrew "Schiz" Buckley. Schiz as in paranoid schizophrenic, not that he was one, as far as I knew. Paranoid for sure, but maybe not schizophrenic. Schiz was a major conspiracy theorist and notorious blogger on the subject. I used to see flyers advertising his blog, Shoot the Messenger, posted around school.

And there was someone else I knew, a tall, slender black kid Parker hung out with on occasion. Quentin something. I couldn't remember his last name. He'd been to our house a couple times, but I hadn't said more than five words to him. Still, something about Quentin was changed from the last time I'd seen him. It was his eyes. There was a stillness in them, a watchfulness. It was almost predatory.

And every single one of the kids in his group had the exact same look.

It was creepy, and what was creepier was the way they seemed to move as one, like they were connected somehow, joined by invisible puppet strings, like birds in formation.

Quentin spoke to the line-cutters, his voice coming out

loud and strong, more adult than I remembered it. "Go to the back of the line."

Pitcher stiffened at the sound of his voice and turned slowly, holding her food tray in front of her like a shield. "Why should we?" she challenged, but her voice no longer carried the note of arrogant assurance it had when she'd spoken to me alone.

Quentin spread his hands, as though in a show of helplessness, but the gesture seemed anything but helpless. My eyes homed in on the center of his palm, on the perfect ring of red scar tissue, about the size of a golf ball.

A scar like Katrina's.

Quentin smiled with his mouth only. "Go to the back of the line," he said again.

Schiz added, "You and your friends are out of order." Schiz smoothed his Dracula-esque widow's peak. He wore a black T-shirt with bold white letters on the front that spelled: TYRANY.

The softball players shared a round of nervous glances, and I thought they would stand their ground. Then Pitcher shrugged and lowered her head, a clear sign of defeat. She stepped out of line and the rest of her gang followed her to the end.

Quentin's eyes made their way to mine, which were about as wide open as they would go.

"Nice to see you back at school, Mia," he said. And then he held out his scarred hand to me.

I shook my head like he'd offered me a loaded bear trap. I wanted to back up, but I was already against a wall.

Quentin frowned. I thought he would drop his hand, but instead he reached out to me, and his long fingers circled my wrist. He held on gently for only a split second before grimacing and letting go. He and his group shared a look, and Quentin nodded. Then they turned in what looked like a military formation, it was so synchronized, and took their seats at an empty cafeteria table where their trays of food saved their places.

I loaded up my tray and found a seat on the other side of the cafeteria, as far as I could get from Quentin and his motley crew. Still, I saw them glancing my way more often than was warranted. I tried to ignore them as I ate. Tried to pretend I was still hungry, but my stomach was twisting and tying itself in knots. Double knots, in fact. Or maybe hangman's nooses.

Parker still hadn't shown up. I had barely touched my food when I stood abruptly and decided to go look for my brother.

"You want the rest of this?" I asked the skin-and-bones boy sitting next to me. He didn't hesitate to take the food off my hands. Couldn't even say thank you, he was so busy stuffing rehydrated mashed potatoes in his mouth.

It didn't take long to find Parker. Maybe I'd known where he'd be all along.

"Hey," I said softly, coming up beside him.

He didn't take his eyes from the wall of the missing.

Have you seen this person? the wall asked a thousand times.

I felt a crawling sensation and glanced behind me, feeling as though the eyes of the dead on the opposite wall were glaring at my back.

"You're going to miss lunch," I said.

Parker looked at me. "They're gone," he said.

"Who's gone?"

"Jake. Kadin. Asher. They left the city. Last time I heard from Asher he said his family might take off, but . . ." He shrugged as if he didn't have the energy to elaborate on how his friends had disappeared without so much as a farewell text.

"Are they coming back?" I asked.

Another shrug, and then his shoulders slumped. "Would you?"

I didn't answer, because the answer was no. We might have left, too, if it weren't for Mom's condition. Travel was not advisable for people with her disorder. Besides, we didn't have anywhere else to go.

I hadn't seen Parker this dejected in weeks. I racked my mind for words of comfort, but came up short.

I hadn't made anything more than acquaintances since moving to L.A. Friendships were complicated, and I didn't need any more complications in my life than I already had. But Parker had made three good friends—or so he'd thought—since moving here. I'd actually felt a little jealous of how close they'd become. Parker and Mom were the only people in L.A. who knew my secrets, and that made them my only real friends. The only two people in the world I could trust.

"I'm sure they would have called to say goodbye if they could have," I told Parker.

"Doesn't matter. They're gone now." The carefully controlled tone of his voice told me that it did matter very much to him.

I considered mentioning that I'd seen Quentin in the

cafeteria. Knowing that one of his second tier friends was still around might cheer my brother up. I opened my mouth and then closed it again, thinking of that weird look in Quentin's eyes, and the strange, synchronized way he and Schiz and those others had moved together.

And that scar.

"Did you see this?" Parker pointed to a flyer tacked in the center of the wall.

EARTHQUAKE SURVIVORS' GROUP
MON–FRI, 6–8 PM
SKYLINE HIGH SCHOOL, ROOM 317

Room 317. Why did that strike a chord?

"Maybe something like that could help Mom," Parker said.

"She won't even leave her room," I reminded him. "You think we could get her clear to the school?"

"We could at least try. Nothing we've done so far has worked." There was tension in his voice. I could tell he was still irritated with me for getting in the way of him playing hero that morning.

There were plenty of other copies of the flyer pinned to the wall. I pulled free the one Parker was looking at. "We'll show it to Mom, see what she thinks."

I folded the flyer and tried to stuff it into my pocket, but it caught on something. I drew out the tarot card Katrina had given me. I'd forgotten about it.

Meet me in room 317.

"Is that a tarot card?" Parker asked.

I stared at the image of the stone tower perched on the

lip of that cliff. The jagged yellow lightning. The falling, screaming people, their eyes open as wide as their mouths. It was unnerving how those eyes seemed to point right at me, like the eyes of the dead on the memorial wall.

"Yeah," I said distractedly.

"Where'd you get it?"

I didn't want to tell Parker what happened in the lounge with Katrina. Didn't want to burden him with another helping of crazy.

"Found it." I stuffed the card, along with the folded flyer, back into my pocket. What I wanted to do was toss the card in the trash and hope I never saw Katrina again. But it looked like an antique. I couldn't just throw it away.

"Mia?" Parker said, his voice somber. "You think Mom's okay alone?"

"I'm sure she's fine." As his older sister, it was my job to lie to him in the name of easing his troubled mind.

"Liar," Parker said (apparently I sucked at my job), and shook his head at me. His heavy blond hair swept the arches of his eyebrows. Probably anyone who saw Parker and me together had no idea we were brother and sister. My hair—which I'd finally grown to the nape of my neck after my last lightning strike seared every strand from my head—was one stop away from black. Parker's eyes were bottle-glass green. Mine were cloudy gray. He looked like our mom. I looked more like our father, who had died of stomach cancer so long ago his face wouldn't stay in my memory. I had to keep referring to the photo albums to remind myself what he looked like, and I always got a little jolt of surprise when I saw my own eyes staring out at me from the pages.

"We should go home and check on her," Parker said. "If we hurry, we'll be back in time for fourth period."

"Parker . . . no. She has to get used to us not being home every second. It might be good for her to have some space without us hovering over her." I tugged on his shirt and started toward the cafeteria. "Come on, you might still have time to get lunch."

Parker followed, but stayed one step behind me.

At the end of the missing persons wall, the twin of the flyer I'd helped myself to caught my eye. At least, I thought it was the twin. There was a slight difference that, when I noticed it, made my stomach drop.

LIGHTNING STRIKE SURVIVORS' GROUP
MON–FRI, 8–10 PM
SKYLINE HIGH SCHOOL, ROOM 317

6

I should have eaten more of my lunch. By the time last period rolled around, my stomach was hollow and I was so exhausted I could barely drag myself to the commons to check the schedule of relocated classes. Electives had been canceled until further notice, but everyone had to show up for daily math, science, English, and history if we wanted to finish the school year and, in my case, graduate. Classes had been rearranged and consolidated on the first floor, partially due to a shortage of teachers and the drastically reduced student body, but also because the upper floors had sustained more damage during the quake than the lower.

All I had left today was English lit with Mr. Kale, the same teacher I'd had before the quake, and also my least favorite. He acted like he was schooling us in military strategy, not flowery nineteenth-century prose and poetry. And he always knew when you studied the CliffsNotes instead of reading the actual book he'd assigned.

There was a disorderly line to check the schedule. I queued up and watched as aid workers in bright orange T-shirts set up tables and organized the mountain of ration boxes they'd be handing out in an hour. Some of the aid workers wore Tasers on their belts, like Militiaman Brent's, or canisters of pepper spray. With several hundred half-starved teenagers to feed, they were smart not to take chances with letting the crowd get out of control.

As the line moved forward, the girl and boy in front of me stepped in sync, their fingers threaded, heads together, whispering intimately.

"So what did you decide?" Boyfriend said into Girl-friend's ear. "Do you want to go?"

Girlfriend's answer was hesitant. "I don't know . . . I want to, but don't you need a password or something to find out where it's gonna be? It moves every night."

I realized they were talking about the Rove and leaned closer to eavesdrop. I thought the Rove, an ultra-exclusive, traveling party that moved to a different location in the Waste every night, was a rumor, something Rance Ridley Prophet concocted to make Los Angeles sound even more corrupt, more worthy of Old Testament–style annihilation. But apparently these two thought it was real.

"My brother's friend is an usher," Boyfriend said. "He gave me the inside info so we can find it. Check it out."

Boyfriend pulled a thin book with a well-worn cover from his backpack. I tilted my head to read the title. *The Waste Land*, by T. S. Eliot. My brows drew together. How was a book of poetry supposed to get you into the Rove?

The couple must have sensed my spying. They glanced back at me with narrowed eyes, and Boyfriend slipped *The Waste Land* back into his bag. "We can talk about it later."

The two of them checked the schedule and left, hands still locked, like they were afraid to let go.

I frowned at their retreating backs, feeling a pinch of

envy. I'd never had a boyfriend, and didn't think I ever would. My freakishness was written all over my body, and I couldn't imagine letting anyone—any *guy*—see that part of me. But it would be nice to have someone to care about . . . someone to care about me. Especially now.

I put the couple and their talk of the Rove out of my mind. I hoped they were wrong and the Rove didn't exist. And if it did . . . if there really was a group of people partying in the Waste where so many had died, where my mom had almost died, I couldn't help but agree with Prophet. Maybe Los Angeles did need to be taught an Old Testament–style lesson.

I checked the schedule and was surprised to see that Mr. Kale was in his usual room on the third floor. He was the only teacher who still had a room up there.

Room 317.

The empty third-floor hallway was covered in a thin layer of plaster dust that had shaken from the ceiling. I hoped it wasn't mingled with asbestos.

Most of the classrooms were closed off with yellow tape. I peered through windows as I passed, and saw glimpses of disarray, shattered windows and desks lying on their sides and papers scattered everywhere. Why had Mr. Kale wanted to stay up here? It was creepy on this floor.

By the time I made it to room 317, the final bell for fourth period was a distant memory.

I turned the knob, ever so gently, and eased the door open . . .

"*—and pour a torrent of light into our dark world. A new species—*"

Mr. Kale looked up from the open book perched in his hands. He saw me in the doorway and his voice cut off, but his face remained expressionless. I could tell when he was annoyed, despite his deadpan demeanor. Mr. Kale had eyes the color of crude oil. They matched his hair, which he wore one length to the nape of his neck, combed straight back. His cheeks were pitted with pockmarks, and the lines around his mouth looked like they'd been carved with a scalpel.

"Welcome back, Miss Price." His gravelly voice put my skin on edge. Mr. Kale always sounded like he'd been gargling broken glass. When he read aloud, whether it was Dickens or Shakespeare, he made the prose seem like it came from a hard-boiled detective novel.

"Sorry, I didn't mean to inter—"

Mr. Kale bulldozed over my apology. "I assume you kept up with the reading while you were away, since I handed out a complete syllabus at the beginning of term."

Seriously? What kind of teacher expected you to make homework a priority during a state of emergency?

Mr. Kale smiled thinly. He seemed to take particular pleasure in torturing me. "Can you tell us, Miss Price, how Mary Shelley's *Frankenstein* relates to the Greek Prometheus myth."

A blank stare was the best I could do. I'd seen every film version of *Frankenstein* ever made—the monster and I had a lot in common—and I still had no idea what Mr. Kale was talking about.

"*A Modern Prometheus* is the novel's subtitle." As much as I wanted it to be, the voice that answered wasn't mine. For one thing, it was male. For another, it knew the answer. I searched for the owner of this voice and found a pair of the most beautifully tortured blue eyes I'd ever seen gazing at me through a pair of black-framed, Clark Kent glasses. And the face behind those glasses . . . angular, with a curvy, elegant mouth. And above those glasses . . . soft, dark hair.

Whoever this guy was, he hadn't been in Mr. Kale's English class before the quake. I would have noticed. Noticing would have been the only thing I *could* do. Like I noticed how perfectly healthy he looked, not skinny and malnourished. Like I noticed how neat and clean his clothes were, as though they'd been ironed. Like I noticed his manicured fingernails.

But if I just focused on the eyes, the tortured blue eyes, I saw someone who had suffered more than any of us.

As I had when I first encountered Katrina, I decided immediately that this guy did not fit. There was something off about him. Or something on.

Mr. Kale turned from me to the guy in the glasses. "Mr. Parish, is it?"

"Jeremy," he said.

Jeremy, a hungry little voice repeated in my mind.

"Jeremy," Mr. Kale repeated. "I understand that you're new to my class, and maybe your other teachers exercised a more liberal style of education, but in my classroom you will raise your hand before you speak." Mr. Kale turned back to me.

"Take your seat."

I beelined for a desk at the back of the room, by the bank of windows that looked west, toward the ocean. I had to pass by Jeremy to get to it, and when I did he locked those infinitely sad eyes onto mine. It was like he'd reached out and grabbed me, like his look was as good as a touch. My heart beat erratically, imitating the drum circles that used to gather on Venice Beach, a chaos of percussion. I reached my desk and folded myself into it, thankful that the window nearest me was open a crack, and I could feel cool air, damp from the ocean, drifting into the room.

I dared a glance at the back of Jeremy's head. He had the kind of hair you wanted to touch without permission.

He turned slightly and looked at me.

I ducked my head like I was dodging a bullet.

When I peeked up again, Jeremy was facing front. I sighed and opened my notebook, poised my pen, and tried to look studious. Tried to look anywhere but at Jeremy. I could feel the pull of him like a freaking tractor beam.

Mr. Kale folded his arms and strolled back and forth in front of the class. Actually, a stroll might have been what he attempted, but it came off as more of a march. Mr. Kale seemed incapable of something so unmotivated as a stroll.

"What else, then?" he asked. "Who was Prometheus?"

As if anyone cared. What did it matter who Prometheus was when half the people in this classroom were counting the seconds until their next meal, and the other half had joined a cult whose leader claimed the world was coming to an end?

No one said anything, and the vacuum of silence grew, sucking us in. I lowered my eyes as Mr. Kale scanned the room, searching for someone to call on. I didn't think he'd choose me again, even out of spite, but you never knew. Mr. Kale had never liked me. I wasn't sure what it was about me that got under his skin. Maybe the way I ignored the reading and watched the film versions of books instead, something I was certain he'd caught on to after I handed in an essay on *The Scarlet Letter* that focused mostly on the sex scenes.

Mr. Kale didn't get a chance to call on anyone. Jeremy answered again. He kept both hands planted firmly on his desk.

"Prometheus was one of the old gods of Greek mythology," Jeremy said. "He displeased Zeus when he stole fire from the heavens and gave it to man. Zeus punished Prometheus by binding him to a rock, where every day an eagle came to eat his liver. But every day the liver grew back, trapping Prometheus in an endless cycle of torture. Dr. Frankenstein crossed a similar line. Fire from the heavens is lightning, which he used to bring his monster to life. But the doctor tried to play God, and in the end he was punished, destroyed by the monster he created."

Okay. Wow. Smart and sexy. A dangerous combo. Jeremy sure didn't look like a bookworm, except for the glasses. More like a European underwear model.

Jeremy's answer should have more than satisfied Mr. Kale. He had obviously read the book and had actually understood it. But Mr. Kale only stared at Jeremy.

"Mr. Parish, the next time you speak out of turn, you will be asked to leave my classroom. This being your first day, I suggest you follow the rules if you want me to sign your ration card."

His first day? School had been back in session for over a

week. I wondered why Jeremy had waited this long to start. The only reason Parker and I had delayed our return was because of Mom. But then we ran out of food and with that we ran out of options.

"Lightning," Mr. Kale said, strolling to the other end of the room. "Fire from the heavens. The weapon that allowed Zeus to become king of the gods. That brought a monster to life. What is Ms. Shelley's intent in relating the two stories? Is she saying that humans do not deserve such power? That we misuse it?"

I sank lower in my seat at the mention of lightning.

This time Mr. Kale didn't have to wait for a hand to go up. A Follower named Lily raised hers.

"Prophet says lightning from God caused the earthquake."

"Does he now." There was a note of mockery in Mr. Kale's voice that was impossible to miss.

Another Follower jumped in. "You said it yourself. Fire from the heavens. The weapon of God. It makes perfect sense. God sent lightning to break the sixth seal and cause the earthquake, to punish Los Angeles for its shameless depravity."

"Well then," Mr. Kale said coolly, "let's hope the old saying is true and lightning never strikes twice in the same place. Moving on . . ."

Students shifted uneasily. It wasn't mention of the earthquake that had my classmates on edge. It was the idea that it might happen again.

I didn't know if lightning had caused the quake, but I wasn't naïve, and I couldn't deny certain facts. The day of the earthquake, lightning had *attacked* downtown Los

Angeles. There was no other word for it. I didn't witness it firsthand (although I'd seen footage on the news a few hundred times since) but I felt the attack like a bomb went off inside me each time lightning touched down. Hundreds of people were struck as lightning hammered the ground. Many of them died instantly. And the lightning kept coming, as though the storm were searching for something.

There was a geological survey going on at the time—which, ironically, had something to do with earthquakes—and a crew had opened up a hole in the ground that went way down into the earth, supposedly for miles, all the way to the Puente Hills Fault that runs right beneath downtown. Lightning struck straight into the hole, and immediately afterward there was an 8.6 magnitude earthquake that lasted over three minutes.

The top seismologists in the world had formulated a theory that, hypothetically, the friction along the Puente Hills fault line might have acted like a beacon for lightning. When the fault was struck, it increased the pressure exponentially, setting off the earthquake like a nuke buried miles underground.

The scientists handing out their educated guesses during news interviews were divided. No one could prove the lightning theory, but no one could disprove it either. One thing I had learned firsthand, though, was that you should never underestimate lightning, or what it was capable of. Lightning was the ultimate trickster. Among those who'd been struck, it never affected two people the same way.

The only thing you could be sure of when it came to

lightning was that the whole "lightning never strikes twice" theory couldn't be more wrong. Once an object had been struck, it was that much more likely to be struck again. It had to do with an exchange of positive and negative energy. Something positively charged on the ground reaches out to the negative charge in the clouds. The two charges meet, and you get lightning. So the reason I was struck again and again was because of my overwhelmingly positive energy. Funny, I'd always thought of myself as a pessimist.

When the bell rang thirty minutes later, students crowded around Mr. Kale, thrusting their ration cards in his face for him to sign. If we didn't have signatures from all of our teachers, we wouldn't get our ration from the aid workers.

Katrina had told me to meet her in room 317 after school, and although I was anxious to get out of Mr. Kale's classroom before she showed up, I stayed in my seat, waiting for Jeremy to join the rest of the students so I wouldn't have to pass by him again. But Jeremy remained seated, and I couldn't take my eyes off him. His head was bowed, hands covering his face, and his whole body was trembling. I wondered if he was sick. He looked like he was having a seizure.

Then a flicker of motion caught my eye. The door had opened, and Katrina stepped inside.

I slumped lower in my desk, but there was no one for me to hide behind. The room had already started to clear out.

Katrina saw me and smiled.

Then a lot of things happened at once.

Katrina stepped to Mr. Kale's side. They leaned their heads together, and she whispered something to him. His

7

"I need to talk to you," Jeremy said. From the grim tone of his voice, it sounded like he was about to tell me he'd run over my dog. Not that I had a dog.

"One second." I tore my eyes from Jeremy and about-faced in my seat, pressing my hands against the window-pane. I searched the hazy horizon line where the sky pressed against the Pacific. But there was not a breath of white in all that blue. If clouds were gathering, they were beyond my range of sight.

Not *if*. Clouds *were* gathering somewhere. I could feel it. The storm would be here tomorrow. Maybe the day after that. I couldn't say for sure, but I knew it was coming. Knew it in my warming blood and my tingling skin.

I swiveled back around in my seat.

Jeremy stood at the foot of my desk, gazing down at me. I swept my books into my bag and accordioned myself out of my seat. Over Jeremy's shoulder I could see Katrina and Mr. Kale watching us. Katrina had hoisted herself up to sit on Mr. Kale's desk, and was swinging her booted legs rhythmically.

The rest of the students had cleared out, but Mr. Kale's

door was still open, and two more students walked in. Schiz and Quentin, from the cafeteria.

"Kale, we might have a lead on—" Quentin began, but both he and Schiz froze when they saw me. "Never mind," Quentin finished.

"*I* found her first," Katrina said. "Me."

"No one's giving out awards," Schiz told her.

"But if they were, I'd win."

"Let's get out of here," Jeremy said to me, keeping his voice low. "You don't know me, Mia, but I need you to trust me. You do not want to get involved with these people. They're dangerous."

He had me at *Let's get out of here.*

"Miss Price," Mr. Kale said, "a word, please."

I don't know why I did what I did next, but I did it. Call it lack of impulse control, or temporary insanity, or both.

As I slid past him I grabbed Jeremy's hand to pull him along after me.

A wave of heat washed through me, starting in my hand and coursing up my arm, through my shoulders, boiling up my neck and into my brain.

I had a moment to think, *This can't be good,* before my mind went white. And then dark.

And the dark stayed.

And the heat stayed.

And then I—

—*stood on the roof of a building, high, high above the ground. Out in the open air. The city spread out in patches of light far below.*

I was at the Tower.

In the Waste.

*The wind charged at me suddenly, knocking me off my feet.
I fell back, and my head turned up, and what I saw above me
stopped my heart and then started it beating faster than ever.
Faster than any heart has a right to beat.*

*Black clouds filled the sky above my head, hanging so low I
could reach up and skim my fingers through them if I chose to.
They boiled and grew and spread.*

I felt the charge building.

Inside the clouds.

Inside me.

Opposite charges, needing to connect.

*I got to my feet and held my hands up to the sky, willing the
lightning to come to me.*

"Mia. Mia, look at me."

*I tore my eyes from the massing storm and saw him. Jeremy.
Standing near the edge of the roof, shaking his head.*

"It doesn't have to be like this," he said.

*"But it does," I told him. "This is who I am. This is what I'm
supposed to do."*

"You can change it." He looked so sad it made my heart ache.

But I turned my face back to the storm, still reaching up.

*Light pulsed in the clouds, but it wasn't white. It was red.
Light the color of blood.*

Thunder pummeled my heart.

I—

—opened my eyes. Flat on my back. Blinking up into a
ring of faces. Mr. Kale, and Katrina, Quentin, and Parker—

"Parker?" I sat up so fast my forehead smacked against my brother's.

"Ow," Parker and I said together, rubbing our heads. The bump must have jarred something into place, though, because I remembered what had happened right before things went black and I dreamed . . .

Dreamed of the Tower. And lightning. And Jeremy.

"Are you okay?" Parker asked me. "Did you hit your head?"

I prodded my skull. No sore spots, except where Parker's forehead knocked mine. I looked around for Jeremy. "Where did he go?" I asked.

No one got a chance to answer. Just then Schiz burst back into the room and bent over, panting. "He was too fast," Schiz wheezed. "I couldn't . . . couldn't . . ."

"Couldn't get your atrophied limbs moving faster than a trot without giving yourself a heart attack?" Katrina said. "I would have had more chance of catching him, and I'm wearing three-inch heels."

"Jeremy ran away?" I asked, still foggy.

"Stayed long enough to catch you before you hit the ground," Katrina said. "What a gentleman." She turned back to Schiz. "Did you at least get a read on him before he left you in the dust?"

"No!" Schiz pounded his fist on one of the desks, and it clattered over on its side.

"Calm down, Mr. Buckley," Mr. Kale said, his voice so low it rumbled, reminding me of thunder, of the dream. My heart continued to vibrate in my chest.

"Don't tell me to calm down! He could have been a spy for *them*! Just because he wasn't wearing white—"

"Mr. Buckley!" Kale said sharply, staring him down. The

air felt suddenly prickly as some unspoken communication seemed to pass between them. It wasn't my imagination. I could feel the static in the air, the way I could feel the electric energy in an approaching storm.

Schiz folded his arms across his chest. "Okay, I'm cool. See? I just can't believe he got away."

"I can," Katrina said. "Ever heard of a treadmill?"

"Screw you."

"Careful, or I'll ask Uncle Kale to fix you so you can't talk back to me."

"And I'll say no," Mr. Kale told her stiffly.

"It's my fault," Quentin said. "I should have gone after him, too. I got distracted." Quentin nodded at Parker. "Didn't expect to see you here, man."

Parker shook his head, confused. "I still don't know what I'm doing here."

Katrina turned to me with her hands on her hips. "What did he say to you?" she demanded. I was still on the floor, so she towered over me.

I assumed she was talking about Jeremy. "N-nothing," I stammered. "He said he wanted to talk to me." *And that you were dangerous.*

"Are you sure?" Katrina narrowed her eyes.

"Why would I lie? I don't even know him. Never seen him before in my life." But there was something familiar about him, wasn't there?

"Good. Stay away from him," Katrina said. "Don't have anything to do with him."

Funny, he said the same thing about you.

"Katrina, give her some room." Mr. Kale nudged her aside. "Can you stand, Miss Price?"

"I guess so." I couldn't believe I'd passed out. I couldn't believe I'd passed out and then Jeremy had ditched me. Jerk. Beautiful, beautiful jerk.

Mr. Kale offered me his hand to help me up. I caught sight of the ring of red scar tissue on his palm. His hand gripped mine and electricity jolted through me, like I'd grabbed hold of a live wire.

I gasped, tried to take my hand back, but Mr. Kale didn't let go until he'd hauled me to my feet. Then I was stumbling away from him. From all of them. Back toward the bank of windows and the ocean breeze that carried its storm warning.

"What was that?" I demanded. "What did you do?"

The buzzing in my palm where Mr. Kale touched me was suddenly in my head. I slapped my hands over my ears, but I couldn't shut the sound out. The buzzing was *inside*, rattling my brain. My head felt like it was full of flies. Full of static, so loud I could barely hear my own thoughts.

My eyes flew from face to face. Who were these people, and why were they looking at me like they'd found a hundred-dollar bill on the sidewalk and planned to keep it? And what was Parker doing here?

"He was invited," Mr. Kale said. "Like you."

"What?" I lowered my hands from my ears. I couldn't have heard him right.

"You wondered what your brother is doing here. I'm telling you."

"How did you . . . you didn't . . . you couldn't . . ." *I* couldn't. Finish the sentence, that is.

I thought of the way the air had prickled when Mr. Kale

stared Schiz down, and how that prickling had migrated into my skull, and I was suddenly terrified.

He read my mind. He read my freaking mind!

No way. Not possible.

In an instant, the buzzing died down. Mr. Kale's mouth twisted into a knowing smile. A knowing-too-much smile.

I looked at Parker. He reached into his pocket and removed a flat, rectangular card. He flipped it to show me the face. The image. An androgynous person floating in the center of a circle. Another tarot card. Another circle.

I shook my head. "What does it mean?"

Katrina plucked the card from his fingers, produced her deck, and slid it back among the other cards.

"The name of his card is the World," Katrina said, and smiled at Parker. "It's the card he drew. The card that drew him, actually. It's a sign that he's meant to be one of us. Potential Seekers always draw the World, and this deck is never wrong. It's more than two hundred years old. Belonged to my great-great-great grandmother, the founder of our circle, and it always knows what's inside a person. Parker is meant to serve our cause."

I raised an eyebrow at my brother, who held up his hands in a show of helplessness.

"She stopped me in the hall before fourth period and asked me to pick a card," he explained. "Then she told me to come to this room after school. She said you'd be here, too."

My gaze swung to Katrina. She was standing on her heels, arms behind her back, biting her lip in a playful, seductive way. Like Lolita.

"Who *are* you? Do you even go to this school?" I asked her. "I've never seen you before today."

"Oh, I've been hanging around a lot lately," she said. "I thought we'd tested nearly everyone at Skyline for the Spark. I couldn't believe we'd missed you until Uncle Kale told me this is your first day back since the quake."

Now it was Parker who raised eyebrows at me, waiting for an explanation. All I could do was shake my head, but the word she used, the *Spark* . . . that was what it felt like when Mr. Kale touched my hand.

Sparks. Miniature lightning bolts.

Mr. Kale cleared his throat. "We'll explain as much as we can. Mia, Parker, please have a seat."

In my mind, I heard Jeremy say, *You do not want to get involved with these people. They're dangerous.*

"I think I've heard enough," I told them.

"Mia," Parker said. "Let's listen to what they have to say. It can't hurt."

"No. We need to go home. *Now.* Mom is waiting for us. Remember her? Remember *Mom*?"

Parker's face flushed red. He lowered his eyes. "I have a feeling this is important."

"I'll take you home, if you want to stay," Quentin said, that watchful gaze of his steady on my brother.

Parker nodded his head, almost imperceptibly. He seemed mesmerized. "I'm staying," he said, and there was no room for argument in his voice.

"Five minutes," I said to Mr. Kale. "Who are you people?"

As though they'd run through this scenario beforehand—and as far as I knew, they had—Mr. Kale,

Katrina, Schiz, and Quentin raised their right hands like they were taking an oath. Each of them had a perfect circle of scar tissue branded on his or her palm.

"We are members of the Circle of Seekers," Mr. Kale said.

"The Circle of Seekers," I repeated slowly. "Whatever you say. So what are you 'seeking'? Buried treasure? The holy grail?"

"People," Mr. Kale said, and the four of them lowered their hands. "People like you."

Katrina sauntered toward me, hips swaying. "We are the answer to a question you have yet to ask. Who is going to save Los Angeles from the false prophet and his Followers? Who is going to save the world?"

"That's two questions," I pointed out.

She ignored me. "Answer: *We* are."

My gaze traveled from one face to the next as I tried to judge whether they were serious. But Parker was nodding silently to himself, as though Katrina had confirmed something he suspected all along.

"Did you know about this?" I asked Parker.

His nodding turned to a head shake, but it was a hesitant transition. "I—" he began, and then scrubbed a hand through his hair. "I don't know. Ever since the quake, I've felt—"

"Like the earthquake was only the beginning," Schiz said. "The precursor for something worse."

Nodding again, fervently now. "Yes."

The whites of Schiz's eyes were veined red, like he hadn't

slept in days. "We felt it, too, like this sense of inevitability. Like there's something we're meant to do, and the earthquake was our wake-up call. And it was. There's a war coming, and we need every soldier we can gather before the big day arrives. Consider yourselves drafted."

"Why us?" Parker asked.

Quentin slapped Parker lightly on the shoulder. "I guess you could say you both have certain qualities we're looking for."

Parker's eyes were wide. "The Spark?" he said. "I have it?"

"Well . . . not exactly."

Some of the eagerness went out of Parker's eyes. "Oh."

"Hey, don't worry about it. I don't have the Spark either, but that doesn't mean my role isn't important. I'll play my part in this, and I'm glad to do it."

"What exactly is your part?" I asked. Curiosity was starting to get the better of me.

The Seekers shared a glance, but it was Mr. Kale who answered, looking at my brother as he spoke.

"Seekers who don't possess the Spark can still sense it in others, as you sensed it in me when I touched your hand, Mia. But all Seekers, once they're bonded to us, act as conductors for the Spark."

My head pendulumed slowly back and forth. Bonding? Conductors? Sparks? I knew the meaning of these words, of course, and I knew about conductors. A conductor transmitted energy. "Conductor" was another word for a lightning rod, and being a human lightning rod myself, I was also, technically, a conductor. It sounded simple enough, and yet I didn't understand any of it.

"Okay, I'll bite," I said. "What's the Spark?"

"Simplest explanation," Mr. Kale said. "The Spark is energy. Electricity."

"Can I geek out for a second?" Schiz said, looking to Mr. Kale for permission. The teacher nodded, and Schiz's eyes lit up. He spoke so fast I could barely keep up. "It's like our bodies produce this electromagnetic field, and when the voltage is high enough, it extends *beyond* the body. Did you know every thought you have creates an electrical impulse in your brain? Imagine if you have a hundred times more electricity in your body than a regular person. Or a thousand times. A hundred thousand! Get it? You can learn to use the energy by will alone. Imagine what you could do with a single thought!"

Parker and I shared a glance, and I knew he was thinking about what happened in Lake Havasu City before we fled. I looked away first.

"Let's say this Spark actually exists," I said. "What does it have to do with saving Los Angeles? It's a little late for that, isn't it?"

"The Puente Hills Quake was a warning," Quentin said. "You've heard of the seven seals from the Book of Revelation?"

I'd heard more about the Book of Revelation lately than I cared to. It seemed to be the only book in the Bible that Rance Ridley Prophet was interested in.

"Well, they're not actual, physical seals," Quentin said. "They're signs. Portents. White horse, red horse, black horse, pale horse, and pale rider. These stand for war and famine and death and all the other badness that's going on in the world. And in this city."

"What's the fifth?" Parker asked.

Quentin and the others shared a guarded look. "That would be the, um . . . vision of martyrs."

"What do martyrs have to do with the end of the world?"

Mr. Kale cleared his throat. "That's not something we talk about with those outside our circle. If you choose to join us, we can tell you more."

"What about the sixth seal or sign or whatever," Parker asked, obviously fascinated. "Can you tell us about that one?"

Quentin spoke again. "In the Bible it says when the sixth seal is opened, the sun will turn black, and the stars will fall from the sky, and there'll be a mighty wind, and every mountain and island will be moved, which is another way of saying there's gonna be a catastrophic storm followed by an even worse earthquake."

I suppressed a shudder, thinking of what I'd felt when that breeze pushed its way into the room. That a storm was coming. Another storm.

"But there already was a storm," I reminded them. "And an earthquake. Doesn't that mean the sixth seal is already open? And, look, we're still here. The world hasn't ended."

Mr. Kale fixed me with a hard gaze. "When the sixth seal is truly opened, it won't merely affect Los Angeles. The entire world will feel it."

"And the seventh?" Parker asked, sounding like he wasn't sure he wanted to know.

"The seventh is the end, the destruction of the earth and the annihilation of all who inhabit it."

"To stop that from happening, we'll need every person we can find who has the Spark," Katrina said. "And we'll need you, Mia. Show them the card you drew."

My fingers felt numb as I pulled the card out of my back pocket and laid it down on the desk.

"The Tower," Mr. Kale said.

Schiz and Quentin stared at me, eyes wide.

"She drew it twice in a row," Katrina said.

"What does that mean?" Parker asked.

"It doesn't mean anything," I said, though chills were running up and down my spine. "It's a stupid tarot card. It's a game. And what do tarot cards have to do with Bible revelations anyway? One has nothing to do with the other."

"That's where you're wrong, Mia." Katrina picked up the card on my desk and inserted it back into her deck. "Everything is connected. Absolutely everything. There are no straight lines, only circles that go round and round and always end up back where they began. And we're all points on that circle. Even you, Mia." She shuffled. The soft cards whispered. "Let me tell you a story," she said.

I glanced at the clock. Was Mom okay?

Katrina continued shuffling.

"This deck belonged to my ancestor, the founder of the Circle of Seekers and the most powerful seer of her time. She traveled across the ocean with her Romany tribe, and the moment she set foot on American soil, she fell to her knees, struck by a vision."

Shuffle.

"She began a reading, using every card in this same deck. The reading went on for a full day and night as she laid out the cards in a circle around her. At the end of the reading, she told her people she had seen the end, the destruction of the world and of humankind, and that it would begin here, in the New World."

Shuffle.

"She said there would be signs to warn us, that one of the last signs would be an earthquake that would lay low the towers of a great City of Angels . . . all but one. And a false prophet would rise to power on a tide of destruction."

Shuffle.

"But there would be a way to prevent the ultimate end of this world. My ancestor formed the Circle of Seekers to gather people with the Spark when the time came, and to build an army to fight the false prophet. But when she finally traveled to the City of Angels she had seen in her vision, she knew the end would not come for over a hundred years, because the towers that would fall had not even been built. But she knew where they *would* be built, and she went there."

Shuffle.

"When she came to the area where the towers would rise and fall, she felt the charge in the earth. The power. She was once again struck by a vision of the end."

Katrina stopped shuffling.

I stopped breathing. Even my heart seemed to pause between beats.

"Before she died," Katrina said, "she told her children what she'd seen."

"What was it?" I asked, hating the breathless sound of my own voice.

"A girl standing atop the last tower, surrounded by a raging storm and lightning made of blood."

I remembered the dream I had after I touched Jeremy's hand, the red lightning, and the chills living on my spine raced over the rest of me.

"The arrival of this girl would be the final portent before the end. She said we would know her because her skin would be marked, and she would always draw the Tower card."

Katrina tilted her head and considered me, eyeing my gloves. My turtleneck. "Or the Tower would choose her."

I stood frozen as Katrina set the deck of cards down on a nearby desk. She cut the deck and moved the bottom half to the top.

"Choose," she said.

I shook my head. "Parker, we're leaving. Come on."

I didn't wait to see if he followed. I bolted for the door, but Parker caught up to me before I could turn the knob.

"Mia, wait." He grabbed my arm. "What if it's true?"

I shook him off. "You know how long people have been saying the world is about to end? Since the beginning. I'm sick of hearing about the end of the world."

"But—"

"Parker." I took hold of his shoulders and spoke gently but firmly, like Mom did when she had a point she wanted to get across for the last time. "They're a cult. They're no different from the Followers."

"We are nothing like the Followers," Mr. Kale growled.

"I wasn't talking to you," I growled back. We sounded like a couple of guard dogs.

His expression hardened, and I felt a sort of tingling in my head, like I'd stood up too fast.

Watch your tone, Miss Price. I'm still your teacher.

The voice that spoke inside my mind did not belong to me.

Kale's eyes narrowed on mine.

*I know who you are. I know what you are. And I know
about the lightning.*

I felt my eyes getting bigger. I shook my head, like I
could shake Mr. Kale loose.

"No," I muttered, covering my ears. "No, no, no. This
isn't happening."

*It is happening. It's all connected, Mia. It's energy, and it's
everywhere. You can't escape it.*

"Mia?" Parker's brows drew together. "What's wrong?"

*Is it really so hard to believe? There have always been people
who could do inexplicable things. Psychics and healers. Mind
readers. People who can move objects or start fires with their
thoughts. People who have visions of the past or the future.
These people had the Spark, and so do you.*

"No . . ."

*What can you do, Mia? Isn't it time you found out? Or do
you already know?*

Mr. Kale's eyes were oil-dark and blazing. Mesmerizing.

I tore my gaze from his, grabbed Parker's arm, and
hauled him out the door, slamming it behind us. The buzzing in my head ceased, and Mr. Kale's voice died with it,
but I kept on running, dragging Parker with me, until we
reached the stairs. Then he finally dug in his heels and
stopped us.

I expected Parker to demand we go back, hear the rest,
but the look on my face must have convinced him to let
it go.

"You're white as a sheet," he said, brows drawing together in worry. "You're not gonna pass out again, are you?
Do you need to sit down?"

I shook my head, keeping my eyes on Mr. Kale's classroom door, praying it wouldn't open.

"Can we please go home? Please, Parker?" I was begging. I didn't care. I wanted to get as far away from room 317 as possible.

Parker, too, glanced down the hallway at Mr. Kale's door. Then he sighed and nodded. "Let's go home."

8

"What's he still doing here?" Parker asked as we turned the corner onto our street. He pointed at Militiaman Brent, standing on the sidewalk in front of our house. His posture was very bodyguard, legs wide, arms crossed high on his chest.

When I saw him, my stomach lurched. Had something happened? Had someone tried to break in?

I parked at the curb and killed the engine. Militiaman Brent didn't turn around. Didn't move a muscle. He was like one of those soldiers on guard at the Queen of England's house.

Parker eyed Militiaman Brent warily. "I'll go check on Mom." He skirted around the man, unlocked the door, and slipped inside. I grabbed the small box containing our rations off the backseat.

"Hi, Mili—hi, Brent," I said, approaching.

He nodded. "Mia."

"Have you been here since this morning?"

"Left at noon to go home and make a sandwich, but I came right back after that."

"You know, when I asked you to keep an eye on the

house, I didn't mean to enlist you as a permanent guard. If you have other things you need to do—"

"Saw the kid with the glasses, the one's been watching your house."

Words went solid in my throat. I had to cough them out. "Are you sure it was him?"

"Boy about your age, here not fifteen minutes ago. When he saw me he got real nervous and walked away. He had glasses on, but not dark ones like you told me he wore. More like the ones the yuppies wear."

"Square with black frames?" I asked, my mouth going dry.

"Yep, those're the ones."

"And dark hair? Really, *really* good-looking?"

Brent puffed out his chest and drew back his head so far that it became part of his neck. "He had dark hair, yeah."

I swallowed hard. It was Jeremy. It had to be.

"You know the kid?" Brent asked.

"I think so. I have a class with him."

Brent's eyes got small. "This guy have a crush on you?"

Heat sizzled up my neck. "No," I said quickly.

The corners of Militiaman Brent's mouth tugged down. "Sounds like you got yourself a stalker." He reached into his pocket, took out a small canister, and handed it to me.

I read the words on the label. "Pepper spray?"

He nodded. "All you gotta do is point and press the button. But make sure you don't point it at your own face on accident. And try not to breathe any of it in, or you'll feel like you took a shot of napalm."

"Well . . . thanks."

"You see that stalker of yours, don't hesitate. Just spray."

Militiaman Brent's words followed me up the walk and into the house. Jeremy, a stalker? No way. A guy like Jeremy didn't need to stalk.

When I opened the front door, I heard a strangled cry and immediately fumbled the can of pepper spray. So much for the point and shoot.

I ran for Mom's room.

Mom was on her bed, knees pulled into her chest and surrounded with her arms, her whole body shuddering. She broke into bouts of terrified screams that quickly left her throat hoarse, so she could only produce strained wheezes. The scar tissue on her cheeks and chin stood out in stark relief, bunched and waxy.

Parker hovered over her, unsure what to do. Whether to keep his distance or touch her to try to bring her out of the flashback. Back to this reality. The one where she was safe in her own home, not buried alive, waiting to die.

I sprang into action. I couldn't say I'd gotten used to these episodes over the past month, but they no longer left me paralyzed.

"Get the Thorazine from her medicine cabinet," I told Parker. He rushed to Mom's bathroom. I heard him riffling through bottles of pills. Heard things clatter as they fell into the sink below the cabinet.

I bent to Mom's ear and spoke softly to her. "Mom, it's Mia. Can you hear me? I'm right here with you, in your bedroom. You're safe. You can come back. I promise this is a safe place. Nothing bad will happen to you here."

If she heard me, she gave no sign. Still, I kept whispering my words of comfort. But all I could think was "This shouldn't be happening. This shouldn't be happening." I was no pharmacist, but the amount of Thorazine and Xanax I had Mom on should have ended these episodes.

The TV was on, and Prophet's face filled the screen. The opaque globes of his eyes seemed to bore right into mine as he spoke.

"I do not relish being the bearer of these bad tidings," Prophet said, his crooner's voice more somber than usual. "I wish with my whole heart that it had not come to this. But know, my Followers, that you need fear no evil, for we will walk together through the Valley of the Shadow of Death, and we will emerge into the light on the other side. If you have surrendered your soul to God and pledged yourself to His service, then you will be protected from the coming devastation. While the world falls down around you, while the storm rages, you will be safe in the eye. On April 17, three days from now, the storm will arrive, but you will be saved."

All at once, Mom's wheezing cries ceased, and her rigid body unclenched. She sat up, blinking at the TV, backhanding tears from her face. She didn't even seem to realize I was there. Her eyes were for Prophet only. It was his words that had brought her out of the flashback, not mine.

Parker appeared in the bathroom doorway, his hands full of pill bottles. "Is she—"

"I'm fine now," Mom said. Her voice was the clearest I'd heard it since the quake. She sounded . . . not like her old self, but at least like someone who was present. Who was not mumbling through a dream.

She looked at me, squinting, as though my face refused to come into focus.

"Mia." She said my name like she was trying it out, seeing if it fit. "Parker."

She touched one of the scars on her face, and then nodded, as though accepting something. "I need to be alone."

She looked at the door, a clear cue for Parker and me to leave. But neither of us moved. Mom hadn't been this lucid in weeks, and I was afraid if I so much as blinked I'd miss the moment.

"Please," she said, her tone sharpening. "Leave me alone so I can think."

Parker looked like he'd been slapped. The anger I'd felt toward Mom that morning, the crazy-making frustration that had been building inside me for a month, surged to the surface.

"We're trying to help you." I didn't quite shout the words, but close enough.

Mom's eyes held mine, unblinking. "You can't help me," she said, her voice regaining some of its usual slow dreaminess. "I'm lost. Lost in the dark. In the Valley of the Shadow."

She looked at the TV. At Prophet.

"He says a storm is coming to finish what was started. The storm that will be the end of all things. He says it is God's will and God's plan."

The tiniest of smiles lifted one corner of Mom's mouth.

"He can protect us."

I punched the power button on the TV, and the screen went dark. "He's nothing but a televangelist, Mom. See how powerless he is? I push a button and he disappears."

She flung herself at me, arms flailing, and I was sure she was going to hit me.

But she didn't hit me. She pushed me. Pushed me to the side, out of her way, and turned the TV back on. Once again Prophet's face filled the screen.

She breathed deeply and smiled into his empty eyes. "Go away," she said to Parker and me without taking her eyes from Prophet's.

"What happened?" I asked Parker when we were in the kitchen, where Mom couldn't overhear us.

He shook his head. "I went to check on her. She seemed calm enough. She was sitting there on the bed, watching *The Hour of Light*. Then Prophet started talking about how a storm was coming, and when it arrived it would bring another earthquake. Mom heard that, and she freaked."

Quentin's words played through my mind. *There's gonna be a catastrophic storm followed by an even worse earthquake.*

Everyone was singing the same tune these days.

My jaw began to ache, and I realized I was clenching my teeth. Of course it had been Prophet who set Mom off. That was his MO, wasn't it? Scare people into submission. And he'd picked the perfect way to do it. Everyone wondered whether lightning striking the Puente Hills Fault had caused the quake. And whether it was even more likely to happen again when this new storm arrived, with the ground in the Waste cracked open in rifts that went down for miles, exposing the fault line.

And a false prophet would rise to power on a tide of destruction.

"Mia," Parker said, his eyebrows angled with worry, "we have a problem."

"Last I checked we had more than one."

"Well, add this to the list." He shook the half-dozen pill bottles in his hands. I expected a sound like maracas, but there was no sound at all.

They were empty.

I grabbed one of the bottles out of Parker's hand and held it up in front of my face. "Where did they go?"

"Maybe Mom's been taking too many."

I started to shake my head, and then stopped. Usually I oversaw Mom taking her meds to make sure she got the right dosage. But I left the pills in her medicine cabinet, and she spent plenty of time alone in her bedroom. She could have taken more pills at any time.

I remembered how she'd snapped at me that morning when I asked her if she was sure she'd taken her meds. I wanted to march into her bedroom and confront her, but not right now. Not after the way she'd screamed at Parker and me to leave her alone.

Acute Stress Disorder wasn't normally supposed to last more than four weeks, but even then it often transitioned into Post-Traumatic Stress Disorder, which was nearly as bad. Parker and I couldn't take care of her unless she was doped up.

"I'm going to see the Dealer," I told Parker, and pounded up the stairs to my bedroom to raid my rapidly diminishing store of cash.

Parker followed on my heels. "You promised you wouldn't go back there after what happened last time."

"It wasn't that big a deal. People get mugged every day."

I grabbed the wad of cash I kept hidden inside the Monopoly box in my closet. I counted out the bills. Two hundred and seventeen dollars. Enough for another week's supply of Xanax and Thorazine, but I'd have to forgo Mom's sleeping pills.

"Maybe there's some other way to help her," Parker said. "Like that earthquake survivor's group at school. She might not even need the meds anymore. She seems a little better . . . sort of."

"She had another episode," I reminded him. "With the amount of Thorazine she's taking—*over*taking—that shouldn't happen anymore."

"Then let me go instead!"

"No. The Dealer won't sell to you. He doesn't know you." The Dealer only accepted patrons by referral, and I'd lucked out in making a connection to him through one of our neighbors, a woman who now bought her insulin on the black market for ten times the amount she used to pay. But it was either fork over the money or go into diabetic shock.

I shoved the cash deep into my pocket. "I'll be careful," I said, but where I was going, it wouldn't matter how careful I was.

On my way out the door, I grabbed the can of pepper spray and slipped it into my other pocket.

9

There was no other place in the world like the Ocean Front Walk on Venice Beach. If you took a circus, a hippie commune, an insane asylum, a homeless shelter, a gypsy caravan, and an inner city ghetto, mixed them up until they were jumbled together, and then set them down in front of a beach polluted by sewage where people still dared to surf and sunbathe, you'd have the Ocean Front Walk.

Of course, that had been before the quake.

Strolling down Ocean Front Walk was no longer an amusing way to spend a sunny afternoon. Now it was a good place to get mugged or beaten or maybe shot.

Here's what happens when several square miles of the poorest, highest-crime areas of Los Angeles are destroyed, and the city offers the former inhabitants of those areas no alternative but to migrate west, away from the ruins of their homes; offers them nowhere to stay, nothing to eat, no clean water to drink, no showers but those used to wash sand and saltwater off after a swim in the ocean or a day of sunbathing.

Here's what happens . . .

* * *

I did my best not to look conspicuous as I struggled through the crowd on the boardwalk, trying to reach the other side, where beyond a small, grassy rise lined with swaying palm trees lay the beach and Tentville. Getting across the congested boardwalk wasn't much easier than attempting to walk through a concrete wall, and it was difficult not to stand out when you were one of the only people in sight who'd showered in the last couple weeks. I noted several sets of eyes following my progress, and I knew what the owners of those eyes were wondering.

What does she have that I need, that I might take?

I met those eyes with defiance. I couldn't let them think I was weak. I'd made that mistake before.

You don't want to mess with me, I thought as I met the eyes of anyone who paid too much attention to me. *I came prepared this time.*

I touched the bulge in my pocket, the can of pepper spray. I understood now why Militiaman Brent touched his Taser so lovingly.

Fighting my way across the flow of people packing the boardwalk was like trying to swim through a fast-moving river. The rank smell of unwashed bodies filled my nostrils. And the noise . . . so many voices talking at once. Loud. Angry. Children crying. Babies shrieking.

I didn't normally have problems with claustrophobia. Small spaces didn't bother me, but crowds . . . crowds were another story. Having so many people surrounding me, pressing against me with their unfamiliar dirty bodies, panic began to override all other brain functions.

I came to a standstill. I couldn't move, and no one else seemed to be moving either. Faces were the only thing

I could see. Faces everywhere. And eyes. All looking at me. Seeing me for what I was. Not one of *them*. I didn't belong here and everyone knew it.

A baby screamed next to my ear.

My paralysis snapped.

I broke through to the other side of the boardwalk and stumbled up over the grassy knoll, past the palm trees, where I could look out over the expanse of sand to the water.

Over the weeks, Tentville had come to resemble a sort of medieval village, only it was vast, stretching as far as I could see in either direction. A pall of smoke hung low over the area, fed by constantly burning cook fires. People huddled around those fires, even during the warm hours of the day, just staring into the flames. Children wandered lethargically through the space between tents, slow with hunger and exhaustion, their cheeks streaked with soot, ashes in their hair, their clothing getting looser by the day.

Many of the tents had been brightly colored nylon when Tentville was first founded, but were now gray and faded from smoke. But one tent stood out from the others. This one was as broad as a small house, and large enough to stand up in. A heavy, canvas army tent, only it was not camo-colored. It had been painted a deep shade of purple. The color of royalty.

The Dealer thought highly of himself.

"Do you have an appointment?" The guard standing outside the Dealer's lair looked like a retired linebacker.

"No," I said. "But I have cash."

He stared past me. His arms were so large and lumpy with muscle, he appeared to have babies stuffed up his sleeves. The Dealer probably gave him a discount on steroids.

"You need an appointment," the guard said. "The Dealer is a busy man."

"I'm a regular. Doesn't that give me some sort of privileges or something?"

"No."

"Look, just poke your head in there and tell him Mia Price is here. He'll see me, I swear."

For a moment I thought the guard would choose to ignore me completely. But he turned and stuck his head through the tent flap. I heard him mutter something, and the high, almost whiny return of the Dealer's voice, and then his cackling laugh, making my spine go rigid. The Dealer's laugh always gave me the creepiest of creeps. He sounded crazed. Unstable. He had access to all these psychotropic meds; he ought to try some, instead of whatever he used that made his pupils dilate to the size of M&M's.

"Send her in," I heard the Dealer say in a lilting singsong.

His guard held open the flap for me.

I squinted as my eyes adjusted to the shadowy interior of the tent. The purple paint that had been used to coat the canvas blocked out the light, and most of the air, too. It was so hot and stuffy inside, I began to feel faint and sick to my stomach. I could still smell the paint fumes. The chemical scent combined with the smell of the Dealer's jasmine candles to make the inside of my head feel like it was full of bees and clouds.

"I think this place is violating a few fire safety codes," I said.

The Dealer lounged on a patchwork pile of colorful pillows at the back of the tent, looking like some kind of ghetto maharaja. Most of the candles were placed behind him, so his face stayed in shadow. His hand rested on a huge black rottweiler that let out each breath in a rumbling growl.

"Didn't think I'd see you again so soon, Mia Price. Mia, Mia, Mia Price," he sang, and then cackled. "It's always a pleasure to see you, though, m'dear. You're one of my favorite customers."

"I'm honored." I wasn't sure how I'd come to be a favorite, but if it got me what I needed, I was happy to accept the status.

"Come," the Dealer said, patting the pillows. "Have a seat. Tell me what I can do for you."

"Actually, I'm kind of in a—"

"Have a *seat*."

The rottweiler growled and licked its chops with a pink tongue the width of a shoe.

I sat, keeping as much distance as I could between the Dealer and the rott and me without seeming impolite. Or afraid. Showing fear was as dangerous in this tent as it was on the boardwalk. The Dealer fed on it.

"Closer," the Dealer said. "I'm not going to bite. I can't speak for Rosemary here, though." He patted the rott's thick skull.

I told him what I needed.

He whistled, impressed.

"You went through that fast, girl."

"It's not for me."

"Mm-hmm."

I shook my head. It didn't matter who the Dealer thought the meds were for. All that mattered was that he sold them to me. I pulled out my cash and counted two hundred dollars. A hundred dollars per bottle.

I handed the money over. Rosemary watched my hand like it was a steak dripping blood.

The Dealer counted the money, and then shook his head sadly. "It's not enough."

I blinked at him. "But that's how much I always pay."

He sighed as though it broke his heart to tell me. "Stock is low. I've had to raise prices."

My chest felt tight. "I can pay a little extra." I shoved the remaining seventeen dollars at him, but he kept on shaking his head.

"You know how many desperate people there are in this city? People who need what only I can provide, and will do whatever it takes to get it? I'm afraid prices have doubled, dearest. Two hundred per bottle."

The walls of the tent seemed to be collapsing around me. "I . . . I can't pay that much. You said I was one of your favorite customers. Can't you cut me a deal this time or something?"

"Spoken like a true addict," he said, his eyes laughing and cruel. He was enjoying this.

"I'm not an—"

"You know what I tell addicts like you, the ones who come to me and turn out their pockets and it's still not enough, and they ask me, 'Isn't there anything I can do?' I tell them . . . yes. Yes, there is."

The Dealer's eyes lowered from my face and scanned down my body. My hand inched toward the pepper spray in my pocket, but froze when Rosemary snarled a warning.

"She likes you," the Dealer said. He reached out and curled a hand behind my neck. His pupils were enormous black marbles. "I like you."

Fear gripped my heart until I thought it would burst. "Never mind," I said. "I don't need the pills. I'll . . . I'll just go."

The Dealer's smile dropped off his face. "No," he said. "I'm going to give you what you came for. What you really need."

My hand raced for the pepper spray and lost.

I didn't have time to scream. It wouldn't have done any good even if I had. This was Tentville. The residents were used to screams.

The Dealer lunged on top of me, pressing me into a pile of pillows until I thought I would disappear, that we would both sink below the surface of them, sucked under like we were in water.

I struggled, fought, scratched, kicked, snarled, swore, but the Dealer had nearly fifty pounds on me, and whatever drug was pumping through his system had made him strong. I tried to scream, but he clamped a hand over my mouth. I bit down hard and tasted blood and tried to spit, but I couldn't because his hand was still on my mouth, and his other hand was pulling at my shirt and working at the zipper of my pants.

The taste of blood in my mouth became the taste of copper wires humming out the flavor of electricity.

The heat inside me came crackling to life, and for once I didn't try to calm it. I let it rage.

"What's this?" the Dealer said, sounding mystified. I felt his hand on my bare stomach. So he'd seen the lightning scars. I should have cared, but I didn't, because the fire in me had taken over and was traveling through my arms, and it was hard to care about anything when you were about to explode.

"You got some kind of disease?" the Dealer said, suddenly repulsed.

"Yeah," I said, my voice faint to my own ears. "You want some?"

He sat up, his face twisted with fury. "You weren't gonna tell me, you little whore?"

He hauled back to hit me. Before the blow could land, there was a sound like a baseball bat hitting a grapefruit, and the Dealer grunted, and his eyes bulged. Droplets of blood flew like splattered paint, and he fell flat on top of me. Smothering me. I shoved at his limp body, but he was dead weight and I could barely budge him.

And then someone grabbed the Dealer and rolled him off me. It was so dark I couldn't make out who stood over me. An image flashed behind my eyes. There was something familiar about the silhouette, but I couldn't place it. The guy looming over me had something clutched in his hand, but in the memory trying to climb to the surface of my mind, there had been something else in his hand. Something shiny and—

"Mia," the silhouette panted. "Are you all right?"

"Jeremy?" My mind went blank with surprise, and the recollection I'd been struggling to capture said goodbye.

"Are you all right?" he demanded.

"Yeah. Yeah, I'm fine." I was getting there, anyway. The fire in me dimmed, making it easier to form a clear thought.

Jeremy turned his eyes away. I looked down and saw that my pants were undone, and my shirt was pulled up to just beneath my bra. I sat up, scrambling to right my clothes. Had he seen my lightning scars?

"Let's get out of here before he wakes up," Jeremy said. He scowled at the Dealer's prone figure. In one hand he held a heavy, cast-iron skillet that he must have grabbed from someone's cook fire. The way his fingers clenched so hard around the skillet's handle made him look like he wanted to bash the Dealer's head with it a few more times. I'd thought earlier today that Jeremy had the saddest eyes I'd ever seen. Now I thought he had the angriest.

But how had Jeremy gotten past the guard? And how had he known I was here?

He started to reach out his free hand to me to help me up, and then withdrew it, so my hand fell short.

He shook his head. "Sorry. I can't." Can't what, he didn't say, but I got the point. The last time I'd touched his hand, I'd woken up on the floor of Mr. Kale's classroom.

I started to climb to my feet on my own, but a low, rumbling growl like the sound of a motorcycle idling froze me in place.

Jeremy and I both looked toward the sound. Rosemary's moist black eyes glinted in the candlelight.

"No sudden moves," Jeremy said, but I immediately reached for the pepper spray. I had to fight to get my hand into my pocket. Damn skinny jeans!

I wrested the can loose and we began to ease slowly toward the tent flaps, the huge black dog's eyes following. Then she grumbled a warning, but too late. A hand grabbed my ankle and jerked my leg out from under me. I landed flat on my stomach in the sand. The breath was pounded from my lungs.

The Dealer's eyes were wide open. Full of rage. But I was prepared this time. I pointed the pepper spray right at his eyes—at least I hoped the nozzle was pointed in the right direction—and pushed the button.

Sssssss!

The Dealer roared and released me to clap his hands over his eyes. He started coughing like he had a lung stuck in his throat. My own throat began to burn, and then I was coughing, too. And so was Jeremy. I doubled over, feeling like I'd swallowed a handful of fire ants that were eating their way toward my lungs. My eyes teared up and oozed fat droplets that felt thick as oil.

The Dealer grabbed blindly at me again. I crab-scrambled through the sand.

Rosemary barked. The sound was earsplitting, and seemed to make the walls of the tent shudder. Then she leaped, knocking over a scented candle onto the pile of pillows. Flames erupted instantly and spread to the tent wall as though the whole place was doused in gasoline, which it might as well have been considering the recently applied coat of purple paint.

Rosemary's teeth sank into the Dealer's arm. She shook her head violently, like she was trying to snap his bones, and the Dealer screamed.

I found my feet and looked down at the Dealer. "You were right," I rasped, my throat ragged from the pepper spray. "She does like me."

The fire consumed the mountain of pillows and had nearly enveloped the far wall of the tent. The heat was reaching unbearable levels. Still, I considered attempting a quick search for the meds before remembering the Dealer kept them locked in a safe.

Covering his mouth with his shirt, Jeremy waved me toward the tent's opening.

I felt the weight of defeat on my shoulders. The meds were gone.

A crowd of onlookers had gathered around the Dealer's tent, but no one made any attempt to put out the fire. The Dealer had not allowed anyone to set up a tent within thirty feet of his, so they must've figured the fire wouldn't spread. Apparently the Dealer didn't have a lot of friends among the residents of Tentville. Even his guard had gone MIA, or so I thought until I saw him lying unconscious on the sand a few feet from the tent. No . . . not unconscious. His eyes were open, but twitching, as though he was experiencing some sort of waking REM sleep.

"What happened to him?" My voice clawed its way through my throat. Tears continued to seep from my stinging eyes.

Jeremy shrugged and looked away. "Maybe he's epileptic."

"That's convenient." Before I had time to fully express my suspicion that Jeremy had done something to the guard,

Rosemary shot from the Dealer's tent and charged into the crowd.

"Doggy!" a little boy with a severely runny nose shouted. His mother pulled him out of Rosemary's path just in time to avoid his getting rammed.

The growing crowd surrounded us.

"We should probably run now," Jeremy said.

"Definitely," I agreed.

We took off through the path the rottweiler had cut and didn't stop until Tentville was behind us.

10

As soon as we stopped running, I started crying. I couldn't help it.

I had failed. I didn't get Mom's meds, and now my only black market connection might be dead.

Dead. Because of me.

At least my tears cleared the remnants of pepper spray from my eyes.

About a block from my house, I was able to get control of myself. I sniffed and wiped at my face and avoided Jeremy's eyes. He was so quiet I finally had to say something to break the silence. I didn't really feel like talking, but I figured it might help me get my mind off the fact that I was probably directly responsible for a man's death.

I had so many questions for Jeremy; I didn't know where to begin. But when I opened my mouth, what came out was more of a statement. "You're not actually enrolled at Skyline, are you."

He took his time deciding on an answer. "No."

"And you weren't there for aid."

"No."

"So what were you doing there?"

He glanced at me, but for once his eyes were unreadable.

I decided to switch to a different line of questioning. Or accusing. "You've been hanging around my house."

Jeremy staggered a little and looked alarmed. "You saw me?" The blood disappeared from his face.

"No, my mom saw you. And Militiaman Brent saw you after school today. He thinks you're a stalker."

Jeremy looked confused for a second, and then strangely relieved. "Outside," he muttered to himself. "They saw me outside." He took a breath and let it out. "I'm not a— Who's Militiaman Brent?"

"One of the neighborhood militia guys. His name is Brent. He likes his Taser a lot, so you might want to steer clear of him."

Jeremy nodded, and the anger gathered in his eyes again. "I remember him. If he hadn't run me off, I could have—" He stopped.

"You could have what?"

He ignored my question. "So you never saw me . . . at your house? Not that you remember?"

"You I would have remembered," I said, and then felt heat fill my cheeks. "I mean, because you don't look like one of the Displaced, so you would have stood out to me. Not because of any other reason. Just . . . never mind."

Jeremy wrinkled his brow at me as though I were some foreign language he was trying to translate.

We moved aside as a band of the Displaced approached on the sidewalk. They looked at us with pleading eyes. They all had the same hollow cheeks, and their eyeballs seemed loose in the sockets. Several of them had the raw, seeping sores around their lips and nostrils that came with earthquake fever.

"Can you spare a few dollars?" asked a woman with ashes in her hair, holding the hand of a little girl sucking her fingers, like they might provide some sustenance.

A few dollars wouldn't even buy this woman a loaf of Wonder Bread anymore.

Parker gave away enough money to the Displaced for both of us, so I said, "I'm sorry, I—"

The woman cut me off. She spoke quickly, trying to get the words out before I could escape. "We're so hungry. If we can't get food today, we'll have to go to the White Tent, and I don't want to take my daughter there. I hear what goes on inside. People like us go in, and then come back out . . . different."

Chills shimmied up my spine.

The other Displaced surrounded Jeremy and me, and I felt a surge of panic. I hated to think it, but I was reminded of feeding pigeons at the park. Once one of them realized you had bread, the rest of them gathered around and followed you wherever you went.

I didn't want to reach into my pocket and pull out my two hundred seventeen dollars in cash, afraid that one of these people might snatch it and run. But then I realized I didn't have two hundred seventeen dollars in cash anymore. I didn't have a single dollar in cash. The money I'd given the Dealer had gone up in flames in his tent.

I clenched my fists at my sides. For a second I thought the tears would return at the realization of yet another failure, but the well was dry for the time being.

"Please?" the woman begged. Her daughter continued to suck her fingers. Drool ran down the sides of the little girl's mouth, cutting muddy trails through the dirt on her face. The Displaced pressed closer around us. Others began to hold out their hands. As one man murmured his plea for aid, the sores on his lips cracked open and oozed a mixture of blood and pus.

"Please," they said. "Please help us. Don't make us go to Prophet."

"He does something to people like us."

"He changes us. Puts his hands on us and changes us."

"We hear the stories."

"Don't make us go to him."

"I'm sorry," I said, swallowing my guilt. It filled my stomach, heavy and acidic. "I don't have any money. I really don't."

"Here," Jeremy said, and pulled a wallet out of his pocket. He began removing bills one at a time, and turning in a circle, handing out one to each of the Displaced. I caught flashes of Benjamin Franklin's face before the hundred-dollar bills disappeared.

I stared at Jeremy with my mouth open.

"Thank you," the woman said, breathless with gratitude. She moved awkwardly toward him like she wanted to hug him or something, and then thought better of it and backed off. "Thank you so much."

The rest of the Displaced echoed her sentiment, one of them bowing a little like Jeremy was royalty.

"Stay away from the White Tent," was all Jeremy said in response.

When they were gone, I turned to him. "Do you always carry a wallet full of hundred-dollar bills?"

He shrugged, avoiding my gaze as he put away his wallet.

I'd had enough of Jeremy's evasive maneuvers.

"Look," I said. "You've been watching my house, and you've obviously been following me. I appreciate you helping me out with my, um . . . situation at the Dealer's, but I could have handled it myself."

"No, you couldn't have," Jeremy said with such certainty that it made me blink.

"What?"

"He would have hurt you. He would have beaten you, broken your jaw, and dislocated your shoulder. Then, when you were unconscious, his bodyguard would have dumped you in an alley, and . . . the Displaced would have done the rest."

I stared at him, stunned. "You don't know that."

"I do."

I shook my head to clear it. Why did he seem so certain? Maybe something *like* that would have happened if Jeremy hadn't shown up, but he'd been so specific.

"Fine," I said. "Whatever. You saved me. You're a hero." I narrowed my eyes at him. "What did you do to the bodyguard? And don't tell me 'nothing,' because I know you did something. Is it like what happened in Mr. Kale's classroom?"

He put on a blank stare, and I sighed.

"You're going to make me say it then, huh? Okay, here goes. After English, you know, when we were talking, and I . . . um . . . I touched your hand—which I didn't mean to do, by the way—I passed out and had this weird dream, and when I woke up you were gone. Is that what you did to the guard? You . . ." I felt ridiculous even thinking it. "You forced him into some kind of dream state?"

He put a hand on the back of his neck, kneading. "They're not dreams," he muttered.

"Then what are they?"

"You won't believe me if I tell you. You're not ready to hear it yet."

"How do you know what I'm ready for? You only met me a few hours ago."

"I just—"

"You just know," I finished for him, my voice rising. "Does this have something to do with the Seekers? You know, those crazy people you said you wanted to get me away from, and then instead you left me unconscious with them. Do you have any idea what they told me once I woke up from your little dream that's not a dream?"

Jeremy's hand went from his neck to his forehead, his thumb massaging one temple and his fingers the other. The fingers quickly moved to the bridge of his nose, pinching there. His neck strained like he was in pain.

"I'm sorry I ran out on you," he said. "I didn't know what to do."

"How about *not* run out on me?"

His cheeks reddened. "I said I was sorry. Be angry with me if you want, but you have to listen to me, Mia." His fingers pinched harder on the bridge of his nose. His eyes squeezed shut. "You have to stay away from the Seekers."

"That's what they said about you."

"Don't listen to anything they say."

"Why not?"

"They're dangerous."

"You said that already. How are they dangerous?"

"Now that they know who you are, they'll try to use you." His teeth clamped so tightly it seemed they might shatter like glass.

Jeremy's words took me back a step.

"Who am I?" I asked in a voice so soft my own ears barely picked it up.

Katrina's words played through my mind.

A girl standing atop the last tower, surrounded by a raging storm and lightning made of blood . . . the final portent before the end . . .

"I told you, I can't explain it," Jeremy said. "But—" He lowered his hand. "I could show you."

Jeremy took a single step and closed the distance between us. I sucked in a breath as I felt a sort of tingling heat pouring off him, making fever erupt all over my skin. Was this the Spark? It sure didn't feel like it. What it felt like was fire. Not like the fire that had turned the Dealer's tent into an oven. Some other kind of fire. The kind you wanted to put your hand in. The kind you invited to burn you.

Jeremy raised his hands. He was shaking. "Don't be afraid," he said.

But I was, and I opened my mouth to tell him so. Then his palms pressed over my eyes. The thrill of his touch sank through my skin, and I was suddenly dizzy. I felt like I might fall to my knees. My mind filled with light, and then darkness and then—

It was like one of those little picture books with images that become a movie when you flip the pages.

Only these pages were about me.

* * *

I was surrounded on all sides by crumbled mountains of concrete and glass. There was a thick carpet of cement dust beneath my feet. Ahead of me in the torn and ruined street I saw the white pillar of the Tower, jabbing into the night sky like a blunt needle. I was in the Waste.

Flip.

I took a step and the ground beneath me disappeared. I looked down and saw I had stepped into a chasm in the street. My stomach rose to my throat as I began the fall into darkness, knowing this was my last moment alive.

Flip.

People dancing. Their bodies pressing in around me, moving in epileptic paroxysms to the heart-thumping electro beat. A beat like thunder. No . . . not like thunder. I turned my face up. We were on the roof of the Tower. The sky was heavy with wet black cotton clouds. Not like *thunder. The beat* was *thunder. Lightning flashed . . . red lightning like blood-filled veins growing through the sky. My eyes burned. I blinked until I could see again.*

Flip.

The dancers were running. Running for the edge of the Tower as lightning attacked the roof. Some of the dancers leaped into nothingness. I heard them scream through their fall. But others joined hands in a ring that grew until it circled the Tower. There weren't enough of them to close the circle, and I was glad, because I knew somehow that if they closed the circle they'd be able to break the storm. And I didn't want them to break the storm. This was my *storm, and I wanted to live it. I raised my hands to the sky, feeling the thrill of what was to come.*

Thunder crashed.

I felt my charge rising up to meet the lightning. To connect.
To—
   Flip.

"Hey! You! Get your hands off her!"

Jeremy withdrew his hands. I found myself blinking as though a bright light had been shone directly into my pupils.

"Back off, pervert!"

Jeremy stepped back, holding up his hands again, only now to show they were empty and innocent.

We stared at each other, both breathing like we'd come to a sudden halt after a sprint. But Jeremy was no longer shaking, and the pain was gone from his eyes.

"Now do you see?" he asked. "Do you understand?"

My skin sang with such intensity it seemed Jeremy would have to hear it. My whole body was burning with fever. I told my heart to cool down. It felt like a lightbulb about to pop.

"Are you listening, kid? I said back up!"

I turned around and saw Militiaman Brent jogging toward us, Taser in hand.

"It's okay," I called to him.

"The hell it is! He's the stalker!"

I turned to Jeremy again, and found him backing away, down the sidewalk. "What was that? What did you do to me?"

"Get over here, kid!"

"I better go," Jeremy said, glancing nervously at Militiaman Brent. He began walking quickly back the way we'd come. I tried to grab his arm, but he kept moving.

He looked at me over his shoulder. "Don't go to the Waste, Mia. Stay out of the Waste and away from the Seekers."

He turned a corner and disappeared. I would have run after him, but Militiaman Brent reached me at that moment, looking pleased with himself.

"Think I might have scared him off for good this time," my self-appointed bodyguard said, puffing out his chest.

I glared at him. "Yeah," I said. "Thanks a lot."

"Come on." He patted me on the back. "I'll make sure you get home safe. Now aren't you glad I gave you that pepper spray?"

I set aside my annoyance with him and nodded. "You have no idea."

11

Parker must have been watching out the window for me, because he opened the front door the second I came within sight of the house.

"You should go," I told Militiaman Brent. "We'll be okay now."

"You sure?" He cocked an eyebrow. "What if the stalker comes back?"

"He's not dangerous." I forced a smile. "He actually kind of came to my rescue today. I'm pretty sure he's one of the good guys."

Militiaman Brent nodded. "If you say so. Take care, Mia Price." Parker reached me at that moment. "Keep an eye on your sister, kid," the militiaman said, and slapped Parker on the back hard enough to make him stumble. "You two stay out of trouble."

He saluted sharply before departing.

"What happened?" Parker demanded when Militiaman Brent was out of earshot. "Your eyes are red. Have you been crying?"

"I didn't get the meds." My voice scratched from my throat, still raw.

I expected an *I-told-you-not-to-go* from Parker, but he

only nodded. "It's okay. We'll figure out something else for Mom." He hung his arm over my shoulder and walked me into the house. I realized for the first time Parker was now taller than me by at least an inch. When had that happened?

Inside, I stared at my reflection in the decorative mirror that hung on the wall in our foyer. The mirror had fallen during the quake but had stayed miraculously intact, except for one long crack running diagonally through the glass. At least it hadn't shattered completely. I figured that exempted us from the seven years' bad luck clause.

I barely recognized the face gazing back at me from the cracked glass that divided my image with a jagged, lightning-shaped line. My hair was frizzed out and gray with ash and sand. There was soot streaked on my cheeks. My eyes were more than red. They were blazing with veins, like the lightning scars on my skin had crawled into them.

I turned my back on that image. I didn't want to see myself that way.

"How's Mom?" I asked in a shaky voice.

Parker shrugged. "She hasn't come out of her room, but I don't hear the TV. I think she's asleep."

I nodded and moved to the kitchen, where I opened the freezer door. The memory of Jeremy's heat was still alive on my skin like a sunburn. I stood there with the door open, bathing in frosty plumes of air. I wanted to climb inside and shut the door behind me, shut out the world and exist in the cold and the dark for a little while. Sometimes the heat of my own body became so unbearable I just wanted to turn it off. Turn everything off.

"What happened with the Dealer?" Parker asked.

"He stole my money and kicked me out," I said, keeping it simple.

"All of it?"

"Yep."

"What are we going to do now?"

I didn't have an answer. I closed the freezer door. "I'm going upstairs for a while."

"Mia?"

"Yeah?"

"I was thinking . . . don't be mad, okay. I'm just suggesting something. Maybe . . . maybe we should take Mom to one of those revivals. The ones on the beach."

It took me a moment to register what he was saying. The revivals on the beach . . . *Prophet's* revivals.

Don't make us go to Prophet.

He does something to people like us.

He changes us. Puts his hands on us and changes us.

A cannonball-sized weight landed in my stomach. "Why would we do that?"

"Well . . ." He took a deep breath and launched into his pitch. "I've been reading about religious mysticism. There's all kinds of weird stuff that's happened in churches and cults and whatever. People with tumors the size of softballs get a blessing and suddenly the cancer is gone, like it was never there. Or people walk through fire or across broken glass or get themselves bitten by deadly snakes and don't get hurt. And there are tribes in Africa that do rituals to bring rain during a drought, and sometimes it works. A storm will just appear out of nowhere."

"Parker . . ."

"Some people think it's God working through these people to perform miracles. But others think it's like . . . like you get enough people together who believe the same way or want the same thing, and what they want just *happens*. It's called concentrated will or collective consciousness or something like that. You *will* something to happen and it does. Maybe it's like the Seekers were saying about the Spark, and how it's all about concentrated energy and the power of thought. It's like these miracles are about what you believe and how strongly you believe it, see?" he continued. "So that might work with Mom, like it's worked with those people who had earthquake fever. She believes in this stuff Prophet keeps saying, so maybe if she believes he can heal her—"

"No," I said.

"Why can't we try? We could take her to one of Prophet's revivals and see."

I shook my head at him. I felt vaguely angry, somewhere down deep. But mostly I felt exhausted.

"You really want to take Mom to see Prophet?" I asked him. "You think we should encourage her belief in a televangelist cult leader who claims the world is going to end in three days?"

I watched the enthusiasm drain slowly from his eyes. "I want her to get better."

"She will," I said, forcing myself to sound certain when I wasn't. "It just takes time."

"What about the earthquake survivors' group, then?" Parker asked.

"What about it?" I brushed past him, heading for the stairs that led up to my bedroom.

"You said we could talk to Mom about going, see if she's willing to try it."

I didn't want to tell Parker the real reason I was reluctant. I doubted he remembered the room number listed on the flyer.

Room 317.

Mr. Kale's room.

I was certain that if Parker realized this, he'd be even more determined to go.

I made a show of dragging myself up the stairs. "I'm tired, Parker. We can talk to Mom about it tomorrow." I closed my door behind me, letting Parker know the conversation was over.

I flopped onto my bed, exhausted. I wished I could take a nap, shut down for a while. If I didn't already know Mom's sleeping pills wouldn't do a thing for me—if she had any left—I would have popped one or five. But I'd tried every sleeping pill on the market. Nothing worked.

I grabbed my laptop off the nightstand and opened a browser, did a silent cheer when the Web page loaded. The Internet was slow, but at least it was working.

Out of curiosity more than interest, I'd looked at Schiz's blog a few times. But that was before the quake. Before the Seekers.

The home page was simple, no photos or graphics or ads. Just a white background and black type. There were dozens of posts, too many for me to read them all, so I scrolled through the headlines. It took me about twenty seconds to come to the conclusion that the posts revolved around two subjects: Rance Ridley Prophet and the coming apocalypse.

Rance Ridley . . . Prophet?

Signs of the End Times (plague, war, famine, all that good stuff)

Why Is the Church of Light Buying Property in the Waste?

Rance Ridley Prophet Wants YOU for His Army of God!

The Sky Is Falling, For Realz Bitches!

Where Is Prophet's Twelfth Apostle?

Who IS Rance Ridley Prophet Really?

I started reading that one. The time stamp said it had been posted only five minutes ago.

Who IS Rance Ridley Prophet Really?

He's the man of the hour. The man who predicted the Puente Hills Earthquake on live television minutes before it hit. Who turned Los Angeles into the Bible Belt's long-lost buckle; who's converting people to the Church of Light faster than an army of Mormon missionaries hopped up on Mountain Dew. The man Followers can't shut up about.

He's Rance Ridley Prophet, and he wants YOU to surrender your soul! Doesn't that sound fun? A nice religious lobotomy at one of his famous midnight revivals?

But aside from what everybody knows about him, who is Rance Ridley Prophet really? Where did he come from, and what road did he take to get here? I'll tell you what, I'm pretty good at the whole Internet research thing, but I didn't turn up much about our friend Rance. I even ventured outside my command station and went to ye olde library trying to find out who this bag of douche, self-proclaimed prophet is. Here's what I learned. It ain't much, folks, but it's all I got for ya.

First, Prophet is not the surname he was born with. He's Rance Ridley, son of a guy named Ram Ridley, who just so happened to be the prophet of the Church of Light before Rance took control at the green age of thirteen.

There's fact number two. Rance Ridley became prophet at AGE THIRTEEN! That's insane! But then, we're talking about a religious cult here, and cult followers aren't renowned for their rationality. The Church of Light went through a dozen prophets before they came to good ol' Rance. Each of his predecessors claimed God spoke to him directly, and that the Big Boss told them the date of the end of the world. And each of them was wrong, so each of them was tossed out of the church on his ass. A piece of advice: if you want to remain in control of a doomsday cult, don't give a date for the end of the world unless you're really, really sure it's going to happen. Being wrong tends to undermine your authority.

Okay, so little Rance Ridley takes control of the Church of Light right after he wakes up in the hospital. He was in a coma for three days, but I can't find any record of what put him in said coma. Anyway, he says he saw God while he was near death, and God told him Daddy Ram was to be deposed and Rance instated as prophet. Ram wasn't down with this, but a few days later he dies mysteriously. Convenient, right??

After that, Rance makes Ridley his middle name and changes his surname to Prophet. Then comes a big old time gap where I can't find any information about him. He and his Followers keep to themselves, doing their own thing. He doesn't resurface until he starts adopting all those kids and calling them his Apostles. (Side note: I can't find any adoption or orphanage records on any of these kids. If those records existed once, Rance must have made them disappear. Why? I ask. Why destroy their records? What is he hiding?)

Oh, and while Rance was flying below the radar, his hair turned white and he developed cataracts, which he refuses to have removed, because he claims God put them there. Whatever you say, man.

A year ago, Rance makes his debut as a televangelist on *The Hour of Light*. And if you're even slightly conscious of what's going on in the world around you, you know the rest of Rance Ridley Prophet's story. And you know that today he finally announced the date of the end of the world.

April 17. Doomsday. The End.

Let's hope Rance is no different from his predecessors.

I closed my laptop. I had read enough—enough to make me feel sick to my stomach. A lot of the stuff Schiz wrote about struck me as your typical conspiracy theorist para-noid babble. The thing that bothered me was that Schiz openly admitted he didn't know that much about Prophet. Normally he would have speculated to the point of complete fantasy. But what Schiz said here . . . it must be true if he hadn't tried to fill in the blanks.

I checked the clock on my nightstand. It had been one of the longest days of my life, and it was only five-thirty.

I laid my head down on my arms, closed my eyes, and then a miracle happened.

I fell asleep.

And I dreamed.

Or I remembered.

12

Arizona. Lake Havasu City. One year ago.

Here's the thing about thunderstorms in Arizona: they sometimes appear out of nowhere. Shifting winds bring the tropical moisture from the Gulf of Mexico to collide with the Arizona desert heat. One minute the sky is clear. The next a huge anvil of a cloud has formed overhead. So I had to be careful when I left the house, lest I be caught in the open with a black cloud hanging over me.

But those kinds of storms . . . they can catch even someone like me off guard.

So here's what happened.

There was this girl, a couple years younger than me. Her name was Janna, and she wasn't all there. I won't go into specifics, but she'd been hit by a car. The car broke her arm, but the pavement, when she hit it, cracked her skull and messed up her brain. She wasn't the same after that. She smiled a lot but didn't talk. She tended to wander around town without direction. She made other kids uncomfortable. They called her retarded, but she mostly just seemed lost.

Janna took a liking to me for whatever reason. Maybe she sensed my outcast status and felt like I'd accept her.

And I did. People in Lake Havasu City were familiar with my little problem, and they steered clear of me. Anyone who knows anything about lightning is aware that you don't want to be standing next to a tree when it's struck, and the same principle applies to me.

But the damage Janna's brain had sustained must have wiped out her sense of self-preservation. Her parents warned her to stay away from me, but she kept showing up on my doorstep.

The day of my last strike, the sky was perfectly clear. It was Saturday. I'd checked the weather report and confirmed that the chance of rain was almost nonexistent, so I should have been safe leaving the house.

When I stepped outside, Janna was sitting on the front porch staring off into space, smiling pleasantly at nothing in particular. I asked her if she wanted to go for a walk, and she nodded. Janna loved to walk, more than anything else. Some days she would walk from one end of town to the other, back and forth without stopping, not saying a word.

So we set out. We decided to walk to London Bridge, which had actually been constructed in London and then bought by some rich American. He had it dismantled and each brick shipped to Lake Havasu City to serve as a tourist attraction. It was one of my favorite places in town, this big old hunk of London dropped into Arizona.

Janna and I were on the bridge, peering over the side and watching boats pass by underneath, when I felt an intense prickling on my skin. I looked up, and saw it: a heavy gray cloud forming right over the bridge, spreading like a drop of ink diving into a glass of water.

It happened fast.

So fast.

Every hair on my body stood up. I tasted metal, like I was sucking on a bullet.

"Get back!" I shouted at Janna, but she just stood there, blinking at me.

So I pushed her. All I wanted was to get her away from me.

Lightning struck at that precise moment. It entered through my back, and it was like being stabbed with a sword fresh off the smelting iron. It was pain, but it was more than that. The pain was so enormous that it became something else. It was life. The very essence of everything. And it was filling me. Charging me.

I was too full of lightning to realize what I had done until it was over. Until my hair was falling from my head like black snow.

That was when I saw Janna, lying in the middle of the bridge fifteen feet away. Traffic was stopped. People were pointing. Shouting. Running to her.

I couldn't move.

Janna's clothes were mostly burned away. Her tennis shoes had exploded, leaving her feet bare, the soles bright red. Blistered. Swollen. Her arms and legs were raw, as though the naked skin had been scraped away with a scalpel, revealing raw tissue beneath. Her hair, like mine, was singed to ash. Her scalp was capped in blisters.

And on her chest, near her shoulders . . . two red handprints had been seared into her flesh.

"You!" I heard someone in the crowd shout. "You did this!"

People started turning from Janna to me.

Many people who had been running toward her started running at me.

Terror grabbed my heart and threatened to crush it. My back was against the edge of London Bridge.

The heat of the lightning was still burning inside me, making it impossible to think clearly. A man walked toward me with purpose . . . a man big enough to pick me up and toss me over the edge of the bridge. And he wasn't alone. The mob pressed in around me, hate in their eyes. Hate and fear.

"You're evil," the big man said when he was a few feet away from me. "You killed that girl. You're *evil*." He said it plainly, not as an accusation, but as fact. Everyone knew it. I was evil. I was a murderer.

A monster.

The big man reached for me. I didn't know what he intended to do, whether he would have thrown me over the edge of the bridge, or strangled me, or hit me. The only thing I did know was that he wanted to hurt me. I had to protect myself. I raised my hands, my palms pointed toward him. I was wearing my fingerless gloves, as always, but there was so much heat surging in my hands my gloves were smoking, falling apart, turning to ash and sprinkling the ground. One second my hands were smoking, and the next, red veins of light jumped from my fingertips and connected to the man. He froze. And then he began to convulse on his feet.

The crowd backed up. There was more shouting, but now it was uncertain. More afraid than angry.

The man's skin started to smoke, and a scent came off him, like burning wires and cooking meat.

Stop! a voice pleaded in my mind. *Stop it! You're killing him!*

It was strange. Until that voice spoke up, I hadn't realized it was me hurting the man. I saw the red veins sprouting from my fingertips, attaching me to him like jumper cables, but I didn't make the connection. Nothing like this had ever happened before.

But it was happening.

I was electrocuting this man. Frying him.

There was lightning in me, and I was striking him with it. I was killing him.

Stop!

I felt something snap, like taut wires being cut. The red veins of light sucked back into my hands, and the man crumpled in a smoking heap.

I looked at the crowd, waited for them to rush at me, shove me over the side of the bridge. And this time I would let them. I wouldn't try to protect myself. I deserved whatever punishment they had to give. The man was right. I must be evil.

My eyes went to Janna. I saw her moving, trying to sit up, and relief washed through me. She was alive.

"I didn't mean to hurt her," I told the crowd.

Silence was all I got from them, but their accusation was as loud as a dozen sirens.

Or were those actual sirens?

Flashing lights.

Police.

My instinct for self-preservation came roaring back.

No one tried to stop me as I ran from London Bridge. And by the time the mob came to drive the Price family from Lake Havasu City, we were already gone.

A week later we arrived in Los Angeles, where Mom said we should have moved right away after her mother died. Los Angeles, where it never rained, according to the song.

Mom had our last name changed in case anyone decided to look for us.

I wore a wig to hide my baldness. The lightning didn't always turn my hair to ash as it had done this time. I almost preferred the times the lightning stopped my heart to when it took my hair.

Parker and I enrolled at Skyline High. I tried to distract myself from what I had done to Janna and the man on the bridge, and from what I learned when I called the hospital on the way to Los Angeles.

I dialed 411 and had an operator connect me to the hospital in Lake Havasu City. I asked for Janna Scott's room. Janna answered. I didn't recognize her voice, because until that moment I'd never heard it.

"I'm so sorry," I whispered. Tears streamed down my face.

"Mia," she said. "Is that you?"

It hit me then . . . she was talking. But now I was the one who couldn't form words.

"I'm okay now," she said.

"No, you're not." I choked on a sob. "I saw what I did to you."

"The burns?" she said, sounding surprised. "The doctors say those will heal. I need some skin grafts, but after that I'll be fine. Better than fine. I don't know what you did, but . . . you fixed me. I'm better now."

I shook my head, not quite understanding. "What about the man on the bridge?"

She was quiet for a long moment. "He'll live," she said finally, her voice barely audible. "Someone's coming. I have to go now." She covered the phone and I heard her muffled voice talking to someone else. Then she said, "Thank you, Mia." And she hung up.

13

I woke burning, pouring sweat. My damp clothes clung to my fevered skin like wet paper. I peeled them off as I stumbled into the bathroom, praying the water was still on. When I cranked the bathtub valve, water rushed from the faucet. I plugged the drain, climbed into the tub and lay down in the bottom, letting ice-cold water run onto my feet. I had to cool down before I melted. I winced as steam hissed off my skin, but the fever in my blood began to lessen by slow degrees.

I closed my eyes, trying not to think about the dream. But in my mind I kept seeing Janna's scorched body lying crumpled in the center of the bridge; kept hearing her voice say, *I don't know what you did, but you fixed me.*

It made no sense. But it was true. I'd read about Janna's miraculous recovery in the online edition of *Havasu News*. My involvement was not mentioned. It seemed like Lake Havasu City wanted to forget I'd ever existed. That was fine. There were things I wanted to forget, too, like what I had done to the man on the bridge.

He lived, but it might have been better for him if he hadn't.

I thought of what Rachel said to me that morning in the lounge.

Redemption. That's what you seek, isn't it? Redemption and forgiveness for the wrong you've done.

Maybe she was right. Maybe I did need redemption. But I wasn't going to seek it out in Rance Ridley Prophet's White Tent. If there was any way to redeem myself, it was by getting my family through the next days or weeks or months or whatever it took. To get Mom better. To keep Parker out of trouble. To steer us back toward stability and sanity and all that was normal. How I was supposed to accomplish that little feat, I didn't know, so I decided not to think about that either.

I thought of Jeremy instead.

Jeremy, who touched me and made me see lightning. Made me burn.

I invited him into my mind, and then put myself in front of him and watched what happened.

And watched.

And watched.

I relaxed into the icy water. My fingers traced the lightning scars on my skin, and my blood began to heat again, my skin to burn, until the bathtub water was no longer cold, and I was hotter than ever, but it was the good kind of hot.

A good burn.

14

By the time I dried off and dressed in clean clothes, it was after seven o'clock. I should have been ravenous since I'd barely picked at lunch, but my stomach was too full of worry to leave room for hunger. Still, I knew I needed to eat, and make sure Mom and Parker did, too. Mom wasn't the only one who'd lost weight since the quake. Parker and I could both count our ribs.

In the kitchen, I found that Parker had unloaded our box of meager rations. Our food supply now consisted of two cans each of vegetables, beans, and soup; two loaves of generic bread; four packets of instant oatmeal; one can of powdered milk. Apparently this was all we really needed to survive.

I went in search of Parker to ask him what he preferred for dinner, soup and toast or beans on toast (we could pretend we were in jolly old England instead of post-apocalyptic Los Angeles).

But Parker wasn't in his room.

I stood still, listening, realizing how quiet the house was. How way too quiet it was.

I found Mom's room empty, too. It looked strange

without her in it, like an essential piece of furniture had been removed.

Mom's car wasn't in the garage, but I had a pretty good idea where it was, and where Mom was, and where Parker was. And I had a very good idea what I was going to do to Parker when I caught up with him.

The sun was busy setting as I drove along Ocean Avenue back toward Skyline. I didn't like going out after dark these days—that was when most of the looting went on—and I hoped to have Mom and Parker on their way back home before dusk.

Apparently whoever was in charge at Skyline was also worried about looting. There were sentries armed with Tasers standing guard at every entrance.

"I'm here for the earthquake survivors' group," I told the sentry barring the main door.

He recoiled when I spoke to him, like I'd snuck up and surprised him, though he'd definitely seen me coming from across the street. He looked me over with eyes that were open a bit too wide. "You're her, aren't you?" he asked in a breathy whisper.

"Huh?"

He shook his head, seeming flustered. "Nothing. Never mind. I thought . . . you know where to go, right? Room—"

"Three seventeen, I got it." I felt him watching me until the door swung closed at my back.

The main corridor was dim and deserted, but felt

crowded with the faces of the dead and missing papering the walls. Their eyes followed me as I walked faster.

I'd never been inside Skyline after-hours. I wasn't a member of any clubs or teams or groups of any kind, so I never had reason to be at school one second longer than was necessary. It was creepy here when the halls weren't full of students, when the only thing I could hear were my own footsteps echoing back at me. I kept sneaking glances behind me, thinking I still felt eyes watching my every move.

"I had a feeling you'd be back."

My head snapped forward and I froze.

Katrina lounged against the staircase balustrade.

The muscles in my neck and shoulders, already so tight it felt like they might fray like old rope, tensed a little more. I really didn't think it was possible for this day to get any worse, but apparently my powers of pessimism had fallen short for once.

"I'm not here for you," I told her.

"Oh, I know," she said. "Parker and your mom are with Uncle Kale now. He knows Parker went behind your back to bring her here. And you know how he knows, don't you?" She tapped her temple with one red-painted fingernail.

My spine went rigid and my teeth came together like I was trying to bite through something tough. "You need to stay away from my family."

She held up her hands to show her innocence. "Your brother came to us. Parker isn't like you, Mia."

"What's that supposed to mean?"

"He's not selfish."

The heat in my chest flared to life. I found myself in

Katrina's face. I'd never been a confrontational person, but this girl brought it out in me big-time. "Whatever you think you know about me, you *don't*."

Katrina pressed herself flatter against the wall, shrinking from me. She swallowed hard. "I know you have power," she said. "I know you could use it to do some good in this world, but instead you hide in the shadows, pretend to be a helpless bystander. But that's not who you are. Your brother doesn't have power, but he's still man enough to stand for something. He's not afraid to fight for what he believes in."

What exactly did Parker believe in? The Seekers' cause? Prophet's ability to cure our mom? That the end of the world was coming? I couldn't pin him down.

I stepped back. Katrina tried to hide her relief, but I saw it. I knew what it looked like when people were afraid of me.

"What's it going to take to get you to leave us alone?" I asked.

"How about a trade," Katrina said. "We'll forget about your brother, never bother him again, if you'll join our side and stand against Prophet and his Followers when the storm comes."

"And what if I refuse?" I asked.

Katrina smiled. "You won't."

"Can I have some time to think it over?"

"This is a one-time offer, and it expires in ten seconds. Ten . . . nine . . . eight . . ."

"Give me a day."

"Seven . . . six . . . five . . ."

"I need more time!"

"Sorry, not much time left. Four . . . three . . . two . . ."

"Fine!" I wanted to strangle her, but my shoulders went slack, the fight going out of me. If this was the only way I could protect Parker from the Seekers, protect him from himself, then this is what I had to do.

"I'll join you," I said, "if you—*all* of you—swear to stay away from my family, even if they don't want you to. Parker is off-limits from this point on, got it?"

"Done." She held out her right hand, showing the knotted brand on her palm. "Shake on it?"

I eyed her hand, wishing I'd never shaken it in the ladies' lounge earlier that day. What was I doing, making a deal with these people? Would they brand me, too? That would require me to remove my gloves, to reveal the lightning scars. I couldn't do that. I wouldn't.

Katrina's hand waited. I ignored it.

"I have your promise," I told her, and started up the stairs. I still had to retrieve my stray family members.

Katrina called after me. "We'll see you here tomorrow morning then, bright and early."

"For what?"

"Initiation. Be in Uncle Kale's classroom at seven a.m. sharp. Don't be late."

I stopped outside Mr. Kale's classroom door, which was ajar by a crack, wide enough so I could peer inside without being seen myself.

The desks had been arranged in a circle. There were maybe fifteen people seated. Mom and Parker were among them, along with Mr. Kale. I recognized a few Skyline students and a couple of teachers, one of them my history teacher, Ms. Markovic, who was standing, addressing the circle. That was a surprise. Ms. Markovic had been replaced on the schedule, so I'd assumed she'd left the city. But I could tell by the strain around her eyes and the new streaks of gray in her hair that she wasn't ready to face a classroom again. She looked almost as haunted as Mom, and I wondered what she'd been through since the quake, whom she had lost.

My plan had been to briefly interrupt whatever was going on in Mr. Kale's classroom, grab Parker and Mom, and get out of the school. But before I had the chance, Ms. Markovic muttered, "Thank you for listening," and sat down.

"Thank you for sharing your experience," Mr. Kale said in a softer version of his rumbling voice. "That was very brave. Who would like to go next?"

He began to search the room. I should have backed away from the door, but it really was open just a crack and I didn't think he would notice me.

His eye caught mine and paused.

I wanted to move away before he recognized me, but I hesitated a split second too long. A hum started in my brain, and everything in me grew still.

Stay, his voice spoke in my head. *Listen.*

His gaze unlocked from mine and moved on.

"We have time for one more person," he said. "Someone new?" His eyes fell on my mom, and he offered his hand to her, as though to help her up. "Sarah Price, is it?"

I felt like someone was squeezing the blood out of my heart. "No," I said, lips moving soundlessly. "Don't touch her."

Mr. Kale's voice again, speaking where it didn't belong.

I can't make her do anything she doesn't want to do. Your mother wants to tell her story. Listen, Mia . . .

I made a deal, I thought back at him. *You have to leave my family alone!*

But Mr. Kale didn't know about the agreement Katrina and I had made. She hadn't had a chance to tell him yet, and he hadn't extracted that piece of information from my mind, probably because I hadn't been thinking about it when I felt that humming in my brain. If he really could read minds, maybe his power was limited to surface thoughts.

My mom took Mr. Kale's hand and stood. He released her, and she seemed unsteady on her feet as she glanced nervously around the room. Then she crossed her arms over her chest and her eyes focused on something behind Mr. Kale, like she was gazing at a movie screen no one else could see.

She won't do it, I thought. She wouldn't even tell Parker and me what happened to her during all those days she was buried. There was no way she'd tell a room full of strangers.

Mr. Kale touched her shoulder. "Speak, Sarah," he said. "Tell us what happened." And something changed. It was hard to say exactly what that something was, but I knew it had happened. Mom's posture straightened, and her eyes fixed more determinedly on that invisible movie screen. She filled her lungs and began.

And I listened. There was nothing else for me to do.

"I was downtown during the earthquake," she said. "In the Flower District with a client of mine. Owen. That's . . . that was his name. He hired me to redecorate his office.

That's what I do . . . what I did. Before the—" Her voice dried up, and she had to pause for a moment. "I didn't realize Owen wanted more than a professional relationship until that day. There were signs, but I didn't notice them. I was always so wrapped up in my family, my work. We even went on a date, only I thought it was just dinner at the time.

"Owen wanted an extravagant flower arrangement in his office's front lobby. He insisted on coming with me to the Flower District to show me what he liked, but once we got there he excused himself and went off on his own. He was gone so long I started to think he'd been called away on business. He wouldn't answer his phone. Then he came up behind me and tapped me on the shoulder. I turned around and he had this enormous bouquet of flowers. He said, 'I didn't know what your favorite flower was, and I didn't want to ask, so I bought one of each.' And then—" She covered her eyes with a trembling hand. "He kissed me. He had a hard time reaching me through the flowers. We sort of crushed them between us. I didn't have the heart to tell him I've never really liked flowers, not since my husband's funeral. Doesn't matter which kind. They all smell like death to me. But with Owen, for that moment, the smell of flowers didn't bother me."

She lowered her hand. Her eyes were glassy. "When everything started to shake, I actually thought, 'Oh my God, this kiss must really mean something if it's making the earth move.' And then the shaking went on and on, and people started shouting. Owen held on to those flowers, though. When the building collapsed on top of us, he still had them."

The tears Mom had held back began to pour down her cheeks. I didn't even notice when the same thing began to happen to me.

"He saved my life," my mom went on. "He covered me with his body when everything around us was coming down, and his back was broken by falling debris. He survived the next twenty-four hours while we waited to be rescued. Then he died quietly, in his sleep, without saying goodbye. It took another two days for a rescue team to find us. Or . . . just me, by then. There were others buried with us. Trapped. They all died. They died, and the flowers died, and the smell of that rot . . . every time I think about it I want to scream." She wiped her scarred cheeks with her sleeve and murmured, "I want to scream."

Mom sat down. Beside her, Parker's face was pale, his eyes stunned.

"Thank you for sharing, Sarah," Mr. Kale said. "That was . . ." He faltered, and finished in a mumble. "Thank you."

I walked silently down the hall, in the opposite direction of the staircase, and hid at the end of a row of lockers. I stayed there until I heard the earthquake survivors' group let out. Voices and footsteps moved toward the stairs. I snuck a glance and saw Parker and my mom among them. Good. Parker was taking her home. He wasn't lingering to talk to Mr. Kale about the Seekers.

I stayed where I was until they were gone. I didn't want Mom to know I'd heard everything she said. She obviously didn't want me to know. She'd let Parker in, but not me.

I was about to emerge from my hiding place when I heard more footsteps, a lot of them, coming up the stairs.

I remembered the lightning strike survivors' group that was scheduled to start right after the earthquake survivors' group, and dove back into my hiding place.

When the footsteps ceased, I slid silently down the hall, praying that Mr. Kale's door would be closed so he wouldn't catch sight of me again. Thankfully, it was, but I could still hear the low murmur of voices. And if I crouched down by the crack at the bottom, I could probably make out what they were saying.

Go home now, Mia, I commanded myself. *Go home and deal with your family.*

I wanted to listen to my own voice of reason, but . . . this was a lightning survivors' group, presumably organized for people who'd been struck during the electrical storm the day of the quake, not people like me. But still . . . I was curious. And more than that I was suspicious. What did Mr. Kale want with a bunch of people who'd been struck by lightning?

A bunch of people like me . . .

So I listened. And I immediately heard a voice I recognized. A voice that I'd be happy never to hear again.

Katrina.

"I don't think anyone new is coming," she said. "We might as well take that flyer down. Face it, Uncle Kale, we're never going to recruit anyone this far from the Waste, not with Prophet to compete with. You know where the survivors who'd listen to us are going every night. We should be focusing every Seeker on the Rove."

My brows drew together. The Waste seemed like the last place on earth a lightning survivor would want to go, back to the scene of the strike.

"Not every survivor in this city is drawn to the Rove, Katrina," Mr. Kale said. "The ones who were struck before the quake don't feel the same pull. Can you imagine Mia Price going there? She's the one we should focus on."

I covered my mouth to silence the choked sound my throat tried to make at the mention of my name.

I could hear Katrina's smile in her voice. "Actually, Mia will be here tomorrow morning for initiation."

"No way. You're lying." That was Schiz.

"She just needed the right motivation."

Katrina told the room about the deal she had made. Everyone started talking at once, but Mr. Kale silenced the group.

"There's a problem," he said. "I spoke to Mia's brother briefly, after the last meeting. He doesn't care what his sister says. He wants to be a Seeker. I told him to be here in the morning for initiation."

My teeth came together. Parker and I were so going to have words.

"We need her more than we need him," Katrina said. "It's too bad. He's so eager to be useful."

"Maybe I could talk to him, tell him the situation," Quentin said. "He's a friend of mine. Sort of."

"Don't bother," Katrina said. "I'm sure Mia will deliver the bad news for us."

Mr. Kale sighed so loudly I could hear him through the door. "I don't like this. No one should have to be black-mailed into our circle."

"I did what I had to do." Katrina sounded defensive. "She's the Tower girl, I know it. Without her, this is pointless. You know what my ancestor, our *founder*, prophesied."

"I'm not convinced she's the Tower girl," Schiz said.

"Are you kidding me? You can feel the Spark coming off her without even touching her. She's like a freaking power plant. None of us have a fraction of her energy, not even you, Uncle. We need her on our side if we're going to stand a chance against Prophet and his Followers. If she's bonded to us and we can conduct for her, it'll be like having another hundred sparked Seekers in our circle."

"She's powerful, yeah, but power is nothing if she won't use it," Schiz pointed out. "Besides, you know that's not the real reason we need her."

I leaned closer, waiting for him to elaborate on the "real reason," but everyone went silent for a moment, as though digesting Schiz's reminder.

"Maybe she's the one prophesied and maybe she isn't," Mr. Kale said finally. "We'll know soon enough. Either way, you still have work to do. If you're new to the Rove, stay close to Katrina and do exactly what she tells you. You're dismissed."

The doorknob twisted and my heart jumped into my throat.

I bolted for the stairs and didn't stop running until I reached my car.

Jeremy was right. *Now that they know who you are, they'll try to use you.* That's what he'd told me before he put his hands over my eyes and took me to the Waste. To the Tower.

The question was, what did the Seekers want to use me for? And how could I stop them from doing it now that I'd agreed to become one of them?

15

I'm sure Mia will deliver the bad news for us, Katrina had predicted. I hated to give her the satisfaction of being right, but that was exactly what I intended to do.

At home, I headed straight for Parker's closed bedroom door. I raised my fist to knock, but was distracted by a voice coming from down the hall, from Mom's room. She and Parker must be in there together, probably having a meaningful conversation about what Mom had revealed at the survivors' meeting. And I was being left out. Again.

I crept down the hall and opened Mom's door a crack.

Parker wasn't there, and at first I didn't see Mom either. Then I spotted her kneeling beside the bed, hands clasped. I sucked in a breath when I realized she was praying. I hadn't seen Mom pray in years, and only in Grandma's presence. Never alone.

"—forgive me, Dear Lord, for failing as a mother . . . failing to lead my children to the light. Their sins are my sins. Please, God, forgive my daughter. Show her the light and the way of righteousness. And . . . and please forgive her for what she did to those people in Arizona. Please don't let her hurt anyone else. Please help me forgive her. Please, please take this terrible curse from her—"

Stunned, I backed silently away from her room until I stood in the living room, in the dark.

Cursed? Was that what she thought of me? Granted, I'd referred to myself as "cursed" more than a few times, but Mom was always the first to insist that I wasn't cursed at all. She said I was special. Unique.

She was lying.

I unlocked the front door and stepped outside onto the porch. I needed some air, but the moist ocean breeze carried its pins-and-needles storm warning to my skin, which did nothing to help with my building anxiety. In the distance, I could see hundreds of fires dotting the beach in Tentville, gray smoke tunneling into the sky.

I surveyed the dark street, and wondered . . .

I cleared my throat. "Jeremy?" I called softly, feeling ridiculous. "Are you there?"

As though he'd been waiting for an invitation to appear, Jeremy stepped from behind a hedge like a shadow that had shaken its maker. Again, this version of Jeremy in the dark, this light-rimmed silhouette, reminded me of something, and again I struggled to grasp what that was.

I didn't move from the porch. I let him come to me, and as he approached, the porch light gave him color and the memory slipped away.

"Where's your militiaman?" he asked, glancing around.

"I gave him the night off." I narrowed my eyes at Jeremy. "Why? Do I need protection from you?"

He shook his head, but yellow light from the porch lamp reflected off the lenses of those black-framed glasses, screening his eyes.

"What are you doing here?" I asked.

He shoved his hands in his pockets like he didn't know what else to do with them. His cheeks looked smooth, like he'd just shaved. My fingers wanted to feel them to know for sure, so I trapped my hands in my pockets, too.

"I wanted to make sure you were okay after what happened on the beach, and—" He cleared his throat and lowered his eyes. "After what I showed you."

I didn't know what to say. The truth was, I still hadn't really processed what had happened that day. What was still happening.

"Why do you care?" I descended the steps until we were nearly at eye level. "And why do you seem so familiar to me? Have we met before today?"

Jeremy lowered his chin, turned his face away. He pulled a hand from his pocket and smoothed his hair down over his forehead. He glanced up at me through the tops of his glasses. His voice was soft. Low. "I've seen *you* before."

My cheeks felt warm. "There you go, sounding like a stalker again." But I found myself wanting to stand closer to him. Jeremy's pull was like an opposite charge, asking me to reach out. To connect. It was so similar to that feeling I had when a storm moved in overhead, that need to call the lightning down and let it inside me.

I descended another step. Only one more and I'd be right in front of him, inches of nothing separating us. "Jeremy, have you ever heard of something called the Spark?"

The muscles in his neck tensed. "Who told you about that?"

"You know what it is, then. And you know who the Seekers are." I swallowed. "You're not one of them, though, are you? I mean, you're not trying to recruit me to some . . . some cause or army or something?"

He shook his head quickly. "No, I'm trying to keep you out of that."

"Why?"

"The fewer questions you ask, the better off you'll be."

I ignored this advice. "Can I tell you something, even if it sounds crazy?" I watched for his reaction. "Those people you warned me about, the Seekers . . . they told me the apocalypse is coming, and claimed some fortune-teller had a vision about me a couple hundred years ago, something to do with the Tower." I searched Jeremy's face. He didn't even blink. "Also, I think Mr. Kale can read minds and talk without opening his mouth. Not like a ventriloquist. Like he can talk inside your mind. What do you think about that?"

A ripple of disturbance appeared on Jeremy's face. "I think you should guard your thoughts carefully when you're with Mr. Kale. Or avoid him altogether."

"Doesn't any of this sound the least bit strange to you?" I answered my own question. "I guess it wouldn't to someone who can do what you do."

Jeremy took a deep breath and let it out slowly. "This is harder than I thought it would be."

He stepped closer to me, pulling his hands out of his pockets like he wanted to reach out and touch me. But he kept his arms at his sides, straight and stiff, like he didn't trust them.

"The things I showed you this afternoon . . ."

"The dreams?"

He shook his head. "They're more than dreams. They're warnings. Visions. And I've been seeing them and thousands of others like them for as long as I can remember." His eyes locked onto mine. "You've been in my head for years, Mia. I've seen you so many times, in so many possible situations, I can't remember them all. Now you're right in front of me, and I don't know what to do."

I opened my mouth to say something, not sure what that something would be, but Jeremy raised a hand to silence me.

"Let me finish," he said. "I don't know how to stop the things I've seen from happening. I don't know how to stop any of this without . . . I don't know, tying you up and locking you in a closet until it's over."

"Whoa, whoa, whoa." I eased backward up the steps. "I definitely don't like the sound of that."

He dug his hands into his hair in frustration, clenching fistfuls. "That came out wrong. I didn't mean I would actually do it. Only that I don't know any other way to protect you from the Seekers. And from yourself. I don't think you have any idea what you're capable of, but the Seekers do. And Prophet . . . if he knew about you, he'd—" Jeremy cut off, as though he'd said too much.

"He would what?"

"He would want you," Jeremy said simply. "He would do whatever it took to turn you to his side, and that would be worse than if you joined the Seekers. But if you stay out of everything . . . if you don't get involved—"

I cut him off. "You think I want to be involved in *any* of this? I don't want people having prophecies about me, or giving me tarot cards, or trying to recruit me for Team

Apocalypse. And . . . and I don't want your dreams or visions or whatever they are." I sighed. It was a mistake to come out here. I already had more problems than I could handle without Jeremy and his tortured eyes piling a few more complications on my back.

"Please stop following me," I forced myself to say. "I'm going to need you to leave now. Goodbye, Jeremy."

I was at the front door when he called after me.

"You don't sleep. Not very often, anyway."

I turned around. "How do you know that?"

My head was partially blocking the porch light, casting Jeremy in shadow again, and the memory of where I'd seen him came rushing at me like water from a flash flood.

The dream I'd had, of the boy at my bedside with his knife.

Nightmare Boy.

No wonder I hadn't remembered. I hadn't thought he was real.

"You were in my room," I said before I could stop the words.

Jeremy's eyes widened and I saw the truth in them.

"Mia, I—"

"What were you going to do with the knife, Jeremy?"

"Nothing!"

"Then why did you have it? Why did you break into my house and come up to my room and stand there with a knife like you were going to stab me?"

"I swear I wouldn't have done it. I thought I could. I didn't see any other way—"

"Any other way to what? To protect me from myself?"

He took a step toward me, but stopped when I backed up against the door.

"Mia," he said carefully. "I don't know how else to put this . . . I tried to show you, but I don't think you understand. There is a strong possibility that, within the next few days, you will do something terrible. Something I'm trying to prevent."

I was shaking all over. "Something you tried to prevent by killing me."

"But I didn't go through with it!"

"I don't care," I said, grabbing the doorknob and wrenching it. "Stay away from me. If you come near my house again, I'll call the cops or the militia or whoever will answer."

"Mia, please—"

I didn't give him a chance to finish. I slipped inside and locked the door behind me, watched through the front window until Jeremy went away. Only then did I take what felt like my first breath in minutes.

Before going to my bedroom, I went through the house and checked every door and window.

Even when I was in bed under my blankets, I couldn't stop shaking. I wasn't cold.

I was never cold.

I was terrified.

PART 2

*"Ain't a cloud in the sky . . .
Don't see no sun but don't see no cloud neither."*
—Flannery O'Connor,
A Good Man Is Hard to Find

APRIL 15
Two days until the storm . . .

16

After lying awake all night, stacking up my worries one on top of the other like I was trying to build my very own tower out of them, I got out of bed when the first hint of light touched my bedroom window. It wasn't even six, but I was supposed to be in Mr. Kale's classroom at seven for "initiation," whatever that meant. I had yet to talk to Parker about the deal I'd made with Katrina.

In the bathroom, I turned on the faucet to brush my teeth. Nothing happened. There was only a dry chugging of pipes. The water was off again. Great start to what was bound to be another in a series of bad days. I would have to skip a few steps in my morning routine, but oh well. Who was I trying to impress? Not Jeremy, stalker with aspirations of murder.

I hadn't made good on my threat to call the police and report his B&E&IK (intended knifing), but I had a feeling Jeremy wouldn't be breaking into my house again anytime soon. Still, I had another feeling I hadn't seen the last of him.

I climbed into an outfit that looked identical to what I'd worn the day before—black turtleneck, black jeans, black boots, black fingerless gloves—realized I wasn't sure they *weren't* the same clothes I'd worn yesterday, realized I didn't care, and headed downstairs.

I'd thought I would be the only one awake so early, but I could hear someone in the kitchen. I figured it was Parker. He thought he still had an initiation invitation. I steeled myself for the reaction I was bound to get when he heard how and why things had changed.

I stepped into the kitchen and blinked in surprise. Mom stood at the counter, not Parker. She was dressed in clean clothes, and her hair was pulled back, not hanging greasy in her face as it usually was, hiding her scars. Now they were fully revealed, a pink slash across her forehead, one below her left eye, and a series of them striking her right cheek.

"Morning," Mom said, smiling at me. Two pieces of toast jumped from their toaster slots. At least the electricity was still on. Mom grabbed them, set them on a plate, and inserted two more pieces of bread. "Do we have any butter or jam left?"

I shook my head. I was having trouble accessing basic vocabulary words like "yes" and "no."

Mom made a face. "Dry toast. Hm. Well, I made oatmeal, too." She indicated three bowls of congealing beige mush on the kitchen table.

"Mom?" I said as she stacked the toast on a plate.

She looked up at me. "Hm?"

I wasn't sure what I'd meant to say, so I didn't say anything. Instead I surprised both of us by wrapping my arms around her and hugging her. For a split second she tensed, as though afraid I might hurt her. Then she relaxed and gathered me closer to her.

"I love you, Mom," I told her.

"I love you, too, Mia," she said in a whisper, like she wanted to keep it between us.

She thinks you're cursed, a nasty little voice reminded me.

Parker appeared in the doorway, dressed for school. When he saw us, he stared, looking as dumbstruck as I'd felt a moment before.

"Hungry?" Mom asked him.

"Starved," he said. His eyes met mine for a moment and he grinned. Remembering the deal I had made with Katrina last night, I did not return his smile.

"I have to be at school early," I told him, taking my seat at the table. "Eat quick."

"No, no," Mom said, "I want you two to relax and enjoy breakfast. Whatever's going on at school can wait."

"It's pretty important," I said, still giving Parker sliver eyes as he sat down across from me.

"Mia, please." Mom brought the last of the toast to the table. "This is a special morning. Before we start eating I think we should offer a prayer."

Parker froze with a spoonful of oatmeal halfway to his mouth.

She went on. "There's not much time left. We have to start living right, and we have to start now. You heard what Prophet said about the storm. Only three days—no, two days until it arrives. We have to get right with God before then." Mom's eyes went to me. "Mia, will you pray?"

Parker slammed my car door. "Why couldn't you just say the stupid prayer like she asked? If praying before we eat makes her feel better, we should do it."

"It may make her *feel* better, but it's not going to make her *better*," I said.

"But she is getting better! You saw how she was this morning. She got out of bed, got dressed. She made breakfast for us. She's trying! I bet it's because she's not on all that medication you were forcing her to take."

"I wasn't forcing her to take anything," I snapped, pulling sharply away from the curb. "Besides, she thinks the world is going to end in a couple days. Do you call that a healthy mind? I don't."

Parker stewed in silence.

"Speaking of the world ending . . ." I said casually. "You haven't heard from any of the Seekers, have you?"

"No."

"Good." I nodded to myself. "Now I know you're willing to lie straight to my face."

My brother went still, like a deer hoping it hasn't been spotted by a hunter. Then he released the breath he'd been holding. "Like I had a choice? If I told you, you'd freak out on me, and . . ."

"And what?"

"And I'd join them anyway! I think they're right, Mia! There's something wrong in L.A., and it's bigger than the earthquake. I can feel it. Don't tell me you can't."

"I don't feel anything," I said. "And you're not joining the Seekers."

"I am. It's the right thing to do."

"No, Parker, you're really not."

He stared at me for a long moment, reading me. "You were at the school last night. That's why your car was gone when we got home." His voice came out flat. "What did you do, Mia?"

I told him. It didn't go well.

As soon as we reached the Skyline parking lot my brother was out of the car, running through the crowds of students toward the school.

"Parker, wait!" I called after him.

He didn't even turn around.

17

"I told you she would come!" Katrina said when she opened the door to room 317. She wasn't talking to me, though. She was talking to the roomful of people behind her . . . people wearing long, bloodred cloaks, almost like graduation gowns, but with hoods pulled over their heads, and black, featureless masks concealing their faces. The only ones not wearing masks were Mr. Kale and Katrina, though both were draped in the same red cloaks as the others. Katrina's lips matched her cloak perfectly.

My gloved hands clenched into fists. I glared at Mr. Kale. "You said this wasn't a cult."

Katrina yanked me inside and locked the door behind me. "Secret society," she said. "There's a difference."

"Not from where I'm standing."

"Then have a seat," Mr. Kale said, patting the back of a chair positioned at the center of the room. The desks had been pushed back against the walls, making space for the cloaked, masked people. The lights were off and the blinds drawn, so Mr. Kale's spectacular ocean view was obscured.

I sniffed, smelled something burning.

Katrina grabbed a rectangle of black construction paper with tape already on one side and stuck it to the small window in the door, making it impossible for anyone outside the room to peek in.

The people in the red cloaks watched me silently from behind their black masks. One of them could be Parker and I would never know.

Katrina didn't need her uncle's ability to read my mind. "Parker was just here. Uncle Kale sent him away."

I nodded, as relieved as I could be while still in my current situation. I wondered how long Parker would stay mad at me.

"Where's your mask?" I asked Katrina.

In answer, Katrina picked up two masks off Mr. Kale's desk and handed one to her uncle.

"Thought you might like to see a couple of familiar faces before we begin," she said, and winked before donning her mask.

Mr. Kale, his face now hidden, took a step back from the chair and made an open-armed gesture as if to say, *It's all yours.*

A vision popped into my head of a prisoner being strapped to that chair and a hood pulled over his face and—

I felt that tingling in my brain again, right before Mr. Kale said, "It's a regular chair, Miss Price. There's nothing to be afraid of."

"I'm not afraid," I told him, but my voice wavered. I took a deep breath, like it would have to last me a while, and sat.

Before the Seekers converged around me, I saw one of them lift the ventilated lid of a small black pot, revealing the orange glow from within and releasing a small puff of smoke. And I saw the metal rod resting on its side near the pot . . . a metal rod with a perfect circle at one end.

I didn't think I'd ever seen a branding iron in real life, but I knew instantly what the metal rod was, and fear seized my throat like a choking hand.

Then Seekers surrounded me, a shrinking red circle. Those featureless black faces gazed impassively down on mine, eyes shining from almond-shaped holes in their masks. Each one placed his left hand on the shoulder of the Seeker in front of him.

"What's going on?" My words came out in something approaching a wail.

"Relax," Katrina said. "Like I told you last night, we need to do a little bonding ritual to seal the deal. Then you'll be one of us. We'll know we can trust you and the masks can come off."

A ritual? Had she mentioned a ritual? No, no, no. I would have remembered that.

Mr. Kale moved around in front of me and let his gaze settle on mine. I felt that tingling in my brain again, the feeling you get when one of your limbs falls asleep and then starts to wake up.

The Seekers nearest Mr. Kale placed their hands on his shoulders, so the whole group of them was connected.

"It's going to be okay," a black-masked Seeker said. I recognized Quentin's voice. "We've all been through this. After, you'll be connected to the rest of us. We'll be your conductors."

I thought of the way the Seekers seemed to move as one, like there was some kind of invisible thread connecting them. I didn't want that. I didn't want to be tied to them, bonded and branded as a Seeker for the rest of my life.

"But why is a ritual necessary? I already agreed to join." Something I was regretting more and more every second. I should have listened to Jeremy, even if he had considered killing me. I should have stayed away from the Seekers. "Can't I just take an oath or something?"

Mr. Kale glanced at Katrina over my head. "You said you explained everything to her."

Katrina shrugged. "Maybe she wasn't listening."

"Mia," Mr. Kale said. "The circle is to contain and concentrate our joined energy. I'm going to put my hands on your head now. You will feel some slight pressure and a bit of tingling, but there shouldn't be any pain."

"Wait. Let's slow down and—"

I felt Mr. Kale's hands come to rest lightly on top of my head. The hands settling there were gentle enough, but the buzz of electricity I felt from that touch was like an electric shock. I jerked in the seat. It wasn't like being struck by lightning. With lightning, the pain was so brilliant that it became something beyond pain. This was different.

"You said it wouldn't hurt." My voice came out so thin I doubted anyone but me heard it. Then the pressure began, like someone was squeezing my brain, wringing it out like a sponge.

Let me in, Mia. Stop fighting. Let me make you one of us.

It was Mr. Kale's voice, and a part of me wanted to do what he said, give in and let this happen. But that part was tiny. Minuscule.

No! Get out of my head!

The heat gathered in my chest, crackling energy.

I heard Mr. Kale gasp.

What are you doing?

I didn't know what I was doing. All I knew was that I wanted his hands off me. Wanted that pressure in my brain to be gone.

Please, stop this, Mia. Don't fight me. I'm not your enemy.

A charge vibrated over my skin.

We need you, Mr. Kale said.

I don't need you! I threw the words back at him, and the charge running over my skin pulsed once. Then the pressure in my head was gone. Mr. Kale's hands were gone. The Circle of Seekers widened and broke as they stumbled backward, a few of them gasping, clutching their hearts as though they'd been defibrillated.

I shot to my feet, and a wave of dizziness swept over me. For a moment my vision went black and sparkly, and then it cleared. I turned around. Mr. Kale had his back against the dry-erase board, and he was breathing in heaving gasps. His mask was gone, and his too-long hair hung in curtains over his eyes, only his nose protruding. His hands were up and he was staring at them through the veil of his hair. Wisps of smoke curled from his fingers, like he'd just crushed a handful of smoldering cigarettes.

"Uncle!" Katrina hurried to his side to examine his hands. "What did you do to him?" she snarled at me.

I saw that the skin on Mr. Kale's palms was blackened, crisp and cracking, and my mind reeled backward to London Bridge in Lake Havasu City, to the burns covering Janna's legs, the handprints scorched onto her chest.

When I began backing toward the door, no one tried to stop me.

18

My body went through the motions. Went to class. Sat down in assigned seat. Stared at words and equations on dry erase board. My mind was another matter. It kept returning to Mr. Kale's classroom, reliving what had happened there.

He'd been inside my head, but this time he hadn't merely spoken to me. This time there had been pressure, that terrible pressure, like he was trying to mold my brain into a new shape.

During classes, I kept sneaking glances at the other students, mentally photoshopping black masks onto their faces. I examined their backpacks. Did they seem too full, maybe because they had red cloaks stuffed inside? Were their hands turned facedown on their desks to hide circular brands?

When lunch came, I didn't want to go to the cafeteria, didn't want to risk running into Quentin and Schiz, or worse, Katrina or Jeremy. Didn't want to feel eyes on me and wonder if they belonged to some other faceless Seeker, or some guy who wanted me dead. At least the Followers didn't hide who they were. You could always see them coming.

I found an inconspicuous alcove where I could lie low

and watch as students flowed into the cafeteria, keeping an eye out for Parker. After ten minutes, he still hadn't showed. Where was he? I needed to talk to him, make him understand that the Seekers were not playing around. They did rituals and wore scary masks and did things to your brain, things no one should be able to do.

I went in search of Parker, starting outside on the school's cement front steps, where he and his friends used to eat lunch.

There was a breeze blowing off the ocean, and my skin seemed to shrink around my body when it touched me. The storm was closer now. If there actually was a storm. I'd checked the weather report again that morning. The forecast hadn't changed. The promise of sunny, seventy-degree days stretched ahead of us for the next week.

A group of Followers dressed in white that was blinding to look at in the noon sun were standing on the sidewalk out in front of the school, holding hands and swaying and singing some sort of tinny, high-pitched hymn. The Followers on each end of the line held up white poster board signs glued to wooden stakes.

Only the Righteous Will Survive, one sign read.

My skin ached. My thoughts were scrambling over and over one another like ants racing to the top of their hill.

What if Parker went back to Mr. Kale to beg to join the Seekers?

I hadn't fulfilled my part of the bargain.

I had run away before they could complete their initiation.

Parker was still fair game.

No. I'm the one they want, I reasoned with myself. *I'm the one with the Spark. I'm the supposed Tower girl.*

Reminding myself of this didn't ease my mind. There was only one way to do that, and it was to find my brother. I had already searched for him in all the places I could think to look, except one, the last place I wanted to go, but the first place I ought to have checked.

Room 317.

But when I got there I found that Mr. Kale's door was locked and the lights were off. Had he gone home for the day to treat the burns I'd inflicted on his hands? I didn't feel the least bit sorry for what I'd done. I hoped I had fried the brand right off his palm. That's what he deserved for trying to mind-control me.

I listened at Kale's door for a moment, but heard nothing from the other side.

I did hear voices, though . . . coming from one of the classrooms down the hall. Since I had no other lead on where Parker might be, I decided to investigate. I followed the voices to the source and peered through the small rectangular window in the classroom door.

At first all I saw were the Followers, five of them, their white-clad bodies seeming to blend into one mass. You almost couldn't tell where one of them ended and the next began. They were crowded around someone, and I couldn't see who that someone was. But now that I was right on the other side of the door, I could make out their words.

"—a fight you can't win," said a female Follower with her hair pulled back in a brutally tight bun. Rachel. I recognized the raw, red place on the back of her neck where her tattoo used to be. "Prophet's Followers outnumber your Seekers, and we have God on our side. The sixth seal will open on April 17, and the earth will tear itself apart, and the unrighteous will be destroyed. There will be no after-life for your kind. You will be sucked down into oblivion and exist forever in an eternity of darkness."

Rachel moved slightly, and I caught a flash of black hair and red lipstick. I sucked in a breath.

Katrina.

"We'll see," Katrina said, affecting an air of indifference.

"Prophet *has* seen it! There's nothing you can do to stop the storm!" This from another of the Followers, a guy whose white clothes were so pristine I figured he must carry a bleach pen everywhere he went. His tongue darted to lick his lips, leaving them wet and glossy, pink as raw pork. "It is God's will that the earth be cleansed. Prophet tells us so."

Katrina smiled and told the guy to perform a physical impossibility.

The Follower sputtered, pink lips squirming on his face like a sea creature had attached itself to him. "You can't speak to me that way. I am a Follower of the Light! Show some respect!"

"If your God has a problem with it, what's he waiting for?" Katrina asked. "Tell him to strike me down." She threw her hands in the air and stared up at the ceiling. "Come on, God of the Followers! Let's see what you can do! Show me some wrath!" She cocked her head, as though anticipating thunder, and then smiled. "Nothing."

Pink Lips smiled back. "Our God is too great to trouble Himself with an insignificant creature like you. He works through us, His faithful servants. And I believe it is His will that you learn some humility. Don't you, Sister Rachel?"

"Oh, yes," she said. "I think that's an excellent idea, Brother Anthony."

Katrina's confident expression departed. She looked longingly at the door, as though wishing she were on the other side of it. When she saw me she blinked, her mouth parting, as though she would call to me for help.

But she didn't. She clamped her mouth shut and took her eyes away.

The Followers broke their wall of white and fell on Katrina like a pack of jackals on a wounded gazelle. But Katrina wasn't wounded. She was fully alive and ready to fight. She kicked and punched and struggled and bit Pink Lips on the hand so hard he screeched. I stood like a statue outside the door, my mind racing toward the inevitable conclusion that any second now I was going to have to do something to help this girl I despised.

But I hesitated, and then hesitated some more.

Despite Katrina's savage efforts to free herself, the Followers pinned her flat on her back on the surface of the teacher's desk.

Rachel grabbed Katrina's hair and yanked it until her neck stretched, winding it around her fist. "Such pretty hair. I used to dye my hair black, before I found Prophet, but it never looked like this. It was always dull. Yours is so shiny. I bet you love it, don't you?"

There was a big pair of metal scissors in a ceramic jar on the desk, among the pens and pencils. Rachel grabbed the scissors in her free hand and went *snip, snip* at the air.

Katrina's eyes grew to the size of golf balls.

Something broke in me. Maybe it was because I'd had my hair sheared away by lightning so many times, but I couldn't stand to see it happen to anyone else, even someone I hated.

I swung the door open, but too late. Rachel chopped through Katrina's hair, right next to her scalp.

Rachel let out a cry of triumph as the thick rope of glossy black hair came free in her hand. "Who owns this school now, Seeker?"

The door was on a spring and slammed shut behind me with a *BANG!* startling me almost as much as it did the Followers.

"Let her go," I said, proud of the implied *or else* tone I achieved without having to make an actual threat I probably wouldn't be able to carry through. And it turned out I didn't need threats. My sudden appearance surprised the Followers so much they lost their grips on Katrina.

She tore free of them and shot toward me. Eyes glassy, she reached up and touched what remained of her hair. She appeared younger without that black river swimming down her back, her oil-dark eyes bigger and wider, almost innocent.

The Followers smirked at us. They had formed their unbroken line again, standing shoulder to shoulder.

"You're one of them now, aren't you?" Rachel said. "I told you not to join them. Our numbers are far greater than theirs. The tide has turned in favor of the light. You could have been saved."

"As long as I'm not one of you, I'm happy," I told her.

"Two days," Rachel said. "That's all the time you have

left. When the storm comes, you'll wish you'd chosen differently."

"What are you going to do when the world doesn't end?" I asked her. "Will that prove once and for all that Prophet is a fraud, or will he make some excuse, convince you God was testing your faith?"

"Prophet is a true prophet of God," Rachel said, doing her best to stare me down. I had to admit, she was good at it. "He's never wrong. You'll see."

I spoke with more confidence than I felt. "I can't wait to watch your prophet make a fool of himself in front of the whole world."

Rachel took a step toward me, eyes dangerous. Her arms hung at her sides, one hand still clutching the scissors, going *snip, snip, snip.*

Katrina moved for the door. "Let's get out of here," she said.

For once, I had no problem doing what Katrina wanted me to do.

19

Again, I found myself in the ladies' lounge with Katrina, when I should have been looking for my brother. At least I knew he wasn't with the Seeker I trusted the least.

I leaned against a sink and watched as she picked at the remains of her hair with trembling fingers.

"Maybe we should tell someone what happened," I suggested. "The principal or whoever's in charge now. Rachel and those other Followers would probably be expelled."

Katrina let her arms fall to her sides, giving up. "It won't change anything."

Her eyes began to water. Her face was emotionless. She didn't make a sound. But tears leaked from her eyes one after another. Then her chin trembled, and she broke. A single sob wrenched from somewhere down deep inside her.

"My hair . . ." she said, and covered her face.

My chest felt tight, like my heart had swelled and there was no more room for it behind my breastbone. I couldn't help it. I felt the pressure of sympathy tears trying to pop free. I thought of all the times my hair had been scorched away and I'd been left not just a lightning-scarred freak, but a bald-headed, lightning-scarred freak.

"It's not that bad," I said. "It's kind of cool, actually. You just have to even it out and put some sticky stuff in it. Then you'll look like Audrey Hepburn. Very classy."

Katrina lowered her hands. Black mascara tears cut crooked trails down her cheeks. "Thank you for helping me up there. I know I'm not your favorite person. You could have left me with them, and I don't know if they would have stopped at cutting off my hair."

I looked at the floor, thinking of how long I'd watched at the window, doing nothing. If I had interrupted sooner, Katrina might still have her hair.

"You're welcome," I said humbly. It was easy to be humble when you had nothing to be proud of.

"And I'm sorry," Katrina said. "You know, for blackmailing you and everything. I didn't see any other way to get you on our side."

I wasn't quite ready to forgive her for that one. "How did you end up in that classroom with a bunch of Followers?" I asked, changing the subject.

Katrina shook her head. "It was my own fault. *Sister* Rachel set a trap for me and I fell right into it. She let me see her 'spreading the good word' to a couple of girls near the staircase, and then she took off up the stairs. I followed her. She knew I would. She stayed just far enough ahead of me to make me think I was chasing when she was actually leading."

I hoisted myself up to sit on one of the sinks. "What's so important about Skyline? I mean, why are you so protective of this school?"

"Because the Seekers claimed it first."

"As your recruiting station? And the White Tent is Prophet's recruiting station?"

"Only he keeps trying to invade our territory." Katrina's lip curled in a silent snarl.

"Why use a school, then? Why not set up your own tent on the beach? Lure people in with granola bars or whatever."

"That's not the way we work. We don't bribe people to join us."

"But you do blackmail them."

Katrina frowned. "That was a one-time thing. And I said I'm sorry."

"Uh-huh. So how many Seekers are there, exactly? Was the whole gang present, you know . . . this morning?" I felt awkward bringing up my failed initiation. I didn't want to think about it, much less talk about it.

"Not all of them," she said vaguely. "There are others. In other schools. Young people make the best Seekers. Our senses are more awake, and our minds are more open, for the most part." She glanced at me. "There are always exceptions, though usually not among people who have the Spark."

I shifted uncomfortably. She was obviously referring to me.

"What about Mr. Kale?" I asked. "Is he cult president?"

"More like our general," Katrina said. "He's had the Spark the longest—ever since he was our age—and he's the most powerful. In our circle, the leader is the one with the most power. Before Uncle Kale, it was—" Katrina lowered her chin and stared at her hands. "It was someone else, but she's gone now."

"Gone?" Then it was possible for someone to check out of the Circle of Seekers.

"Dead," Katrina said flatly, and I gulped.

Katrina's eyes went blank for a moment, as though she were trying to figure something out. "I guess if you were to join us for real, you'd take Uncle Kale's place."

I burst out laughing. I couldn't help it. But Katrina didn't even smile.

"Oh, come on," I said. "You're not serious."

"Those are the rules," she said, her tone somber.

My laughter tapered off. "I hate to break it to you, but I only play by one set of rules."

"Let me guess. Yours?"

"Pretty much."

She studied the ground. "It won't matter anyway. You wouldn't become our leader, not if the prophecy—" She bit her lip and shook her head. "Never mind."

Part of me wanted to hear what Katrina was holding back. But I'd been the focus of our conversation for all of thirty seconds, and already I was anxious to change the subject.

"So is Rachel like you?" I asked. "Does she sense the Spark in people and report them to Prophet?"

"I'm sure she would if she could, but she doesn't have a direct line to Prophet. He has too many Followers at this point to give individual attention to each of them. My guess is she has some knack for sensing the Spark, but that doesn't do her any good unless she can convince people to attend one of Prophet's revivals and receive his blessing, like she tried to do with you yesterday."

I shuddered at the memory of the intensity in Rachel's eyes, her strong hand squeezing my arm. I was surprised she hadn't left bruises.

"As long as you stay away from the White Tent, you're safe," Katrina said. "The only people Prophet trusts to do his recruiting are his Apostles, and they have their hands full recruiting the Displaced in Tentville."

I remembered the headline I read on Schiz's blog about the missing Apostle, and wondered if the twelfth was lurking around some high school, searching for people like . . . well, like me.

"By the way," Katrina said, "you haven't seen that guy around today, have you? Uncle Kale checked up on him. There's no Jeremy Parish registered at Skyline."

"No," I said. "I haven't seen him today." I decided not to mention that I'd seen quite a bit of him yesterday, or that he'd been in my room the night before that with a knife pointed at my heart.

"You'll let me know if he comes around."

"Sure," I lied. I didn't trust Katrina any more than I trusted Jeremy. "I should get to class."

"Mia?" Katrina said hesitantly. "Can I . . . can I ask a favor?"

I wanted to say no, but Katrina looked so pathetic with her choppy, shorn hair, I decided to cut her some slack. "You can ask."

"I want you to go somewhere with me tonight. I need your help. If you'll do this one thing for me, I won't bother you anymore. Or your brother. The Seekers will leave you both completely alone forever."

I was about to ask specifics and then turn Katrina down flat, but then two aid workers in their orange polo shirts pushed through the lounge door. Their eyebrows rose high when they caught sight of Katrina's hair.

"I'll pick you up at midnight," Katrina said. Her eyes scanned my outfit. "Wear something else, okay?"

"Like what?"

"Just show some skin for once."

"Hold on, I haven't even agreed to anything."

But Katrina was already on her way out the door. "Midnight," she called over her shoulder.

20

Incredibly, the rest of the day passed like any other school day, which is to say it dragged along as though it had two broken legs. Parker met me at my locker after school, right on time. We got our rations—this time we had a couple cans of fruit cocktail and a chocolate bar—and carried them to my car. Parker didn't say a word to me the whole time, and he didn't meet my eyes once.

I had never felt so alone in my life, and that was saying something.

Parker and I arrived home to the whiny roar of the vacuum. Mom was in the living room, using the hose to suck up the bits of plaster chips and dust that kept coming loose from the cracked ceiling. Her back was to us, and she didn't hear us come in.

Parker and I shared a glance. Neither of us had dared vacuum anything since the earthquake. Loud noises tended to lead to panic attacks. Now, in a single day, everything was different again. I had no idea what to expect from Mom anymore.

"Mom," Parker called over the drone of the vacuum. "Mom!"

On impulse, I reached behind me and swung the door

shut. The slam it made reverberated through the house. I hadn't slammed a door in our house in a month, and it felt better than I'd ever imagined slamming a door could feel.

Mom dropped the vacuum attachment and whirled around, clutching her heart.

"Oh!" she said. "You're home." She punched the power button on the vacuum.

Parker and I stared at her. The slamming door had startled her, but it hadn't terrified her. I hated to admit it, but maybe Parker was right. Maybe the medications I'd had her on only slowed her recovery.

Now that I really thought about it, keeping Mom in a drugged-up, dreamlike state during the last month, while she watched Prophet proselytize three times a day on *The Hour of Light*, might account for why his sermons had affected her so much.

Oh God, I thought. *It's my fault. It really is.*

My fault it took Mom so long to recover.

My fault she's obsessed with Prophet.

"Mia," Mom said, brows furrowing as she looked at my eyes, which were suddenly swimming. Or drowning. "Are you okay?"

I swallowed what felt like a shard of glass in my throat and eked out, "Uh-huh." I turned away quickly. "I'm just going to"—I caught sight of the overflowing trash can in the kitchen—"take out the trash." It was a dumb excuse to escape. Our trash hadn't been collected since the quake. We could barely fit Mom's car in the garage with all the bags piling up, and it was really starting to stink in there.

The vacuum roared to life again and I went from room to room, gathering trash cans two by two and removing them to the garage. We were out of big trash bags, so I'd started pouring the garbage directly into the city container.

I held my breath as I ventured into the reeking garage and opened the city trash container. I tipped the trash can from Mom's bathroom upside down and watched as what looked like tiny white mints hailed down amid wadded-up tissues. It wasn't until the white pellets were at the bottom of the city container that I realized what they were.

My brain went numb.

"Mia?"

I turned to find Mom in the garage doorway. She came down the steps and stopped in front of me. I realized I was hugging the trash can from her bathroom. I forgot about holding my breath and inhaled the rotten stench coming from the bins. I almost gagged, and not because of the smell.

"I want to apologize to you for this morning," Mom said, seeming not to notice the disgusted look on my face. "I shouldn't have asked you to say that prayer. I can't force you to believe the way I do, but I'd like you to try. Maybe we could watch *The Hour of Light* together tonight. Or maybe we could go to a revival, as a family, to see what they're like."

Her words barely registered. "You threw them away. The pills . . ."

She blinked for a moment, as though confused. Then she nodded. "Yes, I had to."

"Why?"

"Prophet says no person who partakes of addictive substances and mind-altering drugs will be saved when the storm comes. Our blood and our minds and our souls have to be clean."

"Do you have any idea what I went through to get those pills for you?"

A deep line formed between her brows. She shook her head, and I realized she wouldn't know, because I had done everything I could to keep that secret from her. Just like, when I was growing up, I had done everything I could not to let her find out what a pariah I was at school, or how people in Lake Havasu City avoided me, walked on the other side of the street when they saw me coming. I hadn't wanted her to worry. I never wanted her to worry about me. I wanted her and Parker to live normal lives, despite my presence in those lives.

"Why didn't you tell me you didn't want to take them anymore?" I asked.

"I don't know, Mia." Mom shook her head. "I've been so confused."

"Mom, you have to stop watching *The Hour of Light*. You have to stop listening to Prophet. He's screwing up your mind."

"No." She shook her head. "No, Mia. He's helped me to see things clearly for the first time in my life. It's not just what happened during the earthquake. It's everything. I've been living all wrong."

"Listen to yourself! He has you completely brain-washed!"

Her mouth tightened, like someone had pulled a draw-string on it. "Watch your tone."

Suddenly I understood how an earthquake felt, pressure building up along a fault line, needing to be released. The pressure inside me had been building for a long time, and with everything that had happened that day it was too much.

"*You* watch *your* tone." I threw her trash can at the wall, knocking over a jar of nails that shattered as it hit the cement floor, scattering nails and glass everywhere. "You know who's been holding this family together for weeks now? *Me*. I get that you've been through something terrible. I know you lost someone you cared about, and you're confused and scared right now, but Parker and I need you. We're scared, too!"

Mom's face went a deep shade of red and her shoulders began to tremble. "You are not allowed to speak to me this way. Children must respect their parents. Prophet says—"

"I don't care what he says! Parker and I are the ones who've been here for you, not him. Not Prophet. *We're* your family."

For a moment, Mom's eyes seemed to soften, as though my words had finally penetrated. Then she grimaced, and her hands curled into tiny fists at her sides. "You. Don't. Understand." She spit the words out one by one. "I've been so lost . . . I feel like I've been wandering through a fog, just . . . *blind*. And I've finally found my way free. I can see again. I understand why it happened, why God saved me when I should have died like the others. So he could show me the way and the truth. So I could change."

I stared at her. "What's the truth, Mom?"

"That if we're not saved, then we are damned. My children are damned." She lowered herself slowly to her knees on the grimy cement floor of the garage, amid the nails and broken glass and the stink of garbage. "Kneel with me," she implored. "Let's pray for forgiveness. Pray that our sins will be lifted."

"What's going on?" Parker had appeared in the doorway.

Mom had her head down, praying under her breath as I pushed past my brother into the house.

I hesitated in the kitchen, wanting to turn back, to say something, do *something* that would change Mom's mind. But her mind didn't belong to her anymore. It belonged to Prophet.

21

I spent the rest of the afternoon and evening locked in my bedroom. I didn't come down for dinner, even though I heard someone banging around in the kitchen. I thought Parker or Mom might knock on my door with a peace offering of a bowl of soup, but that didn't happen.

At five minutes to midnight, I stood in the dark on the curb outside our house. I kept expecting Jeremy to step out of the shadows and try to stop me from going anywhere, but he didn't. Maybe I really had seen the last of him.

Katrina arrived right on time. I heard her door locks disengage with a click, and I got in.

It took an effort on my part not to stare when I saw her. Katrina did not look like Audrey Hepburn, but she had embraced her new haircut and had styled it in jagged, punk-rock spikes. Paired with her smoky eye makeup and her stripper ensemble—her boobs were near to busting out of her red silk corset, and her leather hot pants barely covered her butt—the haircut worked for her.

"What do you think?" Katrina studied her hair in the rearview.

"It's you," I told her. It was as much of a compliment as I was willing to give. "So where are we going?"

"You'll know when we get there."

I sighed and buckled my seat belt. "Whatever. Can we hit the road before someone realizes I'm gone?"

Katrina screeched away from the curb and cackled like a maniac.

"Thanks," I said. "Very inconspicuous."

She fished around in her purse and withdrew a silver flask. She unscrewed the cap and handed it to me. "You need to relax."

I contemplated the flask in my hands. I'd tried wine before, maybe gotten a little buzzed, but I'd never tasted hard liquor. "What is it?" I asked.

"It's good. Try it."

Alcohol . . . one more thing that was in short supply in the city. I bet Prophet was happy about that.

I tilted the bottle to my lips, filled my mouth, and swallowed. I winced at the alcohol taste, but it wasn't too bad and left a nice warm trail down to my stomach.

Katrina stared at me with wide eyes, paying no attention to the road. "You drank that like it was water." She sounded mystified. "You didn't even cough!"

I shook my head. "Was I supposed to?"

"That was white lightning, Mia."

I shifted uncomfortably, as I did whenever the word "lightning" was spoken in my presence. "Why do you call it that?"

"Because it burns like you swallowed fire, that's why. It's homemade whiskey. Moonshine. You know what moonshine is?"

"Of course. I'm not an idiot. Why did you tell me it was good?"

"Because it is good, for hooch. You're a lot more hard-core than I thought you'd be. Maybe I misjudged you."

To accentuate her point, I took another couple of hearty swallows from the flask. They went down smoother with each hit. I was used to feeling like there was fire inside me. "White lightning" was nothing compared to my own special brand of "red lightning." Still, I did feel like kind of a badass. That was, until the alcohol hit my bloodstream. Apparently I was only immune to the burn of white lightning, not its other effects.

I tilted my head back to stare at the ceiling of Katrina's car, feeling suddenly woozy.

"I think you've had enough." Katrina took her flask back and swigged, grimacing.

"Hey! Can you not do that? I don't want to die in a fiery car crash tonight."

"I can handle it," she said calmly, putting the flask away.

"Yeah, and what if we're pulled over. This stuff smells like rubbing alcohol. We'd get busted and thrown in jail or something."

"Jails are full. The cops have bigger problems to deal with than a couple of mildly inebriated teenagers."

As though our conversation had summoned them, a parade of police cars, lights flashing, raced past us on the road, going the opposite direction at full speed and obviously uninterested in us.

"Like I said, you need to relax." Katrina glanced at me, smiling. Then she noticed my outfit and her smile disappeared. "You're wearing the exact same thing you wore to school."

I glanced down at my clothes, but everything was

starting to blur. "Oh . . . right, I forgot, you wanted me to 'show some skin.'" The mere idea of this made me crack up. No one wanted to see my skin.

Katrina scowled. "Put a stocking on your head and you could rob a bank."

I turned to look out the window, even though the city rushing past made my head spin. "So, what's the favor? Why do you need my help?"

Katrina was quiet for a long time before answering. "Because you can sense the Spark."

I looked at her. Both of her. Damn white lightning. No more homemade whiskey on an empty stomach for me.

"We're running out of time," Katrina went on. "Prophet is recruiting at a pace the Seekers can't match. I need you to help me play catch-up."

"But I'm not even one of you."

"Consider yourself an honorary Seeker. Just for tonight."

"I'm honored," I said.

"Is that sarcasm?"

"Very perceptive of you."

Traffic was light as we entered Koreatown, nearing the dark patch of nothingness that was the Waste. Only the white column of a single skyscraper remained standing, bright white in the center of that darkness, the last visible remnant of the downtown skyline. The Tower.

K-town was several miles west of the epicenter of destruction, but the area had sustained major damage. Cracks veined the outer walls of many of the buildings we passed and the streets were split open in places, like gaping wounds waiting to be stitched back together. But what struck me most was the vacant feel of the area. Before the quake,

K-town had teemed with people. Now many of the businesses had turned off their signs and pulled metal gates across their doors. The dark lake of the Waste was spreading to consume everything around it. I wondered if, in a few more months, when the world didn't end as Prophet said it would, people's fear would fade and they would begin to trickle back into Los Angeles until the city was once again bursting at the seams.

I couldn't put off asking any longer. "Katrina, where are we going?"

Katrina's gaze darted to me and then back to the road. She reached up to curl a piece of hair between her fingers and found nothing but nothing. "I think you already know. You were outside Uncle Kale's classroom last night. You heard us talking."

All at once, I felt very sober. "Tell me," I insisted.

"We're going to the Rove."

"Why?" I asked, my voice more air than sound. I felt like I'd been sucker punched in the stomach, even though I should have seen this coming.

"The Rove attracts a certain type of person," Katrina explained. "That type of person is more likely to have the Spark. It's not just the Rove that attracts them. It's the Waste. There's an energy about the place, something magnetic, like . . . well, you'll see."

"Oh, no I won't," I said, shaking my head. "Stop the car."

"But we're almost there."

"Stop the car now!"

I was surprised when Katrina calmly pulled off to the side of the road.

This close to the Waste, the streetlamps were out. The windows of the surrounding buildings were shattered and dark. There were a few abandoned cars, but none that seemed to be occupied. No people anywhere that I could see.

"You want to get out here?" Katrina asked. "Be my guest. These buildings may look unoccupied, but I'm sure you'll find *someone* to help you get home. Granted, that someone will probably not be the type of person you want to be alone with unless you have protection, and I'm not talking about condoms."

Why hadn't I remembered my pepper spray? I could have used it on Katrina and then commandeered her vehicle.

"Turn the car around," I said through my teeth. I could feel fire in my chest, and the whiskey must have loosened something inside me, because my control was slipping.

As though she could feel the heat emanating from me, Katrina drew back against her door.

"I have to tell you something, and you're not going to like it."

A humorless laugh ripped through my throat. I tilted my head back and spoke to the car's ceiling. "There's more not to like?"

Katrina nodded. "I promise, I didn't know anything about it until it was too late, okay? I found out right before I came to pick you up."

She drew in a long breath and let it out slowly. I wanted to grab her and shake the answer out of her.

"Your brother is there."

For a moment, everything in me went quiet. My heart held still. "You're lying," I said. "Why would Parker be at the Rove?"

"He went with Quentin. He snuck out, same as you."

My heart began to beat again. Slow beats, reverberating like isolated explosions in my ears.

"He wants to be a Seeker, Mia. He wants to help us."

My hands were stones in my lap. If I was still drunk, I no longer felt it. I remembered what Jeremy had said to me the day before. *Don't go to the Waste, Mia. Stay out of the Waste and away from the Seekers.*

I looked at Katrina and said one word. "Drive."

22

Katrina drove us as close to the edge of the Waste as the ruined streets would allow, which wasn't far. The Puente Hills Fault was a blind thrust fault, which meant the plates did not move from side to side, but up. The whole of the Waste had been lifted by about ten feet, and now stood on a sort of huge plateau several square miles wide.

When Katrina was within fifty yards of the edge of the plateau—a wall of broken asphalt, concrete, and busted pipes—she turned into a parking lot in the Warehouse District, where several dozen other cars were parked. Ramps had been erected in numerous places around the plateau, but even if those ramps weren't guarded by armed sentries, it would have been unwise to drive a car without reinforced tires into the Waste. When the skyscrapers fell, downtown had been buried in the shattered glass that rained from above. Those mountains of broken glass still lay like drifts of snow after a blizzard. We'd have to walk the rest of the way to wherever the Rove was.

A feverish tingle raced over my skin as I stepped out of the car into the night air. I checked the sky, but its starless surface was without a trace of clouds. There was only the warm lemon moon, flanked by the eye of a roaming helicopter beaming down onto some other part of the city. A typical L.A. sky. No sign of rain, but my skin was tingling worse than ever, aching with fever, as though the phantom storm I sensed was just over the horizon.

Emerging from the driver's side of her car, Katrina noticed my expression. "You feel it, don't you?" She gestured widely at the destruction. "The power of this place. The energy. It's like it's bleeding out of these cracks in the ground." She rubbed her arms, but her eyes were bright with excitement. "It's all around us."

Katrina was right. I felt it, whatever *it* was, like a magnet with an opposite charge from mine, pulling me closer.

We crept silently toward the plateau wall, staying in the shadows. When I spotted the gun-toting sentry walking the perimeter of the plateau wall, I decided my burglar outfit was a serendipitous clothing choice.

"This is a bad idea," I hissed in Katrina's ear. "We should find another way in. I don't want to get shot today."

"They aren't real bullets," she insisted. "It's a tranq gun. Besides, it's not like the sentries are actual cops. They're volunteers. If they shoot at you, they'll probably miss."

It was a testament to how bad things were that this made me feel better.

"Don't worry," Katrina said. "I've done this before."

"How many times?"

"Lots. I know what I'm doing."

We moved closer to the plateau wall and the sentry, and then paused in the shadows. I barely breathed.

Minutes passed, and finally the sentry moved on down the perimeter.

"When I say go, we run. Climb the wall as quickly as possible."

"But what if—"

"Go!"

Katrina took off at a sprint toward the plateau wall, running silently in her spiked-heel boots over a thick carpet of gray cement dust. I rushed after her, my heart pounding so hard it was all I could hear. I smelled the sickly stench of dead flowers, and looked down to see dried petals scattered over the ground, the remains of wreaths and bouquets people had left to honor the dead. They softened the impact of my boots, muting my hurried steps.

We scrambled up the plateau wall, using broken pipes like ladder rungs. I didn't dare look back. Didn't dare look anywhere. I imagined I could hear the sentry running toward us. My heartbeat became the sound of his boots, of his tranq gun firing at us.

Katrina climbed like a monkey, even in her hot pants and corset. I was not so graceful and came close to impaling myself on jagged shoots of metal.

We reached the top of the plateau without getting shot. Katrina took a quick look around before choosing a direction. She headed up Olive Street, toward Pershing Square, still keeping to the shadows.

I breathed. We had made it.

I hurried to catch up with Katrina, scrambling around hills of debris, tripping on the fractured pavement. Parts of the street jutted at haphazard angles, like pieces of a broken iceberg tilting into the ocean. It looked like a nuke had gone off in the heart of downtown.

Katrina and I walked in silence. The only sound was glass crunching underfoot as we made our way along broken streets, avoiding rifts in the asphalt. I had to force myself to keep my eyes on the ground, on the street sparkling with glass dust, like new snow under moonlight. It was so quiet here, like a museum of the destruction rather than the real thing.

"The sentries only guard the perimeter of the Waste, right?" I asked, keeping my voice down.

Katrina shrugged. "Mostly."

I swallowed hard and tried to ignore the crawling feeling on my skin, and beneath it, too. The energy was under my fingernails, on my scalp, behind my eyes. Everywhere. The farther we traveled into the Waste, the more intense the feeling became, like some alien insects had dug their way inside me.

Thirty minutes later, we were approaching Pershing Square, which looked like a construction crew had taken a hundred jackhammers to the cement grounds. The area was located one block south of where the skyscrapers used to be, so the whole place glittered with glass dust. But Pershing Square's most distinguishing feature, a huge lavender column about the size of a small apartment building, still stood proudly among the ruins.

We entered the square, climbing carefully over the shattered cement. Suddenly Katrina stopped, pressing a finger to her lips. "Shhh." She tilted her head to listen, and I heard the slightest shuffling of footsteps.

A voice from behind the purple column called out, "I do not find The Hanged Man."

I froze, looking around, but before my mind could

finish running through all the scenarios of what was about to happen to us, Katrina called back, "Fear death by water."

A figure emerged from behind the column and came straight toward us. He wore black cargo pants and a black flak jacket and carried the tranq gun of a sentry.

I tensed for the impact of a tranq dart.

"It's all right," Katrina whispered to me. "He's an usher."

"An usher?"

"He'll tell us where the Rove is."

"Oh." I remembered the couple I'd eavesdropped on in line at school. The guy had said his brother's friend was an usher and knew where to find the Rove.

Katrina approached the usher, and he whispered something in her ear. Katrina nodded, her eyes getting bigger. Then the usher stepped back behind the purple column and Katrina returned to me. Her dark eyes were shining.

"Let's go," she said, and headed up Fifth Street toward the Financial District. Again, I had to rush to catch up with her. My boots were so much more sensible than Katrina's, and my legs were longer, but somehow she always managed to stay a few steps ahead of me.

"What was that about with the hanged man and death by water?" I asked.

"Rove protocol," Katrina said. "If you don't know the pass phrase, you don't get the location of the Rove. It's always a corresponding line from that poem, *The Waste Land*. T. S. Eliot. Ever read him?"

"Poetry's not really my thing."

"That doesn't surprise me." She smiled without teeth. "You don't strike me as a person who likes to look below the surface of things. Too scary under there."

"Do me a favor," I said. "Stop pretending you know me."

As we walked, I couldn't take my eyes off the silvery-white pillar ahead of us, the Tower spearing the sky. I remembered what Jeremy had shown me; remembered standing atop the Tower as a storm gathered above me.

And then I remembered something else he'd shown me.

Me: walking through the Waste, stepping into nothingness and falling, falling, falling.

I lowered my eyes in time to see the chasm I was about to step into.

My reflexes raced to catch up to my awareness, but it was too late.

I was going to fall.

And I was going to die.

23

I was about to be murdered by gravity, but time slowed enough for me to feel a world of regret for the things I had done wrong, all the bad choices I'd made, the people I'd hurt.

Maybe it was better this way. Easier for everyone if I disappeared into darkness. At least then I wouldn't do the terrible thing Jeremy claimed I was going to do.

My heart and my stomach stayed where they were as the rest of my body began the plummet.

"Mia!"

Katrina grabbed me and yanked me back from the brink of the chasm. She was a lot stronger than she looked. She threw me like I was stuffed with cotton, and I ended up on my butt on a pile of rubble five feet away.

I tried to catch my breath, but my heart seemed to explode every time it beat, eating up all my oxygen.

Katrina was breathing hard, as well. "You've got to watch where you're going! Some of these rifts go down for hundreds of feet! You could have gotten yourself killed!"

"Yeah. Yeah, okay. Thanks. Really." I stood to brush the powdering of cement and glass dust off my pants. I couldn't look at Katrina as I said again, "Thank you."

"Just . . . try to be more careful from now on, okay? We can't afford to lose you." She reached down to help me up.

Don't go to the Waste, Jeremy said in my mind, while the image of me falling, falling, falling into the chasm rode past on a carousel.

Together, Katrina and I approached the edge of the chasm and peered down into its black, fathomless depths. Katrina picked up a fist-sized piece of broken concrete and dropped it into the crack. We listened. And listened.

We didn't hear it hit the bottom.

My legs were shaky as we navigated our way around the chasm and started up Fifth Street again. Both of us kept our eyes glued to the ground until I asked once more where we were going. Where the Rove had taken up residence for the night.

Katrina pointed. My eyes followed the path of her finger.

She was pointing at the Tower.

Of course she was.

As we neared the Tower, other people began to emerge from the darkness, joining us in our march toward the Rove. Our group grew until we numbered about thirty. It was a party on the way to a party, everyone talking and laughing, passing flasks and joints and pipes, seemingly unconcerned about the sentries that might be patrolling the Waste. Katrina informed me—which she should have done earlier—that many of the sentries doubled as ushers, winning themselves free passage into the Rove.

Katrina moved among the rovers as though they were old friends at a reunion, flirting shamelessly with the guys, ignoring scowls from girls she cut in on. I noticed the way she touched people before she spoke to them, testing for the Spark. Though she kept talking and laughing as she made the rounds, her expression was one of extreme concentration whenever she touched someone new.

I searched the growing crowd for Parker, but I didn't see him. Maybe he was already at the Rove.

Katrina made her way back to me. She gestured at the rovers. "Would it kill you to help me out here?"

"You seem to be doing fine," I said. "Besides, I'm not here to help you. As soon as I find my brother, I'm gone."

"Oh, yeah? How do you plan to get home? Walk? Call a cab?"

She had a point.

"Look, I'll make a deal with you," Katrina said, flipping her nonexistent hair back over her shoulder and then frowning as she remembered it was now an inch long.

"You always have a deal in mind, don't you?"

She shrugged and adjusted her corset. Her boobs were dangerously close to freeing themselves. "Find me three people with the Spark, and I promise I'll help you find your brother and I'll take you both home. Otherwise, you're stuck here until I say it's time to leave."

I turned to my right and picked out the person walking closest to me, a blonde wearing peacock feathers tied into her hair. I held out my hand to her. "Hi, I'm Mia. What's your name?"

"Jude."

Her eyes widened as our hands touched. So did mine. I felt a subtle hum of static crackling off her.

That was easy.

She snatched her hand back. I stared at her with my mouth open.

"You felt it, too, didn't you," she said softly.

I forced my mouth to work. "Yeah. Yeah, I did."

Her eyes went to mine, wide and frightened. "There's something wrong with me," she said, keeping her voice low. "It started the day of the quake. I was downtown, you know . . . when it happened." She bit her lip. "Now I come here every night. I don't even know why. I just . . . I can't stay away. It's like something pulls me here. Is that how it is for you?"

Her eyes begged me to say yes, but I didn't want to lie to her. "There's someone you should talk to," I told her instead. "She'll explain everything."

I caught sight of Katrina and started to raise my hand to wave her over when I glimpsed a mark on Jude's shoulder blade, branching out from below her long hair, almost entirely hidden. She saw me staring and moved her hair over the veiny red line on her shoulder.

"It's called a Lichtenberg figure," she said, sounding defensive, as though I'd looked at the mark with disgust. "I've had it since the storm. It should have gone away by now, but . . . it hasn't."

"You said you were downtown during the quake?"

She nodded.

"Were you . . . ?"

"Struck by lightning?" she finished for me. "No, but the woman standing next to me was. She had a heart attack and died on the spot. I tried to give her CPR, but she was gone like that." Jude snapped her fingers. "I felt a kind of jolt when the woman was struck, though, almost like I'd been stung. My doctor said the lightning might have struck me indirectly, jumped off her and landed on me for a second."

"Excuse me," I said to the girl, and left her standing there, looking confused.

I hurried over to Katrina, grabbed her arm and dragged her away from the guy she was hanging on.

"What?" she asked, irritated.

I nodded at the girl, Jude. "One," I said.

Katrina smiled. "That was fast." She started toward Jude, but I wouldn't let go of her arm until she shook me off, wincing as though I'd been pinching her.

"She told me something," I said to Katrina. "During the quake, she was—" I swallowed. "She was struck by lightning."

Katrina nodded. I searched her face for some sign of surprise at this news, but there was none.

"Does that . . ." I had to swallow again. My throat was paper-dry. "Does that mean anything to you?"

I remembered the words Mr. Kale had spoken inside my mind, the ones that had made me want to run as fast as I could away from him.

I know who you are. I know what you are. And I know about the lightning.

Katrina shook her head, like she was disappointed in me. "The Spark has to come from somewhere, doesn't it? I thought you'd have figured it out by now. You really do have a talent for self-deception, Mia."

My hand fell from her arm, and she turned from me.

I watched as she spoke quietly to Jude. I could still see the tip of one branching lightning scar reaching out from beneath Jude's hair.

The energy that had my skin on edge, that magnetism I'd felt since we entered the Waste, only grew stronger as we neared our destination.

We arrived as a group at the revolving front doors of the Tower, which had formerly been glass but were now shattered and boarded up, though one of the plank boards was missing.

My eyes darted nervously as one by one the rovers filed through the door. Everything about this was surreal. The Tower rising above us; the Waste surrounding us; this bizarre mountain range of torn cement and granite and iron, all of it coated in glass dust, sparkling. The devastation was so complete it was almost like it belonged here, like it was the natural landscape, and only the Tower seemed out of place.

Katrina tugged my sleeve, and I followed her into the expansive foyer, lit by the moonlight shining in through the high windows.

"This is the best Rove location yet," she said. "Normally they just use some abandoned warehouse or loft. I talked to a rover, who said some gazillionaire bought the Tower and he's cool with hosting the Rove so long as it stays hush-hush."

I raised an eyebrow. "Corporate sponsorship? How very un-bohemian. Won't they have to change the name if the Rove doesn't rove anymore?"

"Not if it's on a different floor every night."

I thought of what I'd seen when I touched Jeremy's hands . . . when he put them over my eyes. Standing on the roof of the Tower; reaching for the clouds and calling the lightning down.

I swallowed. "What floor is it on tonight?"

"Sixty-nine, of course."

"You're sure it's not on the roof?" I asked, and when she nodded I exhaled the breath I'd held hostage. "But I don't get it," I said as we made our way toward a bank of elevators. "Why would the Tower's owner let a bunch of rovers party here? It doesn't make sense."

Katrina shrugged. "Don't look a gift gazillionaire in the mouth." She nudged me into the crowded elevator and the doors slid closed.

"I guess that explains why the power's on in this building."

I watched the floor numbers climb, tingling with anxiety. Or was it that strange energy radiating from the ground in the Waste that had my skin on edge?

When we reached the sixty-ninth floor, the elevator came to a halt, the doors opened.

I blinked, waiting for my eyes to adjust. There was no light. That would have given away the Rove's location. But black lights were set up around the room, so the relative darkness was filled with creepy, levitating smiles and white eyes that reminded me of Prophet.

There were perhaps two hundred people, not that many considering how packed some clubs got. But the Rove was an exclusive party, if only because it was hard to reach.

We moved into the room. Tandem DJs worked side by

side at the turntables, like fry cooks sweating over a grill, spinning out fat, electro beats. People danced in orgies, filling the wide-open space. The party sprawled across the entire floor, sections of which were still occupied by modular cubicles that were now, I assumed, being used for more private kinds of partying.

A guy wearing aviator sunglasses and an unbuttoned cowboy shirt handed out baggies filled with weed or white powder or tablets of X to the rovers, which they accepted gratefully, and paid for in cash. Apparently, the Rove was the one place in the city where drugs and alcohol weren't in short supply.

The windows on this floor had either been replaced or hadn't shattered during the quake. The city was laid out in every direction below us. Katrina went to one of the windows, and I followed her, finding excuses to touch people as I passed, waiting to perceive the subtle electric buzz of someone with the Spark, searching every face for my brother's.

At the windows, we stared out at the city. The sky was dark, but Los Angeles glittered, an inverted night sky speckled with amber stars. But in a wide radius around the Tower itself all was blackness, as though the building stood alone in the center of a huge moat.

I shuddered and turned my back on the window.

Get this over with, I thought. *Find Katrina's recruits. Find Parker. Get out of the Waste.*

Katrina had her flask in hand, tipped to her lips as she surveyed the room. She offered the flask to me, but I shook my head. No more white lightning for me. I needed to stay focused.

"How do we do this?" I had to shout in Katrina's ear to be heard. "The recruiting, I mean. Do you have a system or something?"

"Find an excuse to touch people," she said. "If they have the Spark, bring them to me and I'll give them the song and dance."

This sounded too simple. "You'll ask them if they want to help save the world?" I asked. "Just like that?"

"Basically. Yes."

"What if they say no?"

Katrina's mouth curled, something between a smile and a sneer. "That doesn't happen as often as you'd think. Most people want to be a part of something larger than their insignificant little selves. They want to believe they have a higher purpose. And rovers, well, they're not the type of people who want to see the world destroyed and remade by Prophet and his Followers." She looked at me pointedly. "So far you've kind of been the exception to the rule. Happy hunting!"

With that, she lifted her arms above her head and danced off into the crowd. A dozen sets of arms enveloped her and she was gone.

"Katrina, wait!" I called after her. But my voice was lost in the driving beat of the music. Great. How was I going to find her again if I did locate someone with the Spark? And how was I supposed to track down Parker in this crush of people?

I had to. That was the only option. I wasn't leaving here until I found my brother.

I cut a path through the dancers with their glowing teeth and eyes, hands out at my sides like plastic flaps in an automatic car wash, touching everyone I passed. I wondered if it would be easier to feel the Spark if I took off my gloves. What I wanted to do was peel off every layer of clothing clinging to my skin and douse myself with ice water. Rovers pressed in around me, their hot bodies bumping and rubbing up against me, their skin slick, sweat making the air damp.

I caught sight of Jude on the dance floor. She was grooving along with everyone else, but her movements were perfunctory, her gaze distant, as though her mind was far away. It wasn't hard to guess what she was thinking about.

"Hey," I said, approaching her. "Have you seen my friend Katrina? She's the one . . . the one I sent to talk to you about . . . you know."

Jude nodded, leaning her head toward mine. "The Spark," she said. "Katrina told me about it."

"Are you going to . . . join up?" I asked.

"Absolutely."

"Really? You don't want to think it over before you make any big decisions?"

"I don't need to. As soon as Katrina told me about the Spark and what it means, I knew she was telling the truth, that I wasn't going crazy. This happened to me for a reason. Now it makes sense."

"It makes sense," I repeated, wondering if Katrina had given a better sales pitch to Jude.

"It's a relief, actually," Jude said. "Now that I know I have something to fight against, I don't feel so powerless anymore. It seemed like the whole world was spinning out of control, and there was nothing I could do about it. But now . . ." She smiled. "You understand."

"Sure," I said faintly. She probably didn't hear me over the pounding beat. I wanted to tell her the truth . . . that I wasn't sure about anything. That I didn't understand any of this. That I felt as powerless as I ever had. Instead, I muttered, "See you around," and drifted off into the crowd.

How could Jude be so sure about her role in Katrina's end-of-the-world scenario, when I had so many doubts?

A hand touched down on my shoulder. Suddenly the temperature in the room, the temperature in my body, spiked. I gasped as the heat overloaded my brain and bleached my vision. I swooned and stumbled, and thought for sure I was going to crash to the ground. Then the pressure of the hand was gone from my shoulder and the heat dimmed.

"I told you to stay out of the Waste," said a familiar voice, speaking close enough to my ear that I sensed that heat again, a fire that taunted me from just out of reach. A fire I wanted to touch, even knowing its source had wanted me dead.

24

I turned and there he was. Jeremy. Eyes gleaming white and furious in the glow of the black light, he motioned me off the dance floor.

I didn't move, remembering the dream that was not a dream at all, Jeremy standing over me with that silver knife.

The fury in his eyes grew when I refused to follow. He really did look like he wanted to kill me now.

"We don't have time for this," he hissed in my ear. "I have to get you out of here."

"I'm not going anywhere with you."

"Oh, yes you are." He grabbed my elbow and yanked me off the dance floor. I stumbled along beside him, with his heat sinking into me like sunlight, waiting for the darkness to follow. But for some reason it didn't, although I felt it *wanting* to happen. Jeremy released me before it could, and as soon as his hand was gone I stopped moving.

We were on the edge of the dance floor now. I crossed my arms over my chest, partly out of indignation, partly because I needed to trap them, keep them from doing what they wanted to do, which was to touch Jeremy. To feel the burn of him. How could I still be thinking this way about a guy who had considered stabbing me to death?

"Please, Mia," Jeremy said, the anger in his voice softening until he was almost begging. "You can't be here."

My folded arms tightened, and I began scanning the room once again. "I'm not going anywhere without Parker."

Jeremy's face froze between expressions. "Who . . . who's Parker?"

"My brother. He's here somewhere, and I'm not leaving without him."

"Oh." Jeremy's shoulders dropped a little, as though he was relieved.

Did he think I was talking about another guy? A non-brother guy?

Jeremy, too, started scouring the room with his eyes.

"Do you even know what my brother looks like?" I asked.

He nodded. "I've seen him before."

My heart lurched. "When? Were you in his room? Were you going to stick a knife in him, too?"

"No! I swear I've never gone near him. You were the only one I . . ." His words fell away, like they'd stumbled off a cliff. He must have realized there was no good way to say, *You were the only one I considered murdering.*

But if he wanted me dead, why was he so intent on saving me?

I let my eyes linger on Jeremy, studying him, trying to decide if I could see past the knife incident to trust him. But the only thing I could think about when I stared at him was how I wanted to keep staring, never take my eyes away. Even with his eyes and teeth glowing, he looked miles beyond good, in a beaten black motorcycle jacket and white jeans that were luminous under the black light. The white jeans threw me off for a second, but on Jeremy they worked.

I pried my eyes from Jeremy and stood on tiptoes to see over the mass of people bunched together on the dance floor. "Let's pretend I would consider going anywhere with you," I said. "I assume you have a car?"

"A bike."

"A bike as in motorcycle?" I shook my head. I wouldn't be ditching Katrina after all. "Where's my brother supposed to sit?"

Jeremy cursed under his breath. His jaw clenched. Fists clenched. "You'll have to go without him."

"No way. Why do you want me to—" My words stopped. I thought of what I'd seen when Jeremy pressed his hands to my eyes, me falling into the chasm. The same chasm I'd almost plunged into tonight. "Something's going to happen, isn't it?" I said, eyes widening. "You saw it."

Jeremy didn't get a chance to confirm or deny. At that moment the elevator doors opened, and a new group of rovers filed into the room.

They were dressed in white. *All* in white. They glowed under the black light like a pack of ghosts.

"This is bad," Jeremy said.

The Followers glided toward the DJ station, their feet barely seeming to touch the ground. They were young. Not one of them looked older than twenty, but that might have been due to the air of innocence they carried in their empty expressions.

Some of the rovers on the elevator side of the dance floor had noticed the Followers, and their movements slowed to a stop, like windup toys that had run down. The two

DJs looked up to see the procession heading straight for them, and they gawked, forgetting their records. They missed a transition, and more rovers took notice. Voices rose in complaint and quickly fell as more and more people saw the Followers.

The two Followers at the head of the procession, a boy and a girl, both with hair so blond it glowed as bright as their whites, came to a stop at the DJ table. I recognized them from *The Hour of Light*. They were two of Prophet's adopted children, the freakishly tall twins.

The rest of the Followers looked familiar, too. I thought of the headline I'd read on Schiz's blog—*Where Is Prophet's Twelfth Apostle?*—and counted them. There were only eleven, but I was sure these were Prophet's adopted children.

I looked at Jeremy, at the grim expression on his face. Had he known Prophet's Apostles were coming? Had he seen it, the way he'd seen me coming to the Waste, falling into the chasm?

Panic twisted my stomach into cruel knots. Where was Parker?

The twins spoke to the DJs for a moment in voices no one else could hear. There was a lot of head shaking on the DJs' end. But the other Apostles surrounded the DJ station, and finally the DJs gave the twins what they wanted.

They handed over their microphones and shut off the music.

The room went so quiet I felt like I'd gone spontaneously deaf.

The twins faced an audience of stunned rovers, glowing eyes empty, smiles lifting the corners of their mouths to unnatural heights.

Jeremy nudged me and jerked his head toward a door on the far side of the room. There was a little plaque next to the door with a picture of a stick figure man walking down a flight of stick-figure stairs.

I shook my head.

"Hello," the she-twin said into the microphone, her voice booming.

"Good evening." The he-twin gave a tiny bow. "You're probably wondering why we've interrupted your party."

Silence from the rovers. I kept expecting the uproar to start, but they seemed to be in shock.

"We've come to deliver an important message from Rance Ridley Prophet of the Church of Light," the she-twin said, her smile stretching wider, though if it continued to grow it would extend the limits of her face. "In two days, you will all die."

I didn't think it was possible for the silence to deepen, but it did. Until the he-twin broke it.

"*Unless*," the he-twin amended, "you come to Prophet with a penitent heart and surrender your souls to his mercy."

"It's not too late," said the she-twin. "You can still be saved. All you have to do is ask humbly, and he will grant you his blessing."

"And the fires of hell will never touch you."

"You will be protected on the last day of earth."

"You will be raptured to Paradise."

"God speaks to Prophet and tells him so."

"But if you refuse to heed this warning . . . if you continue down the path of iniquity . . . you—"

The twins cast their eyes about the room, as did the rest

of the Apostles. I looked at Jeremy and saw his head was lowered, hair hanging in his face. He almost looked like he was praying.

"—*you*," the she-twin continued, "will be the first to die when the sixth seal is broken. The first to perish when the earth is rent asunder and the stars fall from the sky and the moon turns to blood. You will be—"

"Shut up, you psycho bitch!"

The voice rang out like a bell and seemed to reverberate through the room for seconds after it was raised.

The she-twin's smile shriveled. "Who said that?"

The he-twin put his arm around his sister's shoulder. "Who dares speak ill of my sister?"

"Your sister's a freak, and so are you!"

Suddenly the rovers were all shouting at once. Cursing and hurling insults. And the Apostles were shouting back. I couldn't make out their words. It was like someone had turned on a hundred blenders and thrown every voice in.

One of the DJs tried to snatch the mic out of the she-twin's hand. Her brother reacted, lashing out with his fist, connecting with the DJ's throat. Another rover, this one twitchy and wild-eyed and definitely on something, launched himself at the he-twin, knocking him backward onto the floor. The rover landed on top and started pummeling the he-twin with both fists. The she-twin tried to pull the rover off her brother, and he shoved her away. She fell and hit her face on the corner of the DJ table, and when she got to her feet her mouth was gushing blood from a split lip. The blood dribbled down her chin and made dark splotches on her white dress.

That was when the fighting really started.

But all of it was background noise compared to the urgent voice shouting in my head, *Find Parker! Find Parker!*

I searched the crowd, desperate to see him, but—

I spotted someone I did recognize, moving toward the melee with a determined look on his face. I grabbed him as he passed.

Quentin tried to jerk away. Then he saw my face and froze, eyes growing. "Mia? What are you doing here?" He looked at my hand on his arm and grimaced slightly, as though I were hurting him. I wasn't gripping hard, but Quentin was a Seeker. If I really was emitting some kind of Spark, it must not feel good to him.

"Where's my brother!" I shouted at him. "Where's Parker!"

He shook his head, seeming dazed. "How should I know?"

"You brought him here!"

"No, I didn't." His head shaking became more insistent. "If he's here, he didn't come with me." His eyes narrowed. "Who told you I brought him?"

Realization was clearing out a space in my mind.

"Katrina," I said, and Quentin nodded.

"Sounds like something she would pull."

She lied to me. Katrina lied to me. My brother wasn't here.

"Where is she now?" Quentin asked.

"Hopefully getting kicked in the face by an Apostle," I said. There was no real force behind the words. I was too relieved to be angry. "If you see her, tell her to go to hell. I found another way home."

I turned from Quentin to tell Jeremy I was ready to go willingly, but Jeremy was nowhere in sight.

I clenched my fists, like I meant to join the fight. But there was only one person I wanted to punch right then.

He'd ditched me. Jeremy had ditched me . . . again.

I turned back to Quentin to ask him how he had gotten to the Rove and caught a glimpse of the back of his head before he dove into the fray.

I was doomed to be reliant on Katrina for a way out of the Waste.

I had started searching the crowd for her when Jeremy reappeared, and before I could say a word he grabbed me, threw me over his shoulder, and started for the stairwell door.

I would have fought him.

I would have kicked and beaten at him until he let me down.

But almost immediately after he touched me and the heat of him swelled through me, my mind went brilliant white and then plummeted into darkness and then I was—

—rushing through the Waste, with Jeremy at my side. Hollow buildings watched us with the empty, midnight eyes of their shattered windows. The wind was fierce, tearing at me like it would steal my skin.

I held myself, bracing against the wind as it hurled cement and glass dust at us, coating our skin and clothes, trying to bury us.

"Come on!" I said, grabbing Jeremy's hand and running blindly.

We sprinted through the torn, rubble-filled streets, eyes closed against the dust and the wind. I didn't know how long we ran, and I didn't know where we were going. The wind seemed to choose our direction for us, pushing and pulling us.

Then, suddenly, the wind stopped, and I could see.

"No . . ."

We stood at the foot of the Tower. I craned my head to see to its top, and I heard music, thumping bass rumbling the whole building, like every floor was wired with massive speakers.

But when thunder boomed, it drowned the Rove's bass drive.

Clouds. Thick and black as the sky, tall as mountains, seethed into being above the massive building.

Thunder destroyed my thoughts. I felt the charge of the storm. The thrill of the storm.

"It's time for me to go," I said to Jeremy, staring up at the clouds.

I gasped myself back to the present. Or I thought I did. My eyes were open, but all I saw was a solid wall of black.

"Mia, are you back?" It was Jeremy's voice.

"What did you do to her?" That was Katrina's.

Jeremy: "Nothing."

Katrina: "You can't just go throwing girls over your shoulder and carrying them away. Who *are* you? Why did you run away from us the other day? Are you a spy for the Followers?"

Me: "What's going on? Where are we? I can't see a thing."

I blinked and blinked. Shapes started to form in the darkness. I felt the ground. It was cold and hard. Cement. And the wall behind me, the wall I was leaning against, also cement. I reached up and felt a hard, rounded rod. Metal. A handrail.

"We're in the stairwell," Jeremy said.

I used the handrail to hoist myself to my feet. I kept my hand on the rail, felt the way it slanted upward. I could hear distant shouting from several floors above us, beyond a closed door.

The Rove was up.

Parker was up.

I started to climb, and then remembered . . . Parker was not at the Rove. Katrina had lied to me. Manipulated me.

I rounded on Katrina, though I couldn't exactly see her. "Guess who I ran into upstairs? Quentin," I said. "And guess what he told me? Oh, wait, you don't have to guess because you already know, you lying—"

"Mia, I'm sorry," Katrina cut in. "I knew I couldn't get you to come here unless I bent the truth a little."

"It's called *lying*."

"I did what I had to do! We're running out of time, and I needed you to feel how it is here, in the Waste and the Tower. I thought . . . I don't know, that if I just *got* you here everything would fall into place, and you'd accept your destiny."

"Shut. Up." There was a surprising lack of emotion in my voice. "Just shut up, Katrina. We're leaving now."

"All right," she said. "Fine, we'll leave."

"Not you," I said. "Jeremy and me. You can do whatever you want, as long as you stay away from me."

"What? Mia, no! You can't go with him! You don't know anything about him. He could be a spy!"

"Are you a spy, Jeremy?" I asked.

"No," he said.

"Then it's settled. We're leaving. Don't follow me, Katrina."

"Mia, please—"

"Let's go," I said to Jeremy's shadow shape.

I descended into darkness thick as paint, and heard Jeremy's footsteps echo mine. A third pair of footsteps did not follow.

25

Sixty-eight flights of stairs is a lot of stairs to walk down. It seemed like hours passed before we reached the ground level of the Tower. By the time we reemerged into the Waste, my legs were aching and my knees felt like they'd taken a few dozen whacks with a hammer, but that ache was nothing compared to the sensation of electricity crawling over my skin like a horde of biting insects that wanted to eat me alive.

I held my arms, rubbing them like I was cold, willing the prickling to subside, but it refused.

"Are you all right?" Jeremy asked, his voice heavy with concern.

I couldn't answer that question. I didn't know what "all right" felt like anymore.

"I should have listened to you," I said. "I should never have come here." I turned to him. "You're not going to try to kill me again, are you? Can I stop worrying about that now?"

"Yes," he said. "I mean no, I'm not going to try to kill you. And, yes, you can stop worrying."

"And you're really not a spy for the Followers, like

Katrina thinks?" I asked, eyeing his white pants. "I mean, what kind of guy owns white jeans?"

Jeremy shrugged. "They seemed Rove-appropriate. Besides, if I were a spy for the Followers, don't you think I would have found a way to bring you to Prophet by now? It's not like I haven't had the chance."

I studied his face a long time before accepting his explanation. By the time I finished, I had every feature committed to memory.

"Where's your bike?" I asked.

Jeremy had not parked along the border of the Waste, as Katrina had done, but had entered on one of the ramps and driven almost all the way to the Tower. He'd ended up parking his bike in the Toy District, on the east side of downtown Los Angeles and only a few blocks from the Tower.

There weren't many tall buildings in Toy Town, but the district's proximity to the epicenter of the quake meant destruction on a massive scale. Some of the buildings had collapsed entirely, but most only lost chunks of wall, leaving their interiors exposed. Stores had been picked clean of anything worthwhile. Venders in the Toy District did not deal solely in children's playthings, but also in electronics, pirated video games, and all manner of designer knockoffs. The vultures had not been interested in cheap, fall-apart toys lovingly lead-painted in faraway lands. The ground Jeremy and I walked over to get to his bike was littered with broken action figures, headless dolls or bodiless doll heads, and torn stuffed animals that bled cotton.

I spotted a black plastic machine gun, the muzzle

crushed and flaking paint shards. I stopped to pick it up, feeling somehow more secure even with a toy weapon in hand. I tested the trigger. *Rap! Rap! Rap!* I nearly jumped out of my skin and immediately dropped the gun.

Jeremy shushed me. "The sentries could hear."

"Sorry," I said, cringing. "I didn't think it would work."

Jeremy turned down a dark alleyway, the kind that would have been scary to walk down if not for the fact that every street in the Waste was scary to walk down. "This way," he said. "Watch your step. There are—"

My foot came down on something living. It let out a screech and twisted until I leaped off it with a screech of my own. The rat and I scurried in opposite directions, but my foot caught on a crack in the asphalt. My ankle twisted sharply and I nearly fell, catching myself on Jeremy's arm. The moment we touched, heat enveloped me, but didn't wash away my consciousness.

I looked over my shoulder to see the rat squeezing through an exposed pipe, its tail whipping like a spaghetti noodle when you suck it into your mouth. When it was gone, I turned back to Jeremy. The heat radiating off him made it hard to think, but I was still here. Still present. Not stolen away into some strange vision of the Tower and the storm.

Although I had my feet under me, I continued to cling to Jeremy's arm—nice biceps, I couldn't help noticing. His hand rested so lightly on my hip his touch could have been a ghost's. He wasn't much taller than me, so our noses were almost in alignment. Inches of nothing separated our mouths. My heart pulsed fire and sent my blood boiling.

I pulled away from Jeremy, even though I could tell by

the rapid rise and fall of his chest and the intensity in his eyes that he burned for me, too. I was inexperienced when it came to this kind of thing, but still I knew he wanted to kiss me. That didn't really matter, though, did it? If he knew what I looked like, what I *really* looked like, my body etched in red veins, his desire for me would stop.

"Why didn't it happen that time?" I asked.

"What?" Jeremy sounded dazed, breathless.

"You know. The visions, or omens, or whatever. They usually happen when—" I bit my lower lip.

"When I touch you," Jeremy finished, his voice low, a little unsteady, as though he couldn't catch his breath. "Usually I can control them," he said. "Other people don't always see what I've seen when I touch them, not unless I want them to, but . . . it's been harder with you."

"Oh." Blood rushed to my cheeks, and various other places. The giddiness in my stomach was a momentary distraction from the crawling on my skin.

Past Jeremy's shoulder, I could see his bike parked at the end of the alley. I stepped past him and crossed the dozen yards to it.

I stood there surveying the machine, and even though I knew nothing about motorcycles, I couldn't help but be impressed. And terrified. The bike was black and shiny and compact. It looked barely big enough for one person to ride on, let alone the two of us. But Jeremy lifted the seat and removed an extra helmet from the compartment beneath. He handed it to me. I took it, but only stared at it dumbly.

"Are you okay with this?"

"I guess I have to be, don't I?" I raised my eyes to his,

chewing my lip. "What if—" I hesitated, uncertain how to proceed with the question. "What if the thing that happens, you know, when we're touching . . . what if it happens while we're on the bike? I could fall off the back."

"You won't," Jeremy said.

"How can you be sure?"

"I have to touch you with my hands for it to happen." He raised his hands, palms up, as though in surrender. "As long as these stay on the handlebars, you're safe."

"So I can touch you, but you can't touch me?"

He nodded, frowning. "For now," he said, and the implication made my hot blood boil all over again.

Moments later, I was clamped onto Jeremy's back with the insides of my thighs pressed against the outsides of his as we hurtled through the Waste at a speed that seemed suicidal considering the state of the roads. But Jeremy handled the bike as expertly as if he'd ridden the chewed-up streets a hundred times before.

I tensed when we reached the ramp that led out of the Waste, but there were no sentries standing guard and we sailed by without stopping.

After that, I relaxed into Jeremy's back as much as I could when we were driving at breakneck speed. I let go and enjoyed the warmth of him radiating against me, telling myself I had no other choice but to feel it, so I might as well enjoy it while I could, because this was as close as Jeremy and I were ever going to get.

26

"Want to come inside?" The words surprised even me, and I was the one who spoke them. I'd just climbed off Jeremy's bike in front of my house, and I felt I had to say something, but *thanks for the ride, see you later* didn't seem quite right.

Jeremy removed his black helmet, leaving his hair wild and practically screaming to be mussed, but I managed to keep my hands to myself.

"You want me to come in?" Jeremy repeated, and lowered his chin. "Even after . . ." He didn't have to finish the sentence.

I'd decided in the Waste it was time to put the whole murderous intent thing behind us, but the truth was . . . I didn't want him to leave yet. My mom and Parker had turned on me. Everyone in the city had gone crazy. Jeremy was the only person in my life who was still on my side, at least when he wasn't trying to kill me.

"Weren't you planning to hang around out here anyway?" I asked. "You know, to keep an eye on me?"

He peered up at me from under the tangled fall of his hair and nodded so slightly I almost missed the movement.

"Then you might as well be where you can actually see me," I reasoned.

I led him up the front walk, into our dark, silent house, and up the stairs to my attic bedroom. My stomach felt so light, it seemed to be rising in me like a helium balloon. I'd never had a guy in my room before, unless I counted the night when Jeremy broke in and tried to stab me, but I was trying not to think about that.

I was about to close and lock my bedroom door when I heard Parker's voice hissing up the stairs. "Mia?"

My stomach dropped. "Parker," I mouthed to Jeremy, and held up a finger before heading back down to the first floor.

"What's up?" I asked casually, as though there was nothing strange about me sneaking in at four a.m.

"Where have you been?" Parker demanded in a whisper. "And who's that guy?"

"What guy?"

"The one I saw go up the stairs to your room with you."

"Oh, that guy."

"He's the one who ran away from Mr. Kale's classroom, isn't he? The Seekers told you to stay away from him, Mia. They said he might be a spy for the Followers."

"The Seekers say a lot of things that aren't true," I snapped. "Go back to bed and mind your own business."

Parker didn't say anything. He shook his head at me, a silent admonishment. Then he turned and headed back down the hall, leaving me blinking in the dark.

Jeremy wouldn't take the bed, even though I insisted I was too wired to sleep, so I made him a bed out of blankets and my extra pillow on the hardwood floor. He lay down with his motorcycle jacket still zipped to his chin and closed his eyes.

I stretched out on my bed. Minutes passed. I imagined I could hear a clock ticking.

I sat up, leaning on my elbow.

"Jeremy," I whispered. "Are you asleep?"

He cracked one eyelid. "No. I'm like you. I don't need much sleep. Most nights I stay up, reading."

"Me, too. I mean it's hard for me to fall asleep, not that I read a lot. I'm more of a movie person. But I can read, and do, you know, sometimes. I'm not illiterate or anything. I like books." Why was I still talking?

"Jeremy?" I asked tentatively.

"Yes, Mia?"

The way he said my name, with combined formality and familiarity, made my thoughts go fuzzy. "Um . . . do you need anything? Food, water?"

"I'm fine. Thanks."

"Okay."

He sat up, his wavy hair in his eyes. He pushed it away and removed his glasses, folded them and laid them on my nightstand. "Can't sleep with these things on."

It was surprising how different Jeremy seemed without his blocky Clark Kent glasses. But I couldn't see him well enough to get a good look at him. The only light in the room came from the pale moon, now low in the sky with the approach of morning. I was reminded of the other time Jeremy had been in my room, but strangely I wasn't afraid of him anymore. Not even a little.

"Jeremy," I said. I liked saying his name. Liked it almost as much as I liked hearing him say mine.

"Yes, Mia?" There it was again.

I chewed my lip, reforming the question I wanted to ask over and over in my head. "How do your visions work? Do you ever know if . . . if something is certain? I mean, set in stone or whatever?"

"I think of them as possibilities. Some more likely than others." Jeremy lay back down, but his eyes remained open, staring at the ceiling. "The more often I see a particular vision, the more likely it is to occur."

"And you've seen me a lot," I said quietly. I thought of the visions Jeremy had shared with me; visions of me and the Tower and a storm that appeared out of nowhere. I felt my stomach twist in ways I didn't like.

The Nightmare Boy. That was what I called Jeremy when I thought I'd dreamed him. The nickname was still apt. Turned out he had been the one dreaming me.

"Lately you're all I see," Jeremy said. "You in a hundred different scenarios, but always—"

"I always end up at the Tower," I finished for him. "That's what you were going to say, wasn't it? I always end up at the Tower with that storm."

Jeremy was silent for a long time. Finally he said, "Yes." I didn't know why, but I sensed there was more he wasn't telling me.

"So I guess that possibility is looking more like an inevitability," I said.

"Maybe. The details are constantly changing. The only absolutes have been the Tower and the storm. Those things . . . they never change."

"How long have you been like this?" I asked quietly.

His pause was so long I almost asked again, thinking he

hadn't heard me. "Since I was a kid," he said. "The visions started when I was six. They were always terrible. Always about people dying or being hurt. For a long time, I thought I was dreaming awake, or that I was losing my mind. But then when I was eight I . . . I saw my mother in a vision." He covered his eyes. "She was in a hospital. I hardly recognized her. She was wasting away, and her hair was gone. Two months later, she was diagnosed with stomach cancer. The tumors grew fast. If the doctors had caught it sooner . . ." He lowered his hand and swallowed hard. "The visions aren't random. I always see what I see for a reason. I was supposed to help my mom, get her to a doctor sooner. But I didn't understand."

I imagined what it would've been like if my mom had died in the quake, and how much worse it would be to know I could have prevented it. I don't think I could have ever forgiven myself. Obviously, Jeremy hadn't either.

"You were a kid," I said. "You couldn't have understood what was happening."

He looked at me with his eyes full of sadness and pain and so much anger. I was beginning to understand where his intensity came from. But as he gazed at me, his eyes softened. "You know, the first time I had a vision, it was of you." He smiled a little. "Those were the only visions I ever looked forward to, even though . . ." The smile faded. "The things I saw weren't good."

I didn't ask what he'd seen of my life. I wasn't sure I wanted to know.

"So that's why you've been following me?" I asked. "And why you came to my room that night? Because you keep having visions of me and you're supposed to . . . what, change the outcome?"

"Something like that."

"Does it ever work?"

"Sometimes." His voice was heavy. I guessed sometimes didn't mean often. But I thought of how I'd been a hair away from plummeting to my death in the Waste. Had what Jeremy shown me changed the outcome? Had I hesitated, even slightly, instead of stepping right into the chasm?

Yes, I realized. I had remembered at the last second.

Jeremy had saved my life.

But my life wouldn't have needed saving if I hadn't been in the Waste in the first place. If I had done what Jeremy told me.

He really was trying to save my life.

I looked at Jeremy lying on the floor of my bedroom, and the burning in my chest descended to my stomach, and lower, smoldering like coals at their hottest. All of a sudden, inviting Jeremy up to my room seemed like a terrible idea. I wanted him too much. My desire for him was like a thing separate from me, a wild animal with a mind of its own, attacking the bars of the cage I kept it in, looking for a weak spot.

I scrambled under my blankets, though I usually slept on top of them, not needing the added warmth. Being under the blankets made the heat inside me grow, but they were the only thing keeping me from Jeremy, a too easily penetrable, padded wall.

"Good night, Mia," Jeremy said.

"Good night, Jeremy," I managed, without adding, *I want you, I want you, I want you.*

I closed my eyes and pretended to sleep. I didn't know the difference when pretend became real until I opened my eyes in the morning and found Jeremy's makeshift bed empty except for a handwritten note on the pillow.

PART 3

Some say the world will end in fire,
Some say in ice.
From what I've tasted of desire
I hold with those who favor fire.
—Robert Frost,
"Fire and Ice"

27

Mia,

So you do sleep, after all. I'm sorry I left without saying goodbye. I didn't want to wake you. I have to take care of a few things today, but after that I need to see you. Can you meet me after school? It's important.

Jeremy

He'd scribbled an address at the bottom of the page.

I made sure to pocket his note before I went downstairs for breakfast.

I was so distracted by thoughts of Jeremy and his "need" to see me, I forgot about the fight I'd had with Mom in the garage until I walked into the kitchen and found her sitting at the table, staring at a slightly burned piece of sad-looking toast with only one bite out of it.

I studied her for a moment, waiting for her to notice me. She wasn't as put-together as she had been yesterday morning. She was still wearing her bathrobe, and her hair was sleep-matted.

As I watched, a clear drop of liquid ran down Mom's nose and dropped onto her toast. She was crying.

"Mom?" I said.

Her head jerked up, and she swiped quickly at her cheeks. But she couldn't erase her swollen red eyes. "Mia." Her voice was thick. "I thought you were gone. Parker left already."

I blinked in surprise. "Did he take the bus?"

"He said he was riding with a friend from school. He didn't say who." She shook her head, and spoke to her toast. "I didn't even think to ask. I'm a terrible mother, aren't I?"

A friend from school . . . I didn't like the sound of that, but worrying about Parker could wait.

I pulled out a chair and sat down next to Mom. "Why are you crying?"

She said nothing, but her hands began to worry, fingers tangling and untangling. On impulse, I reached across and grasped her hands in both of mine. She looked up, surprised, and her eyes held mine. I looked into them, *really* looked, in a way maybe I never had before, and I saw such immeasurable sadness there, the same thing I saw in Jeremy's tortured gaze. It was like staring into the chasm I'd nearly fallen into in the Waste. It went down and down, and the bottom was nowhere in sight. I realized something then. This sadness . . . it wasn't simply about Mom's trauma during the quake, or about losing a man she cared about. It had been building for years. This was about the dead father I barely remembered, the husband Mom would never forget, never stop grieving. This was about the years of struggle she'd gone through after he was taken from her. About nearly losing me to lightning so many times. About leaving behind everything she knew in Lake Havasu City, starting over in a city where she knew no one.

Why had I not realized before how unhappy Mom was? How unhappy she had been for a long time?

Because she'd hidden it from me, and from Parker. That was why. Because she hadn't wanted to burden us with her problems. I got that. I had attempted to do the same for her.

"Mom, I'm sorry about what I said to you yesterday." My throat constricted. "I'm so, so sorry."

Tears began streaming from her eyes. She squeezed my hands, unable to speak, so she just nodded, and I went on.

"Things will get better, I promise. I'm going to make them better, okay? We'll figure it out." They were the same words I'd said so many times, but they were no longer hollow. No longer meaningless. I intended to keep my promise, and I wanted Mom to believe me this time.

She kept nodding. "Okay . . . okay."

I stood and pulled her to her feet, and I threw myself into her arms and let her hold me and rock me the way she had when I was years younger, another version of myself entirely. Both of us early editions of ourselves. Who were we now? I wondered. Who would we become now that the world we knew was gone?

I had no answers, but I was determined to do what I told Mom I would. I was going to make things better. I didn't know how, but that was what I intended to do.

"You need to go now," Mom said, close to my ear. Her voice was little more than a hint of sound. "Goodbye, Mia."

I was reluctant to release her, but I did. I had to get to school. I was going to do things right from now on, start acting like I had a future, instead of wandering through life waiting for the next bolt of lightning to fry a hole in my world.

I had a future, and I was determined that it would have nothing to do with either the Tower or the storm. According to Jeremy, my future was not set in stone.

It wasn't until I was in the car, on my way to school, that I thought about how Mom had said, "Goodbye, Mia," and how her voice had seemed to contain a note of finality, as though it were the last goodbye.

But then I rolled down my car window to get some air, and the wind rushing through set my skin to prickling, like a thousand tiny needles piercing me all at once. I nearly drove off the side of the road in my hurry to roll the window back up. I slammed to a halt at a stop sign just in time and then I sat there, breathing in short, ragged gasps, rubbing my skin to calm the latent prickling.

I forgot about my feeling that something new was wrong with Mom.

I had checked the weather that morning, as I always did, and nothing had changed. Every weather site predicted sun and more sun.

But my skin told me the storm was closer than ever.

28

A few minutes after the last bell of the day rang at Skyline, I found myself lingering in Mr. Kale's classroom. Well, not so much found myself lingering, as I forced myself to linger. The Seekers and I had unfinished business, but I intended to finish it once and for all.

Mr. Kale stood alone at the west-facing bank of windows, his back to me. The ocean beyond the glass glittered with reflected sunlight, the view only somewhat obscured by the smoke rising from Tentville.

I let the spring-loaded door slam behind me to announce my entrance, but Mr. Kale didn't so much as flinch. He turned slowly around.

"Alone today?" I made a show of scanning the room, as though his masked minions might be hiding under the desks.

Mr. Kale strolled through the center aisle toward me, taking his time. I noticed his hands were not bandaged, and there was no trace of the blackened skin I'd left him with during our last encounter. He lifted his hands to study his open palms, as though trying to recall what had happened to them. "Rapid healing," he said in that grating voice of his. "It's one of the advantages we enjoy."

"Seekers?"

"People with the Spark," he said, looking up. "People like you and me. It's the energy stored inside us. It changes the way our bodies function. I'm sure you've noticed differences."

I shrugged. "I've never been a particularly fast healer." I'd had plenty of experience to draw from, considering my countless strikes. Then again, I had survived what should have killed me many times over. Maybe there was some validity to what he claimed.

"I suppose we're each unique in our abilities." Mr. Kale's mouth twisted down, and I knew he was thinking of what his hands had looked like twenty-four hours earlier, like meat left too long on the grill.

"I didn't come here to talk about this stuff," I told him.

"Then why did you come?"

"You don't know already? Can't you just read my mind?"

"If you like, I can do that."

"I would not like," I said. "Call me old-fashioned, but talking suits me fine."

"Then talk."

So I talked. I told him about Katrina, and how she'd lied to me, manipulated me into going to the Rove. As I spoke, Mr. Kale's expression darkened.

"That girl," he said when I had finished. He shook his head and sighed. Even his sigh sounded rough-edged, more like a growl. "Her behavior reflects badly on the Seekers. I don't mean to make excuses for her, but ever since her mother died, she's been impossible to control."

I blinked at him with my mouth hanging open, no less

stunned than I would have been if he'd slapped me. "When did her mom die?"

"Shortly after the earthquake."

"I–I had no idea."

"Katrina doesn't talk about it. She's thrown herself into her work to take her mind off it."

I steeled myself against the sympathy welling up in me. I didn't want to pity Katrina. I wanted to hate her. "I'm sorry for her loss, I really am, but that doesn't excuse what she did to me."

Mr. Kale nodded. "No, it doesn't, and if I'd known what she was up to, I would have put a stop to it. Katrina is intensely loyal to the Seekers. She's like her mother that way. The Seekers and our cause come before anything else, and she'll do whatever it takes to ensure our victory over the false prophet, even if it means risking another person's safety. Or her own." He ended on a bitter note.

I asked softly, "Katrina's mom . . . she was your sister?"

"My twin. Her name was Irene."

I winced. "Did she die in the earthquake?"

He shook his head. "We needed a Seeker to infiltrate the Church of Light, learn about Prophet and his intentions. Irene assigned herself the task of ingratiating herself into Prophet's . . . well, his private life. To find out his plan, if he had one."

"His private life? You mean . . . ?" I let the question hang.

"Yes. His bed."

"Oh." I shifted uncomfortably. "Sounds like you were barking up the wrong tree. Haven't you ever watched *The*

Hour of Light? Prophet spends half his time talking about how all the 'fornicators' are going to burn in hell."

"What men practice and what they preach are two vastly different things, Miss Price. Few men in positions of such power as Prophet are able to control their appetites for long. There is an irrevocable link between sex and power, and my sister meant to exploit it, and to discover the extent of Prophet's abilities. His Followers say he can perform miracles, healing the sick, casting out demons, and, of course, they say God speaks to him. Not only speaks, but that God exercises His will through Prophet."

"You think Prophet has the Spark?" I guessed.

He nodded. "Irene confirmed it before she died. Before Prophet killed her."

His words made me feel cold all over, not an easy thing to accomplish. "How do you know he killed her?"

"My sister was like me, only much stronger. She could communicate without speech, even over great distances." He was quiet a moment. When he spoke again, his voice was unsteady. It sounded like rocks tumbling down a hillside. "When Prophet killed her, I felt it. Felt the knife slide into her. The blood run out of her. She had only enough time to tell me there was no doubt. Rance Ridley was the one. The false prophet."

"I'm sorry," was all I could think to say.

"It was an honorable death. She died for a cause she believed in, which is more than most people can say."

I remembered what Quentin said about the fifth seal, the vision of martyrs. "Was she one of the martyrs? Did someone, you know, *foresee* her death?"

"Yes," Mr. Kale said, his jaw flexing. "But she kept that a

secret from me. She knew I would have tried to stop her from going to Prophet, but I would have failed. She was our leader, and I didn't have the power to challenge her. She went willingly to her death, and the role of hierophant passed to me."

I remembered what Katrina told me in the ladies' lounge after her unwelcome haircut, something about the old leader having died recently, and Mr. Kale being new to the position. And she'd been talking about her own mother's death like it was the death of an acquaintance. She was obviously much better at compartmentalizing her feelings than I was.

"What's a 'hierophant'?" I asked. I'd never heard the word before.

"It is what we call the leader of our circle. In ancient Greece, a hierophant was a priest, one who interpreted sacred mysteries."

"Katrina said you were more like a general."

"I suppose I'm a bit of both."

I sighed. "Poor Katrina," I said before I could stop myself.

Mr. Kale gave me a sideways look, one black eyebrow raised. "Katrina is proud of her mother's sacrifice. If called on, she would give her life to the cause."

"Not everyone has to die a martyr." I glared at the teacher, heat flaring inside my chest. I was suddenly furious, and not sure why.

"No," Mr. Kale said. "There are many ways to die. But a coward's death . . . that, I think, would be the worst."

Why did I feel like he was directing these comments at me? It wasn't my death we were discussing. Still, the fire living in my heart was getting hotter as I got angrier.

Mr. Kale's gaze on me was level. He let his arms fall to his sides and took a step toward me. "Katrina still believes you are the one spoken of in our founder's prophecy, the marked girl who will always draw the Tower. The girl who will be the deciding factor in whether the sixth seal shatters and begins the apocalypse."

"What do you think?" I asked him.

"I think that girl, whoever she is, is no coward. So, no, I do not think you're the one prophesied." He took another step toward me, his gaze homed on mine, as though he could read my thoughts scrolling across my eyes like closed captioning for the hearing impaired. I felt a slight pressure in my mind, like someone was leaning on it, and a staticky, humming vibration.

"Even if you aren't the Tower girl, you would be such an asset to us, Mia." Another step. Mr. Kale had long legs. He was now a single stride away from me, and the buzzing in my head was like a fly trapped in a jar. And Mr. Kale's voice had taken on a soothing, hypnotic quality. I couldn't help wanting to listen. I barely noticed when he stopped speaking out loud.

You could still join us, Mia.

We need you, Mia.

Stop fighting us.

Stand with us.

Fight with us.

He was close enough now that I could have reached out and shoved him away. But I didn't do that. I couldn't stop staring at his neck. His shoulder-length hair caught on the collar of his shirt, and skin that usually remained covered was revealed for the briefest of moments. Just long enough for me to catch a glimpse of the veiny red mark that reached down Mr. Kale's neck from behind his ear.

Mr. Kale began to take another step toward me. He reached for me, as though to pull me into an embrace. I caught sight of the circular brand on his palm and revulsion swelled in me. Whatever spell Mr. Kale had been spinning inside my head broke. I took two quick steps back, out of his reach. He frowned, and the pressure in my head went away. It was quickly replaced with rage so fierce it was like gasoline thrown on the fire in my heart, and this time I let it burn.

"I know what you're up to," I said. It was strange how cold my voice was, when inside I was molten. "You can do more than read people's thoughts, can't you? You can make them *do* things, like you made my mom tell a bunch of strangers what had happened to her, when she wouldn't even—" *When she wouldn't tell me.* I shook this thought from my head. I didn't want Mr. Kale to have access to it. "That's what you wanted to do to me here, yesterday . . ." I continued. "What your little initiation was all about, your bonding ritual. You didn't think Katrina's blackmail was enough to secure my loyalty, so you decided to try a surefire way to control me."

"I can bend a person's will to mine," Mr. Kale admitted. There was no trace of guilt in his eyes. "But only if a part of them wants to comply. Your mother wanted to tell what happened to her. I could never have influenced her to do so otherwise. Isn't there any part of you, Mia, that wants to help us?"

I shook my head. It was time for me to end this.

"If you bother my brother or me again, if you even look

at either of us in a way I don't like, I'll turn you in to the police, and the principal, and reporters, and anyone who'll listen to me. I'll tell them you're a cult leader, and you're recruiting students to join. And you know what will happen then? You'll get fired. Maybe you'll even go to jail. And you know what I'll do?"

His mouth tightened. "What will you do, Miss Price?"

"Go about my life as though none of this ever happened."

"Do you really think that's possible?" Mr. Kale asked. "Can you ignore what you know to be true? I've seen inside your mind, Mia. I know what you've done. I know about the man you hurt before you came to Los Angeles. But I also know about the girl you saved. Janna was her name, wasn't it? You brought her back, healed her. I know you're afraid of your ability, afraid you'll hurt people in an attempt to help, but that's all the more reason to join us. You need us as much as we need you. If you let me, I can help you control your ability."

They'll try to use you . . .

My fists clenched. I was nobody's tool.

"Katrina told me about your chain of command," I said. "The most powerful Seeker is the one in charge, right? If I were to join your circle, that would be me, wouldn't it? I'd take your place."

Mr. Kale's brow hunched. "Katrina told you that?"

"She told me enough. Is that what you want from me? You want me to lead your cult?"

"Not . . . not exactly." For the first time I could remember, Mr. Kale looked uncomfortable. He dropped his eyes and shifted on his feet, as though he'd been caught and didn't want to admit it.

"What, then! What do you want from me?"

"I can't tell you that."

"Then I'll never join you."

I turned and stalked to the door. I almost made it through before realization stopped me cold.

The vision of martyrs.

I felt a weight on my chest, like someone was standing on it. I could barely breathe.

The vision of martyrs. Jeremy's visions.

They'll try to use you.

Suddenly I knew what the Seekers wanted from me, and it was not for me to lead them into their final battle.

They wanted me to die for them.

Mr. Kale's spring-loaded door slammed behind me with a sound as loud as a shotgun blast in my ears.

Once again, I found myself running from room 317. The halls were empty, so there was no one to get in my way. I pounded down two flights of stairs, not slowing until I reached the main hallway on the first floor, and then I stopped dead.

Every locker in the hallway had a red flyer taped to its front. Bloodred, with black print. An image of the Seekers in their red cloaks and black masks flashed into my head.

Students were lined up in the commons to receive their rations, and I could see that many of them held red flyers and talked excitedly in groups, while Followers in white kept their distance but watched the rest of the students closely.

I decided to forgo my rations for today. I had to get out of this school.

I hurried to my locker to collect my things, not bothering

to read the flyers as I passed. I didn't want to know what they said. In my peripheral vision, the red sheets of paper blurred like a long sweep of blood. But when I reached my own locker, I could no longer avoid the words printed on the flyers.

BEGINNING OF THE END PARTY
APRIL 17
AT THE TOP OF THE WORLD
HURRY UP PLEASE IT'S TIME

"Hurry up please it's time."

I whirled to find Parker reading aloud over my shoulder, holding his rations box. I snatched the flyer off my locker, crumpled it, and tossed it into the nearby trash can.

"You riding home with me?" I asked.

"Sure. Why wouldn't I?"

"I thought you might catch a ride with whoever brought you to school this morning."

"Nope," he said. I waited for him to say more, to tell me whom he'd ridden with, but he left it at "nope."

They'll try to use you.

I wanted to tell my brother what I suspected about the Seekers, what their real reason was for wanting me to join them. But the truth was, I didn't think Parker would believe me. He'd think I was trying to get him back on my side.

He didn't trust me any more than I trusted him.

So I didn't say anything, just turned away to spin my locker combination. But when I opened the door, something small and flat fluttered to my feet. I knelt to pick it up.

It was a tarot card.

No, not *a* tarot card. *The* tarot card. The Tower card from Katrina's deck.

"What's that?" Parker asked.

I slipped the card into my pocket before he could see it. "Nothing," I said, and I meant it. It was nothing to me.

We had to pass through the corridor of the dead and missing to exit the school. I shuddered to see hundreds of red flyers pinned to the walls there. The afternoon sunlight shone through the high windows and reflected off the red paper, painting everything in red light, including us.

29

"I want you to stay here with Mom," I told Parker as I pulled up to the curb in front of our house. "Don't go anywhere. I'll be back soon."

Parker's grip on his rations box tightened, leaving fingertip-sized impressions in the cardboard. "You're going to see that guy, aren't you? What's his name . . . Jason?"

"Jeremy."

"You barely know him, Mia. You shouldn't be . . . doing whatever you're doing with him."

Blood rushed to my cheeks, heating them like little furnaces. "Thanks for the advice, *Prophet*. What makes you think we're doing anything?"

"I heard him leave the house this morning."

"So. He needed a place to crash. We both had a rough night."

"Oh, yeah? What happened?" He sounded too casual.

"I'm guessing you already know." It really was a guess, but his silence confirmed my suspicions. "Quentin told you."

My brother stared straight ahead, still gripping the box like it would come alive and try to jump from his hands. "He said you were in the Waste last night, helping Katrina.

Why do you get to do whatever you want, while I have to put aside what's important to me?"

"First, I wasn't helping Katrina. Second . . . you know a lot less about the Seekers and what they're really up to than you think. They're dangerous, Parker."

"So what? This whole city is dangerous. The whole world is dangerous. You know what's really dangerous? Standing next to you, Mia, but I've done that my whole life, haven't I? I've always stood by you . . . even when a storm was coming."

"Parker . . ."

"I don't want to stand by you anymore." His voice was anguished, but saying the words couldn't hurt as bad as hearing them.

"Pick a side then," I told him, fighting to hold back the emotion ripping apart my insides. "Us or them. But you don't get to have both."

Parker threw open my car door and got out too quickly. The box on his lap tipped and threw its contents onto the sidewalk. Parker kicked a bottle of water across the lawn, but left everything else where it lay as he stormed inside the house.

I sat there with my car running, gripping the steering wheel, my whole body shaking. I sat there until the heat of rage inside me cooled, and I thought I could drive without losing control of the car.

Then I pulled the note Jeremy had given me from my pocket, smoothed it out. I knew I should go inside. Check on Mom. Make up with Parker. So many things I *should* do, but none of them were things I *wanted* to do. Besides, doing what I should hadn't gotten me anywhere so far.

I reread Jeremy's note. My eyes kept fixating on the word "need." *I need to see you.* He needed me. Someone needed me.

And I needed to see him, too. At that moment, there was nothing in the world I needed, or wanted, more.

30

I drove east on Venice Boulevard, away from the beach and Tentville, away from my home and my crazy-making family, searching for the address Jeremy had written on his note. Even with my car windows rolled up, I could feel the storm warning tingling on my skin, like I was wearing it, a coat with pins and needles sewn in, to act as my own personal iron maiden. But the skies were clear, cloudless, relentlessly blue.

What if I wasn't sensing a storm traveling across the ocean, building over the water like it was supposed to? What if the storm I sensed was like the one that appeared out of a clear blue sky the day of the quake?

What if Prophet was right?

I muttered to myself, "No. No, no, no. There is no storm. There is no storm."

The windows of buildings I passed were wallpapered with red flyers, exactly like the ones I'd seen at Skyline. Telephone poles, too. The doors of houses. Apartments. Trees. There were thousands of them, everywhere I looked. I didn't need to read them to know what they said.

Hurry up please it's time.

"There is no storm." I continued the mantra. "There is no storm."

Traffic on the main roads was bumper-to-bumper, like vast, narrow parking lots stretching for miles north and south. It was like half the city had suddenly decided today was the day to get out. Maybe they'd heard Prophet's proclamation, that the beginning of the end was scheduled for tomorrow, and figured it couldn't hurt to put some distance between themselves and Los Angeles.

"There is no storm."

I left the main roads and started winding my way through side streets. The red flyers were everywhere, papering the city. The Seekers had to be behind this. They must be trying to gather as many people as possible for one last Rove. One last recruiting effort, although it was coming a little late in the game if they believed Prophet's storm really would hit tomorrow.

I shook my head. "There is. No. Storm."

The sky was purple by the time I found it, a small, quaint house on a dead-end street in Culver City, only a few miles from my house in Venice, but it had taken me almost two hours to get there.

Most of the houses on this particular street looked, from the outside, either empty or uninhabitable. A few had collapsed. In others, the windows were busted out. Walls were tagged with spray paint. Lawns were yellow. But there were two houses that appeared untouched, the one that matched the address Jeremy had given me, and another across the street with a sign in the window that announced in an old-fashioned, hard-to-read font:

PSYCHIC
Specializing in Palmistry, Auras, and Tarot

I felt in my pocket for the tarot card Katrina had stuck in my locker. Before I knew what I was doing, I had crossed the street and stood at the psychic's front door. KNOCK, read a plaque the size of a stick of gum affixed above the doorknob. I did.

Katrina and Mr. Kale said the Tower girl would always draw the Tower card. I had drawn it twice from Katrina's deck, which was strange, but could still easily be explained by chance. I wanted to prove once and for all that I was not the Tower girl. I would ask this psychic for a tarot reading, and I would see what a deck other than Katrina's turned up.

The door cracked and an eye peered out at me. "Yes? Who's there?" The woman's voice was a deep gurgle.

I put on my warmest smile. "I'd like a tarot reading."

The door swung open. "Come in," said a tiny, hunched figure in a layered, velvet skirt with a knitted shawl around her shoulders. Her hair was long and gray and hung past her breasts. Looked like she hadn't brushed it that month.

Great, I thought. Of all the psychics in L.A., I chose the fortune-teller who looked like an escaped carny. Still, I followed the woman inside.

"What did you say your name was?" the old woman asked as she led me down a dark hallway to a room at the rear of the house. The whole place smelled like onions and made my eyes water. It was decorated in stereotypical fortune-teller motifs, with hunks of crystal displayed in glass cabinets, beads hanging in doorways, patchy pillows and blankets everywhere.

"I didn't," I said. "It's Mia."

"I am Madam Lupescu." Of course she was. "Have a seat."

She gestured to a small round table laid with a lace tablecloth. All it needed was a crystal ball.

I sat down, and she sat across from me and stared at me. Then the awkwardness set in.

"So," I said, needing to fill the silence, "how long have you been a psychic?"

"Is that what you came to find out?" Her eyes peered at me through weathered eyelids that sagged like an elephant's.

"No, I was just—"

"You were being polite. Making small talk. Wasting time when there is so little time left to waste." She smiled, showing yellow teeth that had been worn down to the nubs. She leaned toward me over the table and I smelled the coffee on her breath, and it made me like coffee quite a bit less. "Let's begin," she said.

She produced a velvet pouch from a pocket in her voluminous skirt, loosened the drawstring, and dropped a deck of cards into her hand. Like Katrina's deck, this one looked old. The woman shuffled, her gnarled fingers surprisingly dexterous as the cards whipped through them. She placed the deck facedown on the table. "Cut to the left," she said.

I did as I was told. Madam Lupescu took the deck and dealt five cards, laying them out in the shape of an even-sided cross.

I studied the cards intently, and then exhaled a pent-up breath and smiled.

The Tower card was not among those Madam Lupescu had dealt.

I was not the Tower girl.

I was free. I could get up and leave now, drop my last ten dollars on the table and head for the door. It would be rude to simply walk out. I would sit patiently and hear Madam Lupescu's reading, dismiss it, and then move on with my life.

"Major arcana." The old woman whistled, then pointed with three fingers to the three cards in the middle. "Past, present, future," she said, then indicated first the bottom card and then the top. "Reason and potential."

She pointed to the card that represented my past. It depicted a glowing orb in the sky and two baying hounds. "The Moon. It is fear. Self-deception. Disorientation."

Okay. Fair enough.

She indicated the reason card. I didn't like this one. It showed a horned red beast with a forked tail that wrapped around a man and a woman.

"The Devil. He is the reason for your Moon. Your *fear*. He is bondage and ignorance. Slavery and hopelessness. But this . . ." She pointed to the top card: potential. It showed a man in a red robe that reminded me way too much of the Seekers' cloaks. He was sitting on a throne, holding a golden scepter and wearing a gaudy golden crown. "The Hierophant."

My mouth went dry. "The . . . the Hierophant? That's my—" I had to swallow. "My potential?"

The old woman nodded. "He represents power and knowledge, and commands respect. He sits on the throne between law and liberty, obedience and disobedience. Between heaven and earth."

"What about those two?" I said quickly, pointing to present and future. My present card showed a winged monkey perched on a wheel. "This is the Wheel of Fortune, right?"

"Yes," Madam Lupescu confirmed. "Destiny. It marks a turning point."

I chewed my lip. "What about my future?" I felt a squirm of nervousness in my stomach, like I had swallowed something that wasn't quite dead yet.

My future card showed a naked man and woman holding hands.

Madam Lupescu scowled thoughtfully at the card. She picked at one corner of it and revealed—

My breath stopped.

"Odd." Madam Lupescu peeled the card with the naked man and woman off the card stuck to its back. Then she laid the two side by side.

I still couldn't breathe.

She tapped her fingernail on the card with the naked people. "The Lovers."

She tapped her fingernail on the card she had revealed, which showed a tower on the edge of a cliff. A lightning bolt cleaving it in two. People falling from it, on their way toward the jagged rocks below.

"The Tower," she said.

I shook my head, finding my breath. "It's a mistake, right? The Lovers . . . that's my future."

"Or the Tower. You must choose one or the other, but you cannot have both."

"I have a choice?"

"You always have a choice."

I looked at the Tower card. The falling people with their accusing eyes. "What does it mean?" I asked. "The Tower."

"For you?" Madam Lupescu studied my face, as though the answer were advertised there. "Letting go," she said with a sharp nod. "Exposing what is hidden. Seeing the way of things in a sudden flash. And letting go. Letting everything go."

I nodded. "How much do I owe you?"

"Donation only."

I took my wallet out of my bag. "That's a nice crystal," I said, pointing at the glass case behind Madam Lupescu. When she turned her head, I snatched the Lovers card and stuck it in my wallet, then laid a ten-dollar bill on the table.

"Thanks," I said, and I meant it. Madam Lupescu didn't know it, but she'd set me free.

Once outside, I took the Lovers card and stuck it into my back pocket, next to Jeremy's note.

I had a choice, Madam Lupescu had said.

I took out Katrina's Tower card and tossed it onto the sidewalk. Let someone else pick up the Tower.

I had made my choice. I could see him across the street, waiting for me on the porch.

And I realized something . . . my skin had stopped tingling.

The storm, if it had ever existed, was gone.

31

Jeremy ran into the street to meet me halfway. His blue eyes searched me as though looking for some sign that I'd been accosted.

"What took you so long?" he demanded. "I told you to meet me after school. That was hours ago. I was worried."

My hand rested on the tarot card hidden in my pocket. The Lovers.

The tingling storm warning on my skin remained as silent as if it had never been.

I smiled and shook my head. "There's nothing to worry about anymore."

There is no storm.

Jeremy's eyes narrowed, a divot forming between them. "You're sure you're all right?"

"I'm fine," I assured him. "The streets are completely jammed, that's why I'm late. It's like everyone left in the city is trying to get out." Everyone who wasn't a Follower or a Seeker or a rover.

Jeremy's shoulders sagged, as though he'd deflated. His hair hung over his eyes.

"Hey, what's wrong?" I touched his arm, felt the heat

radiating through his shirt. He'd said I could touch him, but he couldn't trust himself to touch me without dragging me into one of his visions. But even this gesture made heat dance in my stomach and my knees go soft.

Jeremy shook his head, not meeting my eyes. "I screwed up," he said. "I shouldn't have waited so long. Now it's too late."

My feeling that everything was going to be okay began to dissipate, but I fought to maintain it.

There is no storm.

"Let's go inside," Jeremy said. "We'll talk there."

I tried the light switch on the wall inside, but nothing happened. The electricity was off and the sun had set, leaving behind nothing but shadows.

Jeremy navigated his way through the dark house easily, and a moment later I heard the scrape of a match. He ran the flame along a row of candles on the fireplace mantel. Then he placed a few logs on the hearth, crumpled newspaper, and within minutes had a fire going.

I watched him in silence until he was finished. Once there was light, I moved farther into the living room, turning in a circle to take it in. There wasn't much to see. The only furniture was a lumpy couch with a tattered slipcover facing the fireplace. No TV or bookshelves or pictures on the walls. The only item in the room that stood out was a black leather satchel, the kind that looked like it hung on the side of a motorcycle. I guessed this belonged to Jeremy, who was still crouched by the fire, staring into the flames. Orange light flickered in his eyes.

"Is this where you live?" I asked, trying not to sound disbelieving. But it was such a sad, empty little house.

"No." Jeremy blew on the fire, and the flames grew. He shifted the glowing logs with a wrought-iron poker. "The people who lived here left after the quake."

"So you just took over and made yourself at home?" I would have been pissed if someone did that at my house.

"I lived here once. Long time ago, with my mom." He raised his eyes to the ceiling, as though he could see something there that I couldn't. "This was our house before she died. I came back to check on it after the quake, make sure it was still standing. It was empty, so I started coming here. To get away."

I sat down on the lumpy couch. "What are you trying to get away from?" I asked.

Jeremy's neck tensed until I could see the cords of muscle flexing under his skin. "My family," he said. "Especially my father. I hate him. I hate all of them." He spoke through clenched teeth, and with such bitterness I thought he might punctuate his words by spitting into the flames. He gripped the poker so hard his knuckles turned white, and I worried he might start stabbing the fire with it. But then he glanced at me and must have realized from my expression that his reaction had alarmed me. My mom and Parker had pushed me over the edge more than once lately, but not like this. I had never for a moment *hated* either of them.

"I'm sorry." Jeremy dropped the poker and came to sit

by me on the couch, close enough that I could feel the heat of him, as though I were sitting next to the fire. My body wanted to melt into his.

"You don't have to be sorry," I told him. "Every family has its issues."

"We definitely have plenty of 'issues,' but that's not what I brought you here to talk about." He was quiet for a minute. I could almost see his brain working, trying to figure out how to say whatever it was he wanted to say. Whatever he'd waited too long to say.

"There's something I want to ask you." He turned toward me. Our faces were close. For a split second I thought he was going to try to kiss me. I stiffened, wanting him to, not wanting him to. As long as he didn't put his hands on me, I wouldn't see the Tower, would I? Or maybe I would never see the Tower again, now that I had chosen the Lovers. Madam Lupescu said I had a choice, and I had made mine. I had stolen it.

"Ask me," I said, leaning in until my lips were a breath away from Jeremy's. I waited for him to close the gap.

"I want you to . . ." I felt the air of his words on my lips. A shiver ran through me.

"You want me to . . ." I repeated, breathing him in. *The Lovers,* I thought. *This is my choice. This is my future.*

"I want you—" I didn't let him finish. That was all I wanted to hear. *I want you.*

I moved forward a little, and my lips were on his. Warm. So warm. For a moment we stayed like that, unmoving, our lips simply touching. Then his mouth parted, and so did mine, and he moaned softly into me, with something like relief. I let my tongue do what it wanted, taste his, and then something in me, in both of us, broke, and we were kissing with ravenous desperation.

Jeremy's hands found the sides of my face, and his fingers disappeared into my hair, pulling my mouth harder against his. His lips were hot enough to burn. I wanted to tell him to take his hands off me, not to drag me into one of his visions, but I was afraid he would stop kissing me. And I wanted to know . . .

I wanted to know if my future still held the Tower.

I didn't tell him to stop, even when my vision started to fog, like warm breath on a cold window.

I was filled with an explosion of heat. My vision went white, and then cleared.

The wind rushed at me, seemingly from everywhere, as though it couldn't decide which direction to blow. I could barely see through the hair whipping my cheeks.

There was music, a hammer blow baseline, a driving, chaotic symphony of electronic sound. But the music disappeared when thunder rumbled in the sky. It was the sound of hunger, deep and ravenous. Overhead, thunderclouds roiled and bunched, like the fists of an army of angry gods, ready to pummel the world. Those clouds were so close; I could almost reach up and touch them.

The Tower. Again. Always. Standing on the roof of the Tower, surrounded on all sides by bodies, grinding and shaking and throwing their arms in the air to the thunder music.

A piece of paper sailed through the night and slapped against me. I grabbed it before it could blow away and held it up to read.

BEGINNING OF THE END PARTY
APRIL 17
AT THE TOP OF THE WORLD
HURRY UP PLEASE IT'S TIME

Thunder cracked, jarring my bones. The air was electric, and my blood sang in harmony with its vibration. My skin danced, like every cell was in the process of trading places. It burned, but at the same time I had never felt so alive, like the storm was inside me.

Maroon light pulsed on and off in the blue-black clouds, and my singing blood began to cry out, calling for the lightning. Lightning as red as the scars that branched over my skin. I felt my arms lifting. Reaching. I let the wind take the flyer as I turned my chin up to face the clouds.

"Mia."

Through the veil of hair covering my eyes, I saw Jeremy cutting through the crush of bodies, coming toward me.

"You shouldn't have come," he said, and even though his voice was low I heard him just fine. "You're the missing element. You're what he's been waiting for."

"Who?" I asked.

"Him." Jeremy's eyes focused on something behind me.

Someone.

I turned and found myself inches from a pair of milky white eyes.

"Hurry up please it's time."

"No!" I whirled back to Jeremy. "Show me something else! I don't want the Tower."

Lightning split the sky above us. I saw it reflected in Jeremy's tortured eyes, and the thunder that followed shook my bones so hard I thought they might shatter.

"Hurry up please it's time." The voice whispered in my ear.

I grabbed Jeremy's face and pulled it within an inch of mine. "I won't leave here until you show me a different future. Show me what I chose!"

"I don't know how," he said miserably. "This is all there is."

"No. The Lovers. I chose the Lovers. I choose you."

I crushed my mouth to his in a violent kiss, a demand.

Show me something else. Show me something else. Show me something else.

Then we were falling. Jeremy and I were falling from the Tower, rushing toward the ground, faster and faster, plummeting into one of the chasms, so deep, so unfathomably deep, and then—

The wind rushed at me, seemingly from all sides, as though it couldn't decide which direction to blow. I could barely see through the hair whipping my cheeks.

It began again. And ended. And began.

And ended.

And—

My eyes flashed open to find a dark shape looming over me in a lightless room. I drew breath to scream.

"You're awake! Mia, I'm so sorry. I shouldn't have touched you like that. I wasn't thinking."

Jeremy. The dark shape was Jeremy, and we were no longer in the Waste, and I didn't need to scream.

I exhaled hard and sat up, maybe a little too fast, because my head began to spin. I felt like my brain was being sucked down into a whirlpool. I pressed the heels of my hands to my eyes. "What happened? Why is it so dark in here?"

"The fire went out."

I looked toward the fireplace. A single candle still burned on the mantel, but the roaring fire Jeremy built had gone cold. Not even the embers glowed.

"You were out for hours," Jeremy said. "I kept trying to wake you up, but I couldn't get to you. Mia, I'm so sorry. I've trapped people in visions before, but never for so long, and never without meaning to."

"It's not your fault," I told him, remembering my refusal to leave the vision until I got the future I wanted. But I never did. It was the same loop, again and again.

The Tower and the storm. The Tower and the storm.

The Tower and the storm . . . and Prophet.

There is no storm!

I climbed dizzily to my feet. Jeremy looked furious with himself that he couldn't help me up. His hands clenched at his sides, useless.

"Where are you going?"

I stumbled through the dark toward the door and threw it open. The air hit my skin and my weather sense began to thrum with new intensity, making my skin vibrate like I was some kind of human tuning fork.

The storm . . . it was back, and it was so close.

But the sky was still clear.

As I stood there a breeze picked up, and the pins and needles stabbing my skin multiplied. A piece of red paper fluttered along the sidewalk. I raced down the steps and grabbed it before it could blow away.

"Mia?"

Startled, my hands jerked and tore the flyer nearly in half. I handed it to Jeremy and watched the color disappear from his face and his jaw tighten as he read.

"Hurry up please it's time," I said under my breath. "Time for what?"

"It's a line from a poem," Jeremy said. *"The Waste Land.* T. S. Eliot."

And then I understood.

I raised my eyes to Jeremy's. "We have to get out of L.A."

32

I shook the flyer at Jeremy. "Beginning of the End at the Top of the World. That's the Tower, isn't it?"

Jeremy dug a hand through his hair. "It could be."

"It has to be! That T. S. Eliot line is a password to get into the Rove, and whoever made this flyer is just giving it away to everyone. The Rove doesn't advertise. Exclusivity is part of the allure." I tapped the words with my finger, thinking. "Katrina said some rich guy bought the Tower and offered to host the Rove. And on Schiz's blog, he wrote something about how Prophet was buying property in the Waste. It has to be him! The twins . . . the Apostles . . . they said if the rovers didn't repent, they'd be the first to die. Prophet," I said, my throat tightening. "He planned this whole thing, the Rove in the Tower. The flyers."

I realized I was babbling, but I couldn't slow to compose myself. I had to say it to see how it sounded. So far it sounded crazy . . . but possible. More than possible.

"It's going to start in the Tower," I said. "Maybe Prophet has the whole place wired with explosives or something. The whole freaking city! Who knows what these fanatics are capable of! Or maybe . . ." I chewed my lip, not wanting to admit what I was considering. I took a breath and let it out. "Katrina told me there's something about the Waste, an energy, like the Spark, only bigger. It was uncovered during the earthquake, and now it's exposed."

"I felt it," Jeremy said. "It's strongest at the Tower."

I nodded. "Like that place is some kind of . . . I don't know, like an energy nexus. If there's another storm coming, that energy could draw even more lightning than last time. There could be another earthquake, a *worse* earthquake, and the rovers would be the first to go. They're the only people in the city who've openly defied Prophet, and a lot of them have the Spark. Prophet's opposition would be instantly eliminated."

Jeremy closed his eyes, as though it was too painful to keep them open. "So what do you want to do?"

"Do?" I threw my hands up. "There's nothing we *can* do. It's too late." I shook my head, feeling ashamed that I was giving up, but I didn't see any other choice. "I'm getting my family out of L.A.," I told him.

"What about the roads?" Jeremy asked so quietly I could barely hear him.

Jeremy's words echoed in my brain.

I screwed up. I shouldn't have waited so long. Now it's too late.

I stared at him. "That's what you wanted to ask me, if I would leave the city . . . with you."

Jeremy nodded, eyes on the ground. "I didn't think you'd say yes, but—"

"Yes," I said. "Yes, let's get out of this city. Together. We'll find a way."

Jeremy raised his eyes to mine. His hands were once again clenched at his sides, so I knew what he wanted to do with them, that he wanted to touch me. I remembered the heat of his lips on mine, and I wished I could let him.

But we had run out of time for things like that.

We left my car behind and took Jeremy's bike, weaving in and out of traffic like we were on an obstacle course. I kept my eyes closed most of the way and clung to Jeremy's back so tightly I was surprised he didn't end up with a few cracked ribs.

Even though we were able to avoid being stopped by the gridlock on the roads, it was past eleven by the time we reached my house.

My heart was pounding against my rib cage as we ran to the door. What if Mom or Parker refused to come with us? How could I make them understand?

As it turned out, I needn't have worried.

I knew as soon as I set foot in the house that it was empty. I didn't have to check to see if Mom's car was in the garage. I didn't have to call out for her and Parker, or rush from room to room trying to find them. I did those things anyway, but sometimes you just know when you've been left behind, even before you find a note telling you why.

Parker left his note in an envelope on his dresser, addressed to me. I opened the envelope with shaking fingers and pulled out a piece of notebook paper, jagged along the side where it'd been torn out.

Mia,
  I know you're going to be angry with me.
  I know you won't understand why I'm doing

this. I wish you did. I've joined the Seekers, and undergone their bonding ritual, so there's no going back now, and that's okay with me. It was the right thing to do. Please don't come looking for me unless you intend to join our cause. I love you and Mom. I'm sorry things have to be this way. If we win, I'll see you when this is over.

Parker

I crumpled the note into a ball and hurled it against the mirror above Parker's dresser. I wanted to scream.

"They're gone," I said when I returned to where Jeremy waited in the living room. "Parker joined the Seekers. My mom . . ." I thought of how Mom had been that morning, the way she said, *Goodbye, Mia,* with such finality.

I knew exactly where she had gone.

Jeremy took a step toward me and stopped. Two more strides and he could have reached out and touched me, and I really, really wanted him to touch me right then. I wanted the comfort of his warmth. I wanted it more than anything.

But he stayed where he was.

"I have to go get my mom and bring her home," I told him.

"You know where she is?" he said, and I nodded.

"She went to the White Tent."

I headed for the door, but Jeremy didn't move. "Come on," I told him. "It's almost midnight. We have to go now."

"Mia . . . what if your mom doesn't want to leave?"

I held up my hands. I didn't have an answer. "Are you coming or not?"

He ran a hand over his mouth, looking at the floor. "I'll go with you, but . . ." He looked me up and down. "We'll have to change clothes first."

Jeremy had brought his leather satchel inside so it wouldn't be stolen by the Displaced. He went to Parker's room to change. Apparently he'd packed some necessities in case I agreed to leave town with him, and his white jeans were among them.

I had always avoided wearing white, even before the Followers made it my least favorite absence of color. I worried that the red of the lightning scars might show through pale-colored clothes. Mom had a pair of white jeans that fit me well enough, and I found a thick white turtleneck in the bottom of one of her drawers, something she hadn't worn in years, since the last time she went skiing. With no white gloves available, I had no choice but to stick with my usual black.

When I was dressed, I knocked on Parker's closed bedroom door. There was no response, so I opened it.

"Jeremy, are you—oh—"

Jeremy's back was to me, and he was naked to the waist. My eyes roamed up his body, over his long, lean back. Then he pulled on a long-sleeved white shirt, and buttoned it.

He turned to me. His eyes scanned me up and down, and mine did the same to him.

"Good thing you bought those white jeans," I said.

He nodded. I thought he might ask why I didn't take off my black gloves, but if he had questions, he kept them to himself.

33

Bonfires blazed at intervals along the beach, firelight turning the walls of the White Tent an eerie pumpkin color. Hundreds of figures in white streamed like a river of milk over the sand toward it.

"We get in and out without drawing attention to ourselves, okay?" Jeremy said in a voice only I could hear. "If we find your mom, it's important that you don't make a scene."

"*When*," I said. "Not *if*. I know she's here."

He stopped walking and faced me. "I'm serious, Mia. We have to be careful."

I narrowed my eyes at him. "You act like you've been here before."

"I've heard things, that's all."

We stepped from asphalt onto sand. My feet sank to the ankles. Followers kicked off their shoes and went barefoot, and the filthy, almost feral-seeming citizens of Tentville swooped in like buzzards, snatched up the shoes, and scurried away with them.

Despite how uneasy I was surrounded by so many hundreds of Followers, I felt safer among them than I would have if I'd been wearing my normal clothes. Beach dwellers flanked the river of Followers, shouting curses at them, throwing fistfuls of sand in their faces.

I kept my head bowed and stayed close to Jeremy. We were nearly to the White Tent when I felt a hand grip my arm and yank me away from the procession. I found myself face to face with a wild-eyed man who reeked of sour sweat and campfire smoke. His skin was so grimy it was gray, but salted with gritty white dots of sand.

I tried to pull away from him, but he held me tight by the arms. His fingernails needed trimming. I felt them digging through my sleeves.

"Give your false prophet a message for me," the man said into my face. "Tell him Jesus befriended the whores and the thieves and the sinners. Tell him his Old Testament God is dead. God doesn't punish the wicked and save the righteous. God is love!"

"Let her go," Jeremy said calmly, stepping up beside me.

For a moment the man only gripped tighter. "God is love," he whispered. "Tell the false prophet God is love." Then the fight went out of him and he released me, leaving smudges of fingerprint on my white sleeves.

"False prophet," the man muttered to himself as he wandered away. "False God."

Jeremy guided me back into line. "You okay?"

"Yeah," I said, shaky.

We came to the flap that served as a doorway into Prophet's White Tent. Two Followers stood on either side, speaking to each person before offering admission.

"Have you accepted the Word of Rance Ridley Prophet as the Word of God?" one of them, a man with a squeaky clean-shaven scalp and a Cro-Magnon brow asked me.

I glanced nervously at Jeremy. "Y-yes," I said, stumbling over the word.

"Yes," Jeremy said with more confidence. "We both have."

Cro-Magnon smiled warmly, swept the flap aside and allowed us in. "Welcome, Brother. Sister."

We stepped inside the Tent, and my heart sank into my stomach. There had to be five hundred people inside, and more arriving every second.

I stood on tiptoes, scanning the crowd. TV crews were scattered throughout the tent, some of their cameras trained on the stage, some of them conducting interviews with members of the congregation. The whole place hummed with the energy of a beehive. The dank heat created by so many bodies made my white clothes cling to my skin like plastic wrap.

There was a high stage set up in the center of the tent, like a boxing ring without ropes. Several microphones on stands were lined up across the stage. Prophet was currently nowhere to be seen, but the male half of the twin-set was up on the platform, leading the crowd in a rousing hymn that sounded more like a battle march than an ode to God. Piano music was coming from somewhere, though I couldn't see the piano or the player.

I searched the he-twin's face for bruises, thinking he ought to have a black eye or a split lip or something after the brawl at the Rove. Nothing. His skin was miraculously pristine, like Mr. Kale's after I'd fried his palms.

"Let's circle around the perimeter of the tent," Jeremy suggested. "If we don't find her, we'll move in closer to the stage."

We had to fight for every step, our shoes sinking into

the sand and the tent growing more packed with each passing second, everyone pushing toward the stage. It took us what seemed like an hour and a few dozen sets of crunched toes to make our way around the perimeter. There were so many faces, so many people dressed in white, they started to blur together into one giant cloudlike mass.

We delved farther into the crowd. But as soon as we got within twenty feet of the stage, we hit a solid wall of bodies. We could go no farther without prying the Followers apart.

I cursed in frustration, and a dozen eyes turned to glare at me with disapproval. "Sorry," I muttered.

"You promised you wouldn't draw attention to us," Jeremy hissed in my ear.

At that moment the music stopped, and the he-twin onstage announced that the "program" was about to begin.

"We're not going to find her like this," Jeremy said. "We should go back to your house and wait. She has to come home eventually."

I stepped away from him, irritated by his suggestion. "If you want to leave, go ahead. Disappear on me again. You're good at that." I didn't mean it. The last thing I wanted was for Jeremy to leave me here alone.

"Mia—" He reached for me, but knowing what would happen if he touched me, I took another step back. At that moment the crowd surged like a rising tide and closed around me, and the next thing I knew, Jeremy was gone, an impenetrable wall of people between us. I stood on tiptoes, searching for him, but I only saw strangers.

Then a muffled tapping sound came through the speakers. Someone cleared his throat.

I turned toward the stage and saw a man standing in the center . . . a man with long, thick, perfectly white hair, and eyes the color of fog.

Prophet.

The he-twin flanked him on one side, and the she-twin took her place opposite him. Where were the rest of Prophet's adopted children? I wondered. Would the twelfth make an appearance at this revival? It was a special night. According to Prophet, the world wouldn't be around after tomorrow.

Prophet smiled and held blindly to the microphone as he leaned forward to speak.

"Brothers and sisters," he said in a voice both gentle and authoritative; soothing and chilling. "I welcome you at this dark hour, and I call on you, the righteous, to bring light where there is none. To shine with the glory our God has bestowed upon you. Such light as yours makes the darkness seem a fragile thing. So let us shine! Let us bring not a single hour of light, but a whole night of it, on this, our last night on earth!"

A cheer rose from the crowd like a thousand birds screaming into flight. I clapped my hands over my ears and held them there until the noise tapered off. When I lowered them, Prophet was speaking again.

"Some of you came here tonight seeking comfort," he said. "Some of you wish to be healed, or want merely to stand shoulder to shoulder with like-minded people. Some of you want to be told that everything is going to turn out fine. That this wretched world of ours will heal itself."

Prophet closed his filmy eyes for a moment and breathed

deeply. The sound of his breath was wind coming through the speakers.

He opened his eyes again and turned in a slow circle, as though to look on the faces of every person in the crowd. I wondered what Prophet saw when he looked around him. Blurry angels, or nothing more than a murky haze?

People closed their eyes when Prophet's gaze fell on their section, some clasping hands over their hearts, linking fingers in prayer, muttering to themselves. Tears landed on cheeks. Sobs startled the silence.

When Prophet turned to my section, his eyes seemed to bore right into mine, and I found I wanted to lower my gaze. Wanted to, but wouldn't. There was nothing to be afraid of. I was just one more indistinct shape among many.

"I wish I could tell you the things you want to hear," Prophet went on, still turning in his slow circle, the twins turning with him, like they were on the same axis. "But I am merely a conduit for God's words, and I'm afraid God has other plans for this world. Our earth has been wounded by hate. By sin. By carelessness and greed and apathy. The wound has remained untended too long. Infection has set in, and now there is only one solution: amputation."

There was a collective sucking in and holding of breath from the crowd. In the silence that followed, Prophet's voice resounded.

"Rest assured, though, brothers and sisters, God knows who is on His side and who is against Him. God is with us tonight, and He knows each of your faces. He knows that you have chosen His way and chosen wisely. Fear not, for it is always darkest before the dawn. At this moment, things are very dark, in the world at large, but especially here, in the so-called City of Angels. City of Angels . . ." He shook his head, sounding disgusted. "There may be angels still in this city, but they are the minority. Demons have the power here. Hell-A, I've heard people call this place, and how right they are. This is hell, where the demons manufacture their poison and distribute it through the world by satellite, by television and theater, by Internet. The evil begins here, brothers and sisters, but it will begin to end here. A storm is coming! A storm like no other. The earth will be shaken, and the sun will be as ash, the moon as blood. The stars of heaven will fall unto the earth, and every mountain and island shall be moved out of their places. So sayeth the Lord!"

Prophet clasped hands with the twins and thrust their arms into the air, making an M of limbs, and they *did* seem to shine with some sort of light. I didn't want to see it, but it surrounded them like a halo. Another deafening cry of approval went up from the Followers, but this time I didn't bother to cover my ears. I felt numb. Immobile.

"God has spoken to me, brothers and sisters!" Prophet boomed into the microphone, trying to be heard over the uproar of cheering and clapping. The crowd began to quiet down when they heard his voice, hundreds of people shushing hundreds of other people, which was almost as loud as their cheering. Prophet lowered his arms and the arms of the twins, but he continued to grasp their hands tightly at his sides. "God has spoken to me," he said again, more quietly this time. "He has told me His plan, and it is great, and it is terrible. But He has also said He would protect those of you who come to Him to be saved. I tell you God is present in this place tonight. He is here to offer His blessing and His protection to those who will surrender to Him with their hearts and minds open. Will you surrender to Him?"

"Yes!" the crowd roared.

"Then let the first of you come up onto the stage to surrender and receive His blessing!"

Arms waved in the air, like overgrown blades of grass in a hurricane wind. Figures cut through the field of arms. I recognized a face, two, three I'd seen on *The Hour of Light* and at the Rove . . . the Apostles, moving among the Followers, choosing supplicants not already in white and leading them toward the stage. The crowd parted to let them through.

The twins led a man up onto the platform. Even from a distance, I could see the man's lips and eyelids were crusted with the sores that came with earthquake fever, and his posture sagged, as though his bones were made of something less substantial than a normal person's.

"Are you ready to surrender and be saved?" Prophet asked him.

The man nodded vigorously and fell to his knees before Prophet, sobbing. "My wife died in the earthquake," he cried. "She was everything to me. I can't live like this! I can't live without her!"

Prophet palmed the man's forehead, and the man jolted as though he'd been defibrillated.

"Your wife has been accepted into the kingdom of heaven," Prophet said. "And you will join her someday, but not today. God needs you here, to stand on His battlefield and fight. You are saved, Brother."

Prophet removed his hand and the man rose, trembling, eyes large and shining. The twins led him off the stage, and another set of Apostles received him. My eyes stayed on the man's face. Something about it had changed.

The man wiped at his tears, and I blinked, not sure if I was really seeing what I thought I was seeing. The scabs came loose from his eyes and fluttered to the ground, as though they'd been no more than stage makeup glued onto his face. That had to be it. But the sores around his lips . . . they seemed lighter, like they were disappearing, drying up.

"Music," Prophet called. "Let us sing! Let us rejoice in the glory of God's Light!"

The unseen piano player began the first notes of a familiar tune, and then the whole crowd was singing and swaying as a pregnant woman was hauled up onto the stage, her distended stomach extending in front of her like a handshake.

"I'm going to be an unwed mother," she announced into the microphone, cheeks crimson with shame. "I've been a sinner my whole life. I don't want my child to suffer for my sins. Please, Prophet, give him your blessing. Give him God's blessing."

Prophet laid his hands on the pregnant woman's stomach. She flung back her head and convulsed, crying out in ecstasy.

My stomach felt like it was on an elevator, rising toward my throat. I swallowed and swallowed, but it wouldn't go back down. I wanted to get out, but the crowd pressed in around me, and my mom was here somewhere. I couldn't leave without her. Couldn't leave her here with these crazy people, no matter how much she wanted to be among them.

I began searching the crowd again. I was the only one in the White Tent without my eyes glued to the stage.

Then I saw out of the corner of my eye the next suppli-cant the Apostles were bringing onto the platform, and the blood began to pound so loudly in my ears it drowned out everything else.

The man making his way up the short flight of steps nearly had to be carried, though not against his will. He was injured. He should have been in a hospital. In a burn ward.

He should have been dead.

The Dealer's face was warped on one side, like a melted candle, more raw red tissue than actual skin. His wounds seeped, a constant flow of sap-colored liquid, running down the scorched flesh, soaking the yellowing bandages that wrapped his shoulders and torso.

After the crowd's collective gasp at the sight of the Dealer's ruined face, a new silence, deeper than ever, set-tled around us like a blanket.

But Prophet couldn't see the Dealer. He approached the man as he would any other supplicant who came to him.

"Why have you come to me, Brother?" Prophet asked. "Do you wish to surrender your soul to God?"

"I . . ." the Dealer began, and even producing that one letter caused him to moan in agony. "I was told you could heal me," he finished in a rush that made him writhe, and then sob so pathetically that even I, who knew the circum-stances surrounding his injury, had to pity him.

Prophet approached the Dealer. "I offer healing to my

Followers, yes. But you are not one of my Followers, are you?"

"N–n–no," the Dealer sobbed.

Prophet turned away. "I can do nothing for you, then."

"Wait! I will surrender my soul to God anything just heal me please heal me!" Another windfall of words that, this time, left the Dealer too racked with pain to even sob. Only a sound like a muted scream made it past his bared teeth.

Prophet turned slowly back to him. He flicked with his fingers and those of his Apostles in the crowd returned to him like homing pigeons.

"Be still, Brother. There will be pain, but it will be brief compared to what your soul would have suffered in hell for eternity." Prophet laid a hand lightly on the Dealer's head, and the Dealer's near-silent scream increased in volume. Prophet gave his other hand to the he-twin, and the rest of the Apostles joined hands in a circle around the Dealer and Prophet, until the two of them were completely concealed from view.

More circles, I thought. Just like the Seekers. Looked like the Seekers and Followers had more in common than Mr. Kale wanted to admit.

"In the name of God, I accept this man's soul," Prophet said. "Let him be healed!"

I couldn't have breathed if I'd tried.

The Apostles closed their eyes. Their linked hands squeezed tight. A ringing sound seemed to fill my ears, so loud I almost couldn't hear the Dealer's high, whining shrill of a scream. The air around me seemed to vibrate, as though we were all contained inside a bell someone had rung.

And then it was over, and the Apostles released hands and stepped back, and there was Prophet with his hand still resting on the Dealer's head, and oh my God.

Prophet brought his hand back to his side, and cried, "Behold! This man is saved!"

The Dealer's face was whole again. The burns were gone. There was not even the slightest trace of scarring. It was as though the burns had never been.

The Dealer's eyes were rapt as he felt his face. He began to laugh, softly at first, but growing until he was cackling wildly. He tore at the bandages wrapping his arms and torso until he was naked to the waist, his skin unbroken. Perfect.

"I am a new man! A changed man!" he cried, his eyes shining and strangely empty at the same time. "God is good!"

The crowd erupted in cheers and shouts and echoes of "God is good! God is good!"

"Who else wishes to be saved?" Prophet called out, and if the crowd had been frenzied before, it was nothing compared to the hysteria that gripped the Followers now.

An Apostle led the Dealer down from the platform, and the others dissolved back into the crowd. The piano music and the singing started up again.

I couldn't stop staring at the stage. At Prophet in his white suit with his white hair and his white eyes.

It was a miracle. I had just witnessed an honest-to-God miracle. Prophet couldn't have faked it. The Dealer's wounds had been real. The miracle had been real.

It was real. All of it.

"Mia Price? It's you, isn't it?"

I barely heard my name over the singing. I turned, hoping, maybe even praying, I would find my mom's face hovering nearby.

But it was not my mom who'd spoken. It was reformed-goth Rachel, standing a few feet away. She slid toward me through the crowd. Somehow she had no problem doing so. No one seemed to block her way.

Her smile took up half her face. She seemed drunk, her eyes dreamy and rapturous. "Isn't it amazing?" she said. "The energy of so many good people. Can you feel it?"

All I felt was nausea.

"Does your friend like her new haircut?" Rachel asked, her eyes laughing.

I tried to edge away from her, back through the crowd, but she lunged for me. I remembered how strong her hands were. She caught me and held on tight. "Did you come to spy on us, Mia Price? Did you bring some of your Seeker friends with you?"

"You're insane," I told her.

"No," she said, shaking her head slowly. "I'm saved."

Then Sister Rachel began shouting over the song. "Pretender!" she called out.

She shoved me toward the stage. The crowd parted around us.

"This girl is a spy! A pretender!"

Prophet held up his hands for silence, and he got it, so when Rachel shouted "Pretender!" the last time, the word rang throughout the tent.

My blood was on fire, my breath coming hard and fast.

Sister Rachel finally released me, but I was too dizzy to move. I wanted to run, but I was imprisoned by walls of people.

The Apostles converged around me.

Prophet motioned to the twins with a flick of his fingers to bring me onto the stage. They looked at me like a pair of hawks that had found their prey and couldn't wait to rip it to pieces. I shook my head, struggling to move backward through the crowd, but the Followers surged against me, shoving me forward.

The twins reached for me.

I held up my hands in surrender. I didn't want them to touch me. More than that, I was *terrified* of what I would feel if they touched me . . . and what they would feel from me.

I stumbled up the short walk of stairs onto the platform, keeping my distance from the pale-haired twins. They had no eyelashes, I realized, seeing them up close. Their lids were perfectly bald.

Prophet turned toward me, and I couldn't suppress a shudder at the sight of those milky eyes. He stared at me for a long time. I took deep breaths, trying to calm down, but the fire in my blood wanted to take charge.

"Who are you, Sister?" Prophet asked finally. "Did you come to spy on us?"

I looked around, realizing the hundreds of pairs of eyes on me were not the only ones witnessing this moment. Every camera was trained on me.

This was a nightmare. And now it was going to be a televised nightmare.

Was Parker watching, thinking, "If only she had listened to me . . ."

And what about Jeremy? Where was he? I searched the crowd and didn't see him. I was on my own. No Seekers. No Jeremy.

Just me.

"I didn't mean to disturb your . . . your program," I said to Prophet. "I'm not a spy. I came to find someone." My voice was surprisingly steady, considering the circumstances. Considering I felt on the verge of combustion.

"Don't listen to her," a familiar voice shouted from the crowd. The Dealer pointed his finger at me. "She can't be trusted. She's the one who burned me. She's a sinner, an addict."

"No, I'm not." I shook my head. I looked at the crowd and saw how their eyes turned cold. "I'm not an addict!"

There was a familiar buzzing in my temples, the same sensation I'd felt before Mr. Kale went trespassing on my thought property.

But you do have an addiction, do you not?

The voice that spoke in my head didn't belong to me.

Your drug of choice is unique, the voice continued. You *are* unique.

I looked at Prophet and saw he was staring hard at me, as though he could see me clearly through the haze coating his eyes. The buzzing in my temples continued.

"Who did you come here to find, if not yourself?" Prophet asked.

I didn't want to tell him. I would not tell him.

That buzzing again.

"Your mother," Prophet guessed. Or was it a guess? That

voice that spoke in my head sounded just like his. "Does she wish to be saved?"

"No," I said firmly, but another voice called from somewhere in the tent, "Yes! Yes, I do!"

"Send her up," Prophet commanded.

The crowd parted, and I saw her . . . I saw my mom plodding through the sand toward the stage. My heart got stuck between beats.

I had to stop this.

Somehow I had to stop this.

But all I could do was stand there with my feet rooted to the ground and watch her come.

The twins led Mom up onto the stage, each of them taking one of her hands. Mom barely acknowledged them, or me, for that matter. Her eyes were for Prophet. Her face was flushed with excitement, making her scars stand out, shiny and pink.

"Mother and daughter," Prophet pondered aloud. His eyes tracked my mom down. He held out his hand. "Come to me, Sister."

The twins released her hands, and Mom stepped toward Prophet. Instinctively, my hand shot out to stop her, inciting an outraged gasp and a few shouts of protest from the crowd.

My mom finally looked at me. "Let me go, Mia."

"No," I pleaded with her. "Mom, please. You don't have to do this."

She shook me off. "Yes, I do. I want to."

"He can't save you," I said, my voice coming out louder

than I meant it to. The mics picked it up and played it through the speakers. "You have to save yourself, Mom. Please listen to me. Let's go home."

"I can't, Mia," she said so softly her voice was nearly part of the silence. "I can't ever go home. There's nothing left for me but this."

She turned away from me, toward Prophet, and stood before him as he laid his hands on her forehead.

"I was buried alive during the earthquake," she said. "I lay there for days, waiting for death to take me, and it almost did. There was nothing," she said, almost inaudibly. "I thought there would be a light . . . comfort . . . something. But there was nothing after this life for me. Only darkness. But God let me live. He gave me another chance to find the light."

"God had other plans for you," Prophet said, nodding in perfect certainty. His thumbs pressed against her temples, and he drew her toward him. She closed her eyes, but his remained wide and white as he touched his lips lightly to hers. I saw the muscles in her neck clench, and then relax. He took her in his arms and held her against him. His eyes found me over her shoulder.

"Daughter," Prophet said.

I wanted to ignore him, but I felt this pressure in my mind, and a familiar buzzing, and I . . . I didn't. Prophet released my mom, but kept her by his side. Her cheeks and eyes were wet, but shining. Happy. Looking at her gave me pause. She was transformed. The sadness I had seen in her that morning . . . it wasn't there anymore. Had Prophet done that? Had he taken her sadness away? What if I was wrong about him? Wrong about everything? Did I, too, need saving? Would my eyes shine like that if I let Prophet put his hands on me?

Yes, a voice, not my own, whispered in my mind. *I will uncover the light inside you.*

"Come to me, Daughter," Prophet said. "Come closer."

I shook my head, but weakly. I felt that pressure in my mind again. The buzzing of the trapped fly, only the fly was bigger now. Not a common housefly, but a horsefly, or something even larger. A biplane, perhaps.

And then I felt a tug, like someone trying to open a door inside me.

"No," I said. But I felt my feet shambling toward Prophet. I stopped an arm's length from him. He reached his open palm toward my forehead, and I sucked in a breath as I saw the mark on his skin. Jagged red lines, etched on his palm.

Lightning scars.

Surrender, a voice spoke inside my mind. *Let go and be saved.*

Don't fight me.

I jolted back from that hand coming toward me, but it was too late. His fingers gripped my temples. His hand was huge and strong, and his Spark . . . his Spark was like lightning, a bright, hot flash illuminating my mind, burning it white.

I felt him expanding inside my mind, gaining dominion.

No! I pushed at him, tried to think him out of my head.

You are the missing piece, a voice—*his* voice—said. *God told me you would come.*

Get out of my head!

I opened my eyes. All I saw was white, like I was lost in a blizzard.

"I have a message for you," I said, my voice fading.

"What is that, Child?" His voice. Strong. Certain. Like the voice of God.

"God is . . . God is love. And you are a false prophet."

"Shhhh," he crooned. *Time to go to sleep. Sleep and be saved.*

The whiteness complete. Blinding.

I was gone.

I was saved.

I was finally asleep.

I was finally at peace.

PART 4

When there's nothing left to burn
You have to set yourself on fire.
—Unknown

APRIL 17
The storm

34

Awake. That's what I was. I was awake, and it was a new day, and I was a new me. The old me . . . she was still in there, but she was quiet. All her fears, her endless worries and doubts, her anger and her darkness and her desires . . . those were . . . not gone. Asleep. Old Mia was asleep still. New Mia was awake and her eyes were open.

I turned my head to take in my surroundings. Everything was white. Everything was good and clean and safe.

I lay in a cloud of a queen-sized bed, on creamy white Egyptian cotton linens that seemed impervious to wrinkles. I sat up. The room was unfamiliar, beautiful in shades of ivory and snow. A sliding glass door led out onto a balcony. And beyond the balcony . . . the ocean, stretching into a horizon obscured by mist.

It was morning. Still early. Still a bit gray.

There was a knock. It did not startle me. I was calm. I was at peace, and everything was right with the world. I couldn't remember ever feeling this way. So safe. So protected.

"Come in," I said.

The door opened, and in walked Prophet, dressed in a white, button-down shirt, open slightly at the collar, and casual white pants. His snowy, avalanche hair lay in soft drifts on his shoulders. His filmed eyes did not bother me the way they had when I was the old me, the one who feared and hated what she didn't understand. The new me saw Prophet for who he really was . . . a gift from God. A blessing. Maybe even a savior.

"Good morning, Mia," he said. "Did you sleep well?"

I nodded, smiling. "I must have slept the whole night," I said. "I never do that."

"You were exhausted, and understandably. You've been through so much of late. May I sit with you a while? I'd like to talk to you."

There was a chair set against the wall, a few feet from the bed. Prophet must have known exactly where it was, because he went right to it. He moved it closer to the bed and sat, crossing his legs and resting his elbows on his knees, clasping his hands under his chin.

I looked at my own hands, no longer clad in my usual black leather gloves. They had been replaced with soft, white cotton gloves. That meant someone had seen my hands. My skin. My scars.

I felt a twinge of anxiety.

It doesn't matter anymore. This is a safe place. You don't have to hide what you are here.

"Where am I?" I asked Prophet.

"I brought you to my house," he said.

"Oh . . . why?"

"Because you're special. Unique. And I have need of you."

"What about my mom?" I asked, remembering how

Prophet's lips had touched hers and how he had held her and kept her by his side. "Where is she?" *And Jeremy*, I wondered, *where had he gone?*

Prophet smiled, showing milk-white teeth. "I brought your mother here. I thought you'd want to see her when you woke up. She's a wonderful woman, Mia. I grew very fond of her while you were sleeping. She told me about you. It turns out we have something in common, you and me."

He uncrossed his legs and began unbuttoning his shirt cuffs. I watched him with my brow wrinkled. Prophet pushed his sleeves to his elbows. Then he held up his arms, palms facing me. Lightning scars bloomed on his palms like fireworks, tendrils descending over his wrists.

"You have them, too," I said, breathless.

"They are a gift from God. A mark that we are meant to do His good work here on earth, and of the power He has bestowed upon us."

I thought of the lightning scars stretching to cover my whole skin, and felt a warm glow in my chest.

"How many times have you been struck?" I asked, excited now.

Prophet's smile faltered, and I knew I'd said something wrong. "Three times," he said.

"Oh."

He brought back the smile, though now it stayed below his eyes. "But you, Mia . . . you've been struck countless times. That's what your mother tells me."

I nodded, lowering my eyes. I wanted to be humble. So what if I had been struck more times than Prophet. He was *Prophet*. He was God's mouthpiece.

"You have great power, Mia," Prophet said. "That is not something to be ashamed of. Not unless you use that power for the wrong purposes."

I drew in a deep breath and let it out and raised my eyes to meet Prophet's. "I've hurt people," I said.

"Yes, your mother told me that, too. And I saw it."

"You . . . you saw what happened . . . on the bridge?"

"I can see inside you, Mia. Inside your mind. Your mother didn't need to tell me anything about you. I know it all. But you didn't mean to do what you did. You didn't know how to control the power God had given you. It is, perhaps, too great for you to control. That's why you need someone like me . . . to harness that power. To put it to good use."

I nodded. It was true. I needed to be controlled. I needed Prophet.

"How do you know so much?" I lowered my eyes in shame. "Are you like Mr. Kale?" I figured he knew who Mr. Kale was if he really did know everything about me.

Prophet grimaced in distaste, but nodded slightly. "Our power is similar, yes."

Thinking of Mr. Kale, I remembered what he told me about his sister. Katrina's mother. Had Prophet really murdered her? No, I decided. Mr. Kale must have lied. Prophet was good, and I felt safe with him.

Another twinge of anxiety. If Mr. Kale was a liar, and Parker had become a Seeker . . . then my brother was on the wrong side.

Prophet watched me, and I felt that nagging, buzzing pressure in my mind.

When you see your brother again, things will be different

between you, Prophet's voice informed me. *He is no longer your brother. You have a new family, now. A family of people just like you.*

I shook my head. Shook it because old Mia was inside me still, and she was trying to wake up, to assert control, and she was giving me a not good feeling in my stomach.

"You know I'm right, don't you, Mia?" Prophet said. "Your brother has gone against God's will. Against His plan. The world must be cleansed and remade in goodness and light, and your brother and the Seekers would try to prevent that." Prophet paused and cocked his head, seeming to listen to a voice only he could hear.

God speaks to him, I thought.

Prophet shook his head sadly. "Your brother is now the enemy. He is lost to you."

My breath caught in my throat. "No . . ." I shook my head. "No! No, no, no."

"Yes," Prophet said. *Yes. He betrayed you, abandoned you. He rejected you because of who you are, what you are.*

Old Mia stirred inside me. She didn't like what was happening, didn't like what Prophet was saying about Parker. She didn't like it at all.

The peaceful feeling I'd had upon waking was getting chopped up. Old Mia was ruining it. She was coming back, and she was angry. The warm light of God in my heart was now burning with fury.

"You're upset," Prophet said.

"You think?" I snarled.

Prophet stood and leaned over me in the bed.

"Parker didn't betray me. He was only doing what he thought was right." I shrank from Prophet, but there was nowhere to hide. He placed his hands on my head, and I felt him like the light of God shining down on me. Immediately I calmed.

"What did you do?" I asked.

"I gave you a blessing."

"Thank you. I feel better now."

"Are you hungry?" he asked. "It's time for breakfast, and I'd like you to meet your new family." He stood. "I will leave you to freshen up. Come downstairs to the dining room when you're ready. Take as much time as you need. But not too much." He smiled. "There really isn't much time left."

When I was alone again, I climbed out of bed and opened the sliding glass door to go out onto the balcony. The air was cool and smelled of brine and salt and all things ocean. My skin prickled painfully with warning. I could feel the storm beginning to take shape now, to condense as it gathered strength. I felt I should be concerned, but . . . I wasn't.

If it is God's will that a storm should come to Los Angeles, then so be it.

I leaned against the balcony railing and stared out at the beach. I knew where I was now: in one of the luxurious Santa Monica beach houses that stood on the sand along the Pacific Coast Highway. Peering down over the iron railing, I counted three stories below me and whistled through my teeth. A four-story beach house . . . that was one pricey piece of real estate, probably worth millions. Then again, property values had decreased since the quake, and beach houses were probably going for less these days, considering Tentville now stood between them and the ocean.

In the fuzzy morning light, figures scurried among the tents on the beach, tending fires and cooking breakfast in skillets over hot coals. To the south I could see the Santa Monica Pier, shrouded in mist. And I could see the White Tent where Prophet's revival had taken place. When had that been? Last night? It seemed like ages ago. Time was different after a full night's sleep. I felt like I had missed something important, slept through a vital scene in the movie. But that was okay. Prophet's blessing had set me right, made me a new person.

There was an unopened toothbrush and a fresh tube of toothpaste waiting for me in the bathroom, along with shampoo and conditioner, and a stack of fluffy white towels.

I brushed my teeth, and then stripped off my clothes for a quick shower. I cranked the cold water and let it run icy, examining myself in the mirror. In the white bathroom, the lightning scars appeared redder than ever, red as blood, but that was okay. Prophet had them, too, although not as many. He didn't like that I'd been struck more times than he had. I didn't like that I'd made him envious. If being struck was a gift from God, that meant God had favored me more than Prophet . . . that didn't make sense.

Don't think about it.

Fifteen minutes later, I was showered and dressed in Followers' white once again. I wished I had a change of clothes. There were smudgy dark fingerprints on my sleeves from where that man on the beach had held me, telling me . . . what had he said? Something about love?

Don't think about it.

Yes, it was better that way. Thoughts could be dangerous if you thought the wrong ones, and I had been thinking the wrong ones for a lifetime. But Prophet helped me think the right thoughts. He was like Mr. Kale, only better in every way, because Prophet knew God's plan, and he could guide me.

Now I felt calm . . . the kind of calm that came after a storm.

Or was it before?

I left the fourth-floor bedroom and headed down several flights of stairs until I got to the first floor, where I heard classical music and voices.

The smell of food was like walking into a bakery first thing in the morning. My stomach made its presence known with loud rumbles. I followed the music and the voices and the food smells until I came to a room with a soaring, thirty-foot ceiling and glass walls that looked out on a view of water and more water, like we were on a boat at sea. All I could see of Tentville was hazy columns of smoke rising into the air.

There was an enormous fireplace with a crackling fire burning, and a notched wooden table that extended nearly the entire length of the room. Like the Last Supper table, I thought, complete with Apostles. Twelve of them. I recognized them from TV, and from the Rove and the revival, although now the sight of them did not fill me with trepidation. The twins with their pale hair and bald eyes sat shoulder to shoulder. The boy smiled. The girl did not.

Prophet sat at the head of the table, but he was turned toward a woman with dark blond hair that fell forward to conceal her face. Not an Apostle. Prophet's hand lay over hers, stroking softly. When I entered, the woman turned her head to look at me. She smiled when she saw me, and even with the scars that lashed her face she looked strangely beautiful, like a wounded angel in her loose white linen dress.

"Mia," she said, and stood, and came to me. She took my hands. For a long moment we only looked into each other's eyes. Then she pulled me into a tight embrace.

"I'm so glad you're here," Mom said. "I'm so *happy*. I never thought I could feel like this. So . . . at peace."

"Me, too," I said. Over Mom's shoulder I could see Prophet and his Apostles watching us. There was one Apostle in particular who caught my attention. He had dark hair, neatly parted and held behind his ears; dark-lashed blue eyes. It took me a moment to recognize him without his Clark Kent glasses, but once I did I inhaled sharply, as though a fist had rammed into my stomach.

The missing twelfth Apostle.

Jeremy. The Judas. The Betrayer.

But who had he betrayed, Prophet or me?

"Mia, is something wrong?" Mom asked, feeling me tense. She released me and held me back.

"Jeremy," I said. "What are you doing here?" That question again, the one I was forever asking him.

"I brought you here," he answered. "Father wanted you, and I brought you to him."

Prophet put a hand on Jeremy's shoulder. "You never disappoint me, son."

"Thank you, Father."

Prophet stood. "Children," he said, "let us welcome Mia into our fold. God has chosen her, as He chose you, and has gifted her with His power . . . a power we need to carry out the plan God imparted to me. Mia Price will complete our circle as our thirteenth Apostle."

The she-twin twisted toward Prophet. "But, Father . . . thirteen! It's an unholy number! And she . . ." The girl's eyes cut toward me. "She is not yet proven. How do you know she can be trusted?"

Prophet smiled kindly at the girl, but his white eyes had narrowed slightly. "Iris," he said, "when did I lose your faith?"

The she-twin, Iris, went stiff in her chair, as though overcome by sudden paralysis. "You have my faith, Father," she murmured.

Prophet looked over the rest of the Apostles. "We do not fear a number, even the number thirteen. A number has no power. The power is in our hands."

He held up his hands, showing the bursts of lightning scars on his palms.

"The power is in our hands," the Apostles agreed in unison. Each Apostle touched his or her right hand to a different place on the body. Iris placed her right hand on top of her head. Her twin pressed his to his left shoulder. Jeremy touched his heart. I caught him looking at me again, but this time his gaze narrowed a sliver as he searched my face.

"The power is in our hands, and with our hands we do the work of God," Prophet said.

"The power is in our hands, and with our hands we do the work of God," the Apostles parroted.

Iris, still with her hand resting on top of her head, looked at me. "Where did God's Light enter you?" she asked, her tone still laced with a hint of bitterness, a drop of poison.

I shook my head, confused. "God's Light?" I asked.

"Lightning."

My eyes went wide. "You've all been struck?"

"We've been *chosen*," Iris said. "Chosen by God."

The he-twin nodded. "God sent His holy Light to endow us with His power, so that we could carry out His plan. He gave each of us a gift."

"You mean the Spark?" I ventured.

The Apostles glanced at one another, frowning and furrowing brows, shaking their heads, muttering. I had said something wrong again. I tried not to acknowledge my growing frustration, but it was there. These Apostles were ruining my peace.

"Hush, children," Prophet said. "Mia is new to our fold. She will learn." He looked at me. "Mia, sit with us. I will explain."

I did as I was told, taking the open seat at his left, while Mom returned to the seat on his right. Prophet turned toward me. As with Jeremy, I could feel Prophet's Spark—or whatever they called it—without touching him, like standing near a fire.

A holy fire.

"Mia," Prophet said, "you have had encounters with the Seekers. I know this."

I lowered my eyes. There was no sense denying it. Prophet had seen inside my mind . . . he must know. "Yes," I admitted.

More muttering from the Apostles, but Prophet silenced them with the slightest raising of his hand.

"So you know their aim," Prophet said. "To defy God's will, that the earth be torn asunder and then made anew in peace and beauty. To destroy our hope for a New Eden."

"Yes," I said quietly.

"The Seekers would see the world continue to rot, until there is nothing left of it but a black, moldering cancer. A disease without cure. But we have the cure, Mia, and it must be applied now, before it's too late."

I nodded, but my brow was furrowed. "The Seekers have hope for our world," I said. "And hope is . . . bad?"

Deep inside me, I could feel Old Mia tossing and turning, restless.

Prophet's smile was kind and fatherly below his empty eyes. "No, hope is not bad, Mia. In this instance, it is merely false. It is lost. The offense would be to disobey God's will and entertain such false hope."

"Oh."

"If God meant the Seekers to have the power to challenge His will, He would have bestowed it upon them, as He did us. Our power, our *gift*, comes from God and is therefore divine. The Seekers in their arrogance deny God, but aim to possess those who are gifted with God's Light. They endeavor to seize control of that power, to turn those who lack faith against the God who gifted them."

"They lie," Iris said, piercing me with her sharp gaze.

"Yes, they do," Prophet said. "So you see, we do not insult God's gift by calling it by the name our enemy uses. They can have their Spark." He smiled. "We have the Light."

His hands found my face, thumbs pressing against my temples, and it was like sunrise inside my mind. I couldn't help but gasp. I felt myself opening to that light, like a flower waking in the morning. Connected to him, I could sense other energy around me, the light of the Apostles. I could connect to them in this way, I realized, because we were the same. Here was where I belonged, among people whose energy complemented mine.

Still, there was no light that felt the way Jeremy's did. He and I had connected in a different way.

Don't think about Jeremy, a voice inside me warned. I turned off thoughts of Jeremy and focused on what Prophet was saying.

"You are the one we've been waiting for. The one God said would come. You are the missing piece of the plan, the last link we needed to complete the circle that will bring God's storm."

The last link in the circle? I wasn't sure exactly what he was talking about, but that was okay. I didn't need to understand. I only needed to do what Prophet wanted.

Prophet lowered his hands, and the light dimmed in my mind, but not in my soul and my heart.

But there were places in me, still, where darkness waited behind locked doors . . . and for the time being I would keep it that way until I found out what Jeremy was up to.

"Now," Prophet said, "let us enjoy this bounteous meal. We need our strength for what's to come. Tonight we see God's plan through to the end." He placed both of his palms down on the table. "Tonight we bring the storm of God's wrath to this city."

At his words, my heart-fire flared to life.

35

Breakfast was a feast, with steaming platters of eggs and potatoes, toast soaked in butter, melon slices and straw-berries, fresh-squeezed orange juice and thick, cold milk, and tiny Belgian waffles with maple syrup and whipped cream.

I felt guilty eating such a decadent breakfast while out-side Prophet's door there were people starving. Still, I ate like it was my last meal. I couldn't help myself. The anxiety that had been twisting my stomach into knots had finally subsided. I felt like I hadn't eaten in a month.

One by one, the Apostles went around the table and in-troduced themselves. I'd never been good with names, and I forgot most of them as soon as they were said. The twins, Iris and Ivan, were the only Apostles whose names stuck.

"I saw you," I told them, "at the Rove the other night, when the fight broke out. Why don't any of you have bruises or cuts? Did you heal them, Prophet, the way you did for the Dealer?"

"The Dealer?" he asked.

Heat rose in my cheeks and I looked at my plate, ashamed that I knew such a person. "The guy you healed last night, the one with the burns."

"Is that what ailed him?" Prophet asked in a mildly curious tone. "I didn't notice. But, no, I did not heal my Apostles' wounds. There's no need."

Iris sneered at me. "When is the last time you had a simple bruise or a cut that took more than a day to heal?"

I remembered what Mr. Kale had said, that one of the advantages of having the Spark—the *Light*, I had to remember that—was the ability to heal rapidly. At the time I'd dismissed this claim, but now that I thought about it, the only times I recalled being injured were after a lightning strike. But even then the severe burns I sometimes sustained healed completely within a few days, and the only scars I was ever left with were the lightning scars. Even my hair seemed to grow back more quickly than normal.

"It's part of God's gift to us," Ivan said, and I accepted this simple answer.

The Apostles were friendly enough, except for Iris. None of them welcomed me with open arms, and I could tell they were suspicious of me. They gave off a vibe of protectiveness, like they thought I might steal something. And there was some envy mixed in, as well. I didn't begrudge them their right to a little jealousy. I was the missing ingredient, after all. I was the one Prophet needed to make God's storm, to carry out the plan, though I still wasn't clear on what that plan was.

As the introductions went around, I sensed Jeremy's furtive glances. It seemed I could still feel the heat of him from across the table, and the desire to be next to him, to touch him. These feelings were wrong. Old Mia could feel whatever way she wanted about him, but New Mia should have her baser desires, her hot blood, under control.

"And, of course, you know Jeremiah," Prophet said, beaming at his adopted son.

I could no longer avoid looking at Jeremy. I turned my eyes to his, feeling a sort of giddy nausea in my stomach. *You didn't even know his name,* I thought. *There's nothing between you. Nothing real.*

I nodded, lowering my eyes and playing with my fork.

"Jeremiah has been a great help to me," Prophet said. "Where God speaks to me, he shows Jeremiah images of what's to come. I'm sure he told you of the revelations he's had of you for so many years. I sent him to find you."

My hand jerked and my fork scraped across my plate. I searched Jeremy's face. His normally angry eyes, now so serene, looked like they belonged to a different person. Was it true? Had he only come looking for me because Prophet told him to? Had Prophet told him to kill me?

No. Prophet needed me to carry out the plan. He wouldn't have ordered my murder.

I cleared my throat and glanced around at the other Apostles. "So, you have gifts, like . . . like Jeremiah has?"

"And like you have, Mia," Prophet said. "And a very powerful gift it is. The ability to hold God's Light inside yourself. To release it when you need it. Of course, you have not yet learned to control your gift. That is why it is so important you came to me. Each of my children has received a gift through God's Light, but you are special."

If Iris's gaze had been cool before, now it was downright Siberian.

I avoided her eyes and smiled, but the smile felt forced. A gift? Was that really what I had? The only thing I'd ever done with lightning was hurt people. Well, that wasn't true. I had hurt Janna, but then I had helped her.

"Father," Jeremy said, "tell Mia and her mother how God gifted *you.*"

I glanced at Mom, took in the expression of admiration on her face as she waited for Prophet's response.

Prophet placed his hand over Mom's and leaned toward her until their foreheads touched. Then he lifted his other hand to her cheek and cupped her face as he kissed her lightly.

"This good woman already knows everything she needs to know about me," he said when he broke the kiss. "But, very well." Prophet took Mom's hand and held it as he turned to me once again. "God saw fit to gift me threefold, Mia. The first time I was struck, He took my sight, but He gave me the ability to hear His holy word. The second time I was struck, He put the power in my hands to spread His word among the lost and the unrighteous and have it be believed. The third time I was struck, He gifted me again, with the power to link my Light with that of my Apostles, one to another. To connect us, so there is nothing we cannot accomplish. So that we can combine our unique powers to create God's storm." His clouded eyes drew me in. "And I've passed that gift on to you, Mia. I've awakened you and opened you to us. Now you can share your power with all of us."

Prophet squeezed Mom's hand, and she breathed in and sighed out contentedly. "Now God has granted me a fourth gift in you, Sarah Price."

I looked at Jeremy, or Jeremiah, or whatever he wanted to call himself. I wondered what he wanted me to take from Prophet's words. I wondered if he could sense Old Mia's quiet rage, deep below the surface.

After breakfast, I excused myself and returned to my room. I went out onto the balcony to think, even though thinking was . . . uncomfortable. There were so many things I shouldn't think, and every time one of those forbidden thoughts tried to find its way into my mind I felt wrong, like I was betraying Prophet. But they kept trying to get in: thoughts of Mom and Prophet and how he had kissed her. Of Parker as my enemy. Of Jeremy, and how naked he looked with his hair tucked behind his ears and without his glasses, without his disguise. I wanted the other Jeremy back. But that was bad! Jeremiah, the one in white without his Clark Kent glasses, was a traitor to Prophet and his cause. The other Jeremy was a mysterious boy who could have made things so much easier by killing me, but couldn't go through with it. A boy who watched over me, who tried to protect me from a future I didn't want, whose touch awakened things in me that were bad, bad, bad.

I leaned against the balcony railing and let my head fall into my hands. The air gusting off the ocean made my skin tingle with warning, even though I knew now that there was no storm waiting behind the horizon. The storm inside me wanted out. I had a purpose, and it was nearly time to fulfill it. That was God's plan, to tear apart the world like it was no more than a botched drawing on paper, easily tossed aside so we could start again with a fresh sheet.

If Prophet was to be believed—and of course he was—then that was God's will.

So why did I feel like this was all wrong?

"Mia?"

I spun around. "Mom."

"I didn't mean to scare you," she said, coming up beside me and winding her thin arm around me.

"It's okay." I could feel her ribs from the weight she'd lost, and I didn't find the comfort in her that I used to. She was not as substantial as she once was. "Mom, what do you think about all this?"

"All this?"

"Yeah, the . . . the weird stuff. The Light and the storm and everything else Prophet talked about."

"What do I think . . . ?" Mom said, drawing the words out. She sounded the way she had when she was taking her meds. Drugged. Sedated. Far away.

I pulled back so I could look at her face.

"I think," Mom said finally, "that God works in mysterious ways, and that He speaks to Rance"—she smiled and put her hand over her mouth like she'd let some secret slip—"to *Prophet*, and that Prophet understands God's will. We have to defer to him if we want to walk in God's Light."

"What about Parker?" I asked her. "Aren't you worried that Prophet won't let you love him anymore now that he's our enemy?"

Deep furrows appeared in her brow, and the concern in her eyes was finally real. "I will always love Parker."

Relief flooded through me. "You will?"

"Of course." The frown line between her eyes deepened.

"I don't want to think about Parker. It's too confusing." She turned to me and held me by the shoulders. "Mia, what's wrong?"

I didn't want to talk about what was wrong. What was wrong was in my head. In Old Mia's head.

I changed the subject. "What's going on with you and Prophet? You seem . . . close."

"I'm in love with him," Mom said simply.

I took one quick step back, and her arms fell. "But you've only known him a day."

A flicker of discontent crossed her face, and then: "Don't *you* love Prophet?" the question came out like a shove.

"Yes, I love him," I answered quickly. "He's Prophet. He's *the* Prophet. He's God's messenger."

"He's more than that." She raised her hand and her fingers found the lines of scar tissue on her face. "He only sees the good in me. None of the ugliness."

I thought of the lightning scars covering my body and nodded. "That sounds nice."

"He says he wants me with him all the time. He doesn't want me to leave his side, not ever. I had to slip away to see you while he was talking to his Apostles." She frowned a little. "I wonder if he's realized I'm gone. I should get back to him now. He wants me with him all the time."

"You said that already." I watched her force her mouth back into a smile.

"I did, didn't I? I'm just so excited about tonight. This is happening so quickly."

"You mean the storm?"

She shook her head, and her smile turned secretive. "Prophet is a wonderful man."

I opened my mouth to agree with her, but nothing came out. I was saved by a knock on the door.

What was happening to New Mia? I needed another blessing, I decided. I needed Prophet to set my mind straight.

I wondered if there was any way to put Old Mia in a coma. Permanently.

Hesitantly, Jeremy—Jeremiah—pushed open the door. He didn't look at me, but at my Mom. "Ms. Price," he said, "my father requests that you return to him now."

Mom glanced at me. "He wants me with him all the time," she repeated again. Then she hurried out the door, leaving Jeremy and me alone.

Jeremy closed the door behind him.

And locked it.

"We have to talk," he said.

"I don't want to talk to you," I said. "You're a traitor."

The anger was back where it belonged, in Jeremy's eyes. He crossed the room to me, stood so we were chest to chest. My body lit up with his proximity. Jeremy grabbed the back of my head, fingers disappearing into my hair. His touch was rough. But it was gentle. It was contradictory.

And his kiss was the same way.

His mouth opened mine.

His tongue tasted mine.

The heat between us was nuclear. We melted each other; melted into each other; and then—

The world disappeared.

The bedroom disappeared.

Jeremy disappeared.

And—

*   *   *

I opened my eyes at the top of the world, on the roof of the Tower, close enough to touch the night. Hundreds of rovers crowded the roof, their frantic energy making the air simmer, arms whipping and bodies convulsing to the madness of the beat.

I stood in the center of the chaos, each of my hands clasped by the young Apostles in white on either side of me, thirteen of us joining hands to make a perfect circle.

Jeremy met my eyes, and the sadness in them would have torn at my heart if I had been capable of feeling anything at that moment besides the elation of my Light joined with that of the other Apostles.

"The power is in our hands," we chanted. "The power is in our hands and our hands do the work of God."

Our voices were absorbed in the driving beat pumping from the speakers, and the rovers danced on, unaware of what was coming.

What was here.

The storm.

The air had begun to change . . . to move and thicken. I smelled ozone and wind and burning . . . something burning. An electric fire. The pressure dropped. We turned our faces to the sky, and watched black clouds boil where before there had been a clear velvet night.

My heart pulsed fire, and light pulsing in the clouds matched my heartbeat. Thunder crashed, an explosion that drowned the rovers' music. But the thunder only increased their frenzy. They danced on, shouting at the sky, taunting the storm.

I looked at Jeremy, saw he was no longer a part of the circle.

He stood at the edge of the roof, Prophet looming behind him, holding a glinting silver knife against Jeremy's neck. The same knife Jeremy had brought to my room.

"Jeremy!" I shouted over the bass and the thunder. I struggled to loose my hands from those of the Apostles who held them, but our grips seemed fused. Welded together. I shouted at Prophet as I pulled against the circle, "Let him go!"

Prophet shook his head, mouth curved down in sadness. "He betrayed me. I loved him as my own son. I trusted him, and he turned his back on me."

Lightning fractured the sky with bloodred light.

The rovers, finally impressed, screamed. For a moment the lightning blinded me. Then I blinked and color bled back into the world. I looked to Jeremy again, and saw red. At first I thought it was just the afterimage of the crimson lightning. But no, it was darker. Liquid. Blood was pouring from a deep gash in Jeremy's throat, and the knife in Prophet's hand was red now instead of silver. I screamed and broke from the circle, running toward Jeremy, lightning shattering the sky all around us now, the world cracking open like an egg. There was so much blood. So much blood.

"This is the end," Prophet said. "Now we begin anew."

Prophet lifted Jeremy's body. Jeremy's eyes never left mine until Prophet dropped him over the edge of the Tower.

"Noooo!" I reached the ledge and saw Jeremy falling as lightning ruptured the air around him. Far below us, lightning punished the ground, red branches of incandescence reaching into the chasms where the earth had been laid open during the quake. Then the world began its violent tremble, and the trembling escalated to convulsions. The Tower began to sway, and then to buckle, crumbling toward the earth. The storm continued to *rage, and the lightning to hammer the ground, and I knew I had made this happen, but I couldn't stop it.*

It was too late.

This was the end.

I felt a snap inside my skull, like something stretched beyond capacity splitting in two. The pain was tremendous, like having the two halves of my brain pulled apart. I cradled my head in my hands, eyes squeezed shut. I could still see lightning on the backs of my eyelids, red veins of fire. Pressing fingers into my temples, I peeled my eyes open to find myself still in Jeremy's arms, his mouth so close to mine I could feel his warm breath. He had his hands in my hair. His kiss was still hot on my lips. But the vision had ended.

My head was clear.

Old Mia was back. Jeremy had awakened her with a kiss and a nightmare. The peace Prophet had granted me was gone, replaced by fear and hate and rage and desperation, filling me up inside until I felt like I might burst from the pressure. I squeezed my eyes shut again and buried my face in Jeremy's chest. Jeremy held me so tightly it was almost painful, crushing me into him. At some point he moved me to the bed and sat me down next to him. He kept his arm around me, and his heat soaked into me like sunlight but brought no more visions with it.

"You died," I said, my voice raw. "He killed you. Your father killed you."

"I know," Jeremy said.

"That can't happen!"

"Shh. It won't."

"But it did! I saw it! He's going to find out the truth!" And what was the truth? It came to me as I said it. "He's going to find out you betrayed him. That you tried to keep me away from him, not bring me to him."

"No, he's not. Not anymore."

"Why not?"

He turned his head away. "Because you're not going to tell him."

"No . . . I wouldn't have." I shook my head, but I knew the truth. Eventually, I would have told Prophet that Jeremy was a traitor.

But there was still so much I didn't understand. How had Jeremy come to be an Apostle? When had he turned against Prophet, and how had he broken Prophet's hold on him? How had he kept Prophet from finding out he was a Judas among the Apostles? And, most confusing of all, how had Prophet not gleaned the truth from both our minds?

The line of questions went on and on. I didn't realize I was speaking them aloud until Jeremy held up his hands.

"We don't have much time," he said. "The others will begin to wonder what I'm up to if I don't come down soon."

"They don't trust you," I guessed.

Jeremy went to adjust his glasses before realizing they weren't there. I'd always thought it was ridiculous that no one recognized Clark Kent when he was Superman. Now that I'd fallen for such a simple disguise, it didn't seem so ridiculous. No wonder Mom had fixated on him when she'd seen him out the window. And no wonder he'd been so reluctant to accompany me to the revival. But he *had* done it. For me. Because the only way he could have stopped me was to kill me.

Maybe it would have been better if he had. Safer for everyone. For the whole world.

"They sense that something about me is different," Jeremy said. "Iris is the worst of them. She doesn't trust anyone but Ivan and Father."

"I noticed," I said, shivering as I thought back to breakfast, how I'd told myself that Iris would get to know the new me and accept me. Rage swelled inside me at what Prophet had done: brainwashed me so clean I had almost disappeared. And Mom . . . her mind was so fragile. Would it even be possible for her to come back from Prophet's brainwashing?

Jeremy went on. "Iris has reason enough not to trust me. I've been missing a lot lately, and she's still furious about what happened at the Rove."

"About the fight?" I asked.

"About me not showing up for their little demonstration. As far as she knows, anyway. Iris thinks I'm losing my faith. She doesn't know the half of it."

"What did Prophet and the Apostles think you were doing?" I asked. "Those days when you didn't show up for *The Hour of Light*, or when you didn't come home at night? Did . . . did Prophet know you were with me?"

Jeremy shook his head. "Father talks as though he has access to every thought we have, but there's too much going on in a person's mind, too much confusion, for him to sift through all of it. He picks up enough to make us think he knows every secret, but it's a lie."

I breathed a little easier. "So it's possible to hide things from him."

"Yes. But it's not easy. Once you try not to think something, it's usually the only thing you can think. As far as where Prophet thought I was when I was with you . . . for the most part, I come and go as I please. I've always been his favorite." Jeremy's tone was bitter. "He makes allowances for me that he won't for the other Apostles. But when I left yesterday . . ." He looked at me. "I hadn't planned on coming back."

I felt a knife twist of guilt in my stomach.

"It's not your fault," Jeremy said, reading the dismay on my face. "I should never have let you go to the revival in the first place. If I'd been honest with you from the beginning things might have been different. We might have left town days ago with your mom and your brother and none of this would be happening now." He shook his head, a tortured look on his face. "But I was afraid to tell you the truth. Afraid of what you'd think of me."

I picked my gaze up off the floor and brought my eyes to his. "Why?" I asked.

His hands clenched tight, and I sensed the light coming off him start to change. It dimmed, like the sun obscured by smog. He searched my face. I didn't know what he was looking for, but I hoped he found it.

"I want you to understand why I let Prophet use me this way. His predictions . . . those weren't entirely his. They were mine. Or they were half mine. I would see these terrible things that were going to happen, and Father would hear a voice he said was God's telling him *when* they were going to happen, and . . ." He trailed off, looking miserable.

"You were a team," I said softly.

Jeremy lowered his eyes. "If it weren't for me, he would never have grown this powerful. But you have to understand, for a long time I loved him like he was my real father. I put him on a pedestal. If anything, I hate myself for that, even more than I hate him. After my mom died, I was in and out of foster care. When Rance took me in he saved me from some very bad people. I realized quickly that the only reason he chose to adopt me was because I'd been struck by lightning, and because of my ability, but I didn't care. He made me feel safe. Protected." He looked in my eyes. "You understand what that's like now? What he can do to your mind?"

I nodded, and Jeremy took a deep breath before continuing.

"In the beginning, life with Rance was better than anything I'd known, even with my real mother. For the first time I had a family. Not just a family, but a whole congregation of people who seemed to love me. My new life revolved around Bible study and the Church of Light, but I didn't mind. When I got a little older, things started to change. I began to see things differently.

"Father had strange ways of interpreting Bible passages. His notions were always slanted toward the idea that every thousand years or so, the people of the world became so wicked, so corrupt, that there was no saving them, and the only way to keep the world from becoming hell was for God to bring about some kind of cleansing. It had happened before, with Noah and the flood. The others in the church, and especially my adopted brothers and sisters, hung on Father's every word. I didn't want to be the dissenter, so I kept quiet for a long time, but finally I couldn't stand it anymore. During one of Father's sermons, I dared to disagree with him." He paused, took a breath and released it. "That didn't go over well. Father got very quiet, and then finally sent me to my room. I stayed there until he came to see me. He told me I had to set an example for the others, and by contradicting him I had undermined his authority. 'It can't happen again,' he said, and then he . . . he gave me a blessing to strengthen my faith."

My stomach shrank. I knew where this was going. "He brainwashed you."

"He'd been doing it all along, in subtle ways, but I hadn't realized it until then."

"And the suggestions only work if a part of you wants to comply."

He nodded again. "A part of me did. I wanted to be a good son. I didn't want to undermine him. So every few days he would give me a blessing, and I behaved the way he wanted me to."

"How did you break the cycle?" I asked.

Jeremy leaned his elbows on his knees and rested his head in his hands to massage his temples. "From the beginning, he told me I should always come to him after I'd had a 'revelation,' and tell him everything in precise detail, so that's what I did. He'd started his show by this time, but *The Hour of Light* didn't take off until he began using my revelations. That was fine. We were doing something good. Religion was the perfect tool to mask what was really going on, and to get people to listen. And our predictions saved thousands of lives."

He swallowed hard and reached to adjust his glasses again. But the glasses, his disguise, weren't there. It was just him now.

He looked at me with all the sadness and anger one person could contain without losing his mind.

"I had a vision of the Puente Hills Quake. I saw a storm appear in the sky above downtown, and lightning struck the ground, and then everything began to shake and the . . . and the towers, all but one, fell."

My breath slowed. I nodded.

"I saw it a week before the quake hit."

36

It took me a moment to find my voice. "But Prophet didn't warn about the quake until—"

"Until it was too late." Jeremy's whole body was clenched, shaking with rage like he was experiencing his own private earthquake. "As soon as I woke from the vision, I went to Father to tell him what I'd seen. I demanded he inform the mayor first, before he announced it on *The Hour of Light*, so the city could begin evacuation procedures. He agreed to make the call, but before he did anything, he wanted to give me a blessing. I was upset, and he was afraid I might do something rash, go running through the streets, shouting at people to get out of the city." Jeremy's trembling stilled suddenly. "Next thing I knew, I was waking up and the earthquake was over. The city was in ruins and so many people . . . so many were dead. It was exactly what I'd seen. What I was supposed to prevent."

"Jeremy . . ." I couldn't think of anything to say. There was nothing *to* say.

"When I found out what my father had done, I lost it. My brothers held me down while Father explained that it wasn't up to him, God had commanded he say nothing about the earthquake until right before it was to take place. He said God wanted the people of Los Angeles to be humbled. But I *knew* he had acted of his own will, even if he wouldn't admit it. That was the end for me. Whatever hold he had on me was broken. There was no longer any part of me that could be controlled by him.

"I pretended to forgive him. I didn't know what else to do. If I spoke out against him . . . I knew I'd be putting myself in danger. I've seen him angry. I know he's not above hurting the people who cross him. There was this woman who joined the Church of Light after the quake. I liked her, but there was definitely something off about her. Even though she wore Followers' white, she never looked like a Follower, not in her eyes, anyway. She was always hanging around Father, praising him, flirting with him. Then, one day, she disappeared. When I asked Father what happened to her, he smiled. He never answered the question." Jeremy shook his head. "I wish I could remember the woman's name."

"Irene," I said quietly. "She was a Seeker."

"Was." Jeremy covered his eyes.

"Tell me the rest," I said.

Jeremy nodded, taking a moment to pull his thoughts together. "Like I told you before, I've always had visions of you. But after the quake, their frequency increased. There was one day when I couldn't get out of bed, the visions were coming so fast. I stopped seeing anything else. Just you. You over and over again."

"And the Tower," I said.

"That, but I saw other things, too. Flashes of Skyline and your house, your mom and brother. The visions led me to you, and I told you I always have the visions for a reason."

"So you can change things."

"Father was only able to read fragments of my thoughts, enough to know I was getting close to you. He told me to bring you to him, said he needed you to create the God storm. I . . . I thought if I . . ."

"Got rid of me?" I offered, trying for a lighthearted tone that only made Jeremy wince.

"Yes," he said. "But once I actually saw you, alive, right in front of me, not just an image in some vision . . . I couldn't go through with what I had planned. But I couldn't walk away either. I had to keep you safe. Keep you away from the Seekers, away from the Tower, and especially away from my father. The storm that appeared on the day of the quake was his inspiration."

"To create his own storm, and his own earthquake?" I said, sounding dubious. "Do you think it's really possible?"

"A lot of the things he does are impossible, but he does them anyway. He can't accomplish it alone, though. He needs the Apostles, and the Followers, especially those who have the Light in them and have pledged their loyalty to him. And he needs you most of all. You're the one he's counting on to give lightning to his storm. And the lightning will break the sixth seal."

"But I thought the seals were just omens," I said. "Not actual seals. That's what the Seekers told me."

"The sixth is different. It's the Puente Hills Fault, and if it produces a massive enough quake, it will begin a domino effect that will be felt around the world. The Puente Hills Fault will set off the San Andreas Fault, which will set off another fault and another. And earthquakes won't be the only effect. Volcanoes and calderas will erupt, and tsunamis will wipe out whole cities. Destruction will lead to more destruction. That, according to Father, is God's plan to cleanse the earth."

Jeremy stopped talking then, and we sat quietly for a moment before he said, "I'll understand if you hate me."

I stared at him. "Why would I hate you?"

His mouth twisted down at the corners. "So many dead," he said. "And your mother was almost one of them."

"It wasn't your fault! If you had seen a vision of Prophet putting you to sleep so you'd be out of the way, you wouldn't have told him about the quake. But you didn't have that vision. Maybe there are some things you can't change no matter how much you want to."

Jeremy's teeth clamped together. He was shaking again. "I shouldn't have needed a vision. I knew who my father was, but I didn't want to admit *what* he was."

"You wanted to believe he was better than that. You can't take responsibility for what Prophet did. He manipulated you. He used you. *He* did that. You didn't ask to have these visions any more than I asked to be a . . . whatever I am. And we can still change things, right? It's not too late."

He nodded slowly, and a weight lifted inside me.

"The Seekers will come for you," Jeremy said. "Last night's revival was televised. They'll know what's happened."

They'll try to use you . . .

"Are you sure?" I asked Jeremy. "I made it pretty clear I wanted nothing to do with the Seekers."

He nodded, but there was something hidden in his eyes. "I've seen it. Father is holding a final revival at sunset for every Follower; to gather them on the beach where he claims they'll be safe from the earthquake he thinks is coming. But without you, he won't be able to create a strong enough electrical storm to bring on the quake. The Seekers will come for you at the revival. Unless something changes," he added, looking distant.

"Why don't they come now?" I asked. "Wouldn't that be easier?"

Jeremy shook his head. "I doubt they know where you are. Prophet owns so many properties, under so many different names. Their minds aren't the only thing his Followers hand over to him. Many give up everything, including the deeds to their homes and whatever savings they have."

"What about my mom?" I asked. "What about you? The Seekers will rescue all of us, right?"

He held up his hands. "I only see you, but that doesn't mean your mom and I won't escape with you. The only thing I know for sure is that the Seekers will come for you tonight." He forced a smile that didn't reach his haunted eyes. I thought of the cards Madam Lupescu had dealt me. My possible futures. The Lovers or the Tower. Madam Lupescu said I had to make a choice, and I had, and I was sticking to it.

The Lovers.

I leaned toward him until I could feel his heat against mine. Then I opened my mouth against his and kissed him so deeply I felt I had fallen into a fire that burned without pain. Jeremy kept his hands at his sides, but I still felt his light trying to steal my mind away. I refused it, focusing on the feel of Jeremy. The aliveness of his skin. His lips.

We kissed until we forgot to breathe, and when we

finally broke apart, we were both panting. I noticed several buttons of Jeremy's shirt had come open—did I do that?— and I could see the jagged red mark etched on his skin, as though painted by an unsteady hand.

The branch of a lightning scar.

Jeremy saw the way my eyes fixated on the scar. "Do you want to see it?" he asked. I felt his breath on my face, hot enough to burn up the oxygen I was trying to load up on.

My mouth opened, but I was still working to catch my breath, so I only nodded. His fingers went to the buttons and undid three more and parted his shirt. The lightning scar was like some strange, alien rose. I touched it with my gloved fingers.

"It's beautiful," I said, and I meant it. On him, it was beautiful. On him, everything was beautiful.

Jeremy indicated my gloves. "You can take those off now, you know. You don't have to hide from me."

Without thinking, I pulled my hand away. "No," I said, and Jeremy's face fell. "I'm sorry. I'm not ready yet."

"It's all right," he said, but he sounded wounded. He'd let me see his lightning scar, and now I was hiding mine from him. "I should leave now, before the Apostles come looking for me. I've already stayed too long."

He stood, fastening the buttons on his shirt. He turned toward the door.

I was on my feet then, peeling off my gloves and dropping them to the floor. "Jeremy," I said, and when he turned back to face me I was holding my hands out to him, veins of red blazing across my palms, jagged life lines and love lines.

He came back to me, and looked at my hands. "They're

lovely," he said. I had never heard a guy my age say the word "lovely" like that.

I shook my head, wondering what Jeremy would think if he saw my whole body veined in red, and then I stopped thinking as Jeremy's arms wound around me and he pulled me to him again and his lips burned against mine.

He broke the kiss before another vision could blast through my consciousness.

I heard footsteps on the stairs leading up to the fourth floor. My whole body tensed, my spine going rigid.

Jeremy opened the door to find Iris on the other side, reaching for the doorknob. She eyed Jeremy suspiciously.

"Brother Jeremiah," she said, and then looked past him to where I stood.

I offered her my most sisterly smile. "Hello, Sister Iris," I said, adopting the sort of easy tone and slightly blank look I'd been walking around with all morning.

"Sister Mia," she said. Her gaze narrowed slightly before turning back to Jeremy. "Some of us are going out to minister to the Displaced on the beach. Will you join us, Brother? It's been a while since you graced us with your presence." She spoke pointedly, accusing without needing to, but Jeremy acted as though she were being nothing but civil.

"Of course," he said, and stepped out into the hall.

"What about me?" I asked, thinking that if Jeremy and Mom and I went out onto the beach, we might be able to make a run for it. We wouldn't have to wait for the Seekers to come to our rescue. But it would be difficult to drag Mom away. She would put up a fight, slow us down.

But Iris said to me, "Father wants to speak with you in his study." She smiled, and added, "Privately."

37

He'll know. That was the only thought in my head as I made my way to Prophet's study. Prophet would know I wasn't brainwashed anymore, and then he'd . . . what would he do? He couldn't kill me. He needed me. But my mom . . . he didn't need her.

I thought of what Mom had said to me repeatedly. *He wants me with him all the time.*

I was beginning to understand why Prophet brought her here. It had nothing to do with love, and everything to do with controlling me. She was a fail-safe. Even if my psychic brainwashing failed, he knew I wouldn't leave her, and if worse came to worst he could use her as a human shield.

I would just have to hope that worse wasn't about to get any worse.

I knocked on Prophet's study door and waited for him to call me inside. Instead, the door opened and Mom stood there, luminous in a long white satin dress with lace sleeves and lace at the bodice, and pearls and—

Oh, God.

It was a wedding dress.

"What do you think?" Mom asked, which led me to believe she misread the horror in my eyes as surprise.

"Mom, it's . . . where did it come from?" I asked.

"Rance sent out for it this morning." Her smile dimmed a little. "You don't like it?"

I blanked out my eyes and made my voice calm and accepting. "I do," I said, fighting not to cringe. "It's very modest. And classic. Classy. All of the above." *Shut up!*

Mom beamed and waved me inside Prophet's study. I gazed around. It wasn't what I'd expected, a shrine to Prophet's Old Testament God. It was plain. There were bookshelves lining the walls from floor to ceiling, but they contained no books. The only piece of furniture in the office was a mahogany desk with a large, leather-bound copy of the Bible open on its surface. I could see the letters, and they definitely weren't Braille. Prophet must have the passages he was interested in committed to memory.

Prophet sat in a massive leather chair behind the desk, turned away from us, facing the window that looked out on the beach and the ocean.

On the wall behind the desk was a small, empty display case, but if I had to guess what it was supposed to hold, a certain shiny object with a dangerous pointy end came to mind. The knife Jeremy had brought to my room a few nights back, that I'd seen Prophet use to slice open Jeremy's neck in a vision. Where was the knife now? I wondered.

Mom came around the desk to stand by Prophet, a good and loyal pet. He swiveled his chair to face me. "Mia," he said in greeting. Was it my imagination, or was there something different about the way he said my name now? His voice was cooler, more removed, as though—

No. Don't think about it. Be the other Mia. The one he wants you to be.

"Happy news," Prophet said. "Your mother and I have decided to wed."

"Wow," I said, forcing my voice to stay light, not to betray any of the panic that threatened to take hold inside me. "You two only met last night."

Was it me, or did Mom's smile seem stiff? "It's a little sudden, but—"

"Your mother and I feel like we've been together for years," Prophet cut in. "I would say it was love at first sight, but, well . . ."

He smiled at his joke. So did Mom. I hoisted the corners of my mouth as high as I could make them go, but they resisted. "So . . . when's the big day?"

"Tonight," the Prophet said, "at the revival."

My stomach churned. "Tonight? Not . . . you know . . . after the storm, when things have calmed down a bit?"

"God wishes our union to take place tonight. He was very clear about that."

"Great," I said. "Wonderful."

I looked at Mom, at her eyes, searching them for some sign that a part of her knew this was wrong.

"Something troubling you, Mia?" Prophet asked, as though he could see the truth on my face. Or read the thoughts I was doing a terrible job of keeping in check. But if he tried to read me, I would know it, wouldn't I? I'd feel that pressure in my mind, and the buzzing, like a fly trapped inside my skull. I kept waiting for the buzzing to start, but so far I remained the sole entity occupying my head.

"Isn't it bad luck for the groom to see the bride in her dress before the wedding?" I asked, and then wanted to slap my forehead. Prophet blinked his milky eyes at me slowly as a reminder.

"We don't believe in luck, good or bad," Prophet said. "There is only God's will and God's plan, and this is all part of that plan."

"Mia, I want you to be my maid of honor," Mom said. There was a dress bag hanging from one of the empty bookshelves. Mom removed it and carried it to me. "Rance ordered this especially for you and had it rushed over."

She laid the bag in my arms. It was heavy, like the dress was made of lead or something. "Thank you," I said, the words barely making it past my teeth.

"Thank you, *Father*," Prophet corrected.

I met his eyes, and behind the thick cataracts I could see the black of his pupils muted to gray, and I got the telltale-heart urge to rip that muscle out of his chest, not to bury it beneath the floorboards, but to unleash the fire in my own heart and burn it black.

You could do it, a voice spoke inside me. *You could kill him now. Use the fire inside, like you did on the bridge. Strike Prophet down and get it over with.*

But Mom was standing next to him again, and there was no guarantee I could take Prophet down without hitting Mom, too. It wasn't like I'd been practicing. Prophet was right. I had no control over my Spark or my Light or whatever it was.

So I would wait.

"Thank you, Father," I murmured.

He smiled. "Go try on the dress. I do hope it fits."

* * *

It fit perfectly, the long white satin dress with high collar and matching satin gloves, and—oh, God, who knew it was possible?—white satin ankle boots. I hated it, but once I had it on I didn't take it off. I lay down on my bed and watched the light shift on the ceiling as the sun plunged toward the horizon.

Jeremy came for me shortly before sunset.

I held out my arms. "I suppose this is what happens when a blind man picks out a dress for you."

I wanted him to laugh. I'd never heard Jeremy laugh. Maybe he'd lost that ability.

Instead, he brushed the backs of his knuckles along the satin sleeve of the dress. "Mia, whatever happens tonight, the only thing that matters is that you get as far away from Prophet as you can. When the time comes, don't hesitate, even if it means leaving me or . . . or your mom behind."

I shook my head. "It's all of us or none of us."

Jeremy gritted his teeth, as though in pain. His neck muscles clenched. "That might not be an option. Remember what's at stake. Promise me you'll leave us behind if you have to."

"Jeremy—"

"Promise me!" He was shaking, his eyes slightly rolled back in his head, lashes twitching.

"I promise," I said, realizing suddenly what was happening. He was mid-vision, and whatever he saw hinged on my decision to leave without him and my mom if it came to that.

I moved closer to Jeremy, so my mouth was nearly on his. "I promise," I said again, and instantly he stopped shaking.

He looked at me, his eyes haunted. "It's time," he said.

* * *

The sun was setting fire to the horizon by the time our wedding procession started across the beach, through Tentville. Bonfires and cookfires were being lit, and the smells of oily smoke and charring meat hung heavy in the air. Everyone watched us, Followers and Displaced alike, as though we were royalty taking a shortcut through their pathetic little village.

I wondered how many of these Followers had the Spark. How many had Prophet recruited during his revivals? More than the Seekers found in their two hundred years of seeking? Had Parker managed to recruit anyone in the single night he'd had to do it?

As the sky faded from pink to lavender to blue, fog began to roll in off the ocean. It settled around the shoulders of the Followers like wreaths. There were thousands of them on the beach. Tens of thousands, maybe. There was no way they would fit in the tent. They hardly fit on the sand.

Prophet, in a white suit and white silk tie, strode across the beach with my mom on his arm, her dress swishing around her feet. In the blazing light of the setting sun, her skin glowed red-gold, and the scars on her face were almost invisible. She closed her eyes and leaned her head against Prophet's shoulder and let him lead their way.

Jeremy and I followed behind Mom and Prophet. The rest of the Apostles trailed behind us, two by two, Iris and Ivan right behind Jeremy and me. I could feel Iris's glare on my back, like laser beams trying to sear holes in me.

Ahead of us, Prophet's White Tent was already filling

with his Followers. He'd done his final broadcast of *The Hour of Light*, and announced his wedding plans. Every Follower in Los Angeles would be here tonight. All part of Prophet's plan.

I thought of what Parker had told me about religious mysticism, and African rituals that brought rain during a drought, and how if you get enough people together who believe the same thing, miracles can happen. That it was about energy and focus and creating a collective consciousness. What if you packed thousands of people together in one place who'd been psychically brainwashed to believe a storm was coming and the world was going to end? And what if a bunch of those people possessed a sort of mystical power of their own that was all about energy? What then? Would a miracle happen? Would they, through thought and energy and intent, create the future they believed in?

I was about to find out.

Although there were thousands of eyes on me, I felt the prickling sensation of being watched by one pair in particular. I searched the crowd and spotted a boy's face peering out at me from one of the tents. A face framed by a fall of heavy blond hair.

The boy nodded at me.

I turned my eyes away before anyone saw where I was looking.

I supposed I shouldn't have been surprised to see him. Parker wouldn't miss our mom's wedding. Not for the world.

38

The White Tent was already at capacity by the time we entered. A hush settled over the crowd when they saw us, and the Followers parted, opening a clear path to the raised platform at the center of the tent.

Tonight the media had not been allowed inside, but the piano player was present and the music had already started. I found myself falling into step with the song, doing the traditional bridesmaid walk. I pasted a serene expression on my face as I gazed around at the Followers, smiled and nodded at them, playing the part of an Apostle chosen by God. My eyes landed on Rachel and her Follower gang from Skyline. Rachel's hair was pulled back especially tight for the occasion, making her already buggy eyes protrude like a pug's. But when she saw me in the wedding party, her eyes went even wider. I showed her lots of teeth, but I wasn't smiling.

"Congratulations to you and your mother," a high-pitched voice whispered close to my ear. My head snapped toward it and I found the Dealer's face so close to mine I could taste his breath.

I recoiled, my heart hammering. Jeremy took my elbow to lead me along, watching the Dealer like he was a snake whose fangs had been removed but who still found ways of delivering poison.

We ascended the steps onto the platform. Prophet whispered something to Mom, and she nodded and led him to the microphone. Like a flock of birds falling into formation, the Apostles made a half circle behind Prophet and Mom, boys on one side, girls on the other, and Jeremy and I were forced to separate so he could stand right at Prophet's side, and I at Mom's. The best man and the maid of honor. I realized I was still connected to the Apostles in the same way the Seekers were, bonded as conductors of one another's energy. When we were together, we moved as one. Whatever Prophet had done to us had linked us, and that link had not been severed at the same moment as his brainwashing had. I wondered if the bond was permanent. I didn't like that idea, not at all.

Prophet made a cutting motion with his hand, and the music ceased. A heavy silence followed. The crowd was utterly still, thousands of faces staring up at us. I searched those faces for the Seekers, Katrina and Mr. Kale, Schiz and Quentin, and my brother. Were they out there right now, dressed in white so as not to call attention to themselves until the right moment?

The silence stretched. I could hear the ocean beyond the tent, wave after wave crashing against the shore. Outside, a wind had picked up and begun to howl, beating at the White Tent, making the walls flap. I could see the flames of bonfires against those white walls, orange flowers of monstrous size, flickering behind the canvas, throwing their light against it.

Come on, Seekers . . . what are you waiting for, a priest to ask if anyone objects? There was no priest that I could see, but I supposed Prophet being Prophet could handle the ceremony himself.

"Brothers and sisters," Prophet finally spoke into the mic, his resonant voice filling the vast tent. "I welcome you tonight with my whole heart. There are no people in the world I would rather share my joy with than you, God's truest Followers. On this, the last night of earth as we know it, I ask you to join hands, each and every one of you, and share your light with us. Let light blaze from your hearts and hands until it becomes a fire. A holy fire of God!"

I expected cheering, but there was only the *shush* of feet moving in the sand, of fabric brushing against fabric and skin brushing against skin as thousands of Followers joined hands, their expressions a mixture of reverence and eagerness. Their eyes were animated with feverish intensity.

"Tonight," Prophet called out. "On my wedding night, the Church of Light becomes the Church of Fire! Give me your light, good people! Give me your fire! So long as you hold to one another, your fire will burn, and you will be protected as the storm rages!"

I tried not to show alarm, but I was certain my mask of serenity was crumbling. It was bad enough that the tent was so packed people had to stand shoulder to shoulder, but now everyone had linked hands, forming layer upon layer of human fencing around the platform.

Stay calm, I instructed myself. *Jeremy saw the Seekers rescue you. They'll be here. They* are *here.*

But the things Jeremy saw didn't always happen. They were constantly changing.

I'd seen Parker, so I knew the Seekers were nearby, but

that didn't mean they'd be able to get to us through the linked Followers.

Prophet went on. "God has blessed me with the love of this good woman, Sarah Price, whose hand I will take in marriage this night . . ." He took Mom's hand and drew her close to him. "But God has also blessed me with her daughter . . . Mia." His milky eyes located me, and I felt the attention in the room shift in my direction. I wanted to shrink to the size of nothing, disappear and leave the horrible bridesmaid dress standing in my place on the platform.

"I ask now that Mia join hands in a circle with the rest of my children as Sarah and I exchange our vows."

I blinked in slow motion. I looked at Jeremy and saw his eyes widening in shock, and then in realization, and then in dread. He shook his head slightly, as though to negate what he was thinking. What we were both thinking.

In the last vision he'd shown me, there'd been a circle of Apostles atop the roof of the Tower, our hands linked, power vibrating from us until the air thickened. Then the storm had burst into being over our heads. But it wasn't supposed to happen here, at the beach. It was supposed to happen at the Tower!

The Apostles joined hands, their half circle growing around us.

Mom smiled at me. "Go on," she said softly. "Join the circle, Mia."

Prophet's eyes lit on me.

Join the circle, Mia, his voice spoke in my mind. *I need your Light. I need your Fire.*

Oh, no. Oh, God, if you exist, no. Don't do this to me.

Join them! This time Prophet barked his order in my mind. *Do it, or I will take your mother's life and send her soul back into darkness. Do not doubt me.*

My eyes flew wildly, searching the crowd for help, for the Seekers I should have listened to when I had the chance. But if they were present, they weren't standing up to say they objected.

"Mia?" Mom's smile wilted. "Go on. Take their hands."

My gaze fell on Jeremy next, and I saw he had closed his eyes, the muscles of his neck taut, lashes flickering, eyes moving beneath his lids.

Then his eyes flashed wide and found mine and in them I saw that we had made a mistake.

There had been a change of plan.

I didn't move. The crowd began to murmur.

Close the circle, Prophet demanded. *Or you will watch your mother die tonight, and you will know that it happened because of you. Because you refused to play your part.*

I was the missing ingredient needed to make the storm. If I refused to comply, there would be no storm. No beginning of the end. The world would go on.

Mom's face had fallen. She stared at me, her eyes filling with tears. "Please, Mia," she begged in a whisper. "Do as your father says."

I shook my head. "He'll *never* be my father."

Prophet's lips peeled back from his whiter than white teeth, but before he could say a word, something outside exploded and orange light blasted the side of the tent. Screams went up from the crowd as hungry flames began to consume the canvas.

"It begins!" Prophet boomed into the microphone. "Stay where you are, brothers and sisters! Do not run from the fire of our enemies, for their fire is weak and temporal! Do not let go of your neighbor's hand! We must stand together now as a united front against those who would challenge God's will!"

More explosions, on all sides now. It was the bonfires, I realized. The bonfires growing in huge bursts and then receding. Growing and receding, like people were throwing gallons of gasoline onto the flames. I didn't know if that was actually what was happening outside, but I did know one thing for sure.

The Seekers had come for me.

I grabbed Mom's hand and yanked her away from Prophet, darting toward the edge of the platform. My eyes flew to Jeremy to make sure he was coming, but he stayed where he was. It took me a moment to realize why.

The Apostles had closed their circle around us. I could feel their combined power stirring the air until it condensed like fog . . . like clouds. The pressure in the air had dropped, the way it did before a storm, and I could feel every hair on my body rising to attention. My eardrums needed to pop. The Apostles had started without me. But they were missing an element. I was the final ingredient. I was the lightning.

I thought of the game I used to play as a kid . . . Red Rover.

Red Rover, Red Rover, send Mia on over.

Could we break through those linked hands?

Red Rover, Red Rover, send Jeremy on over.

And even if we could, would we be able to make it past the Followers? Their faces were determined, their hands grasped tighter than ever.

We were trapped.

More explosions of fire and light from outside. The walls of the tent were burning slowly. They must have been treated with fire retardant, the opposite of the Dealer's tent, but that didn't mean the tent was fireproof. Still, most of the Followers did not look worried. They seemed at peace with the idea that they might burn to death inside the White Tent . . . meet their end before the world got a chance to be destroyed by their angry, pessimist God.

The only Follower who looked less than content to fry with his comrades was the Dealer. His lips and lids were peeled back, so he was all teeth and eyes. But he couldn't bolt if he wanted to. He was fenced in with the rest of us.

Gray masses of cloud were forming inside the tent. Anyone who didn't know better might think it was smoke from the burning walls, but it wasn't. It was the moisture in the air condensing into clouds.

There was a commotion near the entrance to the White Tent. I saw the bald-headed Cro-Magnon-looking Follower from the night before, shoving at someone, yelling. But he was one of the only Followers not linked hand in hand with the rest, and none of the others would disobey their Prophet and break the circle to come to Cro-Magnon's aid. Cro-Magnon was thrust aside and newcomers began to pour into the tent. Not Followers.

In they came, dozens of Seekers in their red cloaks and emotionless black masks, gliding over the sand. They were an intimidating sight, but the Followers did not release one another, and there were so many more in white than in red. But the Seekers kept coming, until they formed their own red circle around the mass of white.

Where was Parker? I hoped he was safe outside the flaming walls of the White Tent, if there was such a thing as safe anymore.

One of the Seekers spoke then, shouting to be heard above the crackling of flames. I recognized the hard-boiled growl instantly, despite the black mask concealing his face.

"Release your Followers, false prophet," Mr. Kale called. "Their part in this is over."

Prophet only smiled. "Their faith cannot be shaken. They know I am a true prophet of God."

In answer, Mr. Kale stepped from the circle of Seekers, and the two Seekers to either side of him placed their hands on his shoulders. I felt the energy in the room vibrating my skin. The Seekers seemed to shine with an eerie reddish glow, something I could only see if I didn't look for it. But out of the corner of my eye, it was there.

A nervous murmur rippled through the crowd of Followers.

Mr. Kale placed his hands, one on each of two Followers' heads. Prophet must have sensed something happening that was not part of his plan. His smile was now made of gritted teeth.

"Call this a test of their faith," Mr. Kale called, and his hands clamped tight on the Followers' heads. They bucked, and tried to jerk away, but Mr. Kale held tight. The glow of red light coming from the Seekers intensified for a heartbeat, and suddenly the same red light pulsed from beneath

Mr. Kale's hands. The whole outer ring of Followers, not just the two whose heads Mr. Kale had palmed, writhed and cried out. A few screamed in agony so piercing I wanted to cover my ears to shut out the sound.

Then the outer ring of Followers dropped hands. They looked at one another, dazed, saw the flames devouring the tent walls.

And they ran.

"Their faith is not as strong as you think," Mr. Kale called to Prophet. "I'm coming for you."

Mr. Kale grabbed another set of heads and did the same thing, releasing another layer of Follower fencing. Only about fifty more to go. I didn't know if Mr. Kale was breaking Prophet's hold on these people, or simply commanding them to do what a part of them must want to, which was get out of this flaming death trap. I didn't really care, so long as he worked quickly. Fire was rising up the walls, and the air was black with combined smoke and the clouds still condensing in the air. I could barely see the Seekers anymore. But while the clouds were rising, permeating the ceiling of the tent to ascend into the sky, the smoke was trapped inside. The ceiling was high, but it wouldn't take more than a few minutes for the smoke to spread down to us. Already my eyes were burning, my lungs starting to reject the air I breathed.

The Dealer craned his head to see what was happening near the entrance. I saw a look of relief cross his face when he realized what Mr. Kale was doing. But Mr. Kale was still far away, and the Dealer was linked in one of the circles closest to the platform. The smoke was descending, the inside of the tent heating like an oven.

A sudden, wild cry escaped the Dealer's lips. His brain-washing must have been tenuous, because he wrenched his hands from those of the Followers on either side of him and broke for the exit.

He didn't get far.

"Coward!" cried one of the Followers whose hand the Dealer had held, a chubby, middle-aged woman, who had a sweet, round-cheeked face but the deadest eyes I'd ever seen. She kicked the Dealer square in the crotch and he fell to his knees. "After Prophet healed you! Traitor!" she squalled. She linked with the other Follower whose hand the Dealer had dropped, the two of them pummeling the Dealer with their bare feet, smashing at him with their heels. Other Followers within kicking reach joined in the fun. Rachel was one of them. She kicked at the Dealer with manic glee in her popping eyes.

"This is what happens when you defy Prophet!" Rachel shouted, but she threw her words at me rather than the man she'd just stomped.

The Dealer writhed in the sand, and then began to twitch, and finally stilled altogether.

How were we going to get out of here? Mr. Kale couldn't deprogram everyone before we were asphyxiated. Even if I could get past the Apostles, I'd have hundreds of Followers to contend with. They'd beat us to death before we got ten feet from the platform.

I blinked the sting out of my eyes, and when they cleared, I finally saw through the murky air the person I'd been looking for. He'd entered the tent with several other red-cloaked Seekers, and when he saw me he lowered his mask to show me his face. Show me he was here for me.

"Parker!" I shouted, tugging Mom's arm again. "Mom, come on. Parker's here!"

Distracted by the sight of my brother, my grip on Mom's arm must have loosened. She tore away from me. I whirled to see her rushing back to Prophet's side. He curled one arm around her smoothly, as though he'd been expecting her. With the other hand he reached beneath the lapel of his white suit coat. I caught a flash of silver as he withdrew that familiar knife with the smooth, wickedly sharp blade. Mom continued to cling to Prophet, even when he pressed the blade to her neck. She actually sighed and tilted her head back to reveal more of her vulnerable skin.

A part of her wants this. A part of her wants to die.

"No!" I refused to let her go, let her give up.

I moved toward her, but Prophet either sensed my motion or caught the blur of it in his faded vision. He slid the knife blade against Mom's neck and blood appeared and trailed down her throat and beaded on her satin gown, dark pearls among the white.

Some people in the crowd gasped in shock, but they stayed where they were. Even the sight of their beloved Prophet with a knife to an innocent woman's neck did not break the hold he had over them.

The sight of my mother's blood made a bomb go off inside me. Fire charged through my bloodstream until it gathered in my hands. I felt the air around me begin to crackle with the energy.

"Join the circle," Prophet said, this time out loud, and slid the knife farther along Mom's throat, sawing through her skin. More blood streamed. Mom was smiling again. Gazing back into Prophet's milky eyes and smiling.

"I love you," she said.

In answer, Prophet cut deeper.

"Mia." Jeremy was staring at my hands.

I looked down and saw what he saw. My hands were on fire.

No. Not on fire, but glowing with a light the color of blood, and they were so hot. So very hot. Little red threads of energy emerged from my palms and squirmed, as though searching for something to attach to. Halos of red light beamed around my hands.

"Join the circle," Prophet said again, with finality in his voice, and I knew this was the last time he would tell me.

"Mia, you can't," Jeremy pleaded. "You know what will happen."

I met Jeremy's eyes, but only for a moment before I had to look away. Before I held out my hands to the Apostles, my heart exploding with fury and desperation. Prophet would cut my mother's throat if I didn't do this, and I would watch her die. I couldn't let it happen. I couldn't watch my mother die, knowing I had failed to save her. Failed her one final time.

So instead I would fail the world.

Maybe the storm wouldn't bring another earthquake, a part of me thought. Maybe Prophet's plan would fail, even if I gave him the lightning.

But another part of me knew the truth; knew Prophet's plan would work because Jeremy had seen it work a thousand times.

The Apostles broke their circle and received me, and when my hands joined with theirs I felt the crackling fire-storm surge out from my heart, through my arms to my hands and into the circle. Ivan and Iris, the Apostles to my right and left, screamed in agony as I scorched them, but they didn't let go. They couldn't if they'd wanted to. I'd welded them to me. Threads of bloodred energy wound around their arms and grew and lengthened, stretching like my lightning scars to encompass the Apostles. There was terror in their eyes as the energy twisted around their limbs and torsos, wrapping them completely. Cocooning them in blood lightning.

I felt the charge on my skin as the haze of storm clouds above us thickened and bunched, clouds darkening to the color of ink, permeated with electricity. With *my* electricity. The clouds filled the tent and pushed through the ceiling and into the air outside. Rain began to patter on the roof of the tent.

And then crimson light blasted the sky, and thunder detonated.

"Thy will be done!" A maniac grin spread on Prophet's face as lightning lit up the sky and thunder boomed again. And I found I was grinning, too, caught in the thrill of the lightning, feeling it all over my skin, feeling more alive than I ever had before, and I wanted it to go on and on. This was no regular storm. This was *my* storm, and it had been waiting such a long time to get out.

"Mia!"

I barely heard the voice hidden beneath the sound of thunder. If it hadn't been a voice I knew better than any other, I might have missed it.

"Parker." My voice seemed to come from a hundred miles away.

I turned my head to look over my shoulder and saw him there. My little brother, moving toward the platform behind the rest of the Seekers as Mr. Kale cut a path. But slowly. Too slowly.

They were too late. The storm had already begun, and now it was moving. I could already feel it traveling away from us, and quickly, as though something were pulling it, reeling it in.

The Waste. The energy there, humming like a power plant under the ground . . . it was like the Spark or the Light. What you called it didn't matter. It was energy, and certain types of energy attract other types of energy. A positive charge attracts a negative charge. I had given my energy, the energy stored inside me, to the storm, but clouds were not an efficient storage container. Clouds sought to release their energy, to connect to the right source.

And they would find that source in the Waste, deep in the chasms that cracked the surface of the earth.

The sixth seal. The Puente Hills Fault.

But the sight of Parker broke the trance the lightning held me in, and Jeremy, detecting the change, took two steps and stood before me. Red light washed his face. My heart . . . my incinerator of a heart . . . ached for him. I didn't want to cause him more pain, but I seemed destined to do so.

"Mia, take back your hands," he said softly.

I nodded, but when I tried to pull my hands away, to break the circle, I found it impossible. I had fused myself to the Apostles.

"I knew you couldn't be trusted," Iris said through the

pain of being linked to me. "But you played your part any-way, didn't you? You gave Father what he wanted." Her smile was hate. It was triumph.

I tried again to jerk my arms away, and nearly dislocated my shoulder. Merely pulling away from them wouldn't work. I had to withdraw my energy, pull it back inside my-self. But I had no idea how to do that.

The sky lit up, so bright I was momentarily blinded. An earsplitting crack of thunder sounded.

When my vision returned, I saw Prophet over Jeremy's shoulder . . . his eyes wild with rapture. He still held the knife to Mom's throat. "You're too late," he called, and he didn't need the mic to make his voice heard throughout the tent. "The storm is moving toward the Waste! Soon the ground will quake, and the last Tower will fall, and the evil children of this city will fall with it. Here is where the end begins!"

His grip on Mom had tightened as he spoke, and with his last words he convulsed as though in exaltation. The blade of the knife he still had pressed to her neck bit deep and her eyes widened, and blood . . . so much blood . . . poured from her throat.

"Nooo!" I screamed, and in one agonizing rush sucked back the energy that wrapped the Apostles, rent my hands away, and shattered the circle. A great surge of energy went up like a mushroom cloud, and the Apostles cried out and fell back, tumbling off the side of the platform onto the Followers. Pain like my bones were breaking and my muscles snapping ripped through my body. But the pain didn't matter.

Jeremy grabbed me and held me back. I fought and kicked to get free, but he wouldn't let me go.

Mom's body had gone limp in Prophet's arms. Prophet's mouth was parted in confusion. I realized he didn't know what he'd done, didn't understand why Mom had turned into a life-size doll in his arms. He couldn't see her.

Then he must have felt the blood soaking Mom's white dress, spreading until the dress was more red than white, because he shook his head and his mouth formed "No."

Mom's eyes were still open. She looked at me. *She.* The Mom I knew. The one from before Prophet. Before the quake. The one I'd thought was gone forever.

And now she really would be.

She opened her mouth as if to speak, but her vocal cords must have been severed, for nothing came out. She sagged, dead weight in Prophet's arms.

Prophet's eyes rolled upward toward a sky strobing with electricity.

Everything in me turned red. I wrestled against Jeremy's hold and suddenly broke free. Jeremy slumped to the ground, his eyes twitching behind his lids as a vision stole him away.

I left him lying there and stepped toward Prophet. "Look at me," I said.

Prophet brought his blind eyes to mine. "This was not part of the plan," he said. "She wasn't supposed to die."

I raised my hands, heat boiling and crackling in my palms. That bloodred light had seared away my white satin gloves; new veins of light, like incandescent wire, grew from my hands.

"I don't have a plan," I said. I concentrated every ounce of will into my palms, and then . . . I let go.

All the years I had held on, fighting for control, struggling to keep the fire trapped inside me . . . I let it go. Everything I hadn't given to the storm went into Prophet.

Red branches of light thick as rope blasted from my hands and entered Prophet's body. He released Mom and let her slip to the ground, but not before a few stray veins of light entered her as well and made her jolt. Her back arched momentarily as the veins wrapped her and sank inside her.

She slipped from Prophet's arms and landed in the growing puddle of her blood.

Then the lightning was for Prophet only.

Prophet's mouth screamed without sound, but the Followers, so many thousands and thousands of Followers, screamed for him. The tent was filled with their deafening banshee shrieks. Prophet's lush white polar-bear hair sizzled to ash and snowed from his head. His white suit exploded in tatters of black cloth and his skin turned to charcoal, and then cracked to reveal the blood and muscle underneath the charred skin.

I let go and let go and let go until Prophet was unrecognizable as anything that had ever been human. I emptied the fire until there was nothing left.

Then the lightning was gone, and despite the flames that ate the tent walls, everything seemed dark in comparison.

The congregation's collective paralysis broke then. Followers ran for their lives. I saw Iris mowed down. Ivan tried to help her up, and then he fell, too, and I didn't see either of them get up. Rachel with her Skyline gang tried to rally people to stay and fight, but first her gang deserted her, then the rest of the Followers shoved her aside. Prophet's hold on them had been broken, and now everything was chaos and confusion.

Finally, Rachel seemed to realize she was no longer under Prophet's control, and she, too, broke for the exit.

The Seekers fought their way toward the platform, their hands no longer linked.

I registered all of this, and cared about none of it.

I fell to my knees beside Mom's body and gathered her to me. She was so light, but her blood weighted the wedding dress like stones sewn into the hems.

I should have been crying, but I wasn't. I felt hollow inside, like some essential part of me, maybe my soul, had vacated with the lightning. I was distantly aware that my bare hands were now truly bare. The scars were gone. I wondered if they were gone from my entire body now that I'd finally released the lightning.

I held Mom's body and rocked her, and I didn't look up until Parker was beside me. I released a shuddering breath. A breath of giving up. We had to get out of here. The smoke was pressing down toward us and I could feel heat from the flaming tent walls. Time to pick up Mom's body and take her out of here. At least Parker would be with me for that. I didn't think I could do it without him.

Prophet's body could stay here. His Followers and his Apostles had left him. He would remain here alone while everything white turned as black as his charred remains.

I looked at Parker, expecting his face to mirror my own feelings. But he was . . . smiling? No, he couldn't be smiling. Unless he'd lost his mind, or my smoke-filled eyes were playing tricks on me, or—

Or . . .

I followed my brother's eyes to Mom's.

They were open. And they were alive. Not alive on the way toward dead, but *really* alive.

Mom reached up and touched her neck, where Prophet had cut her. But the blood was no longer flowing from the cut. She had a new scar, or what would become a scar in time. The wound was cauterized, a long line of red-black tissue. It wasn't pretty, this cauterization, but it had sealed the wound and kept the blood in.

I thought of those stray veins of light that had wriggled over Mom's body when I struck Prophet. I almost laughed, thinking of the one thing I knew for certain about lightning: it was unpredictable. When it struck, you never knew what effect it would have.

Mom was alive, sitting up. I found I was crying, and Parker was crying, and then we had our arms around each other.

Then lightning lit up the sky, burning through my relief and thrilling my skin, reminding me that this night wasn't over. There was something I still had to do. The storm was traveling to the Waste, and I had to get there first.

I had to take back the lightning I had given to the storm.

People were coughing violently.

"We need to get out of here," I heard someone say. It sounded like Mr. Kale, but maybe everyone sounded like Mr. Kale with smoke in their throats.

Jeremy was easy to spot among the Seekers. He was the only one dressed in white.

"Can you get me to the Waste?" I asked, already knowing what the answer would be.

He nodded. The sadness and rage were gone from his eyes, replaced with grim determination.

I turned to Parker. He had Mom propped up against him, her face as white as her dress used to be. She'd lost a lot of blood before I'd sealed the cut in her neck. It was soaked into her wedding dress, turning it the color of the Seekers' cloaks.

One of the Seekers standing nearby removed her black mask. "Don't worry," Katrina said. "We'll get your mom to a hospital. Do what you need to do."

Her eyes strayed to the hunk of blackened flesh that was Prophet. "Thank you," she said. She leaned against her uncle, and Mr. Kale nodded at me. "Thank you," he echoed.

There was no time for long goodbyes. To Parker, I said, "Take care of Mom."

"Where are you going?" he asked, alarmed, his body tensing like he might try to grab me, stop me from leaving. But he didn't let go of our mom.

I took a moment to touch his arm, and his eyes widened slightly. He looked at my hand.

"I can feel it," he said, his voice awed. "Your Spark."

"Goodbye, Parker." The note of finality in my voice was hard to miss, but Parker didn't try to stop me from what I had to do. He let me go.

I can't say I would've done the same for him.

39

Wind howled through the Waste, and my skin howled with it. The sky overhead was still clear, but I could see the storm moving toward us. How long until it arrived? It was impossible to judge, seeing as how this was no natural storm, but a man-made one.

A Mia-made storm.

There were no sentries with tranq guns guarding the ramp that led into the Waste tonight. Perhaps they'd gotten the word that the rovers were first on God's hit list and decided to err on the side of caution and steer clear of the Rove.

Jeremy navigated his bike through ravaged streets of the Waste, driving so fast that any accident would equal us dead. But if we didn't make it to the Tower in time, we might as well be, anyway.

When he stopped the bike and we got off, my feet stuck to the spot where I stood, my whole body paralyzed by the rush of red-hot pins and needles prickling my skin. With the pain came exhilaration, a kind of euphoria that let me know I was alive, that I was connected to everything, every molecule that surrounded me. There was no point at which my body ended and everything else began. This was the feeling, this longing to join with something larger than myself, that had gotten me struck so many countless times. But I had never felt it this strongly. I had loaned the lightning to this storm, and I could feel it wanting to return to me.

I closed my eyes and let the glass dust shower my face and burrow into my skin.

"See you soon," I whispered to the storm. I promised.

I turned to Jeremy and saw his eyes were closed, too. His lashes flickering. And then his eyes flashed open and I saw fear. Nothing but fear.

He turned his eyes away from mine.

And I returned to aching for the storm.

Jeremy and I ran through the Waste with the wind in our faces, blasting us with cement and glass dust. We shielded our eyes against the spray. Looking down at myself, I saw I was sparkling from the glass particles that clung to my bridesmaid dress.

My skin thrilled as a roiling black cloudbank massed over the city, marching steadily east. Bloodred light pulsed behind the clouds, and my skin throbbed with the charge. But the fire in my chest did not light up. I had released the fire, and now it was burning in the sky.

Lightning flashed. I counted softly. "One-Mississippi, two-Mississippi, three-Mississippi . . ." I reached six and thunder boomed. I felt it, a quake beneath my skin.

The storm was six miles off. Maybe less. We had to

hurry. Had to get to the top of the Tower, as close to the storm as possible. This was one instance when it would not do to arrive fashionably late for the party.

We were close to the Tower now, and faint music could be heard from far above us.

From the top of the world.

But something wasn't right. The rovers had abandoned the use of black lights to mask their locations. A spotlight on top of the Tower revolved and beamed a circle against the sky, and there was light on other floors of the Tower, too. On almost every floor. It wasn't bright, but it was there, and the closer we came, the more I could make out, through the windows, figures moving and dancing. The many pounding beats coming from different DJs on so many floors was a crazy-making pandemonium of noise, especially with thunder crashing around inside my head.

"He filled the Tower," I said in a voice the wind tried to take. "There must be thousands of people in there!" Thousands more dead. But they would be just the beginning. The first to die.

I would not let that happen.

We ran like we were racing the wind, but when we came to the front doors of the Tower, Jeremy stopped me.

"Mia—" His words choked off, thick with emotion.

I frowned. "What is it?"

He shook his head. His eyes slid away. I remembered his dark lashes flickering; his eyes flashing open.

"Jeremy . . ." I still loved saying his name. "Did you see something new? About me?"

A muscle in his cheek jumped. He turned his eyes back to mine. "No," he said, and then so softly I could barely

hear him over the thunder, "nothing I haven't seen before."

I planted my hands on both sides of his face, and felt the
heat of him on my palms. I guided his mouth onto mine,
and the warmth became a fire and the fire melted us until
there was no stop between him and me.

But no vision opened inside my mind. Jeremy wouldn't
let me see it.

I pulled away from him, breathing hard and fast. "Why
won't you show me?"

He shook his head, shook it like he could loose the vision he was keeping from me. I pounded my fists against
his chest. He was a statue, hands clenched at his sides.

I gave up and let my head fall forward. "It doesn't matter," I said. "I already know what you saw." *The vision of
martyrs.* Emotion tried to dam the words in my throat. "I'm
going to die."

At least Parker and Mom would be safe. And the world
would go on. I would make sure of it.

Not everyone has to die a martyr, I remembered telling
Mr. Kale.

Not everyone. But me . . . yes.

I raised my head and looked into Jeremy's eyes, and
I saw my death there. He didn't have to touch me to show
it to me.

I took a deep, shuddering breath, and I kissed him again,
not so that I could see my end, but so I could feel what
might have been.

The Lovers and the Tower.

Maybe there had never really been a choice.

I kissed Jeremy like it was the last time, because it was.

The elevator doors opened onto the roof, and we were assaulted simultaneously by wind and music. I didn't know which was louder, but the rushing air made my skin seem to writhe over my muscles, as though the particles of matter that made me were coming unbound, pulling apart.

I gasped in pain. In agony. And I yearned for it to go on and on. Sensation roared through me. The siren song of the storm played on my skin, in my bones, in my blood.

We stepped out onto the roof. Near the elevator door, a DJ with wild, dirty dreads spun out his beats on twin turntables. The floor was packed with rovers, here to celebrate the beginning of the end at the top of the world.

A brilliant flash of red cut the sky, leaving an afterimage like a bloody wound. Rovers gasped, but kept on dancing, fingers pointed at the clouds.

My heart felt like it would tear through my chest, and my breath shortened to gasps.

"We have to get them out of here," I panted. "The storm will be here any minute!"

Jeremy stepped behind the turntables and grabbed the DJ's mic.

"Not again, man!" the DJ protested, but Jeremy shoved him back. Suddenly, the music went silent, and there was only the scream of the wind and hundreds of confused-looking rovers who wanted to know what had happened to the music.

My heart pounded in swells, each beat a crashing wave.

The storm was nearly here. Black cotton clouds, mountain clouds, anvil clouds were pressing toward us.

Lightning flashed and pulsed. As much light as darkness in the sky.

"One-Mississippi, two-Mississippi, three-Mississippi—"

Thunder shook the air.

We were running out of time. Always running out of time.

Then, a voice amplified through the speakers—Jeremy's voice.

"Listen to me. Everyone listen! It's not safe for you here. Please vacate the building as quickly as you can."

"We're not going anywhere! This is where we belong!" I looked for the owner of the voice and found a familiar face. Jude, the girl I'd helped Katrina recruit the other night. Everyone had stopped dancing, and stood staring at me now. Their eyes were unnaturally calm, and I realized these were not just any rovers. They didn't need red cloaks and black masks to make them recognizable as Seekers. I could see it in the way they ceased dancing at once, the way they had begun to move in formation, like there was some invisible thread connecting them. In fact, the only person who didn't seem to have some idea what was happening was the DJ.

I turned from them and faced west, toward the coming storm. Lightning stuttered through the sky over Koreatown.

"Not long now," I said, and my voice sounded faint, like the voice of someone leaving. Someone almost gone.

Far below, I saw the lights of dozens of vehicles entering the Waste, heading toward the Tower. More rovers? I wondered. They should have come earlier. They'd missed the party.

The storm was nearly here, and I was feeling less and

less whole. I was breaking apart, particles of me starting to rise into the air.

I moved to the center of the roof, amid the rovers. I could feel the Spark humming off them, crackling against my skin. The energy that brought them here in the first place. I thought of the Tower card I had drawn; the people falling to their deaths.

Jeremy dropped the mic and began forcing his way through the crowd toward me.

"You should go now," I told him. "It's not safe for you either."

He shook his head. "I'm staying."

"Then stay back." I looked around at the rovers. Their eyes were for me. "All of you, stay back."

The rovers backed away, but Jeremy didn't move. I looked at him, and for a moment I started to feel whole again, the particles of me that had risen descending toward me.

"Mia—" he began, and then lightning flashed, and thunder rent the air, swallowing his words.

Lightning shot through the clouds, reaching for me, and thunder jarred the night, seeming to shake the Tower to its very foundation. My arms shot toward the sky. The first drops of rain splattered my palms.

As lightning streaked and pulsed and branched across the clouds, my blood screamed for more. My skin itched to drink in the heat.

"One-Mississippi—"

Crash!

The elevator dinged open, and red-cloaked Seekers poured from inside, moving as one. They melted into the circle the rovers had formed around the roof and joined hands, as though the action were instinctual.

Jeremy did not join them. He couldn't, I realized, because he was not bonded to them. He could not share his power with them. He stood separate, as close and as far away from me as he could allow himself to be.

More lightning. More thunder. Light and noise, blinding and deafening.

I felt like my skin was going to peel right off my flesh.

Another spurt of rain splattered the roof, and then the downpour began. The electricity in the air went wild; my Spark responded like my body was strapped with explosives. Every hair stood on end. My ears rang. I tasted copper and knew I'd bitten my tongue.

I turned my face to the clouds. "Come back to me," I whispered to the lightning.

I screamed as it struck, spearing down into the palms of my hands.

And then . . .

I was on fire, and I *was* the fire.

The pain was more than pain. A word had not been invented to describe this pain, because it was also perfect. An agony of pleasure.

The ringing in my ears grew to a shriek. The air sizzled with electricity. Another bolt of lightning shot down from the sky, a great blazing tree growing toward me at the speed of light.

I was struck. Again. Again. Again.

Jagged arms of light reached to embrace me. To hold me. And I grabbed them and held them as long as I could, to take back the lightning I had given.

Light the color of blood beamed around the circle of Seekers. Another circle, a circle of Followers, had created the storm. Would this one, made up of people with the same power but with a different intent, end it?

Maybe, but not before the storm ended me.

The heat tore through me. Shattered me. This lightning was more than I had created—the storm had grown it. I had taken my own lightning back, and then some. I had reached capacity.

I dared a look down at myself and found that the terrible bridesmaid's dress had been incinerated, leaving my skin bare. The lightning scars were back, etching me with red light. The veinlike markings were opening up. I was cracking apart like glass.

Breaking . . . shattering . . . my body lanced by bolt after bolt of lightning, jerking and convulsing. The burned cinders of my clothes surrounded me. The lightning scars blazed like incandescent blood on my skin.

I couldn't take much more.

The red light surrounding the Seekers intensified until I could feel the tremor of it in the air all around me.

And suddenly I realized that the world had gone silent. The thunder had stopped.

I turned my face up to the clouds, saw a hole had formed in their center. The eye of the storm. Only it was growing, expanding, opening wider and wider. The storm was breaking, tearing itself apart, and behind it lay a clear black sky dusted with stars, glittering like glass dust.

I smiled as I felt my heart beat for the last time. And then it was still. Everything was still.

I let go of my life.

My eyes began to close, and my body to fall. Death wouldn't be so bad, I thought. I would finally get some rest.

And then I saw Jeremy dash forward to catch me before I could hit the ground, and fear squeezed my heart so hard it thumped once . . . twice . . .

No, don't touch me! I wanted to scream at him. *"DON'T TOUCH ME!"*

I scrambled back from Jeremy.

Was I still alive? I had to be, didn't I? I could move, and I could feel . . . I could feel so much heat swimming through me, settling into my body to make itself at home.

"I'm sorry," I croaked. "It's . . . not safe . . . to touch me . . . not yet. Too hot . . . still." My heart hammered in my chest, in my head, in my hands and feet. I was so charged. I was lightning incarnate. Again.

Jeremy stared at me, mouth open. "I thought you were dead."

I wheezed out a laugh. "I was, a bit."

We both looked at the sky. The clouds departing, dissipating like smoke, thinning to nonexistence.

I smiled. Then I saw how Jeremy was studying my face, his brow creased with worry. "What?" I asked. "What's wrong?"

He shook his head. "Nothing," he said, and began removing his white button-up shirt.

"What are you—" I glanced down. "Oh." I tried to cover myself, but I didn't have nearly enough arms. The rovers and Seekers who ringed the Tower graciously turned their eyes away from my nakedness, but I caught quite a few of them checking out the strange marks on my body.

Jeremy held out his shirt to me, but he made no effort

to avert his eyes. He was seeing me, naked, lightning scars and all. I searched his face for evidence of revulsion, but there was only him. The lightning scar on his chest stood out starkly against his bare skin, like a red star exploding.

"Can I touch you yet?" he asked, smiling a little.

I took the shirt from him, and, when my touch didn't turn it to ash, I nodded before pulling it over my head.

Jeremy reached out tentatively and ran a finger down the vein of a lightning scar on my neck. He winced, but didn't withdraw. His hand moved to cup my cheek. He ran the ball of his thumb over my skin, and a momentary shadow passed over his face. Then it was gone, and he was kissing me, and all I could do was hope I wasn't burning him.

No vision overtook my mind.

Jeremy touched me, and I touched him.

And it was just the two of us, the Lovers and the Tower.

EPILOGUE

I am not afraid of storms,
for I am learning how to sail my ship.
—Louisa May Alcott

A part of me thought things would go back to normal after that night in the Waste. The night I died a little bit. The night I quit being ashamed of the lightning scars and accepted who I was . . . the Tower girl. The night Mom stopped being afraid all the time, and Parker and Mom and I forgave each other for things that didn't matter anymore. The night I fell in love with a boy who could see my future, and kissed him under a clear night sky in the ruins of Los Angeles while my skin sang electric.

The night I killed a man named Rance Ridley . . . a man who called himself Prophet. Who had purchased the Tower under an alias and offered to host the Rove in his building, even though he'd publicly defamed the rovers. But no one could ask Prophet why he'd done such a thing, because Prophet was dead, burned to black during a freak lightning storm.

Yeah, things weren't quite back to normal.

Returning to Skyline wasn't an option for me. I had changed, and even though I no longer felt the need to hide my lightning scars, I couldn't go back to school the way I was. The scars had grown again, veins of red stretching across my right cheek, between my eyes, and over my forehead.

My eyes were the real problem. The lightning had entered them, veining the whites to red. And my pupils . . . there was light in them, subtle, but definitely there. No matter how much I blinked, it wouldn't go away. I wondered, if I used some of the lightning inside me, if I let go a little, would the red retreat from my eyes? I didn't know, so I was keeping the lightning to myself for now. I had a feeling I might need it again. I wanted to believe I had played my part for the Seekers, but I remembered Madam Lupescu's reading. I remembered that Hierophant card, my potential. Another possible future.

For now, I was content to spend my days with Jeremy. He had nowhere to go now that Prophet was dead and the Apostles scattered. He didn't even want to return to the beach house to claim his things.

"That part of my life is over," Jeremy told me. I knew that wasn't quite true. I could still see the deaths of the people who were killed during the quake haunting his eyes. I wondered if Jeremy would ever be able to forgive himself. I knew firsthand how hard that would be.

Jeremy didn't go back to Prophet's beach house, but I did. Only once. There was something I'd left behind, in the topmost bedroom.

The Lovers card.

That was something I wanted to keep.

Jeremy had been sleeping on our couch since the storm, but because neither he nor I needed much sleep, we spent nights tangled in each other's arms and legs, kissing until the heat became too much to bear and we broke apart, gulped water, and then started over again.

Jeremy was still hesitant about touching me, even though he hadn't had a vision since the storm. Luckily, he had no reservations about me touching him.

So I did.

A lot.

Mom remembered very little from the time she started watching *The Hour of Light* until her near-wedding/near-death. In fact, the majority of Prophet's former Followers were dealing with a sort of mass amnesia. Even people who had only watched his show and never come to a revival in person to receive his "blessing" were foggy on the events of their lives up until his death.

I asked Mr. Kale if Prophet's mind-control ability had been so powerful it worked even through a TV show. He shook his head. "That had nothing to do with his power, and everything to do with the power of his words, and the time he chose to say them. He spoke to people's fear, and the fear listened."

I nodded, thinking of how Prophet had succeeded in brainwashing me, and how he couldn't have done it if a part of me hadn't wanted to listen.

But that was the old Mia. I was different now.

When you've been struck by lightning as many times as I have, you start to expect the worst pretty much all the time. But I had a feeling the worst was behind me, and I think Mom felt the same way. She told me she had died for a moment, after Prophet cut her throat, but it hadn't been like her near-death experience during the quake. She didn't see a light or anything like that, but there had been something . . . a feeling that she was not alone, and that there was more waiting for her after this life than darkness.

One week after the storm, Mom announced that I was having a birthday party. I was turning eighteen. I'd completely forgotten.

The party was small, and Mom was barely able to scrounge up ingredients to make a cake, but it was still bigger than any birthday party I'd ever had. Mom invited Katrina and Mr. Kale, and Parker invited Quentin and Schiz. Jeremy was the only person I invited, though he hardly needed an invitation.

"Happy adulthood," Katrina said when she and Mr. Kale arrived. She handed me a hastily wrapped package, grinning as I opened it.

It was a clear glass bottle, filled with nasty-looking red liquid.

"Katrina." Mr. Kale growled disapproval, but she ignored him.

"If the girl can nearly destroy the world and then save it, she can have a drink to celebrate. I call it red lightning. It's basically the same as white lightning, but with a few minor adjustments. Enjoy!"

"Thanks," I said, touched. I unscrewed the cap and took a swig straight from the bottle. It went down smoother than ever.

Katrina took out her flask and clinked it against the bottle. "To the calm before the storm," she said.

"Don't you mean after?"

She and Mr. Kale shared a secretive glance that made me nervous.

"Yes," Katrina said. "After."

We drank.

"Of course," Katrina added, "there'll always be another storm."

Mr. Kale held a wrapped package as well, though now he was shifting it behind his back, like he wanted me to forget I'd seen it.

"What's that?" I asked.

Katrina elbowed her uncle, suddenly serious. "Give it to her."

"She won't want it," Mr. Kale muttered under his breath.

"Uncle Kale," Katrina said, her voice softening. "It's hers, whether she wants it or not."

My former English teacher nodded and sighed and held out the package to me.

I smiled weakly as I accepted it. "You didn't have to get me anything," I mumbled as I peeled open the wrapping paper. A swatch of red fabric was revealed, along with a black ceramic mask.

"It belonged to my sister," Mr. Kale said. "I hope it fits."

I took another swig from the bottle of red lightning.

It was after midnight by the time the party ended. Mom was exhausted, but pleased with how things had gone. She wanted to start cleaning up, but I convinced her that she had done enough, and Parker, Jeremy, and I would handle the cleanup tomorrow.

"Happy birthday, Mia," Mom said, and hugged me for a long time. She and I had gone for a walk around our neighborhood earlier that day, just the two of us. I brought the pepper spray Militiaman Brent had given me, but there was no need for it. Everything was calm. For now, at least.

Mom had stopped in front of an empty, half-collapsed house. The yard was overgrown, but the flowers were thriving even without anyone to care for them. She knelt down and picked a small bouquet.

"I miss him," Mom had said. That was all. I didn't ask whom she was referring to, Dad, or Owen, or maybe even Prophet. At home, Mom put the flowers in a vase and set it in the middle of the kitchen table. It was amazing how much those flowers did to brighten up the room. Now, with Mom hugging me, I could see the little bouquet over her shoulder, and it made me smile.

"Do you feel older?" Parker asked me after Mom went to bed, and it was just me, him, and Jeremy sitting around the kitchen table.

"Oh, yeah," I said. "Eighty years sounds about right."

Parker didn't laugh. His eyes were serious.

Jeremy, sensing that my brother and I needed a moment alone, excused himself.

"I never told you I'm sorry," Parker said. "For when I said I didn't want to stand by you anymore. I didn't mean that."

I put my eyes in my lap. "It's okay if you did."

"No." Parker shook his head, making his shaggy blond

hair sweep his eyebrows. "I'll always stand by you, from now on. I promise."

I forced a smile. "Okay," I said, even though I hoped neither of us had to choose between family and obligation ever again.

Jeremy was waiting for me in my bedroom. I'd told him earlier that day what I wanted for my birthday. I considered lighting a few candles, but decided Jeremy and I had enough fire between us.

Jeremy came to me and put his arms around me. "Are you sure this is what you want?"

The fire in my blood sang its favorite song.

Yes, yes, yes, yes, yes, yesssss . . .

Instead of answering, I reached up with my mouth and kissed him, a kiss that started gentle and exploratory, but quickly turned to more of a hostile takeover.

We fell onto the bed. My hands trailed over Jeremy's back, and his hands were beneath me, and in my hair.

Then he pulled back.

"What's wrong?" I asked. My blood was begging for more.

"I never saw this," he said. "You and me together. I never saw it coming."

I glanced at my nightstand, where the Lovers card lay faceup.

I kissed Jeremy. "I did."

ACKNOWLEDGMENTS

You know the saying "It takes a village to raise a child"? Well, the same goes for books.

Thank you to my villagers.

To my agent, Jamie Weiss Chilton, for taking a chance on this book and working tirelessly to help me whip it into shape. And for being a friend. Here's to many years of coffee excursions.

To my editor, Janine O'Malley, who is truly a writer's editor.

To my early readers, Ann Masters, D. J. Kirkbride, Lori Hildreth Walker, Christine Lanoie, Sandra Ramirez, Loara Cadavona, and Anastasia Stanecki.

To the J Crew, Julie Weinbach, Jason Porter, Jodi Rothman Moore, and J'Laurie Zerwer. Great company and mediocre food forever!

To the writers who've been there for me even when "Shadow Jenn" took over: Sara Wilson Etienne, Edith Cohn, Lamar Giles, Jessica Brody, and Christine Silk. I'm lucky to have you.

To my parents, for stocking their bookshelves with strange and dangerous books. To my mom, whose voracious reading habits rubbed off on me. To my dad, for all the bedtime stories that sparked my imagination.

To the Bosworth family, who let me into their inner circle.

To the incredibly talented, creative, and hardworking cast and crew of the *Struck* book trailer: Stephanie Rae Anderson, Alix Maria Taulbee, Nicci Faires, Kevin Joy, Sebastian Siegel, Kelly Ryan, Tristan Whitman, Tahlee Booher, Mario Amadeu, Jack Brungardt, Terra Brody, Jackie Fanara, David Chase, Iggy Scarpitti, Oscar Arvizu, Jessica Brody, and Erin Cathcart. To the Rove extras who danced like there was no tomorrow, and to the Followers who braved pouring rain and flooding streets dressed all in white to be on set and look creepy. You know who you are.

To the city of Los Angeles, for being my haven.

And most of all, to my husband, Ryan, for being my greatest supporter, my greatest inspiration, my greatest love. Lightning struck for us.

TURN THE PAGE FOR

STRUCK

BONUS MATERIALS

Struck Discussion Questions

1. We've all heard the Stan Lee quote "With great power comes great responsibility." Mia has both power and responsibility—but wants neither. If given the choice, would you accept great power if it came with a price? Would it be worth it?

2. In *Struck*, the prophet of a doomsday cult has predicted that the end of the world will arrive in three days. How would you behave if you thought the world was ending in three days?

3. Mia refers to herself as a "lightning addict" and is willing to risk everything—including her life—to connect to the power in storms. What parallels is the author drawing between Mia's addiction and other types of addiction?

4. *Struck* begins one month after a massive earthquake has devastated Los Angeles. The city is in chaos, and millions have lost their homes and are deprived of basic necessities. If disaster struck your town, how would you survive?

5. Mia has Lichtenberg figures—veiny, red, lightning scars—that cover her skin from neck to toes. How does this "disfigurement" affect her everyday life? Do you have any scars that you're proud of or ashamed of?

JENNIFER BOSWORTH

What did you want to be when you grew up?

I always wanted to be a novelist. More specifically, I wanted to be Stephen King. Not the *next* Stephen King, but Stephen King himself. Since he already exists, however, I had to settle for being Jennifer Bosworth.

When did you realize you wanted to be a writer?

Before I learned to read. My dad is an amazing storyteller, and when I was a kid he used to tell me these epic, serialized bedtime stories that went on for weeks. I wanted to do the same thing—to wrap people in a fictional world so tightly that they couldn't go to sleep.

As a young person, who did you look up to most?

Stephen King was my hero. Still is!

What was your favorite thing about school?

For most of my school-going career, it was the moment when the final bell rang and I got to leave. I didn't enjoy school, and any kind of math was the bane of my existence. But I did love my high school English teacher, Mr. Thompson. He was an incredible lecturer, and made any subject he taught fascinating.

What was your least favorite thing about school?

Too much sitting. I'm a wanderer. I like to be able to get up and move around whenever I want. School made me feel like I was in a straightjacket.

What were your hobbies as a kid? What are your hobbies now?

Does watching horror movies count as a hobby? Let's pretend it does. My dad owned a video store when I was a kid, and my favorite thing to do was load up on horror movies, find a TV and VCR (yes, it was that long ago) in a dark room, and try to scare myself. I haven't changed much. I still do that.

What was your first job, and what was your "worst" job?

First job was working for my dad in his furniture/video store (yes, you read that right, it was both a furniture *and* a video store), dusting and cleaning. But I tended to grab a movie, hide in the TV sales room, and watch that instead of working. My worst job was as a holiday greeter at a clothing store in the mall, standing in one place and saying "Hi" and "Welcome" and "Happy holidays" for eight hours.

What book is on your nightstand now?

The Locke & Key graphic novels by Joe Hill.

Where do you write your books?

I have an office in my house. Virginia Woolf says we each need a room of our own, and I believe that. I've been trying to shake things up and write at coffee shops, though, so I won't be distracted by dog-walking and laundry.

What sparked your imagination for *Struck*?

The first part of the story that came to me was the setting: earthquake-ravaged Los Angeles. I wanted to write a book that was a sort of love letter to Los Angeles, because I adore this city. Ironically, I destroy the city in *Struck*—but you always hurt the ones you love, right?

Have you ever felt an earthquake?
I've felt quite a few since moving to Los Angeles eight years ago, but none of them higher than a five on the Richter scale. The little ones feel like a mild roller coaster. They'd be fun if it weren't for the terror that freezes you the second they hit.

If the world was going to end in three days, what would you do?
Eat, drink, and attempt to be merry. Maybe throw a three-day party and invite all the people I love.

Have you ever had a tarot card reading?
I studied tarot while writing *Struck*, so I've done many readings for myself and others. Sometimes they're uncannily accurate, especially when I read for complete strangers. I even did some readings for fans on the Fierce Reads tour during our stop in East Lansing, Michigan.

You have an amazing book trailer for *Struck*. Were you involved in the making of the video?
I wrote and produced the trailer, which was a huge undertaking, but it was thrilling to watch my world come to life. The best part about producing the trailer was casting. It's incredibly suspenseful to sit in the casting room and wait for your characters to show up. And when they do, you just know. It's like falling in love.

What challenges do you face in the writing process, and how do you overcome them?
I'm more of a doer than a thinker. When inspiration strikes, I want to sit down and start writing immediately, rather than think a story through from beginning to end. I'm trying to change my wicked, wicked ways, though, and outline like a good girl.

Which of your characters is most like you?

Definitely Mia. We're both cynical and pessimistic, but we desperately want to find something to believe in.

What makes you laugh out loud?

Bonobos. Also (and this will make me sound like a jerk), I love seeing people fall down. I'm highbrow like that.

What do you do on a rainy day?

I live in Los Angeles, so we don't have many of those. But when it does rain, I divide my time between sleeping in, getting soaked waiting for my dog to do her biz, drinking warm beverages, and getting stuck in traffic. When it rains in L.A., everything grinds to a halt.

What's your favorite song?

Anything by Lavender Diamond.

Who is your favorite fictional character?

Roland Deschain, the last gunslinger from Stephen King's Dark Tower series.

What was your favorite book when you were a kid? Do you have a favorite book now?

I was too young to be reading it, but Stephen King's *The Drawing of the Three* was my favorite. Right now my favorite book is *Sharp Objects* by Gillian Flynn.

What's your favorite TV show or movie?

I was obsessed with *Buffy the Vampire Slayer* and *Battlestar Gallactica*, and I'm currently in the market for a new TV show obsession. I can't settle on a favorite movie overall, but my favorite horror movie is *Carrie*, and my favorite so-bad-it's-good movie is *Flash Gordon*.

If you could travel anywhere in the world, where would you go and what would you do?
I've always wanted to visit Transylvania, just to say I've been there. And I'd like to see the aurora borealis before I die. That's a hard one, though, because you never know when or where it will appear.

If you could travel in time, where would you go and what would you do?
I'd be an old West gunslinger.

What's the best advice you have ever received about writing?
Write the book that only *you* can write.

What do you want readers to remember about your books?
Remember the moments when everything falls apart, and the moments when the protagonist figures out how to put it all back together.

What should people know about you?
As a teenager I talked myself out of a reckless driving ticket by pretending I'd been having an asthma attack. In truth I was drag-racing back to the high school after lunch. It was one of my proudest moments.

What do you like best about yourself?
I excel at arm wrestling.

What do you consider to be your greatest accomplishment?
You just read it! *Struck* wasn't my first book, but it was the first book I wrote that *worked*. I rewrote it from scratch four times, and there were moments—hours, days, weeks—when I considered giving up on it. But I didn't, and that's why it is truly my greatest accomplishment: not giving up even when I was sure I couldn't do it.

PROPHET

BY
JENNIFER BOSWORTH

The day Rance Ridley kissed a girl for the first time, his father revealed the exact date of the end of the world.

The girl's name was Olivia.

Later, Rance wondered if his father would have seen "the end" if he hadn't caught his son lying in the field with Olivia, her lips kissed to the color of crushed strawberries.

The two of them were thirteen. They'd known each other since they were babies, born only two days apart in the compound of the Church of Light. But Olivia's mother abandoned her before she was weaned, disappearing from the compound as suddenly as she had appeared back when she was pregnant and destitute. Rance's mother took Olivia in and acted as wet nurse to the baby girl, raising her as Rance's sister. Perhaps that was why his father's face turned red with fury when he found them and saw the way Olivia's demure white blouse was unbuttoned, pulled loose from her long skirt. Or perhaps it was simply because Prophet Ram Ridley claimed that a kiss shared before marriage was an affront to the Almighty and should be punished accordingly.

The prophet caught Olivia by her hair and Rance by the back of his neck and held them apart. Olivia's wheat-colored eyes were huge with fear, and Rance knew his father was hurting her as he wrapped her endless hair in his fist, reeling her in. Olivia's shirt hung open, revealing most of one small, white breast.

"My own son," the prophet sputtered, his face now the color of a bruise. "You defile the purity of this child."

"Father, we were only—" Rance began to say, but the prophet yanked Olivia's hair so violently a sob flew from her throat. Rance hadn't seen Olivia cry since she was a little girl. She had always been strong. It was one of the things Rance loved about her. One of the many things.

"I taught you better than this," the prophet said to his son. "What will your punishment be, eh? The belt? Or shall it be the cellar this time?"

Rance felt his palms go clammy. He had never done anything bad enough to warrant confinement in the cellar beneath the church, but he'd heard stories from those who had spent days locked in the dark with the dead. That's where the compound cemetery was located, in the large cellar beneath a church so white it hurt Rance's eyes to look upon it. There, those who died could forever hear the songs and prayers of the Followers of the Light. The earthen floor of the cellar was damp and loose, and those confined below the church felt themselves sinking into the ground, as if the dead were drawing them slowly into the soil.

Worst of all, and to his shame, Rance was terrified of the dark—had been for as long as he could remember. He always slept with an oil lamp burning, and he longed every night for electricity.

Rance would never be sorry for what he and Olivia had done that day in the waving summer grass of the field, and he knew lying was an unforgivable sin, but the mere thought of being locked in the cellar made him quake. So he hung his head and lied. "I'm sorry, father. It will never happen again. I deserve the belt."

"You've had the belt before," his father said. "It seems not to have made an impression on you. A day or two in the cellar should remedy that."

"No!" Olivia cried. She knew better than anyone how terrified Rance was of the dark. She understood, and did not judge him. "Prophet, I must confess. I brought Rance to the field. I tempted him. Punish me instead. Rance is good, and I . . . I am a wicked girl. I should be taught a lesson."

The prophet considered, frowning. And then he released Rance's neck and shoved him away. But he kept hold of Olivia's hair, and a smile bent his lips.

To Rance, it seemed as though he were the only one who could hear Olivia through the floorboards as the white-clad Followers sang their evening hymns. On the Church of Light's compound, worship services were held three times a day. First at sunrise. Then at noon. And again at the close of day.

Olivia had been locked in the cellar for five hours, and she was still screaming to be let out. Rance wanted more than anything to go to her, to rescue her from the darkness his father had sentenced her to—three days and three nights without food or water. But if he openly defied the prophet, he would end up in the dark himself.

We could run away, Rance thought. *I could rescue Olivia and together we could leave this place.*

But where would they go? How would two thirteen-year-olds survive in a world neither of them had ever been part of? And how long would it be before Ram Ridley sent a team of Followers to drag the two of them back to the compound?

No, Rance could not save the girl he loved. All he could do was sit with his people and sing loudly enough that he couldn't hear her cries.

But when the song ended and there was a moment of silence before the prophet began his evening sermon, Rance heard what Olivia said.

"Rance, pleeeease! Make them let me out! I'm scared!"

A few eyes flitted toward him, and Rance felt his cheeks go red with shame. He was the prophet's son. He was supposed to set an example for the conduct of others, but instead he had let himself be tempted by a girl. No, a woman now. Olivia was thirteen. She had breasts, and she had told him herself that she'd begun to bleed. She was now capable of bearing children. If things had gone too far in the field, Rance might have been the one to get her with child. A kiss before marriage was an affront to God, but a child born out of wedlock. . . . No matter how much he repented, Rance would never be washed clean of that sin. It was too great.

Rance had thought Olivia was lying to protect him when she told the prophet she had purposely tempted Rance. But perhaps she was telling the truth. Suppose she'd intended to exploit the weakness all men felt in the presence of women.

"My dearest Followers," the prophet boomed out in the chapel. He stood behind the podium and grasped the edges with his hands as though to keep himself from falling over. His face was pale but his eyes were bright and reflective, like pond water when the moon shines off it. "I have had a revelation," the prophet told them. "The end is nigh. I have seen it, a storm the likes of which has not been seen since the days of Noah and the flood. But from this storm there will be no ark to carry us away. This shall be a storm of judgment." The prophet's eyes, burning now, found his son. "Only those who are without sin shall be saved."

The storm, his father said, would arrive in three days.

On the third evening, the Followers gathered in the Church of Light and, as Prophet Ram Ridley had predicted, the rains came.

But Rance was not impressed with God's cleansing storm. It started as a light sprinkle of drops, more like a mist than actual rain. But the mist soon became a downpour. Still, it was only rain. Just a summer storm, the kind that usually ended before it began.

But it didn't end.

As water drummed on the roof, the Followers sang their songs. They prayed. Prophet Ridley sermonized and whipped his people into a frenzy, and then they sang some more. Rance could not keep his eyes from the windows. He kept waiting for the rain to stop, but it went on and on.

While lightning split the sky in a hundred places and thunder pounded their eardrums, the Followers around him stomped and threw their hands in the air and praised God. They basked in His glory, but Rance could not think about God. All he could think about was Olivia in the cellar, cold and alone in the terrible darkness. Shivering and wet and—

Wet.

Rance thought back to the last time there'd been a hard rain. The cellar had flooded. And that storm had been nothing compared to what they were experiencing now.

Olivia.

Rance ran from the chapel and into the pouring rain. Droplets smacked his cheeks like pellets and burst apart. He was instantly soaked from head to foot. He heard his father shouting for him to get back inside, but for once he ignored the prophet. He slammed the church doors shut and rammed the only thing he could find, a piece of broken two-by-four, through the handles.

It wouldn't keep his father and the Followers inside long, but it gave him time.

Rance sprinted around to the side of the church where the cellar door was located. But he should have paused to think before rushing out into the rain. The cellar was padlocked.

Rance pounded on the wooden door. "Olivia! Can you hear me? Please answer!"

No sound. And no time to wait for it.

Rance had to break through the door before his father and the Followers stopped him. Before Olivia drowned in the cellar. Before the buried dead were washed loose from their graves, and Olivia floated with them in the dark. In the dark, where he must go to save her.

"Rance!" He heard his father's distant voice. "You stop this! I command it! God must judge us all! He must judge us all!"

Another bolt of lightning drew a jagged line across the clouds, illuminating, for a moment, a shovel lying against the wall of the nearby toolshed. Rance slipped and skidded through the mud and snatched it up.

He raised it high above his head and brought it down on the padlock. It did not break. He tried again. Nothing.

He pictured Olivia's golden-green eyes and sun-bright hair in his mind, and raised the shovel once more before bringing it down with every ounce of strength he had.

He felt the charge before he *really* felt it. It tugged at his hair and woke his nerve endings and made his heart stutter.

The lightning filled him, washed everything to perfect, pristine white. Washed away Olivia's face.

Rance had never been in a hospital, not even when he was born. So when he opened his eyes and found himself in an all-white room with white sheets pulled to his chest, he wondered if he had died. His vision was blurry, which made everything around him appear soft, heavenly. He blinked a hundred times, but the blurriness remained, as though he were looking through a sheet of ice.

Monitors beeped at a slow, steady pace. Rance began to remember what had happened before everything turned white: the storm and his attempt to free Olivia from the cellar, how he'd raised the shovel above his head, turning himself into a perfect lightning rod.

And the lightning had come for him. Come to judge him.

The beeping became faster and faster. Rance's right hand began to feel hot to the point of pain, tingling with a fidgety, electric feeling.

He held his right hand before his eyes and saw, through the

filmy veil that obscured his vision, veins of red on the palm of his hand, like it had been drizzled in blood.

There was a pounding in his head, a buzzing in his ears, and then a voice spoke so clearly inside his mind that Rance thought at first there must be someone else in the room.

Now you bear the mark. There is great work ahead for you. Gather your Apostles, for you are the new prophet of the Church of Light. The power is in your hands, and with your hands you must do the work of God.

Footsteps. Three indistinct figures entered, and the voice ceased speaking.

"He's awake," a woman said, and began touching him, checking the needle he hadn't even realized was in his arm until she jostled it.

"There's something wrong with his eyes." His father's voice filled the room, always deep and booming, the way it was when he gave a sermon.

"I'm afraid he's developing cataracts," another man said. His coat was white, but not his pants. They were black. He was no Follower. "It's not a common aftereffect of being struck by lightning, but it has been known to happen."

"His hair . . . when will its color return?"

His hair? What was wrong with his hair? Rance wished for a mirror.

"We don't know," the white-coated man answered.

"I thought you people were supposed to have all the answers," the prophet said, a sneer in his voice. "What about that mark on his hand? What of that?"

"Lichtenberg figures," said the man in the white coat. "Also caused by the lightning. But they should fade in a few days. The cataracts are . . . another matter."

Rance spoke then, and his voice reminded him of his father's.

It carried a certainty he'd never had before. "I see more now than I ever could before," he told the room. Then he directed his milky eyes toward his father. His father's face was nothing but a smear of features.

"Tell me, Prophet," Rance said. "What became of Olivia?"

She's dead, that voice whispered in his mind again. Strangely, he was already growing used to it. And already he trusted it. *She's dead, and it was this self-proclaimed prophet who took her from you. He is a false prophet, who declared an end that did not come. God does not speak to him. Your father's time is past. You must remove him.*

Rance couldn't agree more.

Rance Ridley took the podium for the first time the day after his father's body was found in the cellar. Apparently the former prophet had tripped and fallen down the steep steps and knocked himself out. He suffocated in the dark with his face shoved into the mud that remained from the rains and the flooding.

"My Followers," Rance said to his congregation. "God sent His light into me the night of the storm, to chase away all darkness. He judged me and found me not wanting. But the same cannot be said of my father, the false prophet Ram Ridley. Let us not mourn the passing of the man who called himself prophet, when God never did. I have heard the voice of God. I have felt His light."

He gazed out at his people, a blur of perfect white. For a moment, he tried to picture Olivia's face, but he found it was already fading.

He blinked back tears and said what the voice had told him to say.

"God has chosen me, Rance Ridley, to be your one true prophet."

KEEP READING FOR

A SNEAK PEEK

OF

THE

KILLING

JAR

COMING SOON FROM

JENNIFER BOSWORTH

PROLOGUE

There is a memory that lives at the bottom of my mind, like someone tied a rock to it and sank it to the floor of a muddy lake. Sometimes I dream it, and on those nights I wake sweat-soaked and panting, until the memory descends back to where I keep it, and I tell myself that I've done nothing wrong. That I am a normal girl.

That I never hurt anyone.

But my sleeping self knows all about the boy with the jar. There's a butterfly trapped inside, its crisp wings black and blue and jade. It's dying, beating itself against the walls of its glass prison until it loses the will to fight for its life, and it droops against the bottom like wilted lettuce. Its delicate body relaxes, gives up.

The boy who holds the jar, the executioner, is mean and cruel, and he smiles with his mouth closed, lips tight, eyes hard and shiny dark, as he watches his tiny, pretty prisoner. He shoves the jar in my face and commands me to watch, too. And I do, with tears dropping from my eyes like water from a leaking faucet. I watch and cry because the boy is older than me, stronger, and I don't know how to stop him.

Then it's over. The butterfly goes slack. It's a dead thing now. A beautiful dead thing, and the boy wants to pin it to a corkboard where he keeps his other kills—grasshoppers and beetles, spiders and moths. And now this beautiful, fragile dead thing would go on his board of seemingly insignificant murders.

I couldn't let him do it. Couldn't let him pin her there.

I had to take back what the boy with the killing jar had done.

My sleeping self remembers how I grabbed the boy, curled my fingers around his wrist . . . and I opened a door. A door in a wall I hadn't known was there. On one side of the door was him;

on the other side was me. When the door opened, there was no separation between us, and I could reach through and take what I wanted. There was nothing he could do to stop me.

The boy went pale, then gray. Shocked white eyes bulged round from their sockets. He swung a hand at me and scratched my face before he fell, his body as limp as the butterfly's had been. The killing jar smashed on the sidewalk and the butterfly jittered into the sky. So alive. As if it had never been otherwise.

My sleeping self knows how I reveled in the feeling that filled me after the boy went gray and fell like the butterfly had fallen. A hurricane of emotion. A raucous, feral energy that almost lifted me off the ground, that told me I could do anything. Run a thousand miles. Swim an ocean. Live forever. Anything. Everything.

But that's just a dream I have. And when it seems too real, I push it away and I tell myself I am a normal girl.

I've done nothing wrong.

I did not kill that boy.

CHAPTER ONE

I rested my forehead against the night-chilled glass of the passenger-side window and watched the road slide by beneath Blake's 4Runner, a fast-moving conveyor belt carrying us home.

My ears felt numb after hours of being hammered by thudding bass, and I was buzzing all over, charged with a kind of energy I hadn't felt since . . . I couldn't quite remember when. It wasn't important, I decided. The past wasn't important, not anymore. My life had begun tonight, ironically, at a party I hadn't even wanted to go to. Blake talked me into it.

Blake. I glanced over at him, perched behind the steering wheel. He felt my gaze and turned his head toward me, smiling with the ends of his mouth.

"Are you tired?" he asked. The clock on the dash claimed the time was three a.m., but it felt early still.

I shook my head. "Not even a little bit. I don't ever want to sleep again."

His slight smile became a grin. "Me neither."

Blake put his eyes back on the road, but I studied him a moment longer, wondering if he understood what tonight meant to me. What *he* meant to me. Blake had moved to Rushing a month ago, and already he'd been invited into the elite inner circle, the upper crust of Rushing's high school society. It was where he belonged, with his easy manner and his stealth good looks, the kind that snuck up on you and then made you feel like a bomb had gone off under your feet, robbing the ground from beneath you.

For him, Elle Harmon's party might have been interchangeable with any other. For me, it had turned out to be something far more important, because Elle wasn't simply the most popular girl at our school. She was—or had been—the cousin of a kid named

Jason Cooper. Jason had been dead for eight years, but the mysterious circumstances surrounding his death continued to haunt the people who'd known him. Especially me.

I tried not to think too much about Jason. I let the rest of the kids I went to school with—and most of the town—do that for me. No one wanted to forget that I'd been present when nine-year-old Jason died inexplicably. There was nothing wrong with him. He simply . . . ceased to be alive. We'd been on the playground at school, and people said they saw me grab Jason right before he dropped to the ground, but I must have been trying to catch him *before* he fell. That was the only thing that made sense.

What didn't make sense was that after Jason fell, I ran off—but not to get help. No. Instead I just kept running. I disappeared for two days. Search parties scoured the town and the woods but didn't find a trace of where I'd gone. Then I just showed up on my parents' doorstep, dirty and disheveled, with leaves and pine needles knotted into my hair, my skin scratched and bruised, like I'd spent my missing days running through a gauntlet of tree branches.

I didn't remember what happened during the forty-eight hours I disappeared. Maybe I was in shock. Seeing another kid die right in front of you could do that.

Everyone might have let it go, chosen to believe Jason's death had nothing to do with me, if it weren't for my blood under his fingernails and the scratch marks on my face. Eight years later, the scars still hadn't faded completely. Three thin shadow lines on my cheek.

Eight years later, and still people looked at me with suspicion.

But not Blake. He'd heard the rumors his first day at school but he didn't believe them, and now his influence had spread, starting with Elle and extending down through the hierarchy of her friends.

Tonight, at Elle's party, I had been accepted, and suddenly

the tragedy that had haunted me for half my life was exorcised from my history. No one cared anymore. I could be normal now.

It was all I'd wanted for the past eight years.

I realized for the first time, while Blake and I danced in Elle's basement, the lights dim and the throbbing music rattling my bones, that I was young and I was alive, so achingly alive. I sensed every cell in my body at work, vibrating, existing. How had I not known I was this electric being, this sparking organism? I felt like I'd been in suspended animation since Jason's death, waiting for someone to give me permission to live again. To defibrillate my heart and start it beating normally.

Blake had done that for me.

I, Kenna Marsden, now had a life.

The 4Runner slowed. We were at my drop-off point, but I didn't want the night to end, and I sensed Blake didn't, either.

We sat there for a while, silent, breathing.

Then he looked at me. His dance-mussed hair, the strawberry-blond color of peanut butter, lay wavy on his brow, and his copper penny eyes were bright and animated. The spicy smell of his cologne made me feel Tilt-A-Whirl-dizzy.

Blake and I had never kissed. I wasn't even sure if he felt for me what I did for him, or if he thought of me only as a friend. I didn't know what he wanted, but I wanted to know.

He killed the engine and reached for his door handle. "I'll walk you."

There was a football field's distance between the road and the rambler my parents had bought on the edge of the Deschutes National Forest. Blake's family lived next door to mine, a short stretch of woods dividing our houses.

My family used to live closer to town, but after what happened with Jason Cooper we started to have . . . problems. People egging and toilet papering our house, writing "Killer Kenna" on our windows with soap. So my parents moved us to the outskirts.

For a while they considered relocating us to an entirely new town, but the bakery my mom had worked so hard to open was doing well, and Dad had tenure at Rushing's small college, so they kept putting it off, thinking people would forget the Jason incident, that the shunning would stop eventually.

Finally, tonight, it had.

Halfway across the wooded expanse of land between the road and my house, Blake froze and took my arm to hold me still. There was an old pickup truck parked among the trees. Whoever owned it was trespassing on either my parents' or Blake's parents' property. It was hard to say which.

"Maybe I should check it out," Blake said, and started toward the truck. Blake had a heroic streak that I suspected might get him into trouble someday.

"Don't," I said. "It's probably kids making out."

"I don't see anyone in the cab."

"Uh-huh . . . even better reason not to take a closer look."

Despite the dark, I saw Blake's neck redden. "Good point."

We kept on, walking in silence over the soft layer of pine needles covering the ground, feet cracking the occasional fallen branch or pinecone. But it was a loaded silence. I could tell there was something Blake wanted to say. Or do.

We reached the edge of the trees, and still Blake didn't make his move.

I turned to face him, presenting myself, making it easy.

"So you had fun tonight?" Blake asked. It was an empty question, a fill-the-silence question. Of course I'd had fun. Wasn't it obvious? Wasn't I glowing, practically radioactive with happiness? But Blake didn't understand what it had been like for me all these years. He'd always been accepted, had a place in the world, no matter where he went.

I could never make him understand. Words wouldn't do.

I stepped closer to him, so close that I could feel him even without touching. I'd read once that blind people learned to sense objects in the same way, developing an almost supernatural sense of touch to help them navigate through life without constantly bumping into things. That was how I felt with Blake, like there was a cushion of energy over him and I could touch it, dip my fingers into it. It was like heat and music on my skin.

I put my mouth so close to Blake's that I was breathing him in, but still we weren't touching, weren't kissing. We were paused in the moment before, balanced on a tightrope between what we were and what we would become if either of us moved.

I moved.

I brushed my lips against his, and felt his mouth sigh open to receive me. It was all so delicate, so restrained. Blake was careful with me, sensed my fragility. But he didn't understand that I had changed tonight. I'd had a taste of what it was like to be a normal, reckless teenager, and I wasn't willing to go back now.

I made my lips softer but kissed him harder, and I felt him hesitate and then respond. His arms wrapped me and his fingers found their way into my hair. Our kiss became less considerate, more impatient and eager. My temperature turned up until it felt like a fever. My fingertips, calloused and always slightly numb from countless hours spent practicing guitar, dug into his back.

Distantly I heard a noise like a cry, but I ignored it. Blake didn't. He pulled back suddenly.

"What was that?"

I cocked my head and listened. I heard it again, though I still wasn't sure what *it* was. The skin on my back prickled in primal, lizard-brain warning. It sounded like someone, a person, crying out in despair or pain. But there were a lot of birds around that made that sort of sound—birds and other creatures. Mountain lions with their feminine, furious shrieks. This close to the forest, plenty of animals confused our property with theirs, some of them more dangerous than others.

But Blake's mind was on a different track. "Could be the owner of that truck."

I wanted to disagree, to insist that the sound was nothing to worry about. That there was no reason we shouldn't stay out here the rest of the night, sneak back into our houses when dawn broke.

But that sound—that cry—there was something terrible about it. Something that made me want to hide behind a locked door and pull my blankets over my head.

"You should go," Blake said, and, when he saw the disappointed look on my face, gave me a lingering kiss that made me forget about trespassers and woodland creatures. Then the cry came again, and Blake unpeeled himself from me and turned me to get me moving. "I'll watch from here to make sure you get in okay. And I'll call you tomorrow."

"Don't call," I said, smiling. "Just come over."

He nodded, reached for my hand, held it for a moment, his thumb pressing lightly into the center of my palm. "Good night, Kenna Marsden."

I caught my lower lip under my teeth. "Good night, Blake Cahalan."

It was our thing, calling each other by first and last name. I wasn't sure which of us had started doing it, and I didn't care. I loved saying his whole name, his every syllable, like I was staking my claim on them.

He released me and I started walking quickly, almost jogging. As reluctant as I was to part from Blake, I wasn't in any hurry to encounter whoever or whatever was making that sound.

I felt Blake watching me as I crossed the distance to the basement window I'd left unlocked when I snuck out earlier that night. It was the easiest way to get in and out without waking anyone. I looked back at Blake's figure in the trees and waved before sliding the window open and lowering myself inside. I eased the window shut and stood there a moment in the dark, leaning against the cold wall. The basement was unfinished, consisting of cement floors and framed-in rooms with drywall and doors, but only pink clouds of insulation for a ceiling in most places.

My stomach was giddy, lodged somewhere between my lungs.

Me and Blake. Blake and me. Together. Just like that. It seemed too good, too easy. What if this whole night was temporary? What if I woke up tomorrow and it all went away? Maybe if I didn't go to sleep I could prevent my life from resetting.

The cry came again. It clawed through my thoughts, sent icicles sliding down my veins.

The sound was louder now. Much louder.

It was coming from inside the house.

CHAPTER TWO

That sound paralyzed me. It had not come from a bird, or any other animal. It came from somewhere in the basement. But all the bedrooms were on the first floor. Why would anyone be in the basement at this time of night?

A more important question: why would anyone—anyone inside my house—make that sound? That mournful, wordless plea of someone suffering. Someone in terrible pain.

Someone who needed help.

I heard something else, then, and it made my heart beat so hard I thought it might crack bones. Heavy footfalls from above. Clomping. Stomping. No one in my family would make that much noise walking around at three in the morning.

That meant there was someone else in the house. Someone big. Someone who wasn't supposed to be here.

The truck . . . the truck parked in our woods.

I tried to rationalize away my fear. Maybe it was a cop upstairs. My parents had probably realized I was gone and called the police, and they were all up there now trying to figure out where I was. No doubt my mom was upset, crying, and that's what I'd heard.

But if that scenario were even the least bit likely, then why hadn't anyone called my cell phone?

My cell phone.

Police.

My brain put those two things together and a plan was born. Call the freaking cops. Don't wait to find out if it's all a misunderstanding. Do it now.

I forced my joints to bend and reached into my purse, fumbling quietly for my phone. Every sound made my nerves snap like those annoying firecrackers people throw at your feet on the Fourth of July. Upstairs, the man, the intruder—I might as well call him what he was—stomped around the kitchen, making no effort to be quiet. What did that mean? Oh God, what did that mean? My parents . . . my sister, Erin . . . one of them had made the sound. The cry.

A sob welled in my throat, and I smothered it with one hand while the other, shaking uncontrollably, dialed 911.

Keep it together, I commanded myself as I waited for the ringing to begin. Gotta stay calm, make sense, be coherent for the operator. My eyes were hot and tight with the pressure of tears.

"911, what's your emergency?" a woman's voice answered. She sounded brusque. Alert.

I opened my mouth and heard a tiny, girlish whisper respond, "There's someone in my house. An intruder. I think he—" *Say it.* "I think he might have hurt my family."

Saying the words aloud made me shake even harder, but the operator was all business. "I'm going to send officers out to you right away, miss. Tell me your address."

For a moment my mind went blank. What was my address?

The answer finally landed in my head and I blurted it out, too loud. I went still. Listened. No movement upstairs. Had the intruder heard me?

A creak from above. The sound our cupboards made. He was looking through our kitchen cupboards. He was getting himself a snack! But at least he didn't seem to have heard me.

"Miss?" the operator was saying. "Miss, officers are en route. Are you in a safe place?"

"He—he doesn't know I'm here," I said.

"Okay, that's good. Stay where you are."

The cry came again, and this time I pinpointed its origin: the north end of the basement, where Mom and Dad had set up their

StairMaster machine and all the other weird exercise equipment they'd bought but rarely used. Infomercial crap. Dad was a sucker for that stuff.

The cry again, weaker now, and more desperate at the same time. I recognized the voice.

Erin. My sister.

"Miss?" the operator said. "Miss, what's happening now?"

More sounds from above. The intruder had walked to the kitchen table. Sound of wooden chair legs scraping across tile. He was sitting down, making himself comfortable. What was he eating? Mom had made lasagna for dinner. There were plenty of leftovers. The intruder had probably helped himself.

Rage boiled to life inside me. It battled with my terror until the two joined and filled me with a chaos of emotions that made it impossible to think straight.

"Miss? Are you there? What's happening?"

"I have to go," I said, and hung up. I silenced the cell in case anyone called, and shoved it into my back pocket. Then I was moving.

There was no light. I walked softly, but every step I took nearly gave me a heart attack. I was sweating and shivering, and I couldn't see a thing. I felt my way along the sheetrock wall and saw dim light coming from the north end. I bolted silently across the floor.

The sounds from upstairs had stopped, but I imagined I could hear the intruder chewing. In my head the sound was as loud as the man's stomping footsteps, the gooey, wet smacking and gnashing of teeth.

I stole the rest of the way to the plain white door with its cheap gold knob that closed off the "gym," as my parents called it. The door was closed and there was light coming from beneath. I reached for the knob, wondering suddenly if it might be locked, then rejecting the idea. The intruder wouldn't have locked himself out. But what if he had an accomplice? I paused and leaned with my ear close to the crack, straining to hear through the wood.

A soft, shuddering whimper penetrated the barrier.

Erin. It was definitely Erin.

I opened the door.

There are moments that change you forever. I'd had one earlier that night at the party, and then with Blake in the woods, and I experienced another one now. But this was not a moment that changed me for the better.

This one broke me.

Ten minutes ago, this was the best night of my life.

That was the thought that snaked through my mind as I took in the horror of what lay beyond the door.

The bare bulb glaring above cast a mean, relentless light over everything. Over the lake of blood that swamped the cement floor. My parents' bodies—that's what they were now, bodies, not people—were propped against the wall like forgotten dolls on a shelf. Their heads fell toward each other, my dad's resting on top of my mom's. Their legs stuck out stiffly in front of them. They looked absurdly peaceful, except for all the red. Dad wore boxers with ducks on them and a once-white, now crimson T-shirt; Mom wore a silky nightgown, the kind of thing I didn't even know she owned. It was ruined now.

I wanted more than anything not to be seeing what I was seeing, but I couldn't tear my eyes from the awful tableau. Then I heard my name.

"K-Kenna."

The voice was barely a voice. It was a wheeze. A gasp.

My sister lay crumpled in the corner of the room, partially hidden by the StairMaster. I skirted around the blood and kneeled beside her.

Suffocated sobs tore at my throat when I took in the sight of her. Her face was a disfigured purple landscape, one of her eyes swollen shut. My hands hovered over her, wanting to help, unsure what to do, or if there was anything I could do.

She wore a camisole, so I could clearly see the stab wound in her back, between her shoulder blades. She needed medical attention—and fast. How long until the police came? How long did my sister have?

Erin opened her mouth and tried to speak again. Blood bubbled on her lips, gurgled in her throat.

"Shhh. Don't talk," I said. "Help is coming. I called the police."

But we lived so far from town. It took me twenty minutes to drive to school every morning. How much time had passed since I'd called 911? Five minutes? Three? I should call again, tell them to send an ambulance. I reached for my phone.

Erin's eye rolled toward me. "Get . . . out," she managed. "He's . . ."

The man upstairs started moving again, and this time his footsteps were tromping down the stairs.

Erin's one eye went wide and she started breathing fast. But her lungs couldn't handle the air, and she started choking until blood speckled her lips.

He was coming. There was no way for me to get back to my hiding place, to get anywhere, before he blocked me in. There was only one thing to do.

I rushed to the door, closed it, and locked it. I spun around, searching for something to prop against the door. The StairMaster was too heavy to move. I went for Dad's thirty-pound barbell instead, hefting it off the rack. But my hands were slick with blood, and the barbell slipped from my fingers and crashed to the floor.

I heard the murderer's footsteps halt for one deafeningly silent moment. Then he ran.

I snatched up the barbell, holding with an iron grip this time, and wedged it under the doorknob just as the man twisted the knob. When it refused to turn, he pounded the door. Pounded with his fists and his foot.

I backed away, my heart thrashing. My vision darkened around the edges with every rapid thud. Afraid I might black out, I retreated to where Erin lay and huddled beside her. Every time the murderer struck the door, my whole body jolted and my teeth ground like I'd received an electric shock.

"He won't get in. The cops will be here soon. Don't worry. Don't worry." I wasn't sure if I was talking to Erin or to myself. I checked her face to see if she was even conscious and heard a moan come from my throat.

Erin was limp. Lifeless.

A memory burned behind my eyes . . . a butterfly gone slack, sagging to the bottom of a glass jar.

My moan became a wail. A banshee shriek of grief. I pulled Erin into my arms and crushed her against me.

The pounding ceased, and then something worse followed.

The man on the other side of the door began to laugh.